Her Passionate Plan B
by Dixie Browning

ⱱ✸ⱱ

She didn't move away fast enough, and somehow, she was in his arms.

"Daisy," Kell rumbled softly. "I was hoping I'd just imagined what happened between us."

Daisy shook her head. She hadn't imagined anything. But before she could reply or even pull away, he was kissing her. Softly at first, a mere brushing of warm lips, then it escalated into something far more intense.

Break away now while you still can, she told herself. *Or you'll never be able to settle for less.*

Daisy twisted her face away from his, her voice uneven as she murmured, "This isn't very smart."

"Believe it or not, I didn't plan for this to happen," Kell said, panting as if he'd just finished a ten-mile run.

"Trust me, sweetie, neither did I."

Her Man Upstairs
by Dixie Browning

It was too late to think rationally as Cole's lips brushed hers.

No pressure, no demand, just…touching.

As the kiss slowly deepened, Marty felt as if she'd been asleep for a hundred years and had woken up in a brand-new world to the tantalizing scent of soap and leather and sun-warmed male skin, to the iron-hard arms that held her breathlessly close.

Her carpenter. Her kissing carpenter, her upstairs man.

"Well," she breathed, unable to think of anything else to say. "Well…"

"I guess we got that out of the way," Cole said, sounding a tad stunned himself. "You want to fire me? I'll understand."

Marty shook her head. Fire him? Things might be infinitely more complicated after this, but if she let Cole walk away, she might lose the opportunity of a lifetime.

Available in March 2006 from Silhouette Desire

DYNASTIES: THE ASHTONS
Society-Page Seduction
by Maureen Child
&
Just a Taste
by Bronwyn Jameson

🔊 ❧ 🔊

Her Passionate Plan B
&
Her Man Upstairs
by Dixie Browning

🔊 ❧ 🔊

Under the Tycoon's Protection
by Anna DePalo
&
Between Strangers
by Linda Conrad

DIXIE BROWNING

Her Passionate Plan B
Her Man Upstairs

SILHOUETTE®

Desire™

*Silhouette, Silhouette Desire and Colophon
are registered trademarks of Harlequin Books S.A.,
used under licence.*

*First published in Great Britain 2006
Silhouette Books, Eton House, 18-24 Paradise Road,
Richmond, Surrey TW9 1SR*

The publisher acknowledges the copyright holders of the
individual works as follows:

Her Passionate Plan B © Dixie Browning 2005
Her Man Upstairs © Dixie Browning 2005

ISBN 0 373 60307 X

51-0306

*Printed and bound in Spain
by Litografia Rosés S.A., Barcelona*

HER PASSIONATE PLAN B
by
Dixie Browning

DIXIE BROWNING

A painter and gallery-operator whose interests include archaeology and astrology, folk music and baseball, Dixie Browning branched out in a brand-new direction in 1976, starting with a weekly newspaper column on art. Since then she's written more than a hundred romances. Now living with her retired husband on North Carolina's Outer Banks where she grew up, Dixie uses the area she knows best as background for many of her stories.

For a personal reply, fans may contact her at PO Box 1389, Buxton, NC 27920, USA, or through her website, www.dixiebrowning.com.

One

Daisy, who prided herself on her dependability, was upset that she arrived late for the graveside service. First the blasted phone wouldn't stop ringing, and then, in the middle of getting dressed, someone had pounded on the front door, causing her to accidentally kick one of her good shoes under the bed. Faylene had been there to answer it, thank goodness—it had been the power people wanting to know when to suspend service.

She had dashed back upstairs in her stocking feet and retrieved her shoe, in the process pulling a run in her only pair of dark panty hose. As a result of all that, plus the fact that her car was always cranky in wet weather, she was already more than ten minutes late.

Standing stiffly apart from the few others gathered at the graveside of her late patient, she felt the cold, blowing rain begin to soak through her raincoat, which was old, but at least it was black. Her yellow slicker had seemed somehow inappropriate.

Egbert, of course, was already there. She'd never known him to be anything other than punctual. Under the cover of a pair of oversize sunglasses, Daisy studied the man she had picked out to marry. When it came to making matches, she was old enough to know what mattered and what didn't. She wasn't about to make the same mistake a second time.

Egbert hadn't a clue, bless his heart. It would never occur to him that any woman would deliberately set out to seduce him into marriage—but then, modesty was one of his better qualities. Daisy had scant patience with overt "testosteronism," or blowhards as she called them.

For the first time, a slight shift in the few people huddled on the other side of the grave gave her a clear view of the man standing next to Egbert. Now, there, she mused, was the perfect example. If that man had a modest bone in his long, lean body, she would be seriously surprised. Even the way he was standing with his feet spread apart, his arms crossed over his chest, spelled *arrogance.*

I came, I saw, so what the hell—I conquered.

She could almost read his thoughts.

She could almost *feel* his thoughts.

Egbert was wearing his usual dark suit along with a nicely cut black raincoat. A sensible man, he had brought along an umbrella. He really was a nice-looking man, she thought objectively. Maybe not Hollywood handsome, but certainly moderately attractive.

Daisy was a firm believer in moderation. Unlike her two immoderate best friends, she didn't have a string of failed marriages behind her, only a single ego-numbing near miss. Once he realized what a perfect wife she would make, Egbert would be her first. Theirs would be a lasting union between two mature professionals, not one of those starter marriages that were so popular these days.

A noisy flock of ducks flew overhead to settle on the nearby river. She followed the ragged chevron until they were out of sight and then her gaze strayed back to the tall stranger.

No sensible raincoat for him, much less an umbrella. Rain beat down on his bare head, plastering gleaming black hair to a deeply tanned brow. For reasons she was at a total loss to explain, she felt a shiver of purely sexual interest. If she'd learned one thing from the past—and she'd learned several—it was that the minute sexuality kicked in, common sense flew out the door.

The man was a full head taller than Egbert, which would have made sharing Egbert's umbrella difficult even if he had offered. And knowing Egbert, he would have offered, because he was not only polite, he was genuinely caring—another big mark in his favor.

Between sneezes, the preacher managed to get in a few words about the man they were there to honor while Daisy wondered some more about the mysterious stranger. If she'd ever laid eyes on him she would definitely have remembered, not just because he was the only one present who was not appropriately dressed.

Although she had to admit that his blue jeans and leather bomber jacket were far better suited to the weather than her six-year-old black dress and leaky black raincoat, not to mention the muddy pumps that were slowly sinking into the wet earth.

It wasn't very cold, but the rain was beginning to

come down in earnest now. Hardly a time to be wearing sunglasses, but then, people often did at funerals, she rationalized, if only to hide eyes that were red and swollen from tears.

Or, as in Daisy's case, to shield open curiosity.

No, he definitely wasn't from around here. She knew everybody in Muddy Landing by sight, if not by name. Besides, if Sasha and Marty had ever laid eyes on him, he'd be heading their list of eligible bachelors. That is, if he was eligible.

She tried to see if he was wearing a ring. He wasn't, but that was no guarantee. He had tucked his thumbs under his belt with his fingers splayed out over a flat abdomen. The phrase *washboard abs* came to mind.

Washboard abs? She'd been watching too much television. Since Harvey, her longtime patient, had died so unexpectedly, she'd had trouble getting to sleep, but from now on she'd stick to the weather channel.

He hadn't moved a muscle. Maybe he was from Fish and Game, checking to make sure no one slipped down to the river for a spot of illegal duck hunting. No uniform, though. Besides, his hair was too long for a fed.

On a day like this, she mused, he could at least have worn a hat. She pictured him in a Stetson—a black one, not a white one, with the brim turned up on one side and a showy cluster of feathers tucked under the band.

Almost as if he could feel her staring at him, the stranger suddenly looked directly at her across the blanket of drowned flowers and artificial turf. Daisy stopped breathing. There was nothing unusual about blue eyes, but when they were set under crow-black brows in a face the color of well-tanned leather, the effect was…well, riveting, to put it mildly.

The service came to a hurried conclusion just as a fresh wave of rain blew in off North Landing River. With no family to console, the preacher sneezed again, glanced around and mumbled a few apologetic words to no one in particular before hurrying to the waiting black minivan. The pitifully small group of mourners began to straggle away—all but two.

Oh, Lord, they were headed her way. *Not now—please!*

Pretending not to hear Egbert calling to her, Daisy hurriedly splashed her way through puddles to where she'd left her car in the potholed parking lot. She was in no mood to have anyone—not a stranger and certainly not Egbert—see her with wet hair straggling down her neck, wearing a six-year-old rayon dress and a soggy raincoat that was even older. Not that she was egotistical in the least, but that would probably set her plans back at least six months.

The timetable she'd set for herself didn't allow for six months. She wasn't getting any younger. Three months from now Egbert would have been widowed exactly a year. Timing was everything. She didn't want to rush him, but neither did she want to wait until some other woman moved in and staked a claim.

She pulled out onto the highway, the windshield wipers slapping time with her disjointed thoughts.

She would finish all the sorting and packing that had to be done, and then she would sit quietly and listen while Egbert explained for the third time all the legal whereases, whereinafters and heretofores that prevented him from simply reading poor Harvey's last will and testament and turning everything over to the beneficiaries. Which in this case were the housekeeper Harvey had shared with Daisy's two best friends, and a loosely organized, poorly funded historical society.

A glance in the rearview mirror told her Egbert was two cars behind, driving precisely two miles under the speed limit. Some devil made her press her foot on the accelerator until she was doing five miles above the speed limit.

Daisy *never* exceeded the speed limit. Caution was her middle name.

"We've *got* to do something about Daisy." Rain droned down outside as Sasha propped her elbows on the table, carefully stroking glittery purple polish on her long fingernails. "She's showing signs of being seriously depressed."

At Daisy's request, neither of her friends had attended the graveside service. They hadn't insisted.

"She's not depressed, she's grieving. She's always like this after she loses a patient, especially a long-term patient. That color clashes horribly with your hair, by the way."

Sasha studied her nails, then looked at her friend, Marty Owens. "Purple and orange? What's wrong with it? You know, the trouble with Daisy is that she takes every case so personally. It's bad enough working all those long hours, but when she actually moves in with a patient the way she did with poor Harvey Snow…" Sighing, she wiped off a smudge of polish.

"I guess it made sense when she got evicted and he had that big old empty house going to waste."

"She wasn't evicted. Everybody had to move out after the fire. Where else would she have gone? The nearest motel still open is in Elizabeth City—that would have added at least forty minutes to her daily commute. Anyway, it probably wouldn't have hit her so hard if either one of them had any other family."

Nodding in agreement, Marty poured herself another glass of wine. She was already over her limit, but weekends didn't count. Trouble was, since being forced to close her bookstore, every day was a weekend. "I never heard her call him anything but Mr. Snow, but you know what? I think she considered him sort of a surrogate grandfather. Who've you got in mind for our next match, Sadie Glover or the girl with the thick glasses who works at the ice-cream place?"

The two women—three, when Daisy was with them—were accustomed to topic-hopping. Sasha said, "How about Faylene?"

Marty's eyes widened. "*Our* Faylene? Well, for one thing, she'd kill us."

"Daisy needs a distraction. Can you think of a bigger challenge than to find a mate for Faylene?"

"She'd be a challenge, all right. The trouble is, we're running out of male candidates unless we expand our hunting range."

"Oh, I don't know—I've got a couple of possibilities in mind," Sasha said thoughtfully.

Several years ago it had been Sasha and Daisy who had lured Marty into helping set up a shy, elderly neighbor with the cashier at the town's only pharmacy. At the time, Marty had just lost her second husband to another woman and needed a distraction. The match had been deemed a success when the neighbor had rented out his house and moved in with the widowed cashier and her seventeen cats.

The three women had toasted their success and begun looking around for any others who might need a deftly applied crowbar to pry them out of a lonely rut. Soon matchmaking had become their favorite pastime. Not simply shoving a pretty single woman into the path of any eligible man. There was no challenge in match-making for winners.

But for those who had given up hope—for the terminally shy, the jilted, the plain and the socially inept—now, there was a worthwhile cause. Without actually planning it, the three friends began identifying needy singles in the area and tactfully offering makeovers and even a few hints on dating protocol where needed. Often all that was required was a simple boosting of self-confidence. Or as Sasha put it, echoing a song from her humongous antique record collection, accentuating the positive and eliminating the negative. After that, they engineered situations that threw the prospective couple together, the local bimonthly box suppers being a favorite venue, and let nature take its course.

"Forget Faylene," Marty said now. "Why don't we just find a man for Daisy?" Of the three women, Daisy Hunter was the only one who had never married. Marty, having buried one husband and divorced another, had officially sworn off men for herself.

Sasha had divorced four husbands and readily admitted to having abominable taste in men, but that didn't keep her from choosing mates for other singles. "Lost cause," she said now. "Daisy knows plenty of men—what about all those doctors she works with?"

"What, after Jerry whatsisname? He of the sockless Gucci loafers? He of the Armani suits and the blow-dried hair, not to mention that god-awful cologne? The jerk who dumped her the night of the rehearsal dinner?"

"Yeah, there is that. You know what? The trouble with the nursing profession is that most of the people Daisy meets are either doctors or patients. When a patient happens to die, it's bound to be depressing, especially when it's one she's had as long as she had old man Snow."

"Well, duh. She's a geriatric nurse, for Pete's sake. She knew what she was getting into when she chose that specialty."

"She chose that specialty," Marty reminded her friend, "because she had the hots for the guy who used to manage that adult day-care center, remember? The one who turned out to be skimming profits?"

Sasha shrugged. "Okay, so she's got lousy taste in men. Join the club."

"That's right, your second husband got sent up for money laundering, didn't he?"

"Hell, no," the redhead said indignantly. "It was my first. I was only eighteen—what did I know?"

Both women chuckled. Marty said, "Right. So while she's grieving, house-sitting and packing stuff up for the thrift shop or whatever, we can start trolling for eligible bachelors between the ages of what, twenty-five and fifty? By the way, who've you got in mind for Faylene?"

Sasha frowned at her nails. "Hmm, it is sort of flashy, isn't it? Okay, two possibilities come to mind, but I thought we might start with Gus down at the place where I just got my brakes relined. I happen to know he's single."

"Gay?"

"You ever heard of a gay mechanic?" Sasha slipped off her sandals and contemplated her unpolished toenails while Marty continued to sip her wine.

"You know what, Sash? If we want to get Daisy involved in another project we really need to wait until she can sit in on the planning session. Maybe if we encourage her to come up with a few candidates on her own, she'll perk up and get involved. But I still say Faylene will have a hissy fit if she finds out what we're up to."

Applying purple glitter polish to a toenail, Sasha slanted her a grin. "She can have all the hissy fits she wants, just so she doesn't quit. You know me and housecleaning."

A few miles outside the small soundside town of Muddy Landing in a handsome old house that had seen far better days, Daisy Hunter packed another box of her late patient's clothing, to be dropped off at the Hotline Thrift Shop the next time she was in Elizabeth City. It would've been better if she'd moved out the day after he'd died, but her apartment still wasn't ready. And then Egbert had suggested she stay on at least until she took on another case, and one thing had led to another.

"The estate will continue to pay your salary while you inventory and pack away personal property. Aside from that, houses left standing empty for any length of time tend to deteriorate rather rapidly," he'd told her. Egbert had a precise way of speaking that, while it wasn't particularly exciting, was certainly reassuring. A woman would always know where she stood with a man like Egbert Blalock.

Up until Harvey's death she and the banker had been only nodding acquaintances. Since then they had met several times to discuss Harvey's business affairs. It was during the second such meeting—or perhaps it was the third—that she'd begun to consider him from a personal standpoint. The more she thought about it, the more certain she was that he was excellent husband material. After all, she wasn't getting any younger, and if she ever intended to have a family of her own—and she definitely did—it was time.

So while Faylene, the three-day-a-week housekeeper, gave the old house one last going-over, including rooms that had been closed off for decades, Daisy made lists, packed away various personal effects and thought about how to go about making a match for herself. She knew how to do it for someone else, but objectivity flew out the window when she started thinking of deliberately engineering a match for herself.

Naturally she hadn't confided in either of her friends. Knowing Marty and Sasha, at the first hint of any personal interest they'd have taken over and mismanaged the whole affair. Sasha tried on husbands the way other women tried on shoes. Marty was not a whole lot better, although she swore she'd learned after her last experience.

Catching sight of herself in the large dresser mirror, Daisy touched her rumpled hair. At least it was dry now, but the color wouldn't attract a dead moth, much less a man. She was long overdue for a trim, but before she did anything too drastic she needed to find out if Egbert preferred long hair or short. Did he like blondes, and if so, how blond? Platinum? Honey? Her hair was that indeterminate color usually called dishwater.

His was a nice shade of medium brown, thinning slightly on top. Not that hair loss was anything to be ashamed of, she reminded herself hastily. These days baldness was a fashion statement. It was even considered sexy. And while Egbert wasn't exactly sexy, neither could he be labeled *un*sexy. Sasha had once called him dull. Daisy hadn't bothered to correct her. Egbert wasn't dull, he was simply steady, reliable and dependable, all excellent traits in a husband. Some women might prefer a flashier type—not too long ago, Daisy would have, too. Now she knew better. Been there, done that, to use a cliché.

Her stomach growled, reminding her that she hadn't eaten since breakfast. Once she'd returned to the house after the service, she had quickly changed out of her damp clothes and gotten to work again, anxious to get the job done so that she'd be ready to set her own plans in motion. A stickler for propriety, she preferred to wait until she was finished here before launching her campaign.

Folding another of Harvey's tan-and-white-striped dress shirts—he must have had a dozen, all the same color and style—Daisy allowed her thoughts to drift back to the brief rainy service and the stranger she'd seen there. Whoever he was, he definitely wasn't a local. She'd have noticed him if she'd ever seen him before. What woman wouldn't? Those long legs and broad shoulders—the high, angular cheekbones, not to mention the startlingly blue eyes. As a rule, eye color was barely discernible from a distance of more than a few feet, but the stranger's eyes had reminded her of glow-in-the-dark LEDs.

What color were Egbert's eyes, she wondered idly—hazel?

Brown. It was Harvey whose eyes had been hazel, usually twinkling with humor despite his painfully twisted body. Bless his heart, he should have had a family with him at the end, only he didn't have a family and most of his friends had either died or moved away. A couple still lived in Elizabeth City, but their visits had dwindled over the past year.

As she went about layering articles in a box, Daisy thought back to the last hour she had spent with her patient. The noise of the television had bothered him, so she'd read him the newspapers. They'd gotten as far as the editorials when somewhere in the middle of Tom Friedman's piece on nation-building he'd fallen asleep. As it was nothing unusual, she had quietly refolded the paper, adjusted the covers and turned off the light.

The next morning she'd prepared his morning meds and rapped on the door of his bedroom. Hearing no response, she had entered to find her patient sleeping peacefully.

And, as it turned out, permanently.

She hadn't cried, but sooner or later she probably would. She'd been closer to Harvey Snow than with other patients, maybe because she'd admired his courage. Living alone with a steadily worsening case of rheumatoid arthritis and then two small strokes, he had never lost his sense of humor.

Sooner or later the tears would come, probably at the worst possible time. It did no good to try to suppress them, this much she knew, both as a nurse and as a woman. Spare the tears and suffer a head cold. The correlation might not have been clinically proved, but she believed it with all her heart.

A deep sigh shuddered through her as she closed the box and taped it shut. Wrenching her thoughts from her depressing task, she made up her mind not to wait any longer to have her hair trimmed, styled and maybe even lightened. She needed cheering up. In fact, she might even take a day off to go shopping, keeping in mind that Egbert's tastes were probably more conservative than her own. But even a classic shirtwaist could be unbuttoned to show a hint of cleavage and maybe a flash of thigh.

As long as she was shopping, she might as well look for something long and swishy in case he invited her to go dancing. The holidays were coming up, and it had been ages since anyone had taken her out dancing. That used to be her favorite aerobic exercise.

Did Egbert even dance? Maybe they could brush up on their skills together. Dancing skills as well as a few other skills, she thought, trying to drum up a twist of excitement.

She was too tired for excitement. It had been a long day—a long, depressing day, but at least it was nearly over. First thing next week she would get on with her own agenda.

In fact, she could get started right now by calling Paul and making an appointment to get her hair done. Nothing too noticeable, just enough to make Egbert take a second look and wonder if he'd been missing something.

She reached for the phone just as the darn thing rang. Startled, she dropped the roll of tape she'd been holding. The calls had started as soon as word got out about Harvey's passing—everything from tombstone salesmen to local historians wanting a tour of the house, to antique dealers and real estate people wanting to know what, if anything, would be sold off.

She referred all calls to Egbert as Harvey's executor. "Snow residence," she snapped. What she needed was an answering machine, only she wasn't going to be here that long.

"Daisy, honey, you sound like you need a massage—either that or a stiff drink and a three-pound box of chocolate-covered cherries. How'd it go today?"

"You mean other than the fact that it was pouring rain and the preacher kept sneezing and only a handful of people showed up?"

"Hey, we offered," Sasha reminded her.

"I know, I'm just being bitchy. Make that chocolate-covered coconut and I might bite." Daisy dropped tiredly down on the sleigh bed that had been moved back into the room after the rental service had collected the hospital bed. She'd been fighting depression for days.

"Look, Marty and I were thinking—it's time we took on another project. Now that she's closed her bookstore she's drinking too much." Daisy could hear the protest in the background. "I know for a fact that she's gained five pounds. You game?"

Smiling tiredly because she knew they were only trying to cheer her up, she said, "Count me out on this one. The last thing I need now is to try to rearrange someone else's life when I'm up to my ears in artifacts that so far as I know, no one even wants."

"Oh, honey—I know it's real sad, but moping's not going to get you anywhere." Sasha had a softer side, but she'd learned to cover it with a glitzy style and an off-hand manner.

"I'm not moping." As a professional, Daisy knew

better than to get too personally involved with a patient. On the other hand, she'd been with Harvey longer than with most of her previous patients.

"How 'bout it, you ready for a challenge?" Sasha teased.

Daisy sighed. She'd been doing a lot of that lately. Better they think she was grieving than making plans for her own future. If she even hinted as much, the next thing she knew she'd be engaged to some jerk candidate they'd found in a singles' bar.

No, thanks. Once she set her mind on a course of action she preferred to manage it on her own, the same way she'd been doing ever since her foster parents had split when she was thirteen and neither of them had wanted her. She had managed then, just as she would manage now. By this time next year she fully intended to be settled in Egbert's tidy Cape Cod on Park Drive, with—in layman's terms—a bun in the oven.

"Da-aisy. Wake up, hon."

"I'm here, just barely. Okay, who've you got in mind?"

"Faylene."

Her jaw dropped. "No way! A new project is one thing, but a lost cause is exactly what I don't need at the moment." For the past several years Faylene Beasley had worked part-time for Harvey and part-time for Daisy's two best friends. As a housekeeper she was superb, but a target for matchmaking? "You're not serious," Daisy said flatly.

"Serious as a root canal. Honey, have you noticed how grouchy she's been getting lately? That woman needs a man in her bed."

Outside, the rain continued to drone down on the

steep slate roof. So much for the Indian summer the weatherman had promised. Daisy's stomach growled, reminding her again that she hadn't eaten since a skimpy breakfast. "Look, call me tomorrow. Right now I'm too tired to think about it. I'm going to grab a bite of early supper and fall into bed. I might have another bachelor candidate for us to work with."

Not for Faylene, though. Oh, no—whoever he was, he had to be someone extra special.

Two

Kell's boots still weren't dry, but at least he'd scraped most of the mud off. As disappointed as he was that he'd arrived too late to meet his half uncle, he had to admit he'd enjoyed watching the mystery woman dancing around, trying to keep from sinking up to her ankles. Not that he was a leg man, but she had nice ones. She was a blonde—sort of, anyway. With her hooded raincoat and shades, he hadn't been able to see much more than half a pale face, a few wet strands and a pair of mud-spattered legs. But she definitely had world-class ankles.

Still reeling from learning that the guy he'd come so far to see had died, Kell hadn't bothered to ask Blalock about the woman who had answered the phone when he'd called from the outskirts of town the night before. The one who had referred him to the banker. The bank had been closed by that time and he'd been forced to wait until this morning.

He should have called back when he'd first discovered a possible connection between the Snows of North Carolina and the Magees of Oklahoma City, but he'd had some things to wind up before he could leave town. Then, too, he sort of liked the idea of turning up unexpectedly, picturing Half Uncle Harvey opening the door, taking one look and recognizing him as his long-lost nephew.

Yeah, like that would have happened. Kell didn't look anything like his dad. They might be built along the same lines, but Evander Magee had had red hair and freckles. The only facial features they shared were eye color and a shallow cleft in a chin that had been likened a time or two to the Rock of Gibraltar.

Okay, so he might've been overly optimistic, taking off without even notifying Snow of his intentions. A pessimist probably wouldn't have bothered to track down a possible relative in the first place. Trouble was, even now, after all that had happened in his thirty-nine-plus years, Kell was a dogged optimist. Back in his pitching days he'd gone into every game fully expecting to win. As a starter, he might not go nine innings, but he'd damned well do seven. So it stood to reason that once he'd started the search, he'd had to follow through every lead.

It hadn't helped when he'd got to Muddy Landing after dark only to find that the town's only motel had been closed ever since Hurricane Isabel had blown through back in September. He'd had to drive miles out of the way and settle for a hole-in-the-wall place where the bed was too short, the walls too thin, the pillows padded with that stuff that fought back. If he hung around much longer he might be tempted to buy himself a camper and a good pillow, only he didn't think the Porsche was rated for towing.

Bottom line—he had found Harvey Snow a couple of days too late, spent a miserable night on a lousy mattress and, as a result, overslept. He had skipped breakfast, showed up at the bank nearly an hour past opening time and then had to wait to see a man named Blalock who had tried to brush him off, claiming he was pressed for time.

Kell was no quitter. Blocking the door of Blalock's office, he'd introduced himself and explained why he was there—that he'd been given his name, and that his father had had a younger half brother named Harvey Snow. And that he needed to know how to locate the man as the phone book listed a rural-route number instead of a street address.

That was when he'd heard the bad news. "I'm sorry to tell you, but the man you're looking for recently passed away. He's being buried today, in fact. I'm on my way to the service now, so if you'll excuse me?"

It had taken Kell a moment to digest the news. He hadn't moved.

"So far as anyone knows," the smug banker had gone on to say, "Mr. Snow left no surviving relatives."

Kell had felt like protesting, *Dammit, I'm a surviving relative!*

Instead he'd ended up following Blalock through a driving rain along miles of narrow blacktop to a country graveyard. After that, he'd followed him back to the bank. Only now, after the banker had called up a few records on his computer and then grilled him like a trout on a spit, was he finally headed out to see where his father had once lived.

Supposedly lived, as Blalock had stipulated.

Kell figured he could spare five days. A week at most. The boys back home could handle things at the store. If not, they had a go-to number.

Somewhere along the line, working with at-risk kids had segued into even more of a full-time job than the sporting goods store he used as a training ground. He was also in the process of turning a working ranch into a baseball camp, so he had just about everything a man could want. Satisfying work, financial security and enough women of the noncommitted variety to keep him happy well into his senior years.

On the other hand, there was this roots thing. Once he'd started digging, he hated like hell to give up. Blalock might have reservations about the Snow-Magee connection, but Kell trusted his instincts, and those were signaling loud and clear that he was right on target. His dad might have spent most of his life in Oklahoma, but Kell would bet his seven-figure portfolio that his roots were in Muddy Landing.

Following the narrow, wet highway between flat fields and a marshy shoreline dotted with private landings and small boats, he was wishing he'd paid more attention back when his old man used to reminisce about bear hunting in the Great Dismal Swamp and fishing on the Outer Banks. Both areas were less than an hour's drive from Muddy Landing. That alone was evidence that he was on the right track.

Trouble was, he'd usually been too impatient to listen. Hanging in the open doorway, baseball glove in hand, he'd been like, *yeah, yeah, look, I gotta run now, the guys are waiting.* He wished now he'd paid more attention when his dad had had a few beers and got to rambling, but at the time about all he'd been interested in was playing pickup baseball and showing off his best stuff in case any girls were watching.

Speaking of girls—or in this case, women—he had a feeling the woman in the black raincoat was the same one he'd spoken to on the phone, the one who'd referred him to Blalock. Hadn't Blalock said that Snow's nurse was still staying at the house, winding up a few things? Kell thought it was damned decent of her to show up at the funeral. Not many others had bothered. Dressed the way she was, with those wraparound shades, she'd reminded him of one of those mysterious women you saw in movies standing alone at some high-class funeral. They always turned out to be the Other Woman.

The question was, whose Other Woman was the lady in black? Half Uncle Harvey's?

If Blalock knew, he wasn't talking. After only a couple of brief conversations before and after the graveside service, Kell got the distinct impression that the banker was reluctant to uncover any possible link between his client and Kell's father. From an executor's point of view, a relative coming in from left field at this stage of the game might muddy up the waters. Blalock struck him as the kind of guy who liked his waters nice and clear with no hidden snags.

Kell should have assured him right off the bat that he wasn't interested in the estate. Now that it was too late to meet his relative, all he wanted was a chance to learn more about his father's early life and maybe even meet a few cousins if any lived nearby.

The trail had split some fifty-odd years ago when sixteen-year-old Evander Magee had left home. Kell, who'd been fourteen when both his parents had died in the fire that had blazed through their double-wide, burning any documentary evidence they might have possessed, had never even thought about his roots until recently. The combination of watching his fortieth birthday barrel down on him and becoming a godfather to his best friend's twin sons had set him to thinking about family.

That's when Kell had first confronted the fact that he was the last in the Magee line. That was a pretty heavy burden on the shoulders of a man who had conscientiously avoided anything that even smelled like commitment.

He thought again about the bedraggled blonde in black. Kell liked blondes. He liked women, period—wearing black or any other color. Better yet, wearing nothing at all. She'd sounded pretty cool on the phone. She'd looked cold, wet and miserable in the flesh.

He wondered if she'd thawed out yet.

The day of the funeral seemed endless. By late afternoon the rain had finally tapered off. While her friends, who evidently thought she shouldn't be left alone, sipped iced tea and leafed through an old issue of *Southern Living,* an exhausted Daisy relaxed in the dark green cane rocker on a screened porch that had been damaged in the hurricane and never repaired. She watched rose-tinted clouds float over the hedgerow, smelled the fresh green scent of broken branches and wet, overgrown pittosporum. This was her favorite place to sit as long as the mosquitoes weren't too bad.

It had been slightly more than two months since Hurricane Isabel had come whipping across the sound, roaring upriver all the way to Muddy Landing and beyond. Things were still in a mess. Construction workers, already pushed to the limit building those little starter houses that were springing up like toadstools, had quit building to repair hurricane damage. The owner of her apartment building kept making excuses as to why the place wasn't ready for reoccupancy, and she understood, she really did, but darn it, she couldn't stay here much longer. She had her own life to get on with.

Sprawled out in the glider, Marty and Sasha were talking about a DVD they had recently rented, arguing the merits of Jude Law over Johnny Depp. Daisy wished they would leave so she could get on with the job of going through closets, drawers and shelves, and helping Faylene give one last cleaning to rooms that hadn't been used in decades. Maybe tomorrow she'd feel more like shopping and doing something about her hair, but not now. Not when she was surrounded by reminders of a gentle man whose entire adult life had been filled with pain and loneliness.

"Stop mooning about that poor man. He lived a full life," Sasha said.

"I doubt it," Marty murmured. "Didn't you say he was bedridden, Daisy?"

"Only the last few months. After his strokes. Before that he got around just fine in his chair. And I'm not mooning, I'm tired. I promised Eg—Mr. Blalock we'd have the house ready to show by the end of next week."

"Show to who? Whom?"

She shrugged. "All those people who've been calling, I guess." She drifted off again, thinking of all that needed doing and where to draw the line. Thank goodness she had never collected much beyond her clothes, a few nice pieces of furniture and a shelfful of her favorite authors, the latter thanks to Marty's generous discount. That was one of the benefits of having a bookseller for a friend.

Sasha said, "Well, he's always been pleasant to me, even when he had cars lined up waiting for service."

Who, Harvey? Daisy jerked her meandering thoughts back to the present. Being nice to a gorgeous redhead was no big deal, but since when had Harvey had cars lined up? He hadn't driven in years. Didn't even own a car anymore.

"His garage is neat as a pin—for a garage, that is. And we know he's honest," Sasha continued.

Oh. They must be talking about Faylene's potential suitor. "How do we know that?" Daisy wasn't particularly interested in the prospective match. If they'd been talking about matching up anyone but Faylene she might have opted out, but none of them could get along without the housekeeper. If Faylene wasn't happy, someone had darned well better find out why and do something about it.

"For one thing," the redhead explained, "when he changed my oil and rotated my tires last week he charged me exactly what he charged Oren." Oren being her next-door neighbor.

"Okay, so it's just barely possible he won't try to con her out of her life's savings." Having once been taken for everything she owned by a man who claimed to adore her, integrity ranked high on Daisy's list of requirements—another area where Egbert scored in the top one percentile. "When it comes to dealing with his customers he might be trustworthy, but—"

"Look, all we're trying to do here is get them together for a first date. They're bound to know each other casually, the same way everybody in Muddy Landing knows everybody else here, right?" Sasha waited for nods of agreement. "So all we have to do is get the two of them up close and personal and see if anything clicks. I mean, Gus is no Joe Millionaire and Faye's certainly not whatsername, fill in the blanks, but they're probably about the same age—fiftyish—and they're both single. Who knows, he might take one deep look into her eyes and—"

"And ignore everything else," Marty said dryly. "Okay, so Gus has all his own hair and teeth, and Faye—well, you have to admit she has great legs."

It went without saying that her hair was a disaster and her face had more wrinkles than a box of prunes. Her exact age remained a mystery, but she wore white sneakers, white shorts and support hose in all but the coldest months so that her legs, which really were shapely, appeared at first glance to be bare and smoothly tanned.

Daisy said, "He'll freak if she takes him home with her." Faylene lived in Crooked Creek Mobile Home Park, the small area surrounding her single-wide graced by forty-seven pieces of concrete sculpture at last count.

"So she collects art." Sasha shrugged. "He probably

collects something, most men do." Two of her three husbands had collected other women.

"Whatever, they can work it out between them. Anyone heard anything about his sexual practices?"

"Does he practice?"

"The question is, how many hours a day does he practice?"

"No, the question is, how good is he?"

The two other women batted that particular ball back and forth until Daisy broke into a reluctant grin. Chuckling, Sasha said, "Oh, hush up, y'all know what I mean. After that last fiasco, we need to be sure of his, uh— persuasion."

Marty said, "Methodist. You reckon he goes to any box suppers? I don't remember seeing him there."

"If he does, that means he probably can't cook," Daisy offered.

"Or that he's big on charity." The box suppers raised money for various charities, most recently for victims of Hurricane Isabel. The three women had found it a handy place to dish a little dirt and scout out matchmaking prospects—or as Daisy put it, victims.

"If he can thaw and microwave, that's more than Faye can do," Sasha reminded them.

"Here, here." Marty lifted her glass of iced tea in a toast. "So are we going to do boxes for the next supper?" We, meaning Daisy. The other two women provided the raw material; it was Daisy who turned it into a delectable feast. "I think it's Wednesday after next—or maybe this coming Wednesday. What's today's date, anyway?"

Daisy's attention had strayed again. Maybe she

should try one of those short, spiky cuts. Or maybe not. Egbert probably preferred a more conservative style. "Hmm? What date? Oh, Faylene's date."

Sasha glanced at her watch, which, depending on the button pushed, revealed everything from the phase of the moon to the Dow Jones averages. "Okay, this is Friday—it's this coming Wednesday. Outside if the weather holds, in the community center if it rains or turns out cold."

"Oh, great," Marty said dryly. "That'll be romantic. Dibs on the table by the john."

"Oh, hush, the weather will be perfect. So...shall we do our usual, only this time four boxes instead of three? I have a big purple gift bow I can donate. All we have to do then is tag one of the boxes with Faylene's name and tip Gus off that the one with the purple bow has all his favorite food inside."

"First we'll have to find out what his favorite foods are," said Daisy, ever practical.

"No, first I'd better do something about her hair." Sasha was into hair. Her own had ranged from apricot to auburn to titian over the past few years. When she'd claimed to have forgotten what her original color was, Marty had suggested she watch her roots for a clue.

"Well, she can't wear those shorts to a church box supper. Her legs might look great from a distance, but once you get closer—" Marty shook her head and grinned.

"As the lucky guy who buys her dinner will inevitably do." Sasha again. "Okay, I'll work on her hair. Marty, you organize something decent for her to wear. That leaves the box. How about it, Daisy?"

The youngest member of the group by two or three years was still gazing out at the soybean fields and hedgerows bounding the Snow property. She would miss the peacefulness once she moved back to her apartment. Muddy Landing had started life as a tiny settlement with only a few farmhouses—one of them being Marty's—a farm equipment dealer and a bait-and-tackle shop. Over the past few decades it had tripled in growth, and now that the Greater Norfolk Area was spilling out across the state line, it was rapidly turning into a bedroom community.

Sasha snapped her fingers. "Earth to Daisy. You still with us, hon? What about it, you want to do your famous buttermilk fried chicken, a few of those luscious corn fritters, maybe some slaw and a couple of slices of that sinful chocolate-rum pie?"

"What? Oh…well, sure, but maybe we should run through a few more candidates first." Daisy might be still single, but she knew how these man-woman things were supposed to work. Chemistry was important, but it would get you only so far. Unless there was something solid underneath, once the initial reaction fizzled out you were left with a total stranger.

Not that chemistry was even an issue where Egbert was concerned. That was the soundest part of her plan. Since there was no chemistry to begin with, it wouldn't be missed when it fizzled out, as it inevitably would. She might not be as experienced as her friends, Daisy assured herself, but that didn't mean she was naive. Far from it. The difference was that, unlike either of her two friends, she recognized good, solid husband material when she saw it.

At least she did now.

The wonder was that they hadn't already added Egbert to their list of candidates. His wife had been dead almost a year now.

When the phone rang inside the house, Daisy groaned and got up to answer it, muttering about what she would do if one more salesman tried to sell her anything.

The moment she left, Sasha and Marty started talking in hushed tones. "Dammit, I told you she was depressed! She can't even keep track of what we're talking about—she just stares out there as if she's lost her last friend," Sasha hissed.

"Well, they were close. He was sort of a grandfather figure, especially once she moved in with him."

"Big mistake. I told you so at the time, remember?"

"Yes, well, spilt milk and all that." Marty looked around for her glasses. They were on top of her head.

"Anyhow, she said Faylene's coming over this evening, so we need to get her to find out what she likes and doesn't like in a man."

"What who likes, Daisy or Faylene?"

"Both. Either. Oh, you know what I mean. The trouble with Gus is he lives over that garage of his. Even if things work out, can you see him toting Faylene up those stairs to get her across the threshold?"

Marty pursed her lips. Sasha had told her more than once that if she'd just get a few collagen injections, she could pass for Julia Roberts, only with bigger eyes. "He could always use the lift—that thingee he uses to get cars hoisted up so he can see all the whatchamadoodles underneath."

"Did anyone ever tell you that for a former bookstore owner, your vocabulary is lamentably lacking?"

Before Marty could come up with a suitably erudite response, Daisy was back.

"That was Egbert—Mr. Blalock," she said. "I've been routinely referring calls to his office since Harvey's lawyer died last fall. He said a man showed up this morning who claims to be a relative."

"Of Harvey's? I thought he didn't have any family," Marty said.

"I don't think he did, at least no one close enough to count. But Egbert—that is, Mr. Blalock's been going over some records since the service this morning and he thinks this one might warrant checking out. He said the man had even insisted on going to the funeral."

Daisy's eyes suddenly widened. Please, not the cowboy! If that's who was claiming to be a relative, she was out of here. Vamoosed. Whatever. All she knew was that she couldn't deal with anyone that distracting. Besides, he hadn't looked anything at all like Harvey.

After a sleepless night and an endless day she looked like something the cat dragged in.

Not that it mattered, she told herself as she hurried to the bathroom to do something about her hair.

Three

Kell Magee neared the house where he was all but certain his father had spent his first sixteen years. If he'd learned one thing over a wildly erratic thirty-nine years, it was to keep his expectations realistic. That was one of the things he tried to pass on to kids who usually preferred to talk about his short career as a starting pitcher. The first thing most of them wanted to know was how much money he'd made, his stock answer being, "Not as much as Greg Maddux or Randy Johnson, but a lot more than I ever expected."

It was late that evening when Kell pulled into the driveway under a row of big pecan trees, taking care to avoid parking under any of several dangling limbs. He checked his notes again. Oh, man, he mused, gazing up at a house that looked like a wedding cake that had been left out in a hard rain. Just to be sure he hadn't made a mistake, he climbed out of the Porsche and walked back to recheck the name on the mailbox.

H. Snow. The small, stick-on letters were starting to peel off.

It was when he turned back toward the three-story house with all the gables, the stained-glass windows and the dangling gutter that he saw the woman standing in the doorway. Even with the sun glaring in his eyes he recognized her as the same woman he'd seen at the cemetery that morning. Something about the way she was standing looked familiar, even though she was considerably drier now and minus the raincoat.

Squaring his shoulders—that bed last night hadn't done his back any favors—Kell ambled toward the front porch. "Hi there," he greeted once he was in range. "You left before Blalock could introduce us this morning, but he probably told you I'd be along." The way she confronted him with her arms crossed over her breast wasn't exactly welcoming. "You must be Ms. Hunter. The nurse?"

She waited to speak until he got close enough to see the spattering of freckles across her cheeks. "May I see some identification?"

At the bottom of the steps he froze. "Sure…" He had the usual stack of stuff crammed into his wallet. He'd left copies of most of it with Blalock. Why the hell hadn't the guy warned her that he'd be coming out to see the place? "Name's Kelland Magee," he said, reaching toward his hip pocket. "I guess Blalock at the bank told you we're pretty sure Harvey Snow was my uncle? Half uncle, at least."

By now Kell was all but certain of the relationship,

even though Blalock insisted on reserving final judgment—probably waiting for a DNA comparison.

Propping a foot on the bottom step, he adjusted his outward attitude, shooting for friendly and nonthreatening, but with subtle overtones of authority. "Did he tell you my dad's mother married a man named Snow from this neck of the woods after her first husband died?" Shuffling through his credentials, he moved up another two steps. Once he reached the porch he stopped and held out a driver's license and his social security card, which he knew better than to use as identification, but at this point he was getting a little desperate. Without moving a muscle, the lady was messing with his mind. This time her ankles had nothing to do with it.

While she studied his credentials, Kell pretended to take in the littered lawn while his excellent peripheral vision roamed over her streaky blond hair and a pair of steel-gray eyes that were about as warm as a walk-in freezer. Early to midthirties, he estimated. Nice mouth. If she ever relaxed so far as to smile, it'd probably be in a class with her ankles.

He waited for her to invite him inside. Finally she looked up, nailing him with a chilly stare. "What did Mr. Blalock tell you?"

"About what?" He scrambled through his two brief meetings with the banker, trying to recall everything that had been said while he'd attempted to convince the man to let him at least look over the place where his father had allegedly grown up.

"About—well, about Mr. Snow." Her voice was soft but firm, and if that was an oxymoron, then so were all those mattress ads. "You said he might have been your uncle. How do I know you're not a—a dealer of some sort."

"Come again?"

Still guarding the doorway, she handed him back his documents and recrossed her arms. And then for no apparent reason, she seemed to drop her guard. "Oh, all right. You might as well come inside, but I'm warning you, if you try to sell me anything, or want to buy anything, you're out of here, is that understood?"

Well, hell. In other words, look but don't touch. "Yes, ma'am."

Kell followed her inside, unable to keep his eyes from widening. The entire place, at least what he could see from the front hall, was crammed with stuff that looked like it all belonged in a museum. In his stellar, if somewhat abbreviated, career as a major league pitcher, Kell had stayed in some fine hotels. He had run with the kind of folks who had money to burn. In fact, for a while he'd burned his share, too—that is, until he'd wised up and started putting it to a better use.

But this was different. This was *real* stuff. The kind that was handed down, not the kind decorators went out and bought when they were commissioned to fill up an empty space. He knew. Once, back in Houston, when he'd gotten tired of staying in an apartment that looked as if he was waiting for the rest of his furniture to show up, he'd hired one. After three months and a whole bunch of money, he'd ended up surrounded by a lot of chrome, black marble, thick glass and white leather. As for the pictures, they had reminded him of the graffiti you saw scribbled on ruined walls in the barrio—not that he'd ever claimed to be an art critic.

"Well, are you coming, or are you going to stand there gawking all day?"

"Oh, yes, ma'am, you lead the way and I'll follow." If her backside looked anywhere near as good as her frontside, he'd follow her all the way up those stairs to the nearest bedroom. Only he didn't think that was what she had in mind.

Nor, he reminded himself sternly, was it what he had in mind. At least it hadn't been until he'd seen her up close and more or less undraped. Funny thing, the way some women could trigger a certain reaction. He'd read somewhere that the average male had seven spontaneous erections over the course of twenty-four hours, five of them when he was asleep.

Oh, man, this could prove embarrassing.

She'd changed into a pair of khaki shorts and a faded blue T-shirt. Hardly mourning clothes, but definitely not Frederick's of Hollywood, either. As for her eyes…

Kell had never been real partial to gray eyes. Several women he knew wore colored contacts, but gray was actually kind of nice. Sort of restful. Might even call it romantic in a mysterious sort of way.

Get with the game, Magee, you're missing the signals.

Bypassing the curving stairway, she led him to a big, high-ceilinged kitchen where an older woman in tight white shorts was stacking dishes in an open box. The woman pointed at him, using a flowered teapot as a pointer. "I know you! Who are you?"

"He says his name is Kelland Magee," the blonde supplied, as if she hadn't devoured every line on the cards he'd handed her. "He says Mr. Snow was his uncle."

"I said he might have been," Kell corrected. "I mean, I'm pretty certain a man named Harvey Snow was my father's younger half brother, but the courthouse was closing just as I got there, so I won't know for sure if this is the right one until we do some more checking." And this was Friday, dammit. "There might've been more than one Harvey Snow around here." He waited, tense as a rookie pitching his first game in the majors.

While his overall education was a little spotty, Kell had learned to trust his instincts. Right now those instincts were telling him that no matter what Blalock said, this house, as different as it was from anything he could have imagined, was where his father had spent his first sixteen years, or near enough.

"I'm pretty sure this is the right place. I mean the right Harvey Snow. The Dismal Swamp—" He nodded in the direction where he thought it might be located, hoping to impress her with his knowledge of the area. If that didn't work, he'd try out his charm on her. Stuff used to work on groupies, but hell—that had been more than ten years ago. The use-by date on any charm he might once have possessed had long since expired.

Taking a deep breath, Daisy did her best to pretend she was wearing a freshly laundered uniform instead of her grunge clothes. Cleaning and packing was hot work. It wasn't enough that the first time she'd seen him she'd probably looked like a witch on a bad day—now she looked even worse. She hadn't had time to do much with her hair, and unless she used a blow-dryer and a big roller brush on it, it always ended up looking like last year's squirrel's nest.

And all this matters…why?

She didn't know why, she really didn't, except that there was something about his voice—and his face. Not to mention his body. Her gaze fell to his pelvic area and she felt heat rush to her face. He had on the same pair of low-rise jeans he'd been wearing this morning, the kind that were cut full in the groin area to accommodate…whatever.

"Miss?"

"Yes, all right!" If anyone had ever offered her even the smallest chance to learn something about her own heritage, she'd have jumped at it. The least she could do was give him the benefit of the doubt. "All right, come on, then. This is Faylene Beasley." She nodded toward the housekeeper. "It's late and we're both busy, but I guess I can make time to show you around." Her slight effort to sound gracious fell about five miles short of the mark.

The Beasley woman squinted at him. "Magee? Sounds kinda familiar. Long drink o' water, ain't you? I bet you played basketball."

Kell shook his head. "Basketball? Sorry, must be some other Magee." The nurse had sailed off down the hall, so he hurried after her. He had an idea the fuse on her patience was burning down fast, but before it fizzled out he intended to squeeze every drop of information from her he could. If nothing else he could enjoy the view.

She stopped beside the polished oak stairs and said, "What did Faylene mean, she knew you?"

"Faylene?"

"The housekeeper you just met. She said she knew you."

Housekeeper, huh? Funny uniform for a housekeeper. More like the *Playboy* bunny from hell. "Beats me. I guess I've got one of those generic faces. Be surprised how many people think they know me from somewhere."

She didn't bother to hide her skepticism.

Amused, Kell considered telling her about his fifteen minutes of fame. It was more like five seasons, three of them going into play-offs, but that might sound like bragging. He had a feeling the lady would not be impressed.

Idly, he wondered what it would take to impress her.

Determined to show him around and get rid of him, Daisy popped open one door after another on the second floor, allowing him to peer inside before she hurried him down the hall. With all her heart she wished that the stranger she'd first seen this morning looked less impressive at closer range. He was setting off alarms in parts of her body that had been peacefully dormant for years.

"They're all furnished more or less alike," she told him, keeping her tone impersonal. They had vacuumed about half the rooms and replaced the dust covers. Reaching a door at the far end of the hall, she popped it open and then started to close it, having had about all she could take for one day. Before she could pull the door shut again, the man who said his name was Magee brushed past her. Intensely aware of the scent of leather, aftershave and healthy male skin, she wished she'd had time to shower and change into something fresher.

No, she didn't! Of course she didn't!

The small room was lit only by light that fell through a west-facing dormer. Not bothering to switch on the overhead fixture, she said briskly, "There's nothing of interest here, so if you're ready?"

Instead of backing out, he stepped into the room.

"Hey, my mama had one of those things back in Oklahoma," he exclaimed, sounding as if the fact that the Snows and the Magees had something in common proved his case beyond a doubt.

The article in question was a treadle sewing machine, its shiny black head gleaming with gilt scrollwork. Surrendering to the inevitable, Daisy moved inside the small room. The sooner his curiosity was satisfied, the sooner he'd leave. She said, "I believe Mr. Snow's mother used this as a sewing room. I don't think it's been used for anything else since then, except maybe for storage." Did sewing machines count as personal property or furniture? She'd have to ask Egbert. "Are you ready?" She would have tapped her foot to illustrate her impatience, only she lacked the energy.

"Those boxes, what do you suppose is in them?"

Oh, shoot. She'd forgotten those. "Probably fabrics. Maybe mending that never got done." And because she was physically exhausted and emotionally stressed, the poignancy of the whole situation suddenly struck her. She could picture it, even though she had seen nothing like it in her entire life: a pile of clothes—shirts and small overalls—stacked beside the sewing machine, waiting for patches to be sewn on and seams to be stitched up.

She didn't need this, she really didn't. She had never even known Harvey's mother. Couldn't remember his even mentioning the woman.

Turning away, she swallowed a sob, only to choke on the next one. There was no holding back. By the time she started making squeaky noises in the back of her throat he was hovering over her.

"Daisy? Ms. Hunter?"

God, how embarrassing! "Go on downstairs. I—I'll just—I'll just…"

His hands came down on her shoulders and he pulled her into his arms. She shook her head. *I don't want this, I really, really don't.*

But she really, really did. Irrational or not, there were only so many tears a body could hold before the dam broke. "Allergies," she muttered while he made small, comforting sounds in a language that was universal.

Even with her nose stopped up she was aware of it again—that leathery, woodsy scent that was so essentially male. She tried to blame allergies for causing her to break down. She'd been allergic to her ex-fiancé's cologne. Jerry, a typical metrosexual who spent more on maintenance each month than she did in an entire year, used cologne lavishly.

Magee was nothing at all like Jerry. Feature by feature, he wasn't even handsome, not by Hollywood standards, yet the sum total was—

She didn't want to think about the sum total, not when all it took was a few comforting words spoken in that dark molasses voice of his to affect regions of her body that had been neglected far too long.

She was a noisy crier, which was one of the reasons she tried not to indulge if there was anyone within hearing distance. Once she got started, she bawled, boohooed and squealed like a day-old piglet.

It didn't help that he kept making those warm, rusty, there-there sounds while his hands stroked her back. His chin was moving over the top of her head, probably searching for her off button. She took a deep, steadying breath but didn't pull away. Another few seconds, she promised herself.

Maybe she'd make him close his eyes first. As if this morning hadn't been bad enough, add red eyes and a wet nose. By now her hair must look as if she'd just lost a battle with a leaf blower.

"Better now?" he inquired softly. The way he was holding her, there was no way she could fail to be aware of every hard, interesting contour of his body. She'd heard of an embarrassment of riches. This was an embarrassment of embarrassment.

"Thanks for your, uh—patience," she said with all the dignity she could muster, which wasn't a whole lot. "If you're through here, Faylene can show you around downstairs." She pulled away and backed into the cardboard box that had started the whole pathetic episode.

Well, hell. Let Faylene deal with whatever was in the box. She could give it away or dump it in the river, because Daisy couldn't handle another decision.

"Why can't you show me around downstairs?" Still the same warm honey tones, but she detected a steeliness now that hadn't been there a moment ago.

"Because I'll be busy in the attic." She'd forgotten about the attic until the box had reminded her.

He followed her out and closed the door, then nodded toward a narrow door in the shadowy end of the hallway. "Is that the attic stairway? Be funny if it turned out my dad had left some stuff up there, wouldn't it? I guess anything he might have left downstairs would have long since been tossed out, but attics…you never know, right?" He sounded as cool and impersonal as if the past few minutes had never happened.

Instead of turning toward the front stairway, he moved toward the attic door. "Why don't we check it out together? It'll only take a few more minutes."

Four

Daisy surrendered to the inevitable. The sooner she satisfied his curiosity, the sooner he'd leave. At least she had herself under control now, pink nose, puffy eyes and haystack hair notwithstanding.

This was turning out to be the day from hell. What more could happen? She'd planned to grab a nap as soon as she got home from the funeral and then start on another closet with Faylene's help, but Marty and Sasha had come by and stayed for almost an hour. No sooner had they left than the Lone Ranger had turned up with his blue eyes and his sexy voice, making all sorts of demands.

Actually, they were more requests than demands. All the same, she didn't need any more stress added to what she was already dealing with. "You can take a quick look, but whatever's up there is just junk. Things that were too good to throw away but not good enough to use. You know what attics are like."

"Matter of fact, I don't," he said, sounding far too guileless for a man who stood more than six feet even without the cowboy boots he affected. "We didn't have one where I grew up."

That's right, she thought, knowing she was being unfair—turn on the boyish charm, why don't you?

Trouble was, it was working. "Oh, come on then, if you must," she grumbled. "But make it fast, I still have a lot to do today."

The steps were narrow, steep and dark with ancient varnish. Four steps, then a landing and four more. She caught up with him on the landing where the pull cord was anchored, but before she could yank on the single bulb at the top of the stairway, he barged ahead.

"Watch out, there's a—"

Too late. He stumbled over the rocking chair she'd dodged the other day when she'd gone searching for boxes.

Bending over to rub his shin, Kell said, "Hey, this thing looks familiar. Maybe I saw it in a picture or something. It's possible, isn't it?"

How could he simply ignore what had happened in the sewing room when every cell in her body was still buzzing with—well, it was hardly sexual awareness, Daisy told herself. It had to be embarrassment. Shrugging, she said, "Sears Roebuck probably delivered thousands of them. A few might even have made it to Oklahoma."

It was as if he'd pulled down the shades on those brilliant blue eyes, shutting off the look of boyish expectation that made him seem younger than the lines around his eyes indicated. "Yeah, I must have seen one just like it in one of the better soddies out there in the panhandle. At our house we used to sit on upturned buckets, but for company, we always brought in the milking stool."

Thoroughly ashamed of herself, Daisy closed her eyes. "I'm sorry, I didn't mean that the way it sounded." She did, but knew she shouldn't have. "I'm tired—I'm in a rotten mood—but that's no reason to take it out on you."

It would help if he weren't so…distracting. She actually found herself wondering what he liked in a woman—whether he'd be attracted to someone neat and practical or someone sexy and wildly impractical. One thing was certain—no man could be attracted to a grungy-looking crybaby who fell apart at the sight of an old sewing machine.

While he examined the rocking chair and prowled the shadowy space under the sloping ceilings, Daisy mentally distanced herself by thinking about her plans for the future. In a few minutes—half an hour at most— he'd be gone.

She tried not to watch him as he moved around, touching things, studying old license plates someone had nailed to the rafters, shaking his head over a pair of dried and cracked rubber waders. Even the way he moved was distracting. Those long legs, that gorgeous gluteus—

Stop it. Just stop thinking about what you're thinking about! Think about Egbert and how thoroughly decent he is. Think about the way he'll smile, shy and a little nervous, when you walk down the aisle with a bouquet of spring flowers. It would be a small wedding, she'd already decided on that much, but definitely in church. Dressy, but not formal, as there was no point in buying an expensive gown and wearing it only once—although Sasha would argue with her there. Her hair would be lighter and probably shorter, but not too short.

Try as she would to bring the picture into focus, the man waiting at the altar wore jeans, a leather jacket and western boots. A man she'd first seen only hours earlier. A man with a crooked grin and a wicked gleam in his eyes, and as she saw him waiting at the altar, all she could think of was—

Too much stress. She had flat out lost her mind.

Recovering her lost train of thought, she looked guiltily at the broken rocker. "I really am sorry, Mr. Magee. It's just that—well, I guess it gets to me, dealing with all these personal effects. As a rule I'm never involved in that sort of thing, but Mr. Snow didn't have anyone else and I hated to think of strangers pawing through his belongings. He was—he had too much pride for that."

He didn't say a word, just stared at her with those enigmatic blue eyes. Flinging her hands out in a gesture of helplessness, she said, "Look, I liked the man, all right? He was my friend as well as my patient, and this is one last thing I can do for him. So if you don't mind—"

"Just get the hell out of the way so you can finish, right?" he said softly.

She turned away, blinking rapidly. Oh, dammit, not again!

Across the room under a small stained-glass window sat a humpback trunk. That, too, would have to be gone through. She'd almost sooner cart it down to the river and throw it overboard unopened.

"Daisy?"

"What!" she snapped without turning around. Daisy the unflappable, known far and wide for her composure, was coming apart at the seams, leaking embarrassing emotions all over the place.

"It's chilly up here and you're not wearing enough clothes. Let's go down and see if what's her name can brew up some coffee, okay?"

"Faylene," she said, grasping any excuse to cut short the tour. "Her name is Faylene Beasley, I told you that twice already. She worked three days a week for Mr. Snow and one day each for my two best friends, and I don't know why I'm telling you all this because I never babble."

He nodded soberly and led the way, probably expecting her to collapse from overwrought nerves. If she happened to fall and break a leg, he'd be just the type to compound the fracture by sweeping her up in his arms, leaping aboard his white horse and galloping off to the nearest emergency room. God save her from amateur heroes.

"My grandmother might have sat in that rocking chair," Kell said quietly after closing the attic door. "I don't know if Blalock explained or not, but my dad and Uncle Harvey shared a mom."

"I believe you mentioned it once or twice." *Uncle* Harvey? Daisy knew exactly what he was trying to do. He was trying to stake his claim. But it wasn't up to her to decide.

They reached the front of the second-floor hall, her rubber-soled shoes squeaking on the newly waxed floor, his worn, western-style boots making whispery sounds.

He continued, saying, "*Half* Uncle Harvey, if you want to get technical. Anyhow, Blalock said Harvey had never married and it's usually women who save stuff. Guys just toss it or cover it up with more junk. So my grandmom was probably the one who stashed that old trunk up there."

"So?" She should have sent him packing when he first showed up. Let Egbert deal with him, this wasn't part of her job description.

Oh, sure—like housecleaning and sorting through tons of stuff was?

"So there might even be a few old pictures of her and her two sons up there, you reckon?"

He waited for an answer and she didn't have one. As far as she was concerned he could have any pictures he found. He could even have that box of mending for all she cared. She'd leave it to Egbert's interpretation of Harvey's will and whatever he found out about the cowboy's claim.

If he thought turning on the charm would win her over he was flat out of luck. She'd already been vaccinated. What had happened upstairs had been a momentary aberration, not a sign of weakness on her part.

Daisy waited for him to leave. When he didn't, she turned toward the kitchen. Let Faylene deal with him.

His leathery-woodsy scent and whispery footsteps were right behind her. "Don't you think it's significant that both Harvey and Evander had names with *V* in them? I mean, what are the chances?"

"What do you mean?"

"You don't hear many names with *V* in them, do you?"

"Victor, Vance, Vaughn, Virginia—Virgil."

"Hmm…never thought of those. Remind me not to play word games with you."

If his smile was meant to disarm, it wasn't working. "I never play games," she informed him.

His smile widened into a grin. "Ri-ight."

They were still standing there when something struck the side of the house. Daisy said, "Oh, no—it's probably a bird. I'd better go see if it's hurt. Sometimes in the late afternoon the sun reflects on the glass and—"

She was hurrying toward the front door when the same sound came again. This time they stared at each other, then both looked in the direction the sound had come from.

Kell said, "Upstairs."

Daisy said, "Outside."

"Might be a branch," he murmured. "The wind's picked up."

"Oh, great. That means more raking. I'd forgotten about the yard." In an unspoken truce, they hurried outside and looked for signs of a stunned bird among all the pecans, pine cones and broken branches littering the unkempt lawn.

"What about a lawn service?"

"Some crews came by right after the storm and collected whatever Faylene and I could drag out to the road. We cleared off the porches and the driveway, but we never got around to doing anything more."

"You do the yard work, too? I thought you were a nurse."

She shrugged. "As long as I'm living here rent free, I try to earn my keep. Anyway, it's easier to do things myself than try to find someone else to do it, especially now."

Especially now after the hurricane? Kell wondered. Or especially now that she was out of a job? "What about gutters?" he asked, remembering the one he'd seen dangling when he'd first driven into the yard.

"Gutters," she repeated. "Well, shoot. I told Egbert they needed repairing, but he said repairs could wait until the estate was settled."

"Which will be…?"

"Six months, I think. I'm not sure—Egbert needs time for any creditors to come forward, anyway, or any other—" She broke off and he finished for her.

"Or any other claimants. Don't worry, I'm not." She shot him a skeptical look—she had it down pat. Kell didn't bother to set her straight. "Place is a mess, isn't it?" he mused.

She flashed him a smile that disappeared almost before it could register. The tip of her nose was still slightly pink, but it didn't affect the impact. Funny, he thought, because he usually liked his ladies groomed to a high polish. She was anything but.

"If it was a chunk of gutter banging up against the side of the house, I might be able to reach it and pull it down." He knew damned well she didn't want him here. The thing was, the more she wanted him to leave, the more determined he was to hang around. "So why don't I take care of it now?"

Right. Magee to the rescue. He knew what gutters were for, everybody knew that. He even knew roughly how they were attached to a house. The rest he should be able to figure out.

Shielding his eyes from the low sun, he stared up at the dangling section of gutter. If he'd needed an entrée, this just might be it. He could offer to tack up hanging stuff and saw off whatever couldn't be nailed back up. Men's work, he told himself, unconsciously bracing his shoulders.

When it occurred to him that researching his family tree might not be the sole reason he wanted to hang around for a few days, he was quick to deny it. No way, he told himself. The lady was…interesting, but not his style. Besides, he didn't do overnighters.

"Oh, yeah, that definitely needs to come down," he murmured as they stood shoulder to shoulder and gazed up toward the eaves. "Lucky thing it didn't hit that window with all the stained glass."

Nodding, Daisy turned toward the back door where Faylene waited with a market basket of assorted hand tools. "Told you that thang weren't gonna stay up there if the wind shifted."

Kell reached for the basket, but Daisy beat him to it. Faylene said, "Want me to help you get the ladder out? While you're up yonder, you might want to whack off that big limb hangin' over the screen porch."

"Where's the ladder? I'll get it," Kell said, all but flexing his muscles to prove his prowess.

"I know I've seen you summers before," the housekeeper said thoughtfully. "You weren't one o' them bachelors on the TV, were you?"

He grinned and shook his head. "No, ma'am, not in a million years, Ms. Beasley."

Granted, he was a bachelor, and he'd definitely been on TV, but never in the context she'd mentioned. Before the housekeeper could recall where she'd seen him he turned away, pausing only when he reached the bottom step and hesitated.

"I wondered if you knew where you were going," Daisy said dryly. "The shed's around back. The ladder's hanging on the outside wall—at least it was before the storm. It might be over in the next county by now."

"No problem. I passed a hardware store on my way here."

"You're not buying any ladders," she said, as if she suspected him of trying to ingratiate himself. Sharp lady. "There it is," she said. "You take one end and I'll carry the other."

"Be easier if I just balance it on my shoulders." He could tell she wanted to argue, but instead, she marched off toward the house, giving him a perfect view of her shapely, well-toned backside. In a starched uniform she might be able to pass herself off as a dragon, but in rumpled shorts, a T-shirt and grimy athletic shoes, with her hair tumbling from the shaggy wad on top of her head, she was—

Suffice it to say that *dragon* was hardly the word that came to mind.

They worked surprisingly well as a team. Having been treated for various sports-related injuries, Kell had seen the way nurses slapped tools into the palm of an attending physician. He wasn't particularly eager to have her slap anything in his hands, especially not a hammer, nails or a screwdriver, so he selected a few basic tools and tucked them under his belt, took a deep breath and started climbing.

Three rungs from the top he braced himself, held on and shifted his weight experimentally, waiting to see if the ladder was going to settle any deeper into the damp earth. Eyeing the nearby stained-glass window, he called down, "She's one fancy house, all right. Tall, too."

Daisy was watching him, shading her eyes with a slate shingle she'd picked up from the debris on the ground. "Be careful up there," she warned.

"I'm always careful. What'd you say it was called, Victorian?"

"I didn't say." Then, as if relenting, she said, "Gothic. I think."

"Ri-ight, that's what I thought it was." When it came to architecture, he didn't know Gothic from gator eggs.

Kell knew better than to look down. Truth was, he wasn't that great on heights. A pitcher's mound was about as high as he felt comfortable unless he was flying, preferably first class, preferably in an aisle seat and preferably with a shot of single-malt whisky in hand to settle his nerves.

Daisy steadied the ladder with both hands while he reached out to unscrew the single screw holding the gutter to the eaves. He called down to warn her to stand back just as the screw came loose and the section of copper gutter fell to the ground.

"Ouch!"

Kell twisted around to see what had happened. When the ladder tilted under him he let out a yell and sailed off to one side. They both ended up on the damp ground, with Daisy frowning at a ten-inch scrape on the outside of her leg where the falling gutter had grazed her. Kell massaged his butt and pulled out the cluster of pecans he'd landed on. The yard was littered with the damned things.

"You okay?" he asked.

"What were you doing, trying to amputate my leg?"

"I warned you to stand back."

"You warned me after the thing was already falling."

He stood up, flexed his limbs to be sure they were still working, then held out a hand. "Sorry, I guess my timing was off. Gutter work's a little out of my line."

Ignoring his hand, she stood and then leaned over to examine her injury. "I'd better go put something on this. Did you break any bones when you fell?"

"I didn't fall, I jumped." He followed her into the house. "That thing's probably going to stiffen up on you once it starts healing."

"Jumped, ha! Nice six-point landing, though."

"Two feet plus two hands equals four, not six. Do the math."

"You left out the two cheeks," she quipped, slipping through the back door he held open. Glancing over her shoulder, she grinned. "Hope you didn't bruise anything valuable."

Well, what do you know? The lady had a sense of humor after all. He liked that in a woman, he really did. He'd been right about that mouth of hers, too. Without a lick of paint on it, she had a smile that could melt steel-belted radials.

Kell asked if she was up on her tetanus shots and she withered him with a look. "I *am* a nurse," she reminded him. "What are you, by the way? You never did say."

"Hungry, at the moment. Kinda tired, too, come to think of it. It's been a long day." He didn't feel like getting into his life story, it only complicated things. He either came off sounding like a failure or a braggart, and actually, he was neither.

"Where are you staying?" Daisy uncapped a bottle of Betadine and studied the scrape on her leg.

"I spent last night at a motel out on the highway. I'm not sure, but I think the owner's name is Bates." He leaned against a counter and watched as she carefully mopped the raw area with a damp cotton ball. "Maybe you can recommend another place, preferably one near a decent restaurant."

"There's a motel in town, but it's been closed ever since the storm. Something about a mold problem."

"What about restaurants? Most of the ones I saw looked closed, too. Don't folks around here eat?"

She capped the bottle and set it aside. "Most of them live around here. They don't have to rely on restaurants. There are some nice ones in Elizabeth City—motels, too. That's only about eighteen or twenty miles on the other side of Muddy Landing."

"Yeah, I found that out when I was exploring the countryside late last night, looking for the Muddy Landing city limits."

"Oh." She glanced at him, then looked away, almost as if she was embarrassed by the fact that he was hungry and homeless and it was growing dark outside.

Kell did his best to look hungry and homeless until finally she broke. "Oh, for goodness' sake, I suppose if you'd like to you could spend the night here. There's certainly enough room."

He barely managed to suppress his triumph when Faylene came in, bristling with mops, feather dusters and cleaning rags. "Plenty of rooms upstairs," the housekeeper declared. "None of 'em made up, but I guess I could dig out some sheets. Daisy, my bingo's at seven and I need to run home and change first, so if you're lettin' him stay, I'll do up that corner room." She measured him with narrowed eyes. "It's got that big ol' bed. I 'speck it'll fit him all right."

"Thanks, I really appreciate that," Kell said before the offer could be withdrawn. "I was thinking about buying a camper and some bedding just so I could get a decent night's sleep."

Daisy knew the minute the invitation left her lips that she'd spoken too hastily. The way she reacted to this man on a purely physical level was totally illogical. "Although I suppose I really should check with Egbert first," she murmured.

He barely hesitated before saying, "Blalock? Good idea. By now he's probably checked out my bona fides. Mind if I help myself to a glass of water?"

The crazy thing was, she knew very well she was being manipulated, only she couldn't quite figure out how he was doing it. How could any man who looked like a cross between George Clooney and that Joe Millionaire Evan Marriott elicit sympathy simply by asking a simple question about motels?

While Faylene put away her cleaning gear, Daisy leaned against the refrigerator and watched him down the glass of ice water he'd poured for himself. All right, so he was tall and well built—what was so unusual about that? And blue eyes were hardly uncommon. They only seemed that way because of his deep tan and his jet-black hair—not to mention eyelashes any woman would envy. As for his body—

She was a nurse, for heaven's sake. She *knew* what men's bodies looked like. Just because those old jeans of his worn low on his narrow hips happened to bag in all the right places and hug in a few others, that didn't mean what they concealed was all that special. Underneath his clothes he was probably bowlegged, chicken-breasted and hairless.

In fact, some men actually worked at being hairless to the point of shaving their heads and waxing their bodies. Personally, she'd always liked a moderate amount of hair on a man's body.

Good Lord, her brain had been taken over by an alien. "What?" she snapped.

"I said, maybe I could buy you dinner?" He set his glass in the sink. "In exchange for a place to sleep, I mean? Or we could order takeout if you're too tired to go out. I can pick it up if delivery's a problem out here."

Daisy dropped down onto a chair, wincing as the wound on the side of her left leg protested. "I told you everything's still closed since the storm. That includes the ones that do takeout."

"Never mind, then. I'm not really hungry. A bed I don't hang off of will be fine. This has been a long day."

Well, shoot. If he was going to be nice about it—"Look, if you don't mind fried chicken, I've got some soaking in buttermilk in the refrigerator that needs to be cooked. How good are you at making salad?"

Five

Kell was a wizard at making salads, especially when the greens were bagged and the other ingredients lined up in order. Dutifully, he chopped sweet onions and bell peppers, hearing behind him the sound of hot grease spattering in a cast-iron skillet. Faylene popped in to say the room was all ready. "ESPN! I knew I'd seen you somewheres before. If she's frying chicken, make her use bacon grease, else she'll use that canoodle oil. Stuff don't have no flavor a-tall."

"It's canola, and you'd better hurry or you'll miss your bingo," Daisy said, but she was smiling. The two women might have different ideas of what constituted a sensible diet, but they obviously liked each other.

"My dad used to like greens boiled with bacon. Mom used to cook up a potful two or three times a week. She was a barrel racer, did I tell you that? Of course, that was before I came along. She was known for her bean bread, too. Best in all Oklahoma."

"Bean bread?"

They discussed the nonthreatening topic of food while Kell divided the salad between two bowls. He glanced around for whatever else needed doing just as Daisy bent over to drag something out of a lower cabinet, offering him a clear view of the back of her thighs.

There was something intimate about a woman's tan line, he mused. Most of the women he knew well enough to be familiar with their tan lines didn't have any. Daisy's tan line was about midway on her thighs.

He reminded himself that Daisy's tan line, no matter how provocative, was none of his business. At least she didn't wear stockings with her shorts like the other one. Now, there was one weird lady.

Realizing she'd caught him staring, Kell blurted out the first thing that came to mind. "Legs—ah, limbs. Tree limbs, I mean. Lots of trees around here. I'll bet Uncle Harvey climbed 'em all when he was a kid. He ever talk to you about the old days?"

Without replying, she placed another drumstick in the hot grease, jumping back when it spattered. "Watch it," he warned. "Stuff can do you some major damage. I knew a guy that got hot grease splashed in his eye."

"Well, gee, I forgot my safety goggles." The words dripped sarcasm, but he had her number now. Her bite wasn't nearly as bad as her bark.

Hips braced against a countertop, he crossed his legs at the ankles, watching her work. "Blalock mentioned that you'd been here for more than a year. I expect you and Uncle Harvey got to know each other pretty well.

He happen to tell you any stories about when he was a kid? Most old folks like to talk about the good old days."

Hell, he didn't know what old folks liked to talk about. His former teammates liked to talk about cars, golf scores and women. As for the kids he worked with, they mostly bragged about what they were going to do—everything from joining the marines to building the world's biggest airplane.

Which reminded Kell that he needed to get on with finding whatever there was to be found here, if anything. This dilapidated old mansion might not look much like the double-wide where Evander Magee had spent his last fifteen years and Kell had spent his first fourteen, but if there was anything here of his dad's, he intended to find it. He didn't have so much as a snapshot of either his mom or his dad. Those had burned along with everything else—his mom's trophies, the long-legged, long-billed birds his dad had whittled that shared space with a bunch of flowered plates and cups in the corner cabinet between the living room and the dining area. He couldn't really see his dad living in a house like this, but he'd like a few more days to try and get a better feel for it.

"Your uncle—that is, Mr. Snow, was physically unable to do much tree-climbing. He was born with rheumatoid arthritis. Are you finished with the salad?"

Kell waited a long, stunned moment. "You mean he was a—"

"He was a wonderful man who couldn't climb trees. Seeing you on a ladder, I'd say you weren't much good at tree-climbing, either. Now, is the salad ready?"

"Already on the table." If he was going to make the

most of his time here, he needed to choose his topics carefully. Evidently a few areas were off-limits. "I was just thinking about some of my dad's stories about hunting bear in the Dismal Swamp. Back then, I didn't even know where the Dismal Swamp was located. Did Uncle Harvey ever mention anything about bear hunting? I doubt if it's something a guy would do alone."

He didn't know if it was or not. Maybe if a guy needed to put meat on the table for his family…

On the other hand, folks who lived in fancy three-story houses probably didn't run short of groceries between paychecks.

"Better watch that stuff," he said just as Daisy jumped back and grabbed her arm. She swore softly and so did Kell as he pulled her away from the danger zone. "Dammit, I warned you. Here, let me see what you've done to yourself."

"I'm all right," she protested, twisting away.

Holding on to her shoulders, he peered around to see the bare forearm she was clutching in front of her body. "Uh-oh, that one's going to blister." Leading her to the sink, he turned on the faucet and held her forearm under the stream of cold water. "You got anything to put on it?"

She shot him a look that reminded him he was here on sufferance, as if he needed reminding. With her hair tickling his chin, he inhaled sharply and then had to wonder how a blend of roses and bacon grease could put him in mind of warm nights and hot, tangled sheets.

"Turn the chicken for me, will you? I'll be back in time to take it up." She twitched her shoulders free of his hands, shoved the fork at him and headed for the door, still clutching her forearm just above the angry red burn.

Kell stared after her, liking the way she moved. Liking even more the feel of her body against his. This made twice now. He was starting to look forward to the scent of her hair and the way her body felt—the contrast between softness and firmness. If he reacted this way after only a few hours in her company, he just might have a problem by the time he headed West again. A smart man, he reminded himself, would clear out before he got hooked.

Laying aside the table fork she'd been using to turn the pieces of chicken, he searched through drawers until he found a long-handled cooking fork. Speaking of smart, any woman smart enough to be a nurse should know enough to use the right tool for the job. While he'd never claimed to be a handyman, even he knew better than to use a short-handled tool to do a long-handled job.

The chicken was browned to a turn by the time Daisy returned. Shoving him aside, she lifted each piece out and placed it on papers to drain. Leaning against the refrigerator, Kell noticed that she'd taken the time to braid her hair in a single rope that was already coming apart. Unruly hair, he mused. What else about her refused to obey the rules?

Her face was damp. Evidently she'd splashed it off, but she hadn't bothered to do any more than that. Not that she needed to. While she might not be the most beautiful woman in the world, something about her definitely made an impression.

An impression. Right. Like a big white light coming at him in a dark tunnel.

One more thing a smart man should know—to get the hell out of the way or else prepare to face the consequences.

They ate in the kitchen. Kell had yet to see a dining room, but there probably was one. Houses like this might even have two, one for family, one for company.

"I suppose you need to check out of wherever it is you're staying," Daisy said.

Kell cut off a bite of white meat. Man, did she ever know how to fry chicken. "Uh, actually, I already did that. I'd planned to find someplace with bigger beds and softer pillows." And maybe a gray-eyed, streaky-haired blonde to share it with me.

She glanced up then, as if she knew exactly what he was thinking. He felt his face growing warm. "How many rooms did you say there were?" he asked hastily. "We never got around to finishing the tour."

Get your mind out of the bedroom, Bubba.

"Just the usual," she said, drizzling balsamic vinegar on her salad.

"That many, huh?" Okay, so he'd try again. Somewhat to his surprise he was far more interested in her reactions to his questions than he was in the actual answers. A house was a house was a house.

But a woman was an eternal mystery. "Do porches count as rooms?" he asked, wondering whether or not to reach for another drumstick.

"If you want to count them. Five rooms downstairs, not counting the porches, the kitchen or servants' quarters. Actually, that's only a small bedroom and a half bath with a shower."

"Why wouldn't you count those?" Was there another conversation going on underneath the words spoken, or was it only his imagination?

She shrugged. "Count them if you want to, it hardly

matters." She reached for her second piece of chicken and so did he.

Kell liked that in a woman—a healthy appetite. Made him wonder about her appetite in other areas.

The moment they finished, Daisy stood and started collecting the dishes. Kell lifted them from her hands. "Let me," he said, his voice dropping half an octave. "You don't want to splash your arm." Without thinking, he'd lapsed into the honeyed tones he used to use on attractive, available women before he'd become famous enough not to need any special tactics.

Funny thing, he mused—the good old days no longer seemed all that great.

"You mentioned bear hunting," Daisy said as she moved around the kitchen, putting away the condiments and wiping off the table. "I think there might've been a stuffed bear's head in the library until a few years ago." She was moving fast and talking fast, almost as if she was trying to outrun something...or someone.

"What happened to it?" He turned on the hot water, squirted a stream of liquid detergent on a plate and scoured it with the sponge. When he held it under the faucet to rinse, water splashed across the front of his shirt.

Her lips quivered on the edge of a smile. "The bear's head? I never actually saw it, but there's a lighter place on the north wall where something big used to hang. Faylene's been working here for years, and now that I think about it, I seem to remember her mentioning a bear's head that was taken down when it got the mange, or whatever happens to stuffed animals. Moths, probably."

"If Uncle Harvey didn't shoot it, maybe my dad did. I think he was only about sixteen when he left here, but that's old enough to hunt." Kell dried the last of the silverware—heavy pieces with an *S* on the handle. "Hmm," he said, holding up an ornate salad fork. "An *M* would have been nice, but I guess that's too much to hope for."

Daisy felt almost sorry for the man. If Kell wanted to find some connection to a place, a man or a family, who was she to deny him? It was only smart to learn about your genetic background. Not that she was particularly eager to meet the woman who had given birth to her thirty-six years ago. The woman who kept her for nearly three years before abandoning her in the ladies' room of a shopping mall with a note pinned to her snowsuit that read, "Her name is Daisy and I can't keep her." She'd been adopted soon after that, but that hadn't worked out, either.

Kell's voice dropped back into that same chocolate-covered-gravel range he'd tried on her before. "How you feeling now? Does your arm hurt? Leg stiffening up on you?"

Daisy knew what he was up to. Trying to soften her up so she'd let him poke and pry until he found something he could twist into an excuse to hang around until he was declared a legitimate heir and could compete with the historical society for whatever was left. In this case it would be loser take all. Between age, more than a century of storms and what she suspected were termites, it was going to take a fortune to keep the place from crumbling into the ground. Thank goodness it wasn't her worry. Kell, Egbert and the historical society could fight it out.

Straightening away from the counter, she refrained

from glancing at her two injuries. She really must be tired. She'd never been particularly accident-prone before. "I'm feeling just fine," she said briskly. "Thank you."

He shot her a skeptical look as he draped the dish towel over the rack and smoothed it out. Rather than meet his eyes, she watched his hands straightening the damp linen to military precision. He really did have nice hands. Square palms, long fingers, clean, neatly trimmed nails.

Not that there was anything at all wrong with Egbert's hands, she quickly reminded herself. They were exactly what one would expect of a white-collar worker: pale, soft—softer than hers, in fact—and flawlessly manicured.

"I don't know about the hunting regulations around here, but even if my dad was too young to get a license, I'm pretty sure he never broke any serious laws. He was basically a good guy."

And so are you, Daisy admitted silently, surprising herself with the thought. "How many times have you washed dishes before this?"

"What, you're not impressed by my technique?" He teased her with a smile and she stared, mesmerized, at his mouth.

"Technique. Is that what you call it? Squirting each piece individually with detergent and then holding it under the faucet to rinse?"

"Hey, if I was doing something wrong, you should've told me."

"I didn't say it was wrong, only different."

"You don't like my style. That hurts."

"I doubt it," she said dryly. The trouble was, she

liked his style a little too much, considering she'd known him only a matter of hours. Inviting him to stay had definitely been a mistake. Evidently being physically tired and emotionally drained was starting to affect her judgment.

She'd give him tonight, she vowed silently. Tomorrow she'd find some way to uninvite him.

They reached for the light switch at the same time. Their fingers brushed and she snatched hers back. *Damn, damn, damn!*

Placing a hand lightly on the small of her back, Kell led her from the old-fashioned kitchen. "How about fishing? Did Uncle Harvey ever talk about that? Fishing's something you can do sitting on a bank. Plenty of those around here."

Arching away from the warmth of his touch, she said, "Not that I recall. Mostly he talked about shipwrecks and how he wished he'd been able to try scuba diving. I think he has books on it—on diving, I mean. He has books on practically everything you can think of, and all of them need dusting." She was babbling again. If she had a grain of sense she'd shove him out and lock the door, and to heck with good manners and genetic histories.

"And you're going to dust every single one of them, right?"

She was. Call it duty, call it closure—Faylene called it foreclosure—Daisy knew only that she wasn't ready to take on another patient. "Mr. Snow would have hated strangers pawing through his personal belongings."

"You said most of the rooms had been closed off for years. Why didn't he just move into a smaller house?"

Kell gazed up at the transoms over the doors that enabled warm air to flow freely throughout the house. "Place must be tough to heat with these high ceilings, let alone the maintenance involved."

"Because he had a deep sense of family responsibility. This house was built by his grandfather."

"Hmm… Kind of makes you wonder why he never even tried to locate his brother if he had such a deep sense of family responsibility."

"*If* he actually had a brother."

"For that matter, I don't know if my dad ever tried to get in touch with him, either. Dad could be…I guess you could call it stubborn."

Daisy didn't want to hear about his family. The man was enough of a distraction without knowing anything about him personally. As a nurse she rarely had trouble maintaining her objectivity, but as a woman she hadn't always been so successful. A little candlelight, a little music and pretty soon you're confiding secrets you've never told a single soul, not even your two best friends. One intimacy led to another, and before you knew it you were engaged to marry a sneaky, lying, conniving jerk with all the moral integrity of a feral cat.

No candles and definitely no music, she warned herself. As for intimacy, she would simply have to…what was that old saying? Gird her loins?

God, no! Don't even think *about loins!*

"I guess this room would be called a parlor." Kell opened the nearest door and peered into the gloomy interior. Without meaning to, she stared at his narrow hips, wondering just how hard he'd landed. Should she offer to rub liniment on his achy parts? Acting strictly in a professional capacity, of course.

"Back parlor," she informed him, unconsciously mimicking the rental agent who had shown her through her apartment seven years ago. "There are two."

She might as well get it over with. Obviously he wasn't going to be satisfied until he'd seen all there was to see. She switched on the chandelier, wishing she'd remembered to replace the burned-out bulbs. The shadows lent the chilly room an intimacy she could do without.

Kell shook his head slowly as he took in the horsehair sofa and matching chairs, a straight chair, an uncomfortable-looking platform rocker and a scroll-based table, its dusty surface taken up by a stuffed owl, a stereopticon and a vase of faded dried flowers laced together with spiderwebs.

"I'm no expert on antiques, but this stuff, heirloom or not, strikes me as flat-out ugly."

"Try shifting it to clean underneath," Daisy said dryly. Surrounding an ugly floral rug in the center of the room, the varnished floor gleamed dully under a layer of dust. "I guess you can tell the cleaning hasn't progressed this far."

"If you're going to clean under all this stuff, you're going to need help. Some of it must weigh a ton."

For the next few minutes they wandered through interconnected rooms while Kell, using skills developed by working with fragile, at-risk kids, drew her out about the kind of man his half uncle had been—the kind of things he'd enjoyed.

"Your father never mentioned Harvey's...um, situation?"

"Situation? I told you, my father never mentioned anything at all about his family. Or if he did, I was too young and too stupid to listen until it was too late."

"Mr. Snow was able to drive until a few years ago, but his library was his real pride and joy, from childhood on." As they entered the library, she nodded toward several shelves of what were obviously children's books. "I don't really know anything about his early life but someone obviously spent a lot on books and board games. We packed up boxes full and gave them to the Salvation Army last Christmas."

"I imagine there were a lot of medical expenses," Kell said quietly. "That might explain why my dad left home—to help earn money in case it was needed."

Or maybe because he was jealous of his needy younger brother, he thought. He would never know, and perhaps that was best.

Daisy said, "I used to read to him. Newspapers were hard for him to handle after his stroke, but books…" She sighed. "He introduced me to some wonderful authors I'd never even heard of. He had a wonderful sense of humor. You'd have liked him."

"Yeah, I probably would," Kell said, wondering if it was true that blood was thicker than water. He sank down on the edge of the ugly tapestry sofa, searching his memory for anything his father might have said about his younger brother.

Damn. If only he hadn't waited until it was too late. To come all this way, after all this time, and find…nothing. A funeral and a houseful of relics.

Daisy yawned. "I wish I could help you, but I only moved out here August a year ago. Before that, Mr.

Snow had a nutritionist and a physical therapist—and Faylene, of course. I came three times a week." She yawned again.

He glanced at his watch, reluctant to see the evening come to an end. By tomorrow she might have changed her mind about allowing him to stay. Or Blalock might find proof beyond a doubt that Evander and Harvey couldn't possibly have been related, in which case, he'd have no more reason to hang around.

Dammit, he wasn't ready to head back. Somewhere over the past few hours his focus had shifted, leaving him off balance and uncertain. Not to mention semiaroused.

It was an uncomfortable combination, he told himself as he studied the woman in the light of three sixty-watt bulbs. Except for a couple of twists up near the top, her braid was all but unraveled. Curly wisps framed her face and nestled at the back of her neck. Unbidden, he pictured her jogging through a flowery pasture in slow motion, like the woman in the allergy medication commercial.

She took a deep breath and he wondered if she was deliberately calling attention to a pair of high, rounded breasts under her faded T-shirt. Probably not, he conceded reluctantly. There was nothing even faintly seductive about either her attitude or her outfit.

"Well…if you'll excuse me, I'm going to turn in. You know where everything is. You're in the first room on the left at the head of the stairs. Bathroom's across the hall."

Kell managed to hide his disappointment that the evening was ending so early. His head was teeming with new questions. No way was he about to leave until he had a few answers. "Just don't try to move any of this stuff without me," he warned.

"How's your back? After your fall, I mean." Standing in the doorway, she yawned. Lifting a hand to cover her mouth caused her shirt to ride up just enough to reveal a sliver of pale skin at her waistline.

"My jump, you mean. Uh—back's fine. Good to go." He swallowed hard and tried not to stare as his body shifted into full-alert status. Like any other red-blooded man, he enjoyed looking at a bare-skinned woman—the barer, the better.

But who'd have thought that under the right conditions, modesty could be an even bigger turn-on than full nudity?

"Great," she said. "Then if you have time before you leave tomorrow you can help us shift some furniture. Most of it hasn't been moved in so long it's probably stuck to the floor."

Had he said anything about leaving tomorrow? "My pleasure," he assured her. And it would be, even if he had to herniate himself shifting that monster of a sofa. He might no longer be a professional athlete, but he'd never let himself get out of shape like a few of the guys he knew who'd quit training once they were out of the game. If he had to, he could still do a session in the batting cage and follow it up with a few fast laps around the diamond.

Or the bedroom. When it came to women, he was an old hand. Although not even a certain sexy meteorologist, whose face he couldn't quite bring into focus at the moment, had ever got him this turned on, this fast, with no more than a quick glimpse of waistline.

Six

It was just past four in the afternoon the following day when Kell let himself into the house again. Hearing voices from the side porch, he headed that way in time to see an attractive redhead lift her glass in a toast. "Thank you, doll—the mark of a true lady, I've always said, is her ability to pour from a mason jar without spilling a drop."

"You never said that in your life," Daisy retorted.

"Comes from emptying bedpans," teased another woman who was less striking, but pretty in a quiet sort of way. "Besides, it's a wide-mouth bottle, not a jar."

"Oh, hush, you two!"

Kell didn't know whether to back out or to join the group. Daisy settled the matter. Catching sight of him, she waved him out onto the once-screened porch and introduced her two friends. Before either of them could voice the questions that were obviously about to spill over, the housekeeper poked her head through the side door. "You want to clean out that library 'fore I leave today or wait till tomorrow?"

Grinning, Sasha said, "Oh, goody, dirty books!"

Daisy's lips twitched in the beginning of a smile. To the housekeeper she said, "I'd just as soon get started now, if that's all right with you."

"I guess that's our cue to leave. When you're finished here, Faylene," said the redhead, "Marty could probably use help finding a place to store all those boxes of paperbacks."

"Just so they're not dirty as them books in the library," Faylene said. "I never seen so much dust. Poor man, he didn't read 'em no more, but he wouldn't let me touch a one of 'em. Said he knew right where ever'thing was, and I'd put 'em back all wrong."

Leaning against the wall, Kell enjoyed the byplay among the four women as the party broke up. A few minutes later Marty and Sasha roared off in a red convertible. Faylene handed him a half-empty box of cheese straws. "Might's well finish these up, else Daisy'll do it and she don't need 'em. He'p yerself to the wine."

A few minutes later, fueled by half a dozen cheese straws, his muscles lubricated by half a glass of a regional wine, Kell followed Daisy and the housekeeper into the library, where he shifted desks, tables and chairs. Under Daisy's instructions, he moved roughly a ton of books so that she could dust the shelves while the housekeeper vacuumed the stacks of books.

By the time it began to grow dark Kell was not only

hot and hungry, he was sore in places that hadn't had a good workout in years. For all her diminutive size—she couldn't be more than five-five and about a hundred-ten pounds—Daisy was a dynamo. So was the housekeeper. "You two in a hurry?" he'd asked, watching the way they worked together.

"Of course we're in a hurry. Don't worry, you'll have plenty of time to look around before you leave." Daisy picked up a daddy longlegs spider, took him to the front door and dropped him on the porch. Faylene just shook her head and said, "Nice lady, but she's sure got some crazy notions."

Seeing the look on Kell's face when she returned a moment later, Daisy said defensively, "They're harmless. They eat mosquitoes."

He nodded slowly and stacked up her eccentricities against her understated sexiness. Sexiness won, hands down.

Daisy lifted an arm to wipe her forehead, then shoved a hand through her hair. "I guess we'd better quit before I get too tired to make supper."

"Not me," said the housekeeper. "I got me a play-off game to watch tonight."

"If you can think of a place anywhere nearby that's still open," said Kell, not wanting Daisy to feel obligated to feed him again, "call in an order and I'll pick it up. I don't mind driving a few miles out of the way."

"More like twenty-five or thirty." Faylene pulled on a bulky pink cardigan embroidered with white poodles. "My game starts in half an hour—I'm outta here. If I was you, Daisy, I'd get me a good hot soak, else you'll wake up stiffer'n an ironin' board."

That might work for Daisy, Kell mused. In his case, though, a cold shower was called for.

Unbidden, his imagination sketched a picture of the two of them in a hot tub, jets going full blast, soft music in the background and maybe a shot of that eighteen-year-old Balvenie single malt he'd left in his office back home. Man, something in the air around here was affecting his mind, big-time.

As soon as the door closed behind the housekeeper, Daisy turned to him and said, "If you have anything else you'd like to see, then see it now, because I don't intend to be here much longer."

"Message received. Now, what about that takeout?" He wasn't going to get sidetracked.

"You really don't mind driving all that way? I can tell you how to get there, but first I'd better call to see if they're still open. They do great barbecue, too."

"Whatever you want, you call it in and I'll go get it. Do we need anything to drink? Beer? Wine?" He grimaced at the memory of that cloying wine.

She smiled then, and as tired as he was, he had to smile back. "No more wine, thanks. I'll make iced tea."

"Baseball!" Faylene exclaimed, pointing a knobby forefinger at him the next morning. Today, instead of a head that resembled a pompom that had been left out in the rain, she was wearing a flowered scarf with her pink sweater, white shorts and stockings. "You used to play with Houston a few years back—or was it Seattle? Told you, I never forget a face. What was it, first base or shortstop?"

Daisy glanced up from the cleaning closet where

she was searching for another can of furniture polish. "You did?"

Kell looked embarrassed. "I pitched a few years. What do you want moved first, the stuff in the middle room?"

Faylene tugged the scarf down over her ears. "'Scuse the stink. Miss Sasha called last night and told me to come by on my way to work 'cause she had something for all them broken ends I was telling you about, Daisy. Goopy stuff stinks something awful, but if it works, I guess it's worth it. I gotta quit wearing my scroogy, though. She said that's what's causing my hair to break off." Without missing a beat, she turned back to Kell. "Did I tell you my sister's boy plays ball? He's good, too."

Here we go, thought Kell. He wanted to say he had no more pull than the next guy when it came to getting a kid noticed, but that wasn't quite true. He still knew a few scouts. He always passed on a tip whenever he ran across a promising prospect. "How old is he?"

"Fourteen. He's small for his size, but he runs fast, and man, can that boy swing a bat! He's playing after school in that empty lot at the crossroads there by the Feed-and-Seed if you want to come watch."

He was small for his size. Ho-kay. And he could swing a bat, too. Connecting might be a different matter. Families weren't always objective where their kids were concerned.

Kell promised the housekeeper he would drop by and take a look, as the place she'd described was on the way into town. He'd been planning to give Blalock another push, anyway. Either the banker was deliberately dragging his feet, or he was a hell of a lot busier than he looked.

Daisy came up with a can of polish and a handful of clean rags. As she led the way, Kell couldn't help but wonder how the two women would have managed if he hadn't come along.

"Okay, you want stuff moved all the way to the center of the room or just out from the wall, or what?" If every piece in the house needed shifting, that might buy him another few days. As to how he'd use the time, that was still open for debate.

He knew how he'd like to use it. In any old bed in the house, with no particular deadline, exploring all the ways a man and a woman could find pleasure. It didn't make sense, but there it was.

"If you can just shift the furniture out and set it on the rug, we can wax and polish underneath," said Daisy. "I don't know about the rug itself—maybe one of those machines you rent at the grocery store—or maybe we'll just make do with a thorough vacuuming."

Across the hall, a telephone shrilled. "Oh, shoot," she muttered.

"You want me to get it?" the housekeeper offered.

"No, I'd better, it's probably Egbert."

Standing in the doorway, Faylene cocked a hip and shook her head. "That there table might not look it but it weighs a ton. Solid oak. You reckon anybody wants them dried flowers? I might could freshen 'em up some with spray paint."

"Couldn't hurt—might help." What the hell did he know about dried flowers? Lifting one end of the sofa, he swung it a few feet out from the wall and then reversed ends, repeating the action, gradually walking it into position.

"I could pick up a couple of cans at the hardware, maybe pink and blue. Monday I'm going shopping with Miss Marty. It's s'posed to be a secret, but I heard 'em talking, her'n Miss Sasha. They're cooking up something and they don't want me wearing my shorts."

"Uh…right. You want to clear off that table?"

"I'll just set them flowers out in the hall. I don't reckon nobody wants that dead owl—I sure don't. What about that other thing, the picture viewer?"

"Better ask Daisy."

"Bank'll probably haul ever'thing off to that hotline place. I don't know about the house—that there society is s'posed to get it. If I was them I'd auction it off and save myself a lot of trouble. I heard one o' them big discount stores is looking for property out this way."

Over my dead body, Kell thought. He was about to step up to the plate to defend his ancestral home when Daisy appeared and handed him the cordless phone. "Here, it's for you."

Lifting a questioning brow, he reached for the instrument that was possibly the most modern piece of equipment in the house. It was still warm from her hand. "Who is it, Blalock?"

She shook her head. "A woman. She didn't give her name, she just asked for you."

Just so it wasn't someone calling to tell him they'd found genetic evidence proving that his branch of Magees was in no way connected to the local Snows. You'd think his being here somehow threatened to topple a dynasty.

"Yeah, Magee here," he said cautiously, still eyeing Daisy. He liked the way her hair curled around her face and neck, no matter how hard she tried to control it. Hair with a mind of its own on a woman with a mind of her own…yeah, he liked that.

"Kell, this is Clarice. Moxie's in jail and I need you to talk to Chief Taylor. He won't listen to me."

He held the phone away to protect his eardrums. "Okay, calm down, honey. How bad is it?" A few of the kids he worked with had a tendency to backslide, fifteen-year-old Moxie being one of the riskiest.

Still holding the phone a few inches from his ear, he listened to the shrill voice on the other end, nodding occasionally. "Uh-huh…uh-huh. No, don't do that." Daisy had led Faylene out of the room to afford him some privacy, but they had to be hearing every word, at least on his end of the conversation. Possibly the other end, too. Clarice had been one of the kids. Now she was opening her own business. She had a tendency to be loud when she was excited.

"Look, I'll call the chief and explain—yeah, right away. He might not buy it this time, though. In that case, Moxie'll just have to hang in there until—" Closing his eyes while he sieved the resulting flood of information for pertinent data, he waited for her to wind down. Then he said, "You quit worrying now, y'hear? Concentrate on getting ready for the big day. I want to see that neon sign all lit up when I get there, okay?" Sighing tiredly, he waited until she'd finished speaking. "Sure I'll be there. I promised, didn't I?"

Pushing the off button, he took a deep breath, then stepped out into the hall where Daisy and the house-keeper were pretending not to have overheard. Forestalling any questions, he said, "Look, this friend of mine seems to have run into a spot of trouble. Mind if I make a long distance call? I'll put it on my home account."

"How did she get this number?" Daisy's eyes weren't icy, but they were decidedly unwarm.

"Seems my cell phone coverage has a few holes in it. Muddy Landing's one of them. I called last night, put it on my tab and gave her this number in case of emergency. I wasn't expecting her to have to use it."

Daisy had that look on her face again. He'd thought they had gotten past her reservations, but maybe not. He'd have to work on it, but first he needed to settle a few things back home.

"I guess it must be an emergency if you're having to talk to the chief. Chief of what, may I ask? Fire? Police?"

"Uh, police."

She didn't say another word. Didn't have to, her eyes said it all. Kell got the message, but he had to do what he had to do. "I'll explain everything, but first I need to call Chief Taylor, so if you don't mind?" He held up the receiver and turned away.

The two women returned to the parlor, allowing Kell his privacy. Faylene said, "I thought you had a hot one there, but now I'm startin' to wonder. Did he tell you he used to be this big baseball star till he dropped out of sight? What with ever'body gettin' traded around an' a few of 'em not gettin' picked up, I never thought to find out what happened to him."

"You and your baseball games," Daisy said absently as she surveyed the disarranged room. She should never have invited him to stay. Egbert wasn't going to like it. At the time, though, it had seemed like the right thing to do.

"You stick to them romance books if you want to, but

there's nothin' I like better when my very-close veins is killin' me than to kick back with a cold brew an' watch a bunch of good-looking guys in tight pants bendin' over the sack."

Thankful that the rain had ended the day before, Marty lugged the last box of books out of the tiny stand-alone building that had started out life as a service station, morphed into a tackle shop, and for the past seven years—until she was finally forced to admit defeat—had been Marty's New-and-Used Bookstore.

"Next time I decide to relocate, remind me to look for a town where at least half the citizens are literate."

"Have you thought about something for Faylene to wear?" Sasha examined her nails for any damage she might have done clearing out the last few shelves of books.

"Still working on it. Close the flap, will you? Who knows how long it'll be before I have a place to unpack."

Sasha looked at her nails, wrinkled her nose and closed the flaps.

"Well, I guess that's it. I'm officially out of business. You know what? I feel like crying," said Marty.

"Well, don't, it'll ruin your mascara."

"I'm not wearing any."

"That's the hell of being a redhead." Sasha affected a dramatic sigh. "You want something to show up, you have to paint it on—anything besides freckles, that is. What are you going to do with a thousand and one used paperbacks?" Without waiting for a response, she said, "I started on Faye's hair this morning. She's supposed to shampoo out the conditioner as soon as she gets home, but even if it works miracles, I don't think she can take a foil job." The housekeeper's hair had been abused so many times with old-style chemicals it was a wonder it hadn't eroded down to the scalp. "I made an appointment with Paul for a trim and maybe an ashy rinse."

"Good. Anything stronger than a temporary rinse and she'll go bald." Marty shoved her own chestnut-brown hair back. It might be drab, but at least it was healthy. "Have you heard anything from Daisy today?" She opened the door of her minivan to let the heat escape. The temperature was only in the low sixties, but there wasn't a speck of shade around.

"No, but the news is all over town about this studly gentleman who's staying out at the Snow place. Evidently Kell and Blalock are trying to find out whether or not he was any kin to old Harve."

"Studly, hmm? Having met him, I'd say that was a slight understatement. Dibs on him if Daisy kicks him out."

"Thought you were immune," Sasha teased. "Now, me, I never claimed to be immune. Besides, my spare room's not stacked full of books."

"What about all those sample books? What about those bolts of drapery material you're waiting to get made up? What about—"

"Yeah, yeah—well, at least we won't have to worry any more about cheering Daisy up," Sasha said as Marty slammed shut the side door of her minivan. "If she knows what's good for her, she'll put him through his paces before she turns him loose."

"Right," Marty said dryly. "And you'll decide to enter a nunnery and I'll write a bestseller and go on *Oprah*."

The voluptuous redhead tested the vinyl seat with her hand before sliding inside. "She definitely needs a man, though. She's got that tight look around the eyes. She needs to pump up her immune system with a little preventive sex."

Marty pulled out of the potholed parking area and headed toward her Sugar Lane address, named, according to local legend, for the enormous sacks of sugar delivered there back when moonshining was in vogue. "According to you, sex is the miracle drug. I doubt if Daisy would agree with you, I know I wouldn't. She didn't seem all that interested in her studly gentleman."

"Don't let her fool you, she was trying a little too hard *not* to look interested." Sasha tilted her seat back and propped her size-five platform sandals on the dash.

"After Jerry, who can blame her for not trusting men?"

"I doubt if she trusts anyone except for you and me."

"And we're plotting behind her back," Marty said with a sigh. "Some friends."

"Well, dammit, somebody's got to take care of her. You want her to end up an embittered old woman, living alone on social security with a houseful of cats?"

"Sounds good to me."

"Well, not to me. It's unnatural. The only men she's dated since Jerry dumped her were losers, and even then she never dated any of them more than twice."

"Well, duh." Marty snickered. "That means she's smarter than you are."

"I'm going to forget you said that. And what about all those doctors she works with?"

"Probably married. You know the drill—first wife puts him through med school, second wife comes along once he's made it and claims the reward. Meanwhile he probably has a mistress waiting in the wings for act three."

"God, you sound jaded."

"I'm not jaded, I'm simply a realist," Marty declared. "Anyway, picking a mate in the same profession almost never works out. My first husband was in publishing. I loved him dearly for the first three weeks, but after that we started disagreeing about everything. He thought what I read was trash—I thought what he read was pretentious crap."

"What kind of publishing?"

"How-to books for computer dumbbells."

"Oh. Then he wasn't actually literary, he was a nerd who knew how to spell."

"Yeah, well—at least he was good at it. He made a lot of money teaching other people how to be good nerds before he got sick."

Both women fell silent, thinking of former relationships that hadn't worked out. Then Sasha said, "Drop me off at the corner—unless you need help getting those boxes into the house?" The two women lived a block and a half apart in a small subdivision that had been built back in the seventies when Muddy Landing had first begun to expand. Marty's house had been built several years before the rest, so it wasn't actually a part of the development that had grown up around it. Pulling over to where a curb would be if the neighborhood ran to such amenities, she said, "I'm going to leave everything in the car for now."

"Whatever. Save the juiciest ones for me, okay? You know the authors I like. I'm doing a new office complex at Kitty Hawk starting next week, which means I'll be running up to Norfolk a lot, but I'll still have plenty of time to read." Sasha was an interior designer. She opened the door and extended one long, silk-clad leg.

"Speaking of prospects…" said Marty.

"Were we?"

"Speaking of prospects, if Daisy doesn't want the studly gentleman, maybe we should add him to our list of candidates." The skimpy list ranged from the barely possible to the enthusiastic hubba-hubba, but not every prospect turned out to be available.

"For Faylene?" Sasha looked horrified. "No way!"

"Didn't we decide on Gus for Faylene?"

"Oh, right. But we'll let Daisy have first pick. What do you think, does wearing western boots and being from Oklahoma make a man a cowboy?"

"Beats me."

"Yee-haw, ride 'em, cowboy," Sasha caroled, wriggling her well padded behind.

Marty laughed. "It'll help if you haven't destroyed what's left of her hair with that smelly goop you call a conditioner."

"Hey. A friend of mine invented that goop. She's trying to get it patented."

"As what? Insect repellant?"

Seven

The air coming through the open window smelled of marshy riverbanks rather than soybean fields and pine woods. Daisy yawned and stretched. Evidently the wind had shifted. If rain was on the way, she hoped it would get it over with by Wednesday. She still had a few reservations about the plans for Faylene and Gus, but now that Marty's bookstore had closed, her friend needed a distraction.

Rolling over onto her side, she slid her foot over the smooth percale sheet. This had always been her favorite time for planning, before the affairs of the day intruded.

One intrusion in particular came to mind. Kell Magee. To have known him no longer than she had, he was making far too large an impression. How long was he planning to stay? If the woman who'd called here was an employee, the sooner he got back, the better. She didn't sound particularly capable, not when he'd had to call the police on her behalf.

It was none of her business, Daisy warned herself.

The trouble was, the longer he hung around here, being helpful, looking sexy and wistful, asking questions she couldn't possibly answer, the harder it was to remain detached.

She moved her foot again on the narrow bed, imagining how it would feel to encounter a warm, hairy calf. Then, with an impatient exclamation, she sat up and rubbed her scalp, trying to restore a bit of circulation to her obviously oxygen-starved brain.

Order of the day, she told herself firmly: get up, finish what has to be done, get out of here and get on with your own plans. "And while you're at it," she muttered, "forget you ever met Magee."

Easier said than done, she admitted ruefully as she went through a few lackadaisical stretching exercises. At least now she was clear on her priorities. With the start they had already made, it shouldn't take long to finish up in the library and whip through the last few rooms. By the end of the week, or maybe even sooner, she'd be finished.

By that time Kell would have wound up his affairs and be on his way back to Oklahoma.

Well, good. That settled that, then. One lucky cowboy would never know how close he'd come to having his bones jumped by a sex-starved female whose brain was on temporary leave.

By the time she'd showered and pulled on a pair of scrubs, Kell was gone. The coffeemaker was cold and empty, and there were no dishes in the sink, which meant he was either going without breakfast or headed out of town.

Whatever, it meant he wouldn't be hanging around, offering to help with whatever job she tackled. Tempting her with quick grins and lazy, drawling double entendres.

Not that they were, it was only that in that dark-chocolate voice of his, a simple question about the local schools sounded like foreplay. "Miss Daisy, you are truly pathetic," she murmured, amused and a little bit alarmed. At least she knew now that the use-by date on her hormones hadn't expired.

The house was almost too quiet as she finished her skimpy breakfast. She washed her bowl and mug and left them to drain dry, bracing herself to tackle the last few things in the library—stacks of periodicals, the photo albums and the big desk. She hated the responsibility of having to be the one to decide what to trash and what to save, but then, that was why Egbert had asked her to do it. She'd known Harvey better than anyone in his latter days.

By late afternoon Daisy was exhausted and grimy up to her elbows. If Egbert wanted the old newspapers and periodicals cataloged along with the books, he could call in a librarian. As for the photo albums, unless Egbert objected, she intended to offer them to Kell. He could take them back to Oklahoma with him and resurrect a complete family history, real or imaginary.

And no, she did not feel sorry for him, not one bit. At least he knew who his parents were. Evander and Lena, the half-Cherokee barrel racer who cooked something called bean bread. That was far more than she was ever likely to know about her own parents.

A few minutes later she was standing by the refrigerator, drinking ice water straight from the container before washing and refilling it, when she heard Kell drive up. If she'd wanted to make a good impression on him—not that she particularly did—but if she had, this was hardly the way to do it.

Painfully honest, Daisy admitted that in the back of her mind a plan had begun taking shape. By the time he returned, having finished the library, dusted under all the doodads in the parlor, she'd imagined herself relaxing on the side porch wearing something casual, but flattering. If he came close enough he might catch a hint of her Tea Rose body lotion, but nothing heavier. Perhaps a hint of blusher and tinted lip balm…

Instead, a light rain was blowing in on the porch, she looked like Cinderella on a bad hair day and reeked of dust, furniture polish and Murphy's Oil Soap. So much for best-laid plans.

"There you are." Kell poked his head into the kitchen, his hair and tanned face gleaming with moisture. He reminded her of one of those sports car advertisements that always showed some flashy guy racing along a winding road at a hundred miles an hour with the top down. All he lacked was a pair of aviator shades.

"You look like you've had a successful day." The observation sounded snide even to her own ears.

"Yep, sure did." One more eye-twinkling grin, Daisy thought, and she'd buy him a damned sports car herself and tell him where he could road test it. The Himalayas came to mind.

"Fine. Me, too." She set the water container in the sink, added a drop of detergent and turned on the tap.

"Had supper yet? I found this service station that has a deli on the side not too far down the road." He draped his damp leather jacket on a chair back, then thought better of it and hung it in the utility room.

Supper? She hadn't even had lunch, not that she intended to admit it. The last thing she needed was for him to offer to feed her when she was obviously in a weakened condition. "Late lunch," she lied. "If you're hungry there might be a few cans of soup left in the pantry."

He was staring at the boxes she had lugged out into the hall, planning to load them in her car once the rain stopped. "What's all this?" he asked, pointing to the stack with the toe of his left boot.

And that was another thing, she fumed. Boots like that were purely an affectation on anyone who didn't ride, and there wasn't a horse in sight. "Stuff to go," she said. "Some to the dump, some to the thrift shop."

"Anything I might be interested in seeing first?"

"I doubt it. I left the photo albums on the table in the library. If you're interested, I'd appreciate it if you'd go through them and take whatever you want, because I'm hauling the rest away first thing tomorrow."

He waited two clicks and then said, "Got a headache, have we?"

"No, *we* do not have a headache." She did. It had come on the moment he'd strolled into the kitchen and caught her looking like a refugee from the city landfill, drinking ice water straight from the container.

"Sit down and let me work out some of that tension," he offered.

"No thanks, I'm not tense, I'm just tired," she snapped, feeling defensive for no real reason.

"Daisy," he taunted softly. "Hey, I've been on the receiving end of a good massage more times than I can count." She'd just bet he had. "Believe me, it helps."

"I know that. I've been giving therapeutic massages for years."

"Can't give yourself one, though, can you?"

Before she could escape, his hands came down on her shoulders and he pressed her down into a chair. Slowly he began to move his thumbs. A soft moan escaped her lips. "You're way too tense."

Her head fell forward. She was tense, all right. Unfortunately, not all the tension was in her shoulders.

"Met some interesting people today," he said as he kneaded the back of her neck, his touch just short of painful.

"Hmm?"

"Couple of guys in Elizabeth City. One of them belongs to the historical society, lives out on Wellfield Road. Fascinating fellow. You wouldn't believe the things he knows. Talk about a walking encyclopedia."

A small sound escaped her lips as he touched a particularly sensitive spot. "That hurt?" he said, softening his touch to stroke the back of her neck.

"A little. It feels better, though. Really." She sighed. Unfortunately, the tension that had left her shoulders had settled in another part of her anatomy.

"What you need now is a long, hot shower. Set it to needle-spray and let it beat down on the back of your neck, and I guarantee when you're through you'll be floating on air."

"If I can move at all," she said, huffing a little laugh

because it was either that or fling herself into his arms and beg him to redirect his therapeutic attentions.

Ten minutes later she had to admit that he'd been right about the shower, at least. Not that she wouldn't have prescribed the same thing for herself. Hearing noises coming from the kitchen, she headed that way, clean and wearing scented body lotion and her last clean pair of scrubs instead of her favorite caftan.

"Soup's on," Kell announced. He had tucked a tea towel under the front of his belt. She stared at it and felt her face grow warm.

Warning: curiosity may be hazardous to your health.

"Taste it. Too much horseradish?" He held out the long-handled cooking spoon he'd been using to stir whatever was in the pot on the front burner.

"Tomato?" She reached for the spoon. Their fingers brushed and she could have sworn she heard the sizzle of an electrical arc.

"With a few of my own gourmet touches. I'm not totally clueless in a kitchen, you know."

She tasted, not because she was hungry—well, she was, but it was more that she couldn't resist a tall, handsome guy wearing lean jeans and a tea towel, regardless of what he was offering.

"Oh, my—oh, wow!" Her eyes watered as she tried to catch her breath.

"Too much horseradish?"

"Funny—I didn't hear the smoke alarm go off."

"Sorry about that. There was a clump in the bottom of the jar and it all fell out before I could catch it."

She fanned her mouth and reached for the milk. Four percent would have been better for putting out the fire, but two percent was the best she could do short of lick-ing out the butter dish. "Dump in another can of soup," she gasped. "Maybe if you dilute it…"

They dined on pyromaniac's delight, Daisy's term for the concoction Kell had made from a perfectly innocent can of store-brand tomato soup, plus a select few incen-diary seasoning ingredients. The heat didn't seem to bother him in the least.

"So what did your historical friend have to say?" she asked when she was sure her tongue would work.

"He knew my dad…at least I think he did. He also claimed to have helped the Wright brothers find a place to park their bicycles while they tested their plane. That would make him pretty precocious, to say the least. He can't be that old. You want to finish up the last of the soup?"

"No thanks," she said hastily.

"How's the tension?"

"Better. Gone, in fact." *But not for long if you don't stop looking at me that way.*

"You feel up to showing me those albums tonight? I'll just put this stuff in to soak and wash it later."

Daisy didn't want to spend any more time alone with him for the simple reason that she wanted it too much. "I need to call Egbert," she said, reminding herself what was important and what was strictly temporary.

"Can't it wait until tomorrow?"

She gave in far too easily. "I guess. I just needed to be sure of what to get rid of and what to leave here."

"Get rid of?" He looked worried.

She found herself torn between smoothing the frown from his rumpled brow and making a run for it while a few of her synapses were still firing. "Donate or recy-cle. I'll check with the library, but they probably already have all the back issues of *State Magazine* and *The Daily Advance* they need."

She let him put the dishes in to soak and then led the way to the library. Looking wary, almost as if he were afraid of what he might find, Kell picked up one of the albums. "While you glance through those," she said, "I'll just finish going through these drawers."

As executor, Egbert had already removed anything pertinent to the estate, but he hadn't bothered to sort through the rest of the contents. She was flattered that he trusted her to handle something that was technically his responsibility.

She started with the middle drawer. A few bent paper clips, a notepad advertising a real estate firm and a let-ter opener. She emptied everything into the trash box and opened the next drawer.

From time to time Kell made a remark as he leafed through the pages of the old photo album. Once or twice, he even laughed aloud.

Glancing up, she seemed to recall that the album he was going through now held mostly black-and-white photos. She'd glanced inside each one before setting it aside, but looking any further had somehow seemed like an invasion of Harvey's privacy. Obviously, Kell didn't feel that way.

"Come here a minute, I want to show you some-thing." He was smiling.

As determined as she was not to involve herself in his odyssey, there was no way she could refuse. "What's so funny?"

The pictures were held in place by those little black corners. He pointed to a deckle-edged snapshot of a young man standing on a ladder behind a half-decorated Christmas tree holding a wreath over his head as if it were a halo. The sheet draped over his shoulders was probably meant to go around the base of the tree.

Daisy had little trouble recognizing him even though he was laughing so hard his eyes were nearly closed. "That's Harvey. The angel on top of the tree," she said softly. "I told you he had a sense of humor, didn't I?"

Her gaze moved to another picture on the same page, this one of a skinny, barefoot boy in baggy overalls pulling another boy in a wagon. The one in the wagon was hanging on to the sides and both boys were laughing. Recognizing the passenger by the distinctive curve of his back, she could have wept.

But it was the other child that Kell pointed to, the one pulling the wagon. "What do you bet that's my dad?" he said softly. The two boys looked nothing alike, but then, it wasn't a particularly good picture.

Without thinking, Daisy squeezed his shoulder before moving back to the desk across the room. Too many shared emotions could be hazardous to a woman's health, she reminded herself as she busied herself sorting through loose rubber bands, a roll of old stamps, more paper clips, dozens of pencils and assorted ballpoint pens, some with caps, most without. She set aside the stamps and tossed the rest.

The next drawer held only a box of personalized stationery. No point in saving that, either, she told herself, adding it to the growing pile in the discard box. She was about to close the drawer when something at the very back caught her attention—a square white envelope. It was not addressed; there was no return address, but there was a twenty-three-cent stamp in the upper-right-hand corner.

Twenty-three cents? Mercy, how long ago had that been? Curious, she turned the envelope over. The flap was stuck, and after only a moment's hesitation she slid her finger underneath and pried it open.

"Oh, no," she whispered as she stared at the heart-shaped Valentine. Handwritten across the pastel face of the card were the words "Roses are red, violets are blue, someone you know is in love with you."

It was signed "Yours truly, Harvey Snow."

Not until Kell touched her on the shoulder was she aware of having read the words aloud. She had no idea there were tears on her cheeks until he brushed them away with his thumb.

One touch was all it took. When the floodgates opened, she turned to him, pressing her face against his waist. He stood beside her chair, patting her shoulder and cupping the back of her head in his hand. "This is so embarrassing," she burbled. "I never cry, honestly."

She had broken down twice in just the short time he'd been there.

"Shh, I know that." He lifted her from the chair by her arms and led her to the sofa. Even after she was able to stem the flow of tears, a matter of a few minutes, she made no move to pull away.

Nor did he make any move to release her. Instead, he leaned back, his arm around her, her face still hidden in the hollow of his shoulder. "Daisy?" he murmured after a while.

She sniffed. "I'm all right now." And she was, truly she was. Any minute now she would pull herself together, get up and apologize for soaking his shirt. Any minute now.

"Daisy, look at me."

"If you don't mind, I'd rather not." She knew very well what she must look like. Was there a woman on earth who looked seductive in scrubs? Add to that bloodshot eyes and a red nose and she might as well throw herself on the discard pile.

Leaning back against the arm of the sofa, he drew her across his chest while his hands moved slowly over her back. He was making those soft rumbling noises again—sounds that were probably meant to be comforting. She could have told him that was hardly the effect they were having.

Sniffing, she drew in a shuddering breath, suddenly aware that she was draped over his torso like a tartan, with one arm flung over his shoulder. What's more, she was far too comfortable to move away.

"Better now?" he murmured, his voice more a vibration than a sound.

"A Valentine." For whom? Why had it never been mailed? "It's just so sad," she whispered.

"Yeah," he said. His thumb moved slowly over the back of her neck. If he was trying to ease her tension again, he was going about it the wrong way. A bucket of cold water might have been more effective.

She sniffed again, inhaling the clean, outdoorsy scent she had come to identify with the man. If the stuff could be bottled and sold, someone would make a fortune.

"I wonder who she was," Kell said softly.

Daisy shook her head. "Poor Harvey." Reluctantly, she steeled herself to get up. She even went so far as to slide her arm from around his neck. That's when she caught sight of his face. Where a moment ago his eyes had been blue, they were now black except for a thin, incandescent rim of color.

When he murmured, "Daisy, I'm going to have to kiss you," she didn't even try to fight it. Some things were simply inevitable.

Long moments later, having been kissed until she was roughly the consistency of Silly Putty, she told herself that the trouble with scrubs was that they didn't button down the front.

The good thing about them was that they fit loosely enough to accommodate a pair of skilled, exploring hands.

When Kell found her hardened nipples they both groaned. Cupping her breasts in his hands, he proceeded to drive her crazy, using his teeth and his tongue, until she was ready to rip off every shred of clothing—his and hers—and do whatever it took to ease the throbbing demands of her body.

I am *not* a sensual woman, she reminded herself desperately.

The trouble was, she had proof to the contrary.

"Bedroom?" he said urgently, his breath steamy on her bare flesh.

She shook her head, then, realizing that he could hardly see her when his face was pressed against her stomach, she said, "Here…now. Please?" If she had to move she might come to her senses, and that was the last thing she wanted to do.

His hand moved between them and, as if by magic,

the tie at her waist came undone. She heard the sound of a zipper just as she felt the cool air on overheated parts of her body. Feeling the dampness between her thighs, she couldn't help but remember the tube of lubricant she'd bought a few weeks after she'd started seeing Jerry. He'd wanted to see if they were suited. At the time she'd thought they were, but evidently he hadn't agreed.

Why was this *happening?* Why did it feel so *right?* Kell's hands were sheer magic. When he replaced his hands with his mouth, she uttered a cascade of whimpering sounds that would have embarrassed her had she even been aware of them. Again and again he brought her to the precipice, only to pull her back before she could fly away.

They were both breathing in jerky gasps when she gasped, "Hurry, hurry…"

At the same time he said, "Are you…?"

"Yes!" she practically shouted.

"On the pill?"

Her head fell back on the padded arm of the sofa. "No, but don't you have…?"

He was nestled between her thighs, hot and hard and ready. With a groan, he whispered, "Back home—bedside table. I'm not carrying."

So disappointed she could have screamed, she squeezed her thighs together, managing to trap a part of him she would have much rather trap somewhere else. "Well, that's really stupid."

"Yeah," he said, making no move to release his trapped "part." He moved his hips slowly, his eyes closed, his teeth clenched. Reaching between them, he whispered hoarsely, "Let me do this for you."

She shook her head, so disappointed she could have wept all over again. "Just let me up…please?"

With the utmost gentleness, he pulled away and smoothed her top down over her naked breasts. His jeans were around his knees. By all rights he should have looked ridiculous. Instead he looked remorseful, frustrated, and so damned desirable she was tempted to pull him back down to finish what they'd started, protection or no protection.

But if he could be sensible at a time like this, she thought despairingly, then so could she. Forcing herself to sit up, she straightened her clothes while he stood and began pulling up his jeans. He wore navy briefs. *Brief* briefs. And he was definitely packing heat!

Eight

Daisy waited as long as possible the next morning before going in search of caffeine. The first thing that caught her eye was the note on the table, anchored with the salt shaker. Knowing sleep would be elusive, she had taken a book to bed. An hour later, unable to remember a word of what she'd read, she'd given up and turned off the light.

Sometime later she had opened her eyes to darkness. The luminous dial on her alarm clock read eighteen past four. She'd listened for whatever sound had aroused her, her heart going triple time. Then she'd heard it again, this time from the kitchen.

A burglar? Hardly. The crime rate in Muddy Landing was minus zilch. There were only two deputies assigned to the area, and both of them spent most of their time reading comic books. Faylene occasionally arrived early, but never *this* early. It had to be Kell.

Dammit, it would serve him right if he'd had as much trouble getting to sleep as she had. What was that old saying about letting sleeping dogs lie? She'd thought all that craziness was behind her. As a nurse she had seen too many tragic results of having one's brain overruled by one's libido—everything from broken marriages to unwanted pregnancies to assault and battery, heartbreak being among the least of them.

Which was why Egbert was so perfect, she reminded herself now. She had no doubt that they'd be compatible in the bedroom. At their ages, sex once or twice a week should suffice, leaving them to focus their energies on their respective careers. She liked being a homecare nurse. It was a portable profession. She happened to know Egbert intended to move up in banking circles, which would certainly mean relocating. When—not if, but *when*—he moved to a larger area, she could easily relocate with him. At least that was the way she had pictured their joint futures before she'd met Kell.

Now all she could think of was what it would be like to be married to a man who could melt her bones by simply staring at her mouth. Or by touching her hair. Or by simply talking about anything at all in that grave drawl of his. As a nurse, she knew that sound waves were no more than vibrations in the air. Certain vibrations could touch off landslides, but she'd never dreamed how they could affect a woman's body.

She must have dozed off again, because when the alarm clock went off, she knocked it over trying to shut off the intrusive sound. She'd been dreaming the kind of dream that left her hot and damp and restless.

Trying to recapture the dream, she heard the clink of

dishes in the sink. A few moments later when she heard the sound of the front door opening and closing, she was torn between relief and disappointment. After last night's farcical seduction scene—and for the life of her, she couldn't have said who had tried to seduce whom— the last thing she needed was to have to face him across the breakfast table.

Part of the trouble was that she liked the man. Honestly, genuinely liked him. They could have been best friends if only something about him didn't set off fireworks whenever she looked at him—or even thought about him.

For one thing, he appreciated Harvey's home even though, as it had been willed to the historical society, he wasn't in line to inherit. That spoke volumes about his character—or maybe about his common sense. It might be charming, even romantic, but the place was a ruin. The slate roof alone would cost a fortune to repair; the half basement flooded whenever it rained; and she was pretty sure termites had already invaded the floor joists. Which meant that sooner or later the whole thing might collapse unless someone poured a fortune into restoring it.

Watching the sky gradually brighten in the east, Daisy lay there wondering how, after mapping out a safe, sane future for herself, she'd managed to get herself involved with termites and sad Valentines and sexy men.

Striding back to the school parking lot, Kell pumped a fist in the air. If he'd just hit the grand slam that had won the World Series he couldn't have felt any better. *Screw you, Blalock, who needs you? I've found what I came for!*

It had taken all day, but it had been worth it. First the courthouse records had been a mess, having been stacked up out of the tide's reach back in September. The clerk who'd been there for years had recently retired and her replacement was evidently in the throes of on-the-job training without a trainer. Following an interesting but largely unrewarding morning, he'd headed for the local high school, and that's where he'd struck gold. The school librarian was still arranging books that had also been stored for protection against the storm. Old annuals were the least of her worries, but she'd come through for him.

He had slipped out before Daisy was up this morning, uncertain of how to deal with what had happened between them last night. Actually, nothing had happened—the game had been called in the early innings because he'd forgotten the first entry in any bachelor's rule book.

Which might have been a blessing in disguise, because he had a feeling Daisy was no gamer. He couldn't afford to set up any expectations as he'd be leaving in a few more days.

Her car was still in the driveway, but the boxes were no longer stacked on the back seat. That meant she'd been busy today, too. Eager to share the good news, he braced himself for what might be an awkward moment. But awkward or not, he had a feeling Daisy would appreciate it more than anyone else. Definitely more than Blalock would, although he looked forward to telling the smug bastard.

"Daisy?" he called as he opened the door. "Are you home?"

"I'm in the kitchen. Wipe your feet, Faylene waxed the front hall this morning."

He wiped his boots on the faded old crocheted rug she had put there for that purpose and headed for the kitchen, caution fighting with elation. "Chicken again? It sure smells good." So much for not setting up expectations. He could easily get hooked on her cooking alone, never mind that she was one of the sexiest women he'd ever met. Her brand of sexiness was all the more effective for being subtle.

Unable to repress a grin, he slapped a thin stack of papers down on the table and pulled out a chair. Aware of a subliminal sense of well-being, he thought, it doesn't get much better than this. The thought made him oddly uneasy, but he brushed the feeling aside.

"I've been trying to use up everything in the freezer before they cut the power off," Daisy explained without looking around. "It was mostly bread, chicken and fish. I tossed the fish. No telling how long it's been in there." She spared him a quick smile that didn't involve her eyes.

He nodded. Speaking of chicken, she looked finger-licking good. He didn't figure she'd appreciate the compliment.

"You look like you struck pay dirt," she said, not sounding particularly interested.

"Are you using a long-handled fork?"

She held up a cooking fork for his approval. "What did you find out?"

Gloating over his success, Kell tried not to stare at the lines of her bra under her thin yellow T-shirt. Why couldn't she wear a sweatshirt like the other one—Faylene? Or another suit of those baggy pajamas she called scrubs.

He thumped the stack of papers before him. "Photocopies. God bless technology."

Glancing over her shoulder, Daisy lifted her eyebrows. Only a shade or two darker than her hair, they made her look innocent, mysterious and seductive all at once—although damned if he could figure out how. Most women relied on cosmetics to turn up the heat.

She said, "Open that grease can for me, will you? Photocopies of what?"

Only too glad of the distraction, Kell leaped to obey. She still wore a bandage on her right forearm, but at least she hadn't added any more burns. Holding a lid on the pan, she drained it, then lowered the heat and set it back on the burner, all without looking directly at him. Kell had a feeling it wouldn't take much to send her running for cover.

"So tell me," she said finally after adjusting the heat and the lid to her satisfaction. "You found something good, right? Does Egbert know?"

Steering his mind back on course, he said, "Not yet. I never set out to prove anything to him, just to myself." While it wasn't quite true, at this point it was irrelevant. "You ready to look at what I found?"

She moved, almost reluctantly, it seemed, closer to the table, still holding the fork. No wonder she was spooked. What had happened the night before had started when they'd shared a few photographs in an old album. Not that those had proved anything conclusively, as there were no captions. The kid pulling the wagon could've been anyone, but Kell knew in his bones that it was a young Evander giving his kid brother a ride.

As for the Valentine…

Ah, jeez. Harvey, I'm sorry, old man.

"Okay, here we go. Exhibit one," he said, cheering immediately when he produced the copy of a page from the R. L. Snowden High School album, class of '69. "Class pictures, eleventh grade. Check it out."

Laying the fork aside, Daisy braced her forearms on the table and leaned over to study the faces, some grave, others smiling. Kell leaned over her shoulder, trying not to be distracted by her warmth, her scent. Dressed in full body armor, she would still be risky business.

"What did I tell you?" he gloated. After all these years of wondering—well, maybe not years; he hadn't started on this quest until a few months ago—he felt like a bottle of champagne that had been shaken and then opened too quickly.

Forcing his feelings back under control, he pointed to the top row, then read aloud the fine print beneath a picture of a boy with unruly hair and a shallow cleft in his chin. "Evander Lee Magee. Childhood Delight—Barney Google." He cocked his head at an angle to look up at her face. "What the hell is a Barney Google?"

Daisy laughed softly and shook her head. "Who knows?" So he went on to read the small print. "Radio club, photo club, archery. Notice the chin? Add a few pounds and a few years—well, maybe a lot of years—and that's my dad. Color would help, but even in black and white you can almost tell he had red hair and freckles."

"You can? I mean, he did?"

"Sure did. Only thing I inherited from him was maybe the color of his eyes and that split on his chin." Kell fingered the shallow cleft in his bristly chin, reminding himself that he was overdue for a shave. It wasn't a fashion statement; he was simply a twice-a-day shaver. "Hey, you know what else? You see these check marks?" He shuffled through several pages and pointed to two other student pictures. "I found both these guys listed in the Elizabeth City phone book." He leaned over her to point out the surviving classmates, and her behind brushed against his groin, setting off a chain reaction. Catching his breath, he inhaled the faint, familiar scent of roses and bacon grease. "You flavored your canoodle oil again, didn't you?" he teased.

When she glanced up, her face almost collided with his. Desire hit his bloodstream like a shot of tequila. Her lips parted in surprise as her eyes widened warily.

"Daisy," he rumbled softly.

"No. Oh, no." But she didn't move away fast enough, and then, somehow she was in his arms.

He said, "I was hoping I'd just imagined it."

Daisy shook her head. She hadn't imagined anything. But before she could reply, much less pull away, he was kissing her. Softly at first, a mere brushing of warm, moist lips that dragged slightly against her own—back and forth, back and forth, tugging her lips apart. The softness quickly escalated into something far more intense, more invasive. The rasp of his beard brought a rush of goose bumps that spread like wildfire down her flanks.

How could his taste be so familiar when she'd known him so briefly? She was reminded for no reason of warm summer evenings, of fresh-cut grass and honeysuckle and fireflies…. When his hands stroked down her back to cup her against his groin, warning bells went off in her mind. *Break away now, while you still can. Else you'll never be able to settle for less.*

This time she didn't even bother to tell herself that Egbert wouldn't necessarily be less.

"Daisy, I stopped off at the drug store. I bought—"

"So did I," she whispered, trying not to feel embarrassed. She'd always prided herself on being sensible, and a sensible woman prepared for the unexpected.

The unexpected?

Hardly. She hadn't been able to focus her mind on a single task after what had happened last night—the way she had come apart in his arms. He could hold seminars on the fine art of kissing alone, she thought, as parts of her body that had lain dormant for too long once again came to life.

She twisted her face away from his, her voice uneven as she murmured, "This isn't very smart."

Panting as if he'd just finished a ten-mile run, he said, "Why not?"

Daisy hung on to his upper arms until the room stopped spinning and then she reached for a chair back for support. Aware of her burning cheeks and the urgency that grew steadily in spite of the fact that he was no longer touching her, she said, "Because—because I need to finish what I was doing."

As pathetic as it was, it was the only excuse she could think of at the moment. She wasn't about to tell him how long it had been since she'd even kissed a man before last night, much less how long since she'd had sex. Or even *wanted* to have sex.

"Believe it or not, Daisy, I didn't plan it this way." His voice was sincere, but his pupils were dilated, his breathing uneven. A quick glance revealed that that wasn't the only evidence of his arousal.

Of course you didn't, she thought, amused in spite of herself. *Neither did I. That's why we both stocked up on condoms.*

Swallowing hard, Kell glanced down at the pages scattered across the table. "I guess I just got carried away, finding all those pictures of my dad. It was better than winning the lottery. You feel like celebrating at a time like that, you know what I mean?"

If that kiss had anything to do with his dad, Daisy didn't want to know about it, she really didn't. Taking another deep breath, she reached for something cool and intelligent to say—something that would put everything in perspective. "I'm sick of fried chicken, but the freezer was full of it and it's all got to go. Bags and bags of it— Harvey liked chicken. Help yourself if you're hungry. Day after tomorrow I'll finish the last of it for the box supper, then I can unplug the freezer."

Well, that ought to cool his ardor, she thought, amused in spite of the fact that she was still aroused.

"Anything I can do to help?" He stacked his copies and ruffled the edges, looking awkward and all the more appealing for it. She wondered fleetingly if that was a part of his seduction technique.

If so, it was working. From wanting to kick him out she'd gone to wanting to—

At this point she didn't know what she wanted, she only knew that irresistible or not, some short-term treats had long-term consequences. Any woman who'd ever tried to lose weight knew that much.

"I suppose now that you've found what you were

looking for, you'll be leaving." Turning away, she began packing fried chicken into a container to take to an ex-patient who lived alone.

"I'm planning to stay a couple more days, but I can move to a motel if you're uncomfortable having me around."

She was tempted to take him up on it, but that would be as good as admitting she didn't trust herself around him. She didn't, but he didn't need to know it. Besides, staying in the house where his father had once lived obviously meant more to him than it was ever likely to mean to anyone else. She had a feeling Harvey would have approved. "Stay if you'd like to," she told him. "Faylene and I plan to wind up things here by the end of the week, so we'll both be busy."

If he was relieved, he hid it well. "Right. I've got a couple of appointments tomorrow, then I'd like to drive around, check out a few places I'm pretty sure my dad mentioned. A lot's probably changed since then, but some things are bound to be the same. I picked up a map showing the Dismal Swamp and the Outer Banks."

He left her feeling a mixture of dismay and relief. At least he wouldn't be underfoot much longer, Daisy rationalized, tempting her to throw away all her plans for a brief, wild fling.

The best medicine wasn't always easy to swallow.

On Monday evening Daisy looked for something to read from Harvey's collection to help her fall asleep. Nothing appealed to her, but at least the books were clean now. Today she'd done the linen closet, packing away scores of yellowed sheets and monogrammed pillow slips, leaving only a pretty spread for each bed. It wouldn't be long before she was ready to move out.

As to where she would move, that was another matter. Her apartment still wasn't ready—something about a mold problem now. If she didn't know better she might think the owner was stalling.

She hadn't seen or heard from Kell all day. Tired and oddly discouraged, she ended up driving into town. As flaky as they sometimes were, her friends never failed to cheer her up.

"How's the studly gentleman?" Marty asked after Daisy had picked out half a dozen romantic suspense titles and set them aside.

"How's who?"

"That's what people are calling him around here. It didn't take long for word to spread. You should've heard Gracie—she moved here from Edenton this past August to take over Miss Hattie's job at the courthouse? Well, to hear her tell it, he looks like that guy from Norfolk—the reality show bachelor, Evan Marriott? Only Kell's taller, broader in the shoulder and narrower in the hips, not to mention—"

"Marty," Daisy wailed. "Don't! Whatever you were going to say, just don't, okay? Granted, he's sort of nice-looking, but—"

"Sort of nice-looking. Right. And Bill Gates is sort of solvent."

"Anyway, he'll be leaving in a day or so."

"Too bad. I was thinking about inviting him to the box supper. Not that I'm interested in anything long term, but I wouldn't mind a little light entertainment."

Daisy thumbed through a Sandra Brown large print,

wondering if she'd read it before. "You'll be too busy stage-managing Faylene's and Gus's opening act. That should be entertainment enough." She glanced up, a spark of amusement lighting her tired face. "She knows we're up to something. How could she not, after all you two have done to her—"

"For her, you mean."

"Whatever. Just don't be surprised if she comes after us with a meat cleaver when she finds out who you've picked out for her."

"Well, jeez, she doesn't have to marry him, all she has to do is show up and eat supper with him. So…what does Egbert think about him?"

"Think about who, Gus Mathias?"

"No, silly, your cowboy."

"Does it really matter? Kell's not interested in the estate. All he wants is to find out something about his father. He's done that, so he'll probably be headed West again tomorrow—that's if he hasn't already gone."

He hadn't. She'd peeked into his room to see. His bomber jacket was hanging on the chair, his open bag on the bed. The room smelled like whatever soap and shaving lotion he used. She'd been tempted to check out the brands, but then she might have done something extremely foolish, like buy a bar or a bottle or a tube of whatever it was just so she could sniff it and remember him.

As if she could forget.

Marty went on stripping covers from new paperbacks to return to the publisher for credit in case she ever opened another bookstore. Glancing up, she said, "I'll bet Egbert wasn't too happy when he came nosing around. Poor sweetie, I knew Egbert in high school. Even then he was a stickler."

"Egbert? I'd hardly call him a stickler," Daisy hedged. "Although in his profession, it's probably required."

"So tell me more about him."

"You've known him longer than I have." Daisy had gone to school in Elizabeth City, which was two counties away.

"Not him, the hottie. We know he drives a Porsche, he has black hair, blue eyes and a truly bodacious bod. Sasha wanted to bet me you'd have him in your bed by now. How about it, do I owe her a seafood platter?"

"Oh, hush up! If that's all you can talk about, I'm taking my books and going home."

"Don't blame you one bit, sugar. If I had what you've got waiting at home for me, I'd be in a hurry, too."

Daisy had to laugh. "And you're the one who claims she's sworn off men?"

"Hey, I can swear on again, can't I? Has Faylene said anything about Wednesday?"

"The box supper? No, but like I said, I'm pretty sure she suspects something. I saw her smirking after we talked on the phone yesterday."

"She'll have a ball, you wait and see. You wanna stick around and help me strip books?"

"No thanks. I'd better go—and wipe that smirk off your face. I'm going to make a peanut butter sandwich, pour myself a glass of milk and go to bed. To *read,*" she stressed.

"Yeah, yeah, I hear you," her friend jeered. "When's your apartment going to be ready?"

"Who knows? Now they're talking about mold, and you know what that means."

"I heard he had a buyer on the hook wanting the property. Those old apartments don't bring in all that much revenue with land values going up so fast. Taxes and maintenance probably eat up any profits."

Well, that made sense, Daisy thought morosely. "The good news just keeps on pouring in, doesn't it?"

"Hey, you're not alone. My wiring's acting up and I can't get an electrician to even look at it, much less give me an estimate. The last one—oh, by the way, he's single and not bad-looking, so I've already added him to the list. Anyway, he said he wouldn't touch it with a ten-foot pole, not even with insulators."

"Tough. Did y'all decide who's going to tip Gus off as to which box to bid on tomorrow night?" With one hand on the doorknob, Daisy juggled her stack of books.

"Sasha said she'd do it. Show me the man who can refuse her anything. The joys of being a redhead."

"Or the joys of having an hourglass figure," Daisy said dryly.

"I keep telling her if she doesn't change a few habits she'll be all butt and boobs by the time she's forty."

Daisy laughed, feeling some of her earlier depression lift. Friends were invaluable, and she had the best. "Thanks for the books. I'll return them as soon as I'm finished."

"Hey, used is used. Just don't drool on the pages if you-know-who happens to pass by on his way to the shower."

Nine

Some two hours later when Daisy pulled into the driveway, the house looked dark and unwelcoming. It hadn't occurred to her to leave a light on, as she hadn't expected to be gone this long. While she was out she'd taken time to drive by a few rentals in case she had to move. Actually, a house would suit her better than an apartment, anyway. With a yard of her own, she might even get a cat or a dog for company.

But then, when she married Egbert, her plans might change. Something temporary, then…

There was no sign of Kell's car. Could he have come back, packed his few things and left without even saying goodbye? One part of her, the sensible part, hoped he had.

Another part—the one that lacked even a single grain of common sense, felt like crying. But at least, she rationalized, she wouldn't be able to make comparisons later on.

She refrained from looking to see if his things were still in his room. She had enough to worry about without wasting time on any adolescent daydreams.

She ended up having half a glass of buttermilk and a few stale saltines for supper. By the time she heard Kell come in, she had read the same page at least three times. Before she could switch off her light and pretend to be asleep, he rapped on her door.

"Daisy?" he called softly. "I'm in for the night. I locked the front and checked the back. All secure."

If the door had been transparent she couldn't have been any more aware of him just on the other side. He lingered, and finally she blurted, "I thought maybe you'd gone back home."

"Nope, not without saying goodbye. I drove down the Outer Banks. I thought as long as I was this close I might as well see where Dad used to fish."

She waited to see if he would leave. When he didn't, she said, "It's probably changed all out of recognition since he was there."

"Probably." Long pause, and then he said, "There's a bag of chicken in the refrigerator. Want me to do something with it?"

"That's the last of it. It's thawing for the box supper. Thanks, though."

"No problem." Even strained through a paneled mahogany door, his voice resonated on every nerve in her body.

Hours later when she finally fell asleep, she dreamed of Kell wearing western boots, a Stetson and nothing in between. He was standing in a kitchen she only half recognized with a cooking fork in his hand, and then he was galloping off on a big white stallion with her sprawled across his lap.

No more reading historical romances in bed—at least, not until the covers had been stripped. While she bore no resemblance to a heroine, Kell was the epitome of every romance hero in the history of the genre.

He was gone when she woke up the next morning. Daisy told herself she was perfectly within her rights to open his door, to see if this time he was gone for good. If so, she could strip his bed and wash his linens along with her own.

And this time she wouldn't inhale.

His leather coat was gone, but there was a shirt on the back of a chair and his soft-sided bag was open on the foot of the bed. The three photo albums were stacked neatly on the dresser. She tried not to wonder where he'd gone this time. He was obviously as eager to avoid her as she was him. Good thing one of them still possessed a working brain.

With Faylene's help the house was almost ready to close up, the freezer was finally empty and unplugged, the pantry shelves all but bare. Stripping down for a quick shower, Daisy ignored the bath gel and went for the plain, unscented soap. The last thing she needed was to get her hormones in an uproar again.

She was drying her hair when someone rapped on the bathroom door. She shut off her hair dryer to hear a familiar creamy baritone drawl. "Daisy, you in there?"

"What do you need?" She'd scarcely seen him since

Monday evening when he'd come home all full of himself for having found his dad's old high school annual.

"I'm headed down to the place that sells subs and barbecue. Want me to bring you anything?"

And that was another thing. He knew she was trying to use up all the food on hand, yet he didn't take it for granted that he was invited to meals. He'd bought a pound of freshly ground Colombian coffee, a box of doughnuts and cereal. Neither of them would be there long enough to use all the coffee. Faylene could have the cereal.

"Daisy? Did you slip down the drain?"

"No, look—there's this box supper thing at the church out on Water Street. Maple Grove? White frame, with a parking lot in front and a picnic area off to one side? You can try your luck there if you don't want to drive all the way to Barco."

"Box supper, hmm? The only box supper I've ever seen is the one in that Broadway show, *Oklahoma!* I'm not much of a dancer and I can't sing a lick. Does that make me ineligible?"

Laying aside her hair dryer, she reached for her comb and started unsnarling her hair. He was still out there, she could feel him just on the other side of the door. "Of course not." Long pause. He was still there. She said, "I didn't know you liked Broadway musicals."

"It was named for my state, so I figured it was my patriotic duty to see it as long as I was in New York for the play-offs, anyway."

Snatching her robe off the hook, Daisy rammed her arms in the sleeves and tied the sash around her waist.

"You ever see any Broadway shows?" he called through the door.

She wasn't about to tell him she'd been too busy baby-sitting, pet-walking, dish-washing and going to classes to take time off for anything more frivolous— not to mention more expensive—than an occasional movie. When she didn't respond, he said, "Well then, I, uh—I guess I'll see you later. That is, unless you want me to move out now?"

She did and she didn't. The weakest part of her didn't. "Tomorrow will be soon enough," she called through the door, trying to sound matter-of-fact but sounding breathless instead. If he left in the morning, she could do the last load of laundry and be gone by to-morrow evening.

"Right. Well, thanks." Still he didn't leave. She could picture him just on the other side of the paneled door, those cobalt-blue eyes half closed, one booted ankle crossed over the other one, arms crossed over his chest. He might appear tame, but if ever a man had *free-range* stamped all over him, it was Kell Magee.

Finally, he said, "So…I guess I'll see you later, then. Have fun at your box supper."

Daisy's shoulders drooped as she stared at herself in the steamy mirror. She could think of several interest-ing ways of spending his last night here, and not one of them involved box suppers.

Holding a hand mirror, Faylene studied her back-side in the full-length mirror on her bathroom door. Truth was, she was disappointed at the way her hair had turned out. She didn't like it near as much as she liked that buffet-style like Dolly Parton's, which is what she'd been aiming for, only all them bleaches made her ends break off, so even when she got the color right she didn't have enough hair left to do nothing with.

But hair would grow out, and Miss Sasha said the wrench would wash right out if she changed her mind about the color. Leastwise, her roots didn't show up so much now.

The pants Miss Marty had bought her fit real good, though, even without her support hose. She didn't need them to sit at a picnic table eating Miss Daisy's fried chicken and corn fritters with a new gentleman friend. That might make a certain Mister Somebody set up and take notice, she thought smugly. Oh, she knew what they were up to, these friends of hers. She let them get away with it on account of it suited her just fine.

Bob Ed would hear about tonight. Yessir, there'd be plenty to tell him that if he wanted to lay claim to Faylene Beasley he'd better hurry up and get in line.

Zipping on her bronze leather ankle boots, she went over in her mind the list of possible candidates. Once they set their minds to matchmaking, they did it so slick you'd swear they hadn't had a hand in it. Good thing they hadn't put Bob Ed on their list. He might not know it yet, but he was already spoken for. That prissy little man down at the bank was single again, too, the one Miss Daisy looked at like she was measuring him for curtains or something. Poor soul, if them three went after him his goose was already stewed.

The parking lot was nearly full by the time Faylene squeezed in between a long-bed pickup and a muddy SUV. Miss Daisy was parked over in the corner, and there was Miss Sasha's fancy red convertible, parked right next to the preacher's minivan. Her and Miss Marty must've come together.

Bob Ed drove a truck he'd built himself practically from scratch. That man could do most anything he set his mind to, she just wished he'd set his mind to marrying himself a wife.

Several people greeted her as she strode up the front walk and around to the side where the picnic tables were set up. This weren't her regular church, but she knew most everybody in town by face if not by name. Smiling, she tried not to appear self-conscious in her new outfit, with her hair right out of one of them ladies' magazines. Pausing at an empty table, she looked around to see who she could spot.

There was Miss Marty. Faylene waved, and then caught sight of her other two ladies up at the front talking to the auctioneer. The table was stacked full of baskets and boxes, all done up to look pretty. She spotted the one with the purple bow right off, the one that was supposed to be hers. Pinching the creases in her new slacks, she sat down and glanced around just as someone turned the volume down on the boom box that had been blaring out gospel music.

Folks stopped talking and turned toward the auctioneer. He was holding up the first basket and just getting started with his gabble-de-gook, sounding like a tobacco auctioneer, when the new coach passed right by her table. Was he the one they'd fixed her up with?

He pretended like he hadn't seen her, but they must've told him which box to bid on. He was new here—he didn't know many folks yet, so when Sara from the bank called out something to him, he set down with her. Sorry, girl, you're too late, Faylene thought smugly. The coach has already got his marching orders.

Just then Miss Marty got up and hurried across to the far side of the picnic grounds. Faylene had to stand to see where she was headed. She frowned. And then her frosted-cherry lips fell open.

Gus Mathias?

She tried to remember if Marty had mentioned any car trouble she'd been having lately. But when her employer pointed to the end of the table where the boxes were stacked, it sure looked like she was pointing right at the box with the big purple bow.

Gus looked at the tableful of boxes, and then he looked straight at where Faylene was sitting. And then he shook his head. Frowning, Marty waved her other two ladies over and the three of them started jabbering up a storm, looking first at her and then back at Gus.

He kept shaking his head. Then, blamed if he didn't walk off, skinny little arse, spare tire, beer belly and all. After he passed within ten feet without so much as a polite "how do" and headed for the parking lot, Faylene turned to glare at her three ladies. The ones she'd thought were her friends. Gabbling like a flock of guinea hens, they were headed her way.

Rising with all the dignity of an independent, self-supporting woman, she turned up her nose and set off toward the parking lot as fast as she could move. They were still trotting after her, calling for her to wait up, when she slammed her car door shut, cranked up her engine and scratched off, displacing a spray of gravel.

Damn near rammed into Gus's tailgate while he waited for a break in the traffic, too. "Serves you right," she muttered. When he honked at her, she stuck her head out the window and yelled, "Take a good look, buster, 'cause this is as close as you're ever gonna get to yours truly!" She couldn't *believe* they thought Gus Mathias was the best she could do! Some friends. Serve 'em all right if she handed in her notice.

Kell recognized the car scratching out of the churchyard just as he turned in. It barely missed a pickup truck that was slower to accelerate. He'd intended to pick up some barbecue and then spend his last evening calling around to see if he could get in touch with another of his dad's old classmates. Trouble was, he couldn't seem to concentrate on anything but Daisy—about the way she'd come apart in his arms and then tried to pretend it had never happened. For that matter, so had he. Tried and failed.

And dammit, he knew better, too. He'd always gone for sophisticated women who were out for a good time—women who were no more interested in anything more than a no-fault relationship than he was.

Daisy, with her bare face, her baggy clothes and her easygoing style, had caught him off guard. He should have been satisfied with what he'd found and headed out yesterday.

Instead he'd waited too late. He'd called and made reservations to fly out of Norfolk for tomorrow, which meant he'd have to fly back to get his car once he sorted out the situation back home, with Clarice and Moxie and Chief Taylor.

He had what he'd come for, or as much as he was ever going to get. As for anything else, he'd like to think that by the time he returned he'd have come to his senses. Or at least gained enough perspective to know if this thing they had going between them was all spark and sizzle, or if there was something solid behind it.

While the very thought of "something solid" scared the hell out of him, he'd never been able to walk away from a challenge. Deliberate or not, Daisy was definitely that.

The shower had still been steamy when he'd heard her drive off earlier, carrying a stack of boxes, the one with a purple bow on top. He'd been invited, he reasoned—so why drive all the way to Barco when there was food available right here in Muddy Landing?

By the time he'd located the church and found himself a parking place, he'd made up his mind. If he had to wipe out his entire money-market account to do it, he was going to buy her damned box and spend his last night here with a certain streaky-haired, gray-eyed blonde who smelled like bacon grease and roses. What happened after that was up to her. If he struck out again, at least he'd go down swinging.

He spotted her right away, in a huddle with the flashy redhead and the woman who looked like Julia Roberts, only with bigger eyes and a smaller mouth. He started to cut through the crowd but decided it might be smarter to wait until he had a legitimate claim to her company. Meanwhile, he'd just keep an eye on that purple bow.

Kell stood back and watched as the auctioneer held up first one supper box and then another one, reading off a name and fielding the bids.

"Now, come on, George, you know Miss Tilly's crab cakes is worth more'n five dollars. Smells like she stuck in a couple of her homemade grape-leaf pickles, too."

The bidding had been going on for about ten minutes when the auctioneer held up the box with the purple bow. Recognizing it as one of those Daisy had carried out to her car on top of the stack, Kell raised his hand just as a familiar voice called out a five-dollar bid.

On the far side of the church grounds, Daisy was wailing, "I can't believe I worked this hard for nothing. Didn't I tell you all this was a crazy idea?"

"Hey, it's worked before," Marty reminded her. The box suppers were one of their favorite venues for getting couples together. Marty and Sasha bought the supplies, Daisy did the cooking, making up an extra box. Then the three women would divvy up the other three boxes, dish a little dirt and look around for their next project.

Sasha checked her shoe heels for mud. "You got the freezer cleaned out, didn't you? Means you're that much closer to moving out of that old mausoleum."

"I'd be even closer if I'd stayed home and worked instead of wasting a whole evening here," she grumbled. "Faylene doesn't want a man, all she wants is a pair of legs that don't hurt and a raise."

"Don't forget hair like Dolly Parton's," observed Sasha.

"So? She can settle for one out of three and consider herself lucky."

"Five dollars, do I hear ten?" came the tinny voice from the loudspeaker.

Someone called out a bid of seven in a voice that could barely be heard over the sound of children playing tag around the picnic tables.

"I guess now that Gus is gone, nobody else is going to bid on it," said Marty. "Raise your hand, Sash."

"Ten!" called another voice before the redhead could comply.

"Fifteen" came the prompt response.

"That sounds almost like…" Daisy stirred uneasily.

"Now, that's right generous of you, sir. Do I hear twenty?"

He heard twenty-five, followed almost immediately by thirty-five. Not thirty, but thirty-*five*. Daisy tried to peer over the heads of the crowd. Marty, the tallest of the three women, stood on tiptoe. She whistled softly under her breath and said, "Well, what do you know—maybe this wingding's not a complete washout after all."

"Look, I know y'all were only trying to cheer me up," said Daisy. She had finally figured it out. "It's not your fault it didn't work, but with Faylene gone, whoever buys her box will have to make do without a partner. I'm going home."

"So we goofed," Sasha said airily. "It's not the first time—probably won't be the last time, either. Hey, how else can three smart women of a certain age have fun in a place like Muddy Landing? This doesn't let Gus off the hook, either. Sooner or later we'll use him, we just have to find him someone a few years younger."

Seeing a football tossed her way, Daisy caught it and threw it back. The preacher's son picked it up and had the good manners to yell, "Thanks, Miss Daisy!"

Miss Daisy. If she'd needed a reminder that she wasn't getting any younger, that did it. If Gus thought Faylene was too old for him, how long before someone said the same thing about her?

"Trouble is, I don't know if he'll ever trust us again." Sasha tugged at the corset top she'd chosen to wear with her harem trousers. "His exact words when he heard who his supper partner was supposed to be were that he wasn't about to waste time on a prune-faced female old enough to be his mother when he could be watching the Wednesday night Braves game down at the volunteer fire department."

"But didn't you tell him Faylene's a Braves fan, too?" Marty was hopping around, trying to get a better view of the auctioneer's table.

"Didn't have time, he took off too fast," Sasha replied. "Who'd have thought his ego would be that touchy?" She shook her head. "Men!"

Daisy was tired to the point of being irritable. "Who'd he think we were fixing him up with, Madonna?"

"Too old. Try Britney Spears."

It was hardly the first time their plans had failed at the last minute, but all the same, Daisy didn't need any further frustration. She'd had enough of that already. "Look, if y'all don't mind, I'm just going to go home, eat a bowl of cereal, finish up the last of the scuppernong wine and go to bed. Whoever buys Faylene's box, you can either join them or explain that she had to leave. Make up something, you're good at it."

Gathering her purse and the cardigan she'd brought in case it turned cooler—which it had—Daisy was already on her feet when, in a sudden lull, the auctioneer shouted, "*Sold!* Sold to the gentleman in the black shirt for one hundred dollars! My saints alive!"

Sasha's mouth fell open. "A hundred *dollars?* Who on earth…?" She climbed up on the picnic bench, grabbed the top of Marty's head for balance and tried to see over the heads of the crowd.

Daisy covered her face with both hands when it dawned on her that she knew "who on earth." Somewhere under all the layers she'd tried to insulate herself with, she had recognized his voice. Peering out the corners of her eyes, she saw the studly gentleman—her rainy-day cowboy—standing just the way he'd stood the first time she'd ever laid eyes on him at Harvey's funeral. Arms crossed, booted feet spread, he was wearing the look of a man who knew exactly what he wanted and wasn't about to go away empty-handed.

I came, I saw, so what the hell—I conquered.

Only this time, instead of a dreary rain, the setting sun gilded his angular cheekbones, turning his tan to pure gold. As for his eyes, even from this distance they looked incandescent.

"Gracious me, if it's not your cowboy again." Sasha climbed down and made a show of fanning her ample endowment. "Shall we invite him to eat with us?"

Daisy forced her gaze past Kell, who was making his way to the auctioneer's table, in time to see another familiar figure. It was Egbert, and he was headed out to the parking lot. "Egbert?" she wailed softly. "Oh, for Pete's sake, what else can go wrong?"

"Who'd you think was bidding against him? I guess it's time to add Egbert to the list, now that he's officially out of mourning." Marty made a show of scratching a name on her palm with her finger.

"It's been almost a year," Sasha said. "Besides, I heard she was thinking about leaving him when she got sick. Sara down at the bank said—"

"Oh, hush up," Daisy muttered. Suddenly—or maybe not so suddenly—this game of theirs didn't seem quite so enjoyable.

"Too late, I've already got someone in mind for him." Marty leaned in closer as she watched Kell dodge through the moving crowd. "You know Carrie Stovall? She's been living with this guy and it turns out he's got a wife up in Suffolk, and they're not even divorced? Carrie needs someone steady."

"Lord knows Egbert's steady," Sasha said with a lift of her penciled eyebrows. "Any steadier and he'd have moss growing on his north side."

"Maybe Daisy knows of a remedy for terminal steadiness. What about it, hon, you want to try your healing arts on Egg-butt?"

Oblivious to the good-natured dishing between her two best friends, Daisy didn't know whether to weep or kick something. To think she could have shared supper with him. It would have been the first step in her campaign.

"Well, hello there," Sasha purred as Kell sauntered up to join them. When Daisy glared at him, she added, "Don't mind her, she woke up on the wrong side of the bed."

Daisy had had enough. Ignoring the grinning Kell, who was carrying a big white box full of the food she'd spent the afternoon preparing, she said, "You know what, Sasha? You're the only woman in the world who would dress like that for a church box supper."

"Honey, let's face it—I'm the only one in town with any fashion sense."

"Which one of you lovely ladies do I have the privilege of sharing supper with?" Kell asked. He was looking straight at Daisy, who was purposefully avoiding his gaze. *As if I didn't know* was implied.

"Oh, God, would you just listen to that. Not only a voice to die for, but manners, too," Sasha murmured. "You get Daisy, but if she doesn't appreciate you, we'll be right over there at the table by the magnolia tree. Won't we, Marty?" She elbowed her friend in the arm.

"We will? Oh, sure."

Ten

At least, Daisy assured herself, she was surrounded by so many chaperones she could hardly do anything too outrageous. All she had to do was behave sensibly for another hour or so; after that he'd be gone and she could try to smooth things over. The good news—the really encouraging news—was that Egbert had bid on her supper box.

"Daisy?" Kell was studying her, a quizzical smile tugging at the corners of his mouth.

"All right," she snapped. A few weeks from now she'd have forgotten all about Kell Magee. By then she should be well on her way to winning Egbert's—well, if not his heart, at least his very good friendship, which, after all, was the best basis for any marriage.

"Look, if I made a mistake and messed up your plans, I'm sorry. I can leave and you can join your friends, just say the word."

She shook her head. "I'm sorry. It's just—oh, I don't know, everything, I guess. I'm tired from rushing to get things ready so we can close up the house, and on top of that, I think my apartment's going to be sold out from under me. And why am I telling you all this?" She shook her head.

"Maybe because you need to unload and I happen to have broader shoulders than either of your two friends over there?"

She relented. It wasn't like her to be snippy. She'd learned a long time ago never to allow her emotions free reign. It was messy at best, disastrous at worst. "Come on, let's find someplace where we're not apt to be hit in the head with a football."

"Lead on, MacDuff."

"Actually, I think that's supposed to be 'Lay on, Mac-Duff.'" Daisy rolled her eyes, and seeing her expression, Kell chuckled. She told herself that if she'd managed to resist his charms while sleeping under the same roof, she should be able to manage sharing a meal in a public place.

Taking her arm, he headed for a table down near the creek. And that was another thing—the way he walked. You'd think every moving part in his body had been greased.

One hundred dollars? For plain old fried chicken tied up with a purple bow? She wished now she'd paid attention to the bidding, but she'd been too busy worrying about Faylene and Gus. How hard had Egbert tried to outbid him? Egbert had a reputation for being a good citizen. He always bought Girl Scout cookies and gave them away because he had a wheat sensitivity.

Oh, shoot. She'd forgotten the flour in the corn fritters, not to mention the flour she'd dusted her chicken with. Not to mention the piecrust and the homemade cloverleaf rolls. She'd like to think fate was on her side for once, but that would be too great a stretch.

"After sampling your fried chicken, I'm really looking forward to supper," Kell said. "This table suit you?"

She wanted to tell him to stop being so damned…decent! How could any man look boyishly innocent and devilishly sexy at the same time? "It's fine with me, as long as you don't mind eating supper next to all those tombstones."

"Not a problem. I don't believe in ghosts, do you?"

"I don't know what I believe in, not anymore," she muttered.

They could always try again with Faylene, but she'd missed a wonderful chance to get better acquainted with Egbert on a personal level. Of course, if he bid a bundle and then couldn't eat a single thing she'd prepared, it would've been embarrassing, to say the least.

A picture-postcard setting. Sunset reflected in the creek. Dark fingers of marsh delineated the shoreline, naked cypress trees were silhouetted against the sky. Kell glanced around and murmured, "Nice."

Stealing a look at his profile, Daisy had to agree. He had a wonderful nose, just the right size, with the slightest arch to give it character. Her gaze moved on to his lips and she quickly looked away. If anyone ever held a kissing Olympics, he'd win gold, hands down.

When he took out a handkerchief and brushed leaves and dried pokeberry deposits from the bench, she told herself he was just too good to be true. Which meant he probably wasn't.

"What about something to drink?" he asked.

"There's a machine in the church basement. Sorry—I should have thought of it sooner."

"No problem. Name your preference and I'll fetch."

"Anything diet."

He was back in less than five minutes with two bottles of water. "Sorry, this was the best I could do."

"It's fine. The diet drinks always go first. You do know this was supposed to be Faylene's and Gus's box, don't you?" She nodded to the white cardboard box she'd saved from the last time she'd bought a bakery cake. "It had her name on it, and Gus Mathias was supposed to bid on it."

"Figured it must be something like that. I saw her drive off just as I was pulling in. She wasn't looking any too happy."

Daisy shrugged. "I guess you think we were meddling." Well, they were, but only with the best of intentions. "It's just that when you see someone you like and you think there's a chance to make her happy, you want to try."

He nodded, then lifted his shoulders in an easy shrug.

She tried unsuccessfully to interpret his mixed signals. "All right, so we have fun matchmaking. There's not a whole lot to do for entertainment in a place like Muddy Landing unless you like hunting, fishing or bingo."

"And you don't, I take it. Man, are those what I think they are?" He took out a cloverleaf roll and sniffed it, closing his eyes.

"They're just plain old yeast rolls."

"Hey, there's nothing plain old about these things," he said, somehow making ordinary bread sound like hot buttered sex.

"Store-bought ones are just as good. I'm just trying to use up all the staples. I hate to throw out good yeast and flour."

Kell pinched off a bit of roll, then searched in the box to see what else it held. "Ah, geez, is that chocolate cake wrapped up in the napkins? So this thing you planned with Faylene and what's his name—it didn't work out, huh? I guess his loss is my gain."

"It's pie. Not cake. Kell, I'm really embarrassed you had to bid so much for the same old fried chicken you've had before."

He bit off a bit of corn fritter, chewed with his eyes closed, then said, "Man, oh, man. Didn't have to. I'd planned on having a sub from that place down the road, but then I passed the church on my way through town."

"Yes, but a hundred dollars?"

"Blalock ran it up to fifty-five. I got tired of playing his game."

When it came to playing games Kell was obviously no slouch, but Egbert? She'd never have pegged him as the competitive type. But then, he was a man. With some men it was a survival tactic, a holdover from the Stone Age when the man with the biggest club won.

"Where'd you learn to cook like this?" He broke off a crumb of chocolate-rum pie, tasted it and closed his eyes. "Don't tell me you learned to bake like this in nursing school."

"I had courses in nutrition, but before that I worked my way through school by helping out in the cafeteria. The women there were wonderful cooks. How about you?"

"You mean where'd I learn to cook?" He shot her a smile that managed to be both teasing and tempting. It occurred to her that she wasn't feeling nearly as tired as she'd been when the evening started.

"Faye said you were a baseball player. Who do you play for? Would I have heard of them?"

"Played. Past tense. I used to play for Houston. Why? Are you a fan?" He had a way of speaking volumes with the lift of a single eyebrow.

"Not really. I never went in for sports—never had time." At age twelve she'd just been getting into track, but then things had started coming apart at her adoptive home. Next thing she knew, she was back in the system again. And while the system might try, it was understaffed and underfunded. "So how'd you get interested?" she asked. "Aren't you a little young to have retired? And now you own a sporting goods shop?" As long as they kept talking, she reasoned, she'd be in no danger of falling under his spell again.

They discussed sports and growing up in a small town and then moved on to choosing a profession versus having one chosen for them. By the time she handed out slices of the sinfully rich chocolate-rum pie with coconut and walnuts, Daisy felt so comfortable she nearly forgot to be disappointed about the way the evening had turned out.

She'd been telling him about one of her cases, an elderly woman who had served in the Coast Guard during the Second World War—back then the women were called SPARS—when she noticed he was staring past her toward the creek. The sun was already down, the afterglow laying long lavender shadows across the mossy old graveyard.

Twisting around on the bench seat, Daisy looked to see what had caught his attention. So far as she could tell there was nothing out there but an old two-plank landing used only by a few trappers and hunters.

Suddenly he rose, stepped over the bench and strode down toward the creek. After only a moment's hesitation, Daisy followed. "Kell? What is it?" Oh, God, she thought, not a child! Kids loved messing around the water, but surely if a child had fallen in they'd have heard the splash. "Kell?"

"Gotcha!" He bent over and came up holding something dark and round in both hands.

"A *turtle?*"

"Slider, if I'm not mistaken. She's been circling around out there ever since we've been here. I don't know much about these critters, but it didn't look like she could see where she was going. She kept running into things."

Much later Daisy would look back on it as the moment she had fallen in love. A muddy little slider, of all things. And Kell had willingly spent the rest of the evening trying to help the poor creature. She couldn't help but wonder if Egbert would have done as much. Or would he even have noticed the poor, blind thing?

It was nearly three hours later when they headed back to Muddy Landing, having left one yellow slider with an eye infection and a serious case of malnutrition at the home of a retired veterinarian in Elizabeth City.

"Kind of makes you feel good, doesn't it?" Kell said quietly as they turned off on Highway 34 at Belcross.

It did, but by that time Daisy was half-asleep, the stress of the past few days having finally caught up with her. "Mmm."

"Good thing you knew that vet. He said you used to pet-sit for some of his clients."

"Mmm-hmm." Dr. Van had retired years ago, but he'd taken one look and confirmed Daisy's suspicions. Too blind to find food, the poor creature would have starved, that is if it didn't blunder out onto the street and get run over.

"You cold?" He turned on the heater, and a current of warm air flowed over her. Once the sun went down, the air had chilled down quickly.

He drove fast, probably above the speed limit, but Daisy was too comfortable to complain, especially after he turned on a CD, lulling her with Vince Gill's dulcet tenor. Why fight it? Feeling warm and safe and—well, comfortable hardly began to describe it, but it would do for now—she gave up and let her eyes drift shut again.

The next thing she knew Kell was lifting her from the car. Coming instantly awake, she started to protest. He said, "Shh, you're in no condition to make it up those steps."

"Wha's hap'nin'? Where are we? Kell, put me down."

"Now, why would I do that?"

Twisting around, she looked to see the familiar turreted silhouette of the old mansion that had been her home for nearly a year. "Lemme get the key out," she mumbled, struggling to find her shoulder bag.

"Already got it."

"How? It's in my purse." Her car. Good Lord, she'd left her car in the church parking lot.

"Daisy—hush up, honey, it's not worth fighting over. I didn't mess with any of your other stuff, just the keys."

"But my car—you should have taken me back—"

"Shh, your car's probably safe enough in a church parking lot. We'll collect it tomorrow."

Evidently somewhere between Elizabeth City and Muddy Landing she had lost her free will, her backbone and her last shred of common sense. She didn't even argue.

"You're bushed, aren't you? You want to turn in now, or do you want a nightcap?"

"Turn in," she mumbled. And then "No, maybe something…" She tried to cut off the thought, but before she could stop it, a picture of a naked couple sharing a bottle of wine and then falling into bed together appeared like a DVD, full of color, detail and animation.

She shut her eyes. It didn't help, so she opened them again. In the dim light of the freshly dusted overhead fixture, his features looked as if they'd been carved from some exotic wood and polished to a satin sheen. "Maybe milk," she said desperately.

"Milk it is. Warm or cold?"

She was wide-awake now. Emotionally confused, physically exhausted, but wide-awake. Shaking her head, she said, "You decide, I can't think straight."

"Cocoa, then. Why don't you get ready for bed while I make it."

She stood there like a stump wanting to say, Forget the cocoa, just come to bed with me. Instead, she said, "We don't have any more mix."

"I'll improvise. You go wash, brush and put on something comfortable and I'll see you in a few minutes."

Kell watched her stumble toward the end of the hall where her quarters were located, then headed for the kitchen. She'd been asleep in the car for the past twenty-five minutes, making soft, puffy little sounds with her lips. He'd been tempted to pull over and try a little mouth-to-mouth, but knowing how exhausted she was, he'd resisted the temptation. She'd been going flat out ever since he'd been there, trying to wind things up so she could move back to town. He'd been torn between trying to stay out of her way and wanting to spend as much time with her as possible before he had to leave. And not just because he liked being in the house where his father had grown up. And then, on top of everything else, she had taken on this box supper thing. Didn't those two friends of hers have any idea how pushed she was?

Behind the cereal he found a tin of cocoa with maybe an inch or so left in the bottom. Without bothering to read the instructions, he poured milk into a pan, dumped in some sugar and emptied the cocoa tin, listening all the while for sounds to tell him how near ready she was. If she got through in the bathroom and fell asleep before the stuff was hot he'd just have to wake her up. One way or another, he intended to share something with her before he left tomorrow, even if it was only a mug of cocoa.

He heard the pump cut on, heard the door of the medicine cabinet open and close. He called softly, "Daisy? This stuff's about ready."

"Library," she called through the closed door.

Uh-huh. She didn't trust him to take it to her bedroom. Smart lady.

Daisy always slept in nylon not because it was sexy, but because cotton pajamas twisted around her. A restless sleeper, especially when she had a lot on her mind, she usually changed positions at least a dozen times during the night. Now shoving her arms in the sleeves of a faded pink terry-cloth robe, she looped the sash twice around her waist and knotted it, then waited until Kell left the kitchen to follow him to the library.

She smelled the cocoa even before she entered the room, the rich, slightly burnt scent intermingled with floor wax and furniture polish. Kell had set it on the desk and was looking over the rows of books, all dusted and ready for the librarian, the historical society, or whoever ended up with them.

"Looks like Uncle Harve had a lot of different interests," Kell said.

It took her a moment to react to the words, she was so busy reacting to the man himself. Even standing there with his back to her, hip cocked and chin resting in one hand, he reminded her of a big, sleepy cat, trying to make up his mind whether or not to pounce.

There was nothing at all sleepy about his eyes when he turned to face her. They were glowing like a pair of blue flames. "Judging from all these titles, I mean."

Titles? Oh—books. Turn on your brain, woman! "Um…yes, he did. That is, he was. It was one of the things I liked best about him—he had such an—an inquiring mind." *Stop looking at me that way!*

"Astronomy, geology, history—what's numismatics?"

"Coins. Oh—did Egbert tell you Harvey left his coin collection to Faylene? It turned out to be only a few hundred Susan B. Anthony dollars, worth face value, but still it was really sweet of him. She'd been with him for nearly fourteen years, you know, even though for the past few years, ever since he closed off most of the rooms, she only worked two or three days a week."

And I'm chattering like a monkey, she thought hopelessly. She should have gone straight to bed and stayed there for the foreseeable future, or at least until she was sure he'd gone back to Oklahoma.

"That's great," he said. Collecting the two mugs of cocoa, he handed her one. "She strikes me as a good worker. Glad Uncle Harvey appreciated her. Here, drink this stuff before it gets any colder. I don't know if it's sweet enough or not, I didn't use any measurements."

"Just so you didn't add any horseradish."

He chuckled, drawing her attention to his mouth. If a mouth could be called tempting, his was. Full lower lip, nice bow, uptilted corners.

Shut up and drink your cocoa, stupid!

A skim had already formed on the top. Ignoring it, Daisy lifted her mug, gulped and tried not to shudder. "I just thought you should know. About the coins, that is. I mean, I don't know how much Egbert told you, but the local historical society is the main beneficiary. They get the house, termites and all. I'm not sure about the furniture. Maybe they can sell it to pay for repairs."

Staring at her lips, Kell took a sip, made a face and set the thing down on the tray. "Ouch. Stuff's pretty bad, isn't it? You don't have to drink it."

"No, it's fine," she insisted, forcing a smile to prove it.

His gaze never leaving her face, he lifted the mug from her hands, set it on the tray and then touched her lips with his thumb. Swallowing hard, Daisy found herself unable to look away. He said something about chocolate and then he leaned closer. A moment before his face went out of focus she closed her eyes.

The taste of bitter chocolate only enhanced a kiss that was sheer seduction, soft, warm and moist. With his tongue, he touched the corners of her mouth, stroked her lips and then went on to rob her of any lingering will to resist.

Kell tried to go slow. The last thing he wanted to do was to spook her into running away from him, because once she shut that bedroom door, that was it. Whatever happened between them had to be mutual or it was no go.

He wanted her so much his hands were shaking, but for all his experience with the opposite sex, he'd never met anyone like Daisy Hunter. For one thing, she had never even tried to attract him. No sexy outfits, no sexy makeup—hell, she didn't even wear perfume, just that lotion stuff she rubbed on her hands and arms. She was…the word *real* came to mind. Not only that, but her entire life was devoted to taking care of other people.

When was the last time anyone had taken care of her? Did she even have someone who cared enough to make her hot cocoa when she was tired and needy? To see that she got enough rest? Someone to doctor her hurts and to lift heavy things for her—to put her to bed and then crawl in beside her and hold her while she slept?

The fact that he wanted to do all those things, especially the last, was downright scary. Over the past twenty-odd years he'd known a lot of women, but he had never entered any relationship feeling the way he felt now. He always took care to spell out the ground rules going into an affair—a no-fault affair where both parties were free to walk at any time.

With Daisy there weren't any rules. He found himself wanting to know everything there was to know about her, starting with what she'd been like as a little girl and ending with what she'd be like when those laugh lines deepened and multiplied, and her hair was more gray than blond.

And if that weren't scary enough, he found himself wondering how she felt about kids.

How she felt about him.

But all that would have to wait. Because right now he had an even more desperate need, one he could only hope was mutual.

Eleven

The sofa was too narrow for what he had in mind, but there was a perfectly good bed going to waste just down the hall. She had moved downstairs once they'd finished cleaning the second floor.

"Your place okay?" he rasped, figuring a trek down the hall might allow him to cool off just enough to do the job properly. He'd never had trouble with a short fuse before, but then, he'd never made love to a woman like Daisy.

"Mmm," she murmured, reluctantly pulling away.

"Race you," he teased. Hell, he wasn't even sure he could crawl, much less run. In the doorway, they paused for another lingering kiss that only served to deepen the hunger, not to abate it.

When she opened the door, his attention zeroed in on the bed. Neatly made, it was obviously too short and too narrow for a good night's sleep. But then, sleep was the last thing on his mind.

She was wearing a fuzzy bathrobe over a scrap of white nylon. The sash had been wrapped around her waist and tied in a hard knot. If she thought that would protect her, she was sadly mistaken.

Obviously she had no such thought, as she plucked at the knot until it came loose and then let the robe slide off her shoulders onto the floor. "I can't believe I'm so nervous," she whispered with a brittle little laugh.

"Just say the word any time and we'll stop." If it killed him—and it probably would.

With unsteady hands he lifted her gown and eased it over her head, leaving her in only a pair of plain white cotton underpants. Not high-cut, not low-cut, and definitely not thongs.

Trying hard to regulate his breathing, he ripped his shirt over his head and unbuckled his belt. "I can't believe—that is, I never knew—" He broke off, shaking his head.

Averting her face, she sat on her hands on the side of the bed. "You can't believe what? You never knew what?"

He tried to take off his pants before he remembered to remove his boots and ended up hopping on one foot. "I forgot what I was talking about." Kell Magee, MVP two years in a row, a man who'd been mobbed for his autograph by countless female groupies, was nervous as a cat in a pound full of dogs.

He said, "I like your underwear," and smacked himself on the forehead. "Ah, jeez, I can't believe I said that!"

Daisy laughed, and then she stood up and shed her plain white cotton underpants. No posturing, no sneaking a look to see if he was enjoying the show, she simply pulled down the elastic, stepped out of the things and tossed them onto a wicker hamper.

Her hips were nicely flared, her waist narrow and flat. She had freckles on her upper chest, small breasts and tan lines all over the place, probably from working in the yard.

And not once, not even in the raunchy bars where lap dancing was the favored sport, could Kell recall seeing anything so seductive. Her breasts fit perfectly in the palms of his hands, that much he already knew. Before this week, if he had drawn up specifications for his ideal woman, Daisy wouldn't have come anywhere close to fitting them. Yet everything about her was right. It was as if he'd found a vital part of himself that he'd never even known was missing.

Instead of lying back on the pillows and striking a seductive pose, she just sat there, looking him over. Making him feel proud and embarrassed at the same time. "Uh…you're not going to change your mind, are you?" he asked anxiously. *Smooth, Magee—really smooth.*

Without taking her eyes from the strip of hair that arrowed down from his chest to the southern hemisphere, she shook her head. "Um—they're in the bedside-table drawer."

His were in his wallet on the floor. Curious to see if she liked plain, ribbed, colored or flavored, he nodded. She stretched out on the bed, still watching him almost warily. He said, "Daisy, are you sure about this? I mean, we don't have to. There's no truth in that old blue-ball rumor. It's just—"

"I know. Kell, I know all there is to know about sex

technically, but I haven't done this in a long time. Please don't expect too much. I never was very good at it."

He swore then, long and quietly. How could any woman this desirable even think such a thing, much less express it? Unless some impotent jackass had deliberately tried to blame her for his own shortcomings.

Easing his arms under her knees and shoulders, he shifted her over to make room so he could lie down beside her. Then, covering both her legs with one of his, he leaned over and brushed her hair away from her face. *Easy, easy—don't rush her, Magee.*

But no matter how much he wanted to take it slow and easy, Kell had a feeling fast and furious was inevitable. At least the first few times.

Using all the skill at his command, plus a tenderness he had never even come close to feeling before, he began searching out each sensitive place on her body, starting with her small pink ears and kissing his way down to the hollow of her throat. The warm hollow under her arm, so personal, so private—the insides of her elbow where the blue veins led from her heart to her hands. Nipping, tasting his way, he returned to her shoulders and then to her breasts. Her small, perfect, rose-scented breasts where her small, proud nipples begged for his attention.

She was exquisitely sensitive there and in the soft place surrounding her navel…and in the shadowy crease of her groin.

When he tasted her there she caught a shuddering breath and gasped, "My turn."

Oh, no, not now, he thought, desperately close to the edge. But obediently, he lay still under her ministrations, the scent of her arousal teasing his nostrils as she fingered her way down his body. First, his nipples, then the arrow of dark hair that led south, lingering at the equator, her fingers playing there while her tongue flicked his nipple until he thought he'd explode. The closer she came to the South Pole, the more rigid he became, his breath coming in tight gasps until he could stand it no longer.

Tense as a bowstring, he lifted her, eased her over onto her back and stared down at her. Her heart was pounding visibly, the aphrodisiac scent of her heat alone enough to shove him over the edge. Trembling, he palmed her mound, forcing himself not to move too quickly. This had to be perfect for her, even if it meant putting his own release on hold indefinitely.

Her face was flushed, her eyes dark and bright as he began his most intimate exploration. She was moist, hot and ready, but still he waited. Slowly lowering his face to her soap-scented belly, he entered her with his finger, moving gently, preparing the way.

Now, now! his body shouted.

"Please," she whimpered.

Delaying the inevitable as long as possible, he used his experience unselfishly for once as he set about driving her out of her mind with pleasure before moving up her body. She was whimpering, gasping for breath by the time he eased inside her. Not until she lifted her hips, her fingernails biting into his shoulders, did his self-imposed restraint break.

Once he began to thrust it ended far too quickly in a cataclysmic release that left them both trembling and gasping for air. Waves of indescribable pleasure washed over them.

Aeons later when her brain cells began to function again, it occurred to Daisy to marvel at how rarely it happened that way. From all she'd learned as a nurse, plus articles she'd read in women's magazines, not to mention the frank talk among friends, she knew that men sought their own pleasure. Only then, if one happened to be skilled enough and generous enough—or even still awake—would he take care of his mate.

Daisy let herself drift through soft clouds of sex-scented darkness until gradually it occurred to her that fate must have had a hand in what had just happened. She'd never been superstitious—she certainly wasn't into any of that New Age stuff. All the same, when she thought about it…

Cause and effect? First she'd taken on Harvey as a patient when she'd had three to choose from. Then her apartment building had been damaged in the hurricane. That led her to moving in with him—fate had nothing to do with it.

But then there was Kell.

Oh, my, yes, she thought, a dreamy smile softening her face as she gazed at the man lying beside her, his angular face slack in repose. Even in the dim light from the hall he looked familiar, as if she'd known him all her life, only she hadn't known where to find him.

Instead, he'd found her.

"Did I ever tell you how beautiful you are?" he murmured without opening his eyes.

Trying for blasé and missing it by a mile, she said, "Don't push it, Magee. Halfway decent I might accept, but no more."

He smiled, still without opening his eyes. "Okay

then, but you're about the most halfway decent woman I've ever had the pleasure of knowing, and that includes centerfolds."

Even as strung out as a fiddle tuned an octave too high, there was no way Daisy could take it as anything other than gentle, good-natured teasing intended to put her at ease. It was almost as if he'd known about the subtly barbed remarks that used to accompany Jerry's rough, hurried attempts at making love. There'd been no love involved, only she hadn't realized it at the time.

Now, after watching a man go to such lengths to rescue a mud turtle, it took only the amazing fact that he could tease her at a time like this to tell her what she'd already suspected.

She was so in love. So head-over-heart-over-heels in love with a here-today, gone-tomorrow man who could set her on fire with just the sound of his voice. So much for all her fine plans for the future.

"'Course, if you'd had the body of a cow and a face like the grill of a Mack truck, I might've had a few second thoughts. Lucky for me, though, you turned out pretty decent."

A gurgle of laughter escaped her just before he turned over on his side and buried his face in her throat. Wedging her head back on the pillow, she moaned softly as he lifted her hips and entered her again.

Kell opened his eyes to darkness, wondering why his backside was freezing. He had a vague recollection of opening a window earlier. Weather must have turned in the night, he thought drowsily. Daisy had rolled up in the covers and he'd been too far gone to claim his share.

Now his butt was freezing, his feet were hanging off the bed and his right arm had gone to sleep.

Overriding all that, there was a warm, sweet woman snuggled up to his groin, smelling of sex and roses, and he was tempted—

Damn, but he was tempted!

But four times in as many hours was stretching it, even for him. It didn't necessarily mean he was getting old, only that he needed a few hours of sleep before tackling anything more strenuous than lying in bed and trying to think of some excuse to get out of a few commitments.

He had his flaws, more than he liked to admit, but going back on his word wasn't one of them.

According to his watch it was already Thursday, and he still had an idea he needed to run past Blalock. His original plan had been to head back in plenty of time to speak with Chief Taylor before Clarice's grand opening and make sure Moxie was in on the festivities. He figured if the kid could be a part of the action from the beginning, even busing tables in a five-table ice-cream shop, it might motivate him to prove something to himself, as well as to the people who'd gone to bat for him.

As it was already too late to head back via I-40, he'd called late yesterday and made reservations on an 11:10 a.m. flight out of Norfolk. Now all he had to do was see Blalock about donating a block of stock to the historical society to be used toward putting the house back in shape and then get to the airport in time to make it through Security.

After dealing with whatever mess Moxie had gotten himself involved in this time and seeing Clarice through her grand opening, he needed to check on the progress out at the ranch. Two days, he figured—three at the most. With any luck he should be back here before Daisy had time to buckle on her armor again.

Last night he had finally found a clue as to why she was so defensive. At first she'd thought he was trying to horn in on Harvey's estate—at least he'd dispelled that notion. But if it turned out he was right and some jerk had done a bad number on her, she was going to need special handling until he could reassure her of his intentions.

Intentions. Now, there was a scary word in any man's vocabulary. Kell wasn't quite sure how to play it. In the first place, Daisy was nothing at all like the women who usually wound up in his bed. No gloss or glamour, no fancy designer labels, no teasing demands for tangible proof of his affections. Her only jewelry so far as he could tell was a businesslike wristwatch.

Above all, no games. With Daisy Hunter, what you saw was what you got. In the beginning it might have been the challenge that had attracted him—he'd never been able to resist one of those. But somewhere along the way things had changed. The tricky part now was keeping her from bolting while he took care of some unfinished business back home.

Talk about playing by the rules—this was a game he'd never played before. Best he could do was take things one step at a time.

Leaning over, he kissed her on the temple, inhaling the essence of soap, shampoo and warm, sexy woman. Then, smiling in the darkness, he eased out of bed. They both needed sleep. He'd never been able to relax enough on a plane to fall asleep, and he needed at least a couple of hours to get him through the next twenty-four or so. Her narrow bed, as inviting as the company was, didn't make the cut. One roll in either direction and he'd end up either on the floor or on top of her. In the latter case, sleep wasn't even a faint possibility. As tempted as he was, he wasn't up for an all-nighter, not with everything he had to do in the next few days.

A brief cooling-off period was probably best for all concerned. If this thing they had going here turned out to be real, it should last until he got back. If not...

Oh, hell, he just didn't know. Some of his friends changed women almost as often as they changed shirts. Others married young, stuck it out and actually seemed to enjoy it. Kell was closing in on forty—too late to marry young. On the other hand, maybe this old dog could still learn a few new tricks.

Cold air fell through the window he'd cracked open after they'd steamed up the place for the second or maybe the third time. He lingered, listening to her slow breathing, reluctant to move away.

He had a chance to build something solid—something that would last the rest of his life, if he played it right. Other people did it. Hell, his own parents had done it. They'd had their squabbles—his dad had had a redhead's temper and his mom had stood up to him whenever she'd thought he was in the wrong. As a kid, he'd hated their fights. He'd been embarrassed because you could hear them all over the trailer park. But thinking about it now, he remembered the way they used to look at each other after they'd both run out of steam. They'd both burst out laughing and he'd be invited to go outside and play. Before he was even out the door, they'd disappear into the bedroom.

He had laughed with Daisy, too. They'd laughed together, which only seemed to make the sex better—richer. It was a hell of a time to have to leave, but they both needed a little space.

Things had happened too fast—maybe he needed to back off and see how he felt in a day or so—in a week or so. Because he'd learned a long time ago that false promises were worse than no promises at all.

Quietly, he collected his clothes and boots from the floor and left, pulling the bedroom door almost but not quite shut. He didn't know if she usually closed it or not. There was so much he still didn't know about her. That was part of the problem. But one thing he did know—they weren't finished yet. Three days from now—four at most, he'd be back and then they could get to the bottom of whatever this thing was between them. All he knew at this point was that it was like nothing he'd ever experienced before.

For the third time, Daisy scanned the note she'd found on the table anchored by the salt shaker. Damn him. Damn him! "Daisy, I've got to handle a few things back home. See you in a few days. K. M."

Like hell he would, she fumed, not believing for one moment he would be back. If he'd planned to come back, he would have woken her and told her he was leaving instead of sneaking out like a thief in the night. He was just like Jerry. Try out the merchandise, and if it doesn't suit, return it, no questions asked.

She read it again. Not even so much as a Dear Daisy, just "Daisy, see you in a few days."

"I don't think so," she muttered under her breath as she rumpled the note and crammed it into her pocket.

"So he's cleared out, has he?" Hands on her hips, Faylene was openly gloating. It was Thursday, the day after the box supper fiasco. "Serves you right for what y'all tried to do to me."

"For what we…? Oh, you mean the box supper." She blinked rapidly, willing herself not to cry.

"You're doggone right I do. If I wanted to eat my supper with a man who don't even bother to trim the hair in his nose, I coulda done it without no help from you three." She pulled a forgotten cast-iron skillet from the oven and slammed it down on the counter, endangering the forty-year-old Formica. "I thought y'all was settin' me up with that new coach there at the high school."

"Faylene, I'm sorry. You know how it is with us— we didn't mean any harm. We just thought it might be nice if—"

"Huh! You don't never mean no harm, but that don't mean harm don't get done. I got feelings, you know. I might not be as smart as you and Miss Marty or as pretty as Miss Sasha, but that don't mean I can't get me no boyfriend. I got one, so there, too!" she said triumphantly. "Only reason I won't let him move in with me is I don't have room for all them decoys and them guns o' his." Using one finger, she scratched her head, cracking a part in her heavily lacquered hair. "When's the power gonna be shut off, today or tomorrow?"

Daisy momentarily forgot her own problems. "Guns?"

"Oh, don't worry, Bob Ed ain't no bank robber or nothing like that. He just happens to be the best guide 'tween here and the Currituck Banks. What's more, he can cook, too, so he don't need me to keep his belly happy." She opened her mouth to say something else and then shook her head. "I notice you three ladies don't have no men hangin' round *your* doorsteps. I passed that ballplayer, driving like a bat outta hell. He didn't even toot at me."

He didn't toot at me, either, Daisy thought morosely a few hours later as she sealed up the final box for delivery to the thrift shop. Sasha and Marty had brought her car back, but left soon after that since Daisy informed them she was far too busy with last-minute duties to chat.

"Oh, but, hon, just wait till you hear who we've got picked out for Gus. Did you know he plays fiddle?"

"Not now—please," Daisy had pleaded.

"Okay, then I'll see you tonight," Marty told her. "Key's under the bird feeder if I'm not there." Marty had offered her a room until she found another place.

"I keep telling you, you're going to lose that key one of these days," Sasha warned as they headed out the front door. "You know that squirrel-proof feeder in my backyard? Well, believe me, even wing nuts are no problem for a determined squirrel."

"You're both nuts and you're both squirrely," Daisy called after them, laughing in spite of her growing depression.

By noon the kitchen was as clean was it was ever going to get. Faylene had wiped out the refrigerator and taken what she wanted from the pantry. The phone had already been disconnected. Now Daisy waited only for the power company to cut off service. With the wiring as old and probably as neglected as everything else, she didn't dare take chances when there was no one around to hear the smoke detector.

"You sure you don't want none o' this stuff? A can of soup or something in case you don't get away before dinner?" The housekeeper had apparently forgiven her for her part in the botched matchmaking attempt.

"I'll be leaving as soon as they disconnect us," Daisy told her. "I'm staying with Marty for the time being, so I'll see you there."

"I guess you heard they was planning to bulldoze your apartment, probably put up another batch o' them ugly places that all looks alike. You can come stay with me till you find you another apartment if you need to. I'll even help you pack up and move out. My place ain't fancy, but it's clean."

"Oh, Faye…after yesterday I can't believe you'd still have me."

"I wouldn't, not permanent, but a few days won't do no harm. Thanksgiving's coming on. If you like stewed goose with rutabagas and dumplin's and all, Bob Ed's plannin' on cooking up a mess at my place."

Unexpected tears dimmed her eyes, but Daisy shook her head. "I love stewed goose—" She'd never even tasted stewed goose, but she recognized a generous act of forgiveness. "Marty and Sasha and I have already made plans to drive to Virginia Beach and eat Thanksgiving dinner at that restaurant Sasha just finished decorating. They told her she could bring as many guests as she wanted, on the house. But I'll see you Monday. Monday's Marty's day, right?"

"If I ain't still mad at her, I reckon. I know it weren't your idea—leastwise, you didn't start it, them other two did." The housekeeper shook her head and smiled as Daisy held the door for her and her box of canned goods, cold drinks, dried flowers and assorted condiments. "Don't you stay here no longer'n it takes to lock up after they cut you off, y'hear?"

"I promise. See you soon."

Lingering at the front door, Daisy felt the emptiness close in on her. "Goodbye, Harvey," she whispered. "Don't worry, they'll take good care of it."

And they would, she assured herself. The members of the historical society might not agree on much, but they all knew the value of a house that had been a landmark in Currituck County for more than a century.

With the temperature dropping some twenty degrees overnight, the house was already growing cold. She had let the furnace run until the man from the gas company had come to disconnect it and take the tanks.

"What else?" she mused, missing the presence of someone else in the big, empty house.

Missing Kell. The scoundrel.

Packing the last few items—her soap and shower cap from the bathroom, her rose-scented hand lotion from above the kitchen sink—she made a mental note to stop by the post office on her way to town and tell them to hold her mail until she had a new address.

She made a deliberate effort to think of any loose ends. Windows all locked, inside doors and transoms opened to keep the air from growing too stale. Once she left, she had no intention of ever coming back. Besides, she'd be far too busy to dwell on what had happened last night. So the sex had been unbelievably good. So having a generous lover had made all the difference in the world. So she had learned things about her own body that *Gray's Anatomy* had never even hinted at, much less tried to describe.

"You can think about all that tomorrow, Scarlett."

Since she had to stop by the bank on the way to Marty's, she might as well drop off the keys.

Twelve

Swearing under his breath, Kell punched off his cell phone and tossed it onto the seat beside him. What the hell had happened back there, another hurricane? The number had sure as hell been in service when he'd called the airport to make reservations.

He was tempted to turn around and go back, just to see what kind of game she was playing now. More than once he'd heard her fielding calls, sounding like one of those computer-generated voices as she referred callers to Mr. Blalock at the bank unless the caller happened to be one of her friends.

Had he told her he'd be back by the first of the week? Or had he just said he'd see her soon? Added up to the same thing, but he had a feeling he might have screwed up. He'd never been much of a letter writer. He must have used up half the tablet she used for grocery lists, trying to strike just the right tone. Nothing mushy, because that wasn't him, but nothing too cool, either. Because cool was the last thing he was feeling. In the end, he'd settled for stating the facts, knowing he could say more once he'd had time to put things in perspective.

Still, it wouldn't have hurt to use the word *love*. People used it all the time—no big deal. Like I love baseball, or I love country music? Stuff like that? People signed letters "love, so-and-so," even to casual friends.

But "love, Kell"—that would have been a big deal. So big it scared him just to think it, much less to write it.

Much less to say it.

Marty showed her where to put her things, then lounged in the doorway while she unpacked. "You mean he just up and *left?* No warning or anything? Are you sure he's not just out somewhere checking on another sprout on his family tree?"

Faylene knew the truth. She'd been there when Daisy had found the note. But Daisy hadn't told either of her friends that Kell was gone for good. "No more sprouts, nothing left to do. He found out what he came to find, so there's no reason to hang around."

"But yesterday—I mean, what the devil happened between you two? Last I saw, you were headed off across the church grounds looking as cozy as grits and gravy."

"Yoo-hoo, anybody home?" Sasha let herself in the front door, bringing in cold air and a whiff of Odalisque.

"We're in the guest room," Marty called. "Come on back."

"I tried to call out at the house, but the service has

already been discontinued. Daisy, I thought you weren't going to leave until tomorrow."

"I hadn't counted on all the utilities being cut off so fast. Usually when you call the office you have to wait until they have someone in the neighborhood."

"Oh. I thought they did all that from the office." Sasha plopped herself down on the guest bed, tipping over the stack of freshly laundered scrubs Daisy had just unpacked. "Hey, if the hysterical society wants to get rid of anything, I want first crack. Client of mine just bought a McMansion on the beach and now he wants me to make it to look like it's been in his family for generations. Where's Kell, by the way?"

Marty shook her head, a warning expression on her face, but Daisy saw no point in trying to evade the issue. "He left this morning before I was even up."

Sasha's eyes widened. "But he's coming back, right?"

Daisy shrugged. "Who knows? He's not in line to inherit anything. Harvey's will was pretty specific about who gets what."

"Yes, but—" Sasha looked at Marty, arched her eyebrows and then asked the question both women had been skirting around. "I thought you and Kell were… well, you know."

Fighting tears, Daisy said, "I've got to go start moving out of my apartment. Anybody want to help?"

Kell watched the board as flight after flight was canceled due to a squall line moving through Central Oklahoma. He checked his watch again, felt a familiar burning sensation in his belly and wondered if he was getting an ulcer. He'd been in too big a hurry to get to the airport to bother with breakfast. Probably all he needed was food. On the other hand, with everything that had happened over the past three days, he'd damned well earned himself an ulcer.

After a few last-minute emergencies, the opening had gone off without a hitch. Clarice was in hog heaven, as she'd announced at least a dozen times. He'd managed to get Moxie another chance and hoped to hell he'd impressed on the kid that this was it—one more screwup and he was down for the count.

He'd tried at least a hundred times to call Daisy. He'd even called the phone company, only to be told—again—that the number was no longer in service.

She had a cell phone, but dammit, like the dumb ox he was he hadn't bothered to get the number. There'd been no need while he was there, and once he'd left, it was too late.

He'd tried to remember the last names of her two friends. One was an Owens, he couldn't remember the redhead's last name if he'd ever heard it. There were dozens of Owenses in the directory, not one of them a Sasha or Marty. Women used initials, he remembered hearing that somewhere. To keep jerks like him from finding out they lived alone.

He left the concourse and went in search of a pharmacy—any place where he could get a dose of antacid. If he didn't already have a hole in his gut, he probably would by the time he reached Norfolk. He had never handled frustration well, especially frustration brought on by his own stubbornness. It was one of the reasons his career had ended prematurely. Hurting like hell, he'd kept on insisting that he was good for another few innings and then argued each time he was taken out of a game. He'd been on the DL—the disabled list—for almost an entire season after surgery, first on his shoulder, then on the elbow of his pitching arm.

Ten years later he still didn't handle frustration as well as he should, but he was learning. Working with at-risk kids had taught him a lot. This thing with Daisy was teaching him even more.

At least this time he'd managed to get a direct flight. Now all he needed was for the weather to cooperate. *Come on, Mom, put in a word for me. Do a sun dance up there or something.*

The first place he found that sold antacids happened to be a café that specialized in chili. Cause and effect? At any rate, he bought a bowl of the stuff, ate it standing up, along with the bag of chips that went with it, then downed three antacids and chased it all with a mug of scalding black coffee.

Thunder rumbled like a thousand-car freight train, but the sky to the west was finally showing a few patches of blue. A few flights were already starting to move as he found a seat as close to the boarding gate as possible.

Where the hell are you, Daisy? What's with the phones?

If she'd already closed up the house and moved to town, where would she stay? Last he'd heard, her apartment was still shut down. The only motel was probably out of business for good if the sign on the door was anything to go by. He hoped to hell she hadn't left Muddy Landing, because one way or another he was going to find her even if he had to go door to door.

* * *

"How long does it take you to read one page, if you don't mind my asking?" Marty glanced up from the financial page of the *Virginian-Pilot* and waited for her friend to show some sign of life. Daisy had been staring at the same page of a paperback book for the past five minutes.

"Sorry. Did you say something?"

"Honey, he'll be back. I'll bet you anything you can name he's been trying to reach you."

Daisy gave up and laid the book aside. "I've been right here all day. My phone hasn't rung. You didn't bring me a letter. Shall I go into a trance and see if anything comes through on the ESP channel?"

"Did you call the registry about another assignment?"

Daisy nodded, her gaze still unfocused.

"Well?"

"Anytime I'm ready. Multiple sclerosis in E. City, problem pregnancy in Whitehall Estates, recovering suicide attempt near Point Harbor."

"Take the pregnancy," Marty advised.

"I said I'd check back in a couple of days." Daisy yawned, stood and stretched. It was barely eight o'clock, but she felt as if she'd been drugged. She'd slept until almost nine this morning and hadn't done anything worth mentioning all day.

"You wanna hear my big news, or are you going to flake out on me again?"

But before either of them could speak, the phone rang. Marty reached for it, never taking her eyes off her friend. "Owens's residence," she said briskly.

And then a smile started in her eyes and spread to her generous mouth. "Well, hi there, cowboy. Where you calling from?"

Daisy refused to pack up and move out entirely, but at least she threw a few things into her overnight bag. Kell took that as a good sign. He'd called from the airport, having run through every Owens in the phone book with *M* as either a first or second initial. By the time he reclaimed his car from long-term parking and drove all the way to Muddy Landing, following Marty's directions, nearly two hours had passed.

Grinning like a jack-o'-lantern, Marty had invited him in and offered him her sofa, a pillow and blanket. "It's nearly eleven, you don't need to drive any farther tonight."

Kell had thanked her, knowing damn well she didn't expect him to take her up on it. "Thanks, but I rented a cottage at Southern Shores."

"A whole cottage?"

"Yeah, well…I didn't have much choice. Sounds like things are in a pretty big mess down there."

Even after agreeing to hear him out, Daisy wasn't saying a word, just standing there, arms crossed over her chest as she looked from one to the other. Kell didn't want to think he was responsible for those shadows under her eyes. At least she'd agreed to hear what he had to say.

Finally he managed to escape. Taking her bag, he steered her out to the car, stashed her bag and settled her in the passenger seat, all without a word being spoken between them. Truth was, he didn't know where to start.

He only knew that the reason he was back had nothing to do with any relatives, dead or alive. He had a feeling she knew it, too.

"So…you closed up the place," he ventured as they headed south on Highway 168.

"I understand the historical society sent somebody out there yesterday—or maybe the day before. And guess what? An anonymous benefactor just donated enough to do almost everything that needs doing. Isn't that wonderful?"

"To do what? Clean up the yard? Fix that section of gutter?"

"Oh, much more than that. Egbert said they're already looking for someone who does slate roofs." As long as they talked about the house, Daisy told herself, she could handle it. She didn't want to be here, she really didn't, but her head and her heart had been fighting it out ever since he'd left. Her heart had evidently won.

If he wanted to sleep with her again, she probably would because she had nothing more to lose.

Nothing she hadn't already lost.

"I've been thinking," he said as he tooled along the dark highway at five miles over the speed limit. "The place is going to need a lot more fixing up. How well funded is this outfit?"

"The historical society? Not very, according to Egbert. I think there's a lot of squabbling among the members over which places to take on. There's a school and a couple of churches that are even older than Harvey's house, but they're probably too far gone to restore. Besides, this mysterious donor specified the funds have to be spent on Harvey's house." She shot him a significant look.

Ignoring it, he slowed up for a stoplight near Barco. "You hungry?"

"Mmm-mmm."

"Is that a yes or a no?"

She sighed audibly and said, "Actually, it's a yes. I didn't eat supper tonight."

"Me, neither. I had a bowl of chili before I left home. Remind me not to eat chili for a while."

"Why'd you rent a whole cottage. Are you expecting company?"

Lights from the dashboard glinted on his teeth as he grinned at her. "Frankly, I had to pull in a favor to get the place at short notice. As for company, I consider her more like…family."

Daisy sucked in her breath. Charlene or whatever her name was? Surely he hadn't—he wouldn't—

Suddenly he swerved into a convenience store. "What's it going to be? This place has pretty good subs and some other stuff."

Kell ordered a triple-dip cone for himself and a six-inch Italian sub for Daisy. She said, "Is that all you're having? I thought you said you'd skipped supper?"

"Yeah, well…I told you about the chili. I thought this might put out the fire."

"Oh, Kell…" She shook her head, her look all but saying, "You need a keeper."

By the time they reached the monster beach house, Daisy knew she was fighting a losing battle. Of all things, she found herself wanting to manage his diet—not to mention everything else in his life. She tried to tell herself it was the nurse in her, not the woman, but she knew better.

The cottage had five bedrooms, five baths and a hot tub. Kell tried hard not to show it as he led her from bedroom to bedroom, offering her a choice, but he was suffering.

"Oh, anyplace, it doesn't matter," she said. "Now, let's take care of what ails you." He cocked an eyebrow and attempted a careless grin. It didn't quite come off as convincing. "How long have you had an ulcer?"

"Hey, it's not a full-fledged ulcer. The doc just said it might help to cut down on stress and run a few miles every day."

"He didn't say anything about your diet?" Daisy opened her overnight bag and took out her toiletry case.

"He said whatever I liked was bad for what ailed me."

"I'll bet, seeing how you season your food. It's probably stress, though. Any idea where it comes from? Your sporting goods store? Your social life? Your—"

"Try my love life."

Her hands froze in the act of opening a bottle of antacid. "No thanks."

"Daisy, let's cut to the chase, shall we? Dancing around an issue is stressful, in case you haven't noticed."

"Are we dancing?"

"You wanna dance?"

She looked at the blue bottle she was holding, wondering if her own nerves could get any tighter. "Do you?" she whispered.

"With you? I'll dance as long as it takes, but right now I can think of something else I'd much rather do."

He stood there, looking much the way he had the first

time she'd ever seen him. Feet planted apart, thumbs hooked under his low waistband so that his fingers were angled toward his fly. He looked tired, even pale, but the tiredness in no way affected the intensity of his eyes.

I came, I saw, so what the hell—I conquered.

He opened his arms and Daisy walked into them. In a cold, empty beach castle, with no music other than the muted roar of the nearby surf, he began to sway. Daisy swayed with him, inhaling the aphrodisiac of leather, healthy male skin and whatever soap he'd last bathed with—something green and piney. Her breathing was rapidly becoming erratic, but then, so was his.

"The bed's not made," he said, his voice registering on her sensitized body the way it had from the first.

"Is there a blanket?"

"Will we need one?"

"Probably not," she murmured, making no move to resist as he led her toward a king-size bed with a view of the ocean that neither of them was in any condition to appreciate.

Naked in seconds, she dived under the quilted spread and watched as he unbuckled his belt, unbuttoned his black flannel shirt and unfastened his fly. "Don't forget your boots," she reminded him.

She snickered. He looked chagrined for a moment, then he laughed. "Be a hell of a time to trip and break a leg."

"Don't you dare," she whispered as he stripped off the last of his clothes and came down beside her.

"Later let's try out the hot tub," he said as he lifted and swung her over his thighs. "It's been a long day. You care to do the honors?"

"Oh, my…"

Daisy did the honors—at least, it started out that way. In the rough-and-tumble tangle of bare limbs that followed, with panting laughter interspersed with mind-blowing pleasure, neither of them could find the energy to try the hot tub.

Kell had a few scars—old injuries and surgeries from his playing days. One on his back that occasionally gave him trouble even now. Daisy explored them all, first with her fingertips, then with her lips. She didn't ask questions about them, which was a good thing, because he wasn't sure he could have spoken if his life had depended on it.

He sucked in his breath as she grew bolder. For a woman who was supposed to know all about anatomy, she was surprisingly awkward. Touchingly, endearingly awkward. When she leaned over to kiss her way down his throbbing body, he nearly lost it.

Back, don't give out on me now.

And then it was his turn. Leaning over her, he took it slow and easy, touching, exploring—finding and exploiting all the secret places on her body that set her off, made her close her eyes and moan. She was hot and wet and tight, and that alone nearly catapulted him over the edge. Carefully he positioned himself and eased inside her. Eyes closed, fists knotted, he braced himself to hold out as long as it took to bring her along with him.

It was going to be a close race. Slowly, carefully, he withdrew. She clutched his shoulders and whimpered sounds of protest.

He thrust again, shaken to his very depths by the avalanche that threatened to consume him. Trembling, he lowered his mouth to taste her lips again. Sweet, sweet addictive…

He willed himself to hold back—not rush her. But when he felt her tighten around him, any chance of holding back fled. They were in the race together from start to finish. And in this particular race, there were no losers.

A few hours later hunger drove them on a pilgrimage to locate the kitchen. "My friend had the heat turned on and the refrigerator stocked. I guess he didn't tell the rental agency to have the bed made up, not knowing how many people would be staying here with me."

"You have a friend here at the beach?"

"Actually, he lives in D.C. now, but he owns a few cottages between here and there."

"Nice friends."

"Yep."

They had made the bed together sometime between the second and the third time they'd made love. Afterward they had showered together, which had taken another half hour. Kell had insisted on covering every inch of her body with suds, then massaging them into her skin.

"Can't afford to miss a place," he'd rumbled, on his knees in the eight-foot-square shower stall as he traced a path from her toes to her inner thigh. "Always pays to work the kinks out after a game. Trainer told me that my first year in the minors."

"Not like this, I hope." Leaning against the tile wall, she'd had trouble breathing, much less speaking. "Ke-*ell?*" Her voice ended in a squeak as his hands toyed with her damp curls, then slipped inside her.

This time he braced himself in the corner and lifted her until she was clutching his shoulders, then he lowered her slowly until he was inside her. She bit his shoulder, trying not to cry out. They were both trembling with the effort to make it last, but there was no holding back.

It was a wonder they hadn't slipped and broken something. Moments later, Kell slowly settled with her still on his lap.

The scent of ginger lilies and sex permeated the air as the water began to grow cooler. Evidently, not even a million-dollar cottage had an endless supply of hot water.

"Did we ever get around to talking?" Daisy murmured now as she filled the coffeemaker.

"We never got around to a lot of things, but we will. I've got this place for two weeks. If it takes any longer than that, we might have to move somewhere else, but I'm not leaving until you promise…"

"Until I promise what?" Her heart lodged in her throat.

Don't be a fool—don't get your hopes up. Just because he came back for his car…

"That you'll marry me. That you could learn to love me enough to pack up and leave your friends and your home and whatever else you've got around here. That you—"

Daisy placed a finger over his lips, but there was no escaping his eyes. They were openly pleading. "Oh, Kell—oh, yes!"

"Yes what?" he whispered when she moved her hand so that she was cupping his face. Her thumb traced the shallow crease in his chin. He needed a shave, either that or he needed to let his beard grow out.

"With or without, I'll love you," she said, feeling

giddy with relief and sore in places that had never been sore before.

"With or without what?" he asked cautiously.

"Your beard. Whatever. Kell, don't you know how much I love you? Couldn't you tell?"

"I hoped. I wasn't sure. Love's not something I've had any experience with. If you want to know the truth, I was afraid I'd screw up."

"You did. Next time you walk out on me, at least wake me up and tell me you're going so I can ask questions if I want to."

So then he told her about Clarice and Moxie, and about a few other kids and the sporting goods shop in town where he trained them, and the baseball camp he was building on a ranch out in the panhandle where he hoped to retire in a few years and concentrate on the ball camp.

By the time he finished, they were lying in bed sharing turkey, cheese, bacon and apple sandwiches and a quart of full-fat milk.

"If all those boys are going to be living out there— at the ranch, I mean—then it seems to me you need a nurse in residence."

"Can you do that? Practice in another state, I mean?"

She set her plate on the bedside table, took his and stacked it on top, then curled into his arms again. "I expect it can be arranged," she murmured. "As long as I have to keep you from ruining your digestive system, I think I can manage to look after a few children, mop up their bloody noses and doctor their cuts and bruises."

He could have told her it might be more than that, but he figured she would learn soon enough.

Sighing, she stroked his naked chest. Neither of them

was wearing any clothes. And while it wasn't exactly a new experience for Kell, he had a feeling making sandwiches, checking out the wine supply and the view, all without a stitch on, had been a first for Daisy.

Just as his eyes began to close, she twisted a curl of chest hair around her finger and whispered, "You sleepy?"

His body's response was answer enough.

They looked at each other and both started laughing.

Hey, Mom—Dad—I think I know why you two were laughing....

* * * * *

HER MAN UPSTAIRS
by
Dixie Browning

OFFICIAL OPINION POLL

ANSWER 3 QUESTIONS AND WE'LL SEND YOU
2 FREE BOOKS AND A FREE GIFT!

0074823 |||||||||||| |||||||| |||||||

FREE GIFT CLAIM # 3953

YOUR OPINION COUNTS!

Please tick TRUE or FALSE below to express your opinion about the following statements:

Q1 Do you believe in "true love"?

"TRUE LOVE HAPPENS ONLY ONCE IN A LIFETIME."
○ TRUE
○ FALSE

Q2 Do you think marriage has any value in today's world?

"YOU CAN BE TOTALLY COMMITTED TO SOMEONE WITHOUT BEING MARRIED."
○ TRUE
○ FALSE

Q3 What kind of books do you enjoy?

"A GREAT NOVEL MUST HAVE A HAPPY ENDING."
○ TRUE
○ FALSE

YES, I have scratched the area below.

Please send me the 2 **FREE BOOKS** and **FREE GIFT** for which I qualify. I understand I am under no obligation to purchase any books, as explained on the back of this card.

D6CI

Mrs/Miss/Ms/Mr _____ Initials _____

BLOCK CAPITALS PLEASE

Surname _____

Address _____

_____

Postcode _____

Visit us online at www.millsandboon.co.uk

NO STAMP NEEDED!

THE READER SERVICE™
FREE BOOK OFFER
FREEPOST CN81
CROYDON
CR9 3WZ

NO STAMP
NECESSARY
IF POSTED IN
THE U.K. OR N.I.

One

Marty allowed herself ten minutes, start to finish, to shower, shampoo the stink out of her hair, dress and get back downstairs in time to meet the fourth carpenter. *If* he even bothered to show up. What the devil had happened to the work ethic in this country?

She knew what had happened to her own. It fluctuated wildly between gotta-do, gonna-do and can't-do. Between full speed ahead and all engines reverse, depending on the time of the month.

At least she had no one depending on her for support. Not even a cat or a dog, although she was thinking about getting one. Something to talk to, something to keep her feet warm in bed at night while she read herself to sleep. But then there were all those shots and flea medicines and retractable leashes and collars and tons of kibble.

So maybe a couple of goldfish…?

She checked her image in the steam-clouded bathroom mirror, searching for signs of advancing age. "At least you're not paying rent. Except for the phone bill, the power bill and property taxes, you don't owe a penny to anyone."

On the other hand, her split ends were in desperate need of a trim and the sweater she was wearing dated back to her junior year in college. Even if she could've afforded to update her hairstyle and her wardrobe, she lacked the interest, and *that*—the lack of interest—was the scariest of all. She was sliding downhill toward the big four-oh, which meant that any day now, the guarantees on various body parts would start running out. Oh sure, her teeth were still sound, and she could still get by with drugstore reading glasses, but she plucked an average of three gray hairs a day; she was collecting a few of what were euphemistically called "laugh lines"; and lately her back had been giving her trouble.

Of course, moving a ton and a half of books and bookshelves single-handedly might have had something to do with that.

Bottom line, she wasn't getting any younger. Her income was zilch minus inflation, her savings account had earned the lofty sum of a buck eighty-seven in interest last month, and with the least bit of encouragement she could become seriously depressed. She read all those magazine articles designed to scare women and sell pharmaceutical products. The trouble was, scare tactics worked.

Frowning down at her Timex, Marty decided she'd give him ten more minutes. Traffic jams happened, even in Muddy Landing, population just shy of a thousand. She'd forgotten to ask where he was staying, when he'd called late yesterday to see if she still needed a builder. If he was coming from Elizabeth City and happened to get behind a tractor or a school bus, all bets were off.

Squeezing the moisture from her thick chestnut-colored hair, she tried to hedge against disappointment by telling herself that he probably wouldn't show at all, and even if he did, he probably wouldn't be able to fit her into his schedule anytime soon. If he did manage to fit her in, she probably couldn't afford him. But the biggie was her deadline. If he couldn't meet that, then there'd be no point in even starting.

"Well, shoot," she whispered. When it came to looking on the bright side, she was her own worst enemy. So what else was new?

The first time the idea had occurred to her, she'd thought it was brilliant, but the longer it was taking to put her plan into action, the more doubts were seeping in.

Was that a car door slamming?

She gave her hair a last hurried squeeze with the towel and then felt in the top drawer with one hand for a pair of socks. Having long since gotten out of the habit of matching her socks and rolling them together, she came up with a short and a long in two different colors. Tossing them back, she raced for the stairway, bare feet thudding on the hardwood floors.

At least she no longer reeked of polyurethane. If the cinnamon had done the trick, neither would her house.

The phone rang just as she hit the third step down from the top. Swearing under her breath, she wheeled and raced back to catch it in case it was her carpenter asking for instructions on how to find her address.

"Hello! Where are you?"

"Is he there yet?"

Her shoulders drooped. "Oh, Sasha." If there was an inconvenient time to call or drop by, her best friend would find it. From anyone else Marty might think it was a power thing. "I thought you were someone else. Look, I don't have time to talk now. Can I call you back?"

"You're talking, aren't you?"

"But I'm in a hurry—so can it wait?"

"Is he there yet?"

"Is who there—here?"

"Your carpenter, silly! Faylene said Bob Ed said he was going to call you yesterday. Didn't he even call?"

Marty took a deep breath, drawing on the lessons of a lifetime. Patience was a virtue, right up there with godliness and cleanliness. At various times, she'd flunked all three. "Somebody's here, I just heard a car door slam. It might be him—he. Listen, later I want to know exactly what you two have been up to, but not now, okay?"

If you couldn't trust your best friend, whom could you trust?

"Wait, don't hang up! Call me as soon as he leaves, okay? Faylene said—"

Marty didn't wait to hear what Faylene had said. The trouble with a small town like Muddy Landing was that aside from fishing, hunting and farming, the chief industry was gossip. By now probably half the town knew what she planned on doing to her house, who was helping her do it, and how much it was likely to cost her.

Slamming the phone down, she peered through the front bedroom window to see a ratty looking pickup with a toolbox in back and a rod-holder on the front bumper, a description that fit roughly half the vehicles in Muddy Landing. There was probably a gun rack in the back window, too, and an in-your-face sticker peeling off the back bumper.

Well, so what? If the guy could read a blueprint and follow simple instructions, she didn't care what his politics were or what he drove or what he did in his spare time.

Not that her drawings bore much resemblance to blueprints, but at least she'd indicated clearly what she wanted done. Not only indicated, but illustrated. If he could read, he should be able to do the job. If it weren't for all the red tape involved with permitting and such, she could probably have done it herself, given enough time. There were how-to books for everything.

She watched from the window as a long, denim-covered leg emerged from the cab. Putty-colored deck shoes, Ragg socks, followed by leather clad shoulders roughly the width of an ax handle. Judging by all that shaggy, sun-streaked hair, he was either a surf bum or he'd spent the summer crawling around on somebody's roof nailing on shingles. All up and down the Outer Banks, building crews were nailing together those humongous McMansions on every scrap of land that wasn't owned by some branch or another of the federal government. She'd like to think of all the tourists who would pour down here once the season got underway as potential customers. Trouble was, there were enough bookstores on the beach so that few, if any, tourists were likely to drive all the way to Muddy Landing, which wasn't on the way to anywhere.

She was still watching when her visitor turned and looked directly at the upstairs front window. Oh, my…

As she flicked the curtains shut, it occurred to Marty that living alone as she did, inviting all these strange men into her home might not be the smartest thing. This one, for instance, looked physically capable of taking out a few walls without the aid of tools. *He's a construction worker, silly!* she told herself. *What did you expect, a ninety-seven-pound wimp?*

She was halfway down the stairs when the doorbell chimed—three steps farther when the smoke alarm went off with an ear-splitting shriek. "Not now, dammit!"

She galloped the rest of the way and reached the bottom just as the front door burst open.

"Get out, I'll take care of it!" a man barked. He waved her toward the open front door.

Swinging around the newel post, Marty collided with him in the kitchen doorway. She stood stock-still and stared at the billowing smoke that was rapidly filling the room.

"Try not to breathe! Where's your fire extinguisher?"

"Beside the drier!" Marty yelled back. Racing across the room, she jumped and slammed her fist against the white plastic smoke detector mounted over the utility room door. The cover popped off, the batteries fell out and the ear-splitting noise ceased abruptly.

In the sudden deafening silence they stared at each other, Marty and the stranger with the shaggy, sun-bleached hair and the piercing eyes. The stranger broke away first, wheeling toward the range where clouds of pungent smoke rose toward the ceiling.

"Get out of my way!" Marty shouldered him aside and grabbed the blackened pie pan with her bare hand. Shoving open the back door, she flung it outside, took two deep breaths and hurried to turn off the burner.

The stranger hadn't said a word.

Trying not to inhale, she clutched her right hand and muttered a string of semi-profane euphemisms. God, she could have burned her house down!

"You want to tell me what's going on here?" Fists planted on his hips, the stranger stared at her warily.

He wanted answers from *her?* She wasn't the one who'd burst into a house uninvited and started shouting orders. At least he wasn't wearing a ski mask over his face and carrying an AK-whatchamacallit—one of those really nasty guns.

Of course, she'd been expecting a carpenter. And he did have a toolbox in the back of his truck. But for all she knew, the thing could be full of nasty weapons of mass destruction.

A big fan of hard-edged suspense, Marty often let her imagination get the better of her. Not only that, but she'd been under a growing amount of stress, which always tended to affect her common sense.

"Sorry about that," he said quietly, pulling her back to reality. "I thought you had a real fire going." He waved away the pungent fumes with one hand.

Trying not to breathe too deeply, she leaned over the sink and held her stinging fingers under cold running water. Ow-wow-ee!

She felt him right behind her and tried not to react. He *had* to be her carpenter—either that or a fireman who just happened to be passing by 1404 Sugar Lane and smelled smoke.

Or the answer to a harried maiden's dream?

Not that she was a maiden. Far from it.

Way to go, Owens—so much for getting your head together. You nearly burn down your house and now you're checking out the vital statistics of the first man on the scene.

"Uh—maybe I'd better leave, okay?" The voice was rich and gravelly, if somewhat tentative. Pavarotti with a frog in his throat.

"No! I mean, please—I need you. That is, if you're the carpenter I was expecting. You are...aren't you?" She turned, still clutching her wrist to keep the pain of her burned fingers from shooting up her arm.

He was staring, probably trying to decide if it was safe to hang around. "Ma'am, are you sure you're all right?"

He'd called her "ma'am." Pathetically un-PC, but sweet, all the same. Conscious of her dripping hair and her naked feet, Marty tried to look cool and in control of the situation. *Oh, Lord, did I remember to fasten the front of my jeans?*

In case she hadn't, she tugged her sweater down over her hips. A smile was called for, and she did her best, which probably wasn't very convincing. At least, her would-be rescuer didn't look convinced. Any minute now he'd be calling for the butterfly squad.

Deep breath, Owens. Get it in gear. "Sorry. I'm usually not this disorganized." At least, this time of day she wasn't. Early mornings were another matter. She was a zombie until she had her fix of caffeine and sunshine. "It's just that everything happened at once. First the phone, then the doorbell, then the smoke alarm."

He nodded slowly. Then he sniffed, using a really nice nose. Not too big, not too straight—just enough character to keep the rest of his features from looking too perfect. "What *is* that smell?"

Marty sniffed, too. The air was rank. "Polyurethane and paint thinner, uh, laced with fried cinnamon. Actually, not all my ideas work out the way they're supposed to. You ever have one of those days when everything goes cronksided?"

He continued to watch her as if he suspected her of being a mutant life-form. His eyes, she noted, were the exact color of tarnished brass. Sort of greenish blue, with undertones of gold. Looking uneasy, he was backing toward the front hall, and she couldn't afford to let him get away.

"I left the burner turned on the lowest setting, thinking sure I'd have time, but…" Despite appearances to the contrary, she tried to sound intelligent, or at least moderately rational.

Fat chance. She sighed. "Look, I've been painting bookcases in the garage and I left the side door open so I could hear the phone, so that's how the smell got into the house, okay? I was just trying to cover it—while I showered—with cinnamon."

"You showered with cinnamon."

Was that skepticism or sympathy? Time to take control. "Yes, well—I probably should have used something heavier than one of those aluminum foil pie pans. Pumpkin. Mrs. Smith's. I hate to throw them away, don't you? They come in handy for scaring deer away from the pittosporum."

Nodding slowly, he backed a few steps closer to the hall door, watching her as if he expected her to hop up on a counter and start flapping her wings. "This *is* the right address, isn't it? Corner of Sugar Lane and Bedlam Boulevard?"

Bedlam Boulevard wasn't even a boulevard, just a plain old street. She'd almost forgotten the developer's love of all things British: Chelsea Circle, Parliament Place, London Lane.

She snickered. And then watched as his lips started to twitch. And then they were both grinning.

Marty said, "Could we start all over, d'you think?"

"I guess maybe we'd better. Cole Stevens. I was told you needed some remodeling done?"

"Martha Owens. I'm mostly called Marty, though. Come on into the living room, the odor shouldn't be so strong there. I'd open a window, but we'd freeze." Ignoring her stinging fingers—she'd probably burned off her fingerprints—Marty led the way, pretending she wasn't barefoot and dripping and utterly devoid of any claim to dignity she might once have possessed.

Following her, Cole wondered if he wouldn't be better off leaving now. He'd never worked for a woman before—at least, not directly.

He wondered if the fact that she was barefoot had anything to do with the way she moved. Hip bone connected to the thigh bone, thigh bone connected to the—

And then he wondered why he was wondering. Why he'd even noticed the way she walked—or the way she'd scrooched up her mouth when she'd hurled that blackened pan outside. For a crazy woman, she was sort of attractive.

It wouldn't hurt to stick around for a few more minutes, seeing as he was here. He hadn't planned on going back to work this soon, but that didn't mean he couldn't change his mind. The one thing he was, was flexible.

When he'd set out earlier this week, he'd had some vague idea of cruising south until he saw someplace that appealed to him. Less than a day out of his old mooring place on the Chesapeake Bay, he'd had some minor engine trouble and looked for a place to lay over. He'd radioed a friend of his, who had recommended Bob Ed's place near the neck of Tull Bay on North Landing River. He'd limped along on one engine, located the place, liked its looks and rented a wet slip for a week, with options.

Yesterday he had exercised his option for another two weeks. One of the things he liked about the place was the fact that, other than a few local commercial fishermen, it was empty. Add to that the fact that, while it was off the beaten track, it was relatively close to a metropolitan area in case he ever needed something that couldn't be found in the sticks.

Hell, there was no law that said he had to keep on running. No family, no job to hold him back. Not much of a reputation either, but the lack of a haircut over the past few months should keep anyone from recognizing him as the whistle-blower who'd brought down the third largest developer in southeastern Virginia.

What he hadn't counted on when he'd pulled up stakes and headed south was having so much time on his hands. When a guy didn't have a real life, things got boring real fast.

He'd been considering moving on when he saw the old guy who ran the place trying to replace a rotten window frame. He'd offered to help, and had been pleased and somewhat surprised to discover that he hadn't quite lost his old skills. By day's end they had replaced three windows on the northeast side of the rambling unpainted building that housed Bob Ed's Ammo, Bait and Tackle, and Guide Service. He'd met Bob Ed's lady, Faylene, briefly yesterday when she'd come to bring a stack of mail from the post office.

Now there was one strange lady. It was largely due to her that he was here today, actually considering signing on for a construction job. Too much fried food had evidently affected his brain.

Either that or too much solitude.

Cole followed the Owens woman into a comfortable, if slightly cluttered living room, where she turned to confront him. He stood six foot two to her five feet plus a few inches, yet she managed to look down her nose at him.

Haughty as a maître d' in a five-star restaurant, she said, "May I see your résumé?"

His résumé. Cole didn't know whether to laugh or to leave. A few minutes ago leaving had seemed the better option, but sooner or later he was going to have to jump-start his career. Living alone aboard his boat with no real structure in his life wasn't going to do it. This job, small as it was, sounded like a good first step if he planned to stay in construction, which was all he knew.

Hands on, though. No more management.

"My résumé," he repeated. He cleared his throat. "Short version—the firm where I worked for the past thirteen years recently went bankrupt, so my résumé would be pretty worthless." He didn't bother to add that the firm had belonged to his ex-father-in-law, who had pushed him into an area of management he had been unprepared for. Deliberately, he'd later learned. The result being that by calling a spade a spade—or in this case, calling a crook a crook—he'd lost his wife, his job, and any ambition he'd once had to be the best damn builder in the business.

"Would I have heard of it?" she asked.

"Were you watching the local news last spring?"

"Local? You mean Muddy Landing?"

He shook his head. "Norfolk. Virginia Beach, specifically." The state line was less than forty-five minutes away. Northeast North Carolina got most of the news from Norfolk feeds.

The way she was eyeing him, she was probably reconsidering her job offer. With no résumé and no referrals, he couldn't blame her, but now that he'd come this far, he was determined not to let that happen. Something about big, cloudy gray eyes and soft, pouty lips…

Oh, hell no. Any decision he made would be based on his

own needs and not on the appeal of any woman. He'd gone that route once before, and look where it had landed him.

"Look, I'll be honest with you," he said.

"For a change?"

Cole didn't particularly like being called a liar, especially when he wasn't, but having been grilled by experts, he let it pass. "I can leave now or we can go on with the interview, your choice," he said quietly. "I'd intended to head on down the Banks and points south in a few days, anyway."

"Then why did you bother to apply?"

Had he thought gray eyes looked soft? At the moment hers looked about as soft as stainless steel. "I'm beginning to wonder," he muttered, half to himself. The lady was as flaky as one of the Colonel's biscuits. "All right, fair question. First, I did a small repair job for a guy who owns the marina where I've been living aboard my boat. Yesterday a friend of his happened to mention that she knew somebody who needed a small remodeling job done in a hurry, and asked if I was interested in earning some maintenance money."

Actually, despite appearances, he had a fairly decent investment income considering his simplified lifestyle. But the market tended to be schizophrenic and, as someone once said, a boat was a hole in the water into which the owner poured money.

"You said that was your first reason. What else? Is there a second reason?"

A second reason. If he said "instinct," she was going to think he was as big a nutcase as she was. As to that, the jury was still out, but until he had more to go on he'd just as soon not have to defend himself.

It had been instinct that had first tipped him off that

Weyrich was dirty. Long before that, it had been instinct that told him Paula was bored with their marriage and looking for bigger fish to fry. Frying them, for all he knew. By that time it had no longer been worth the effort to find out.

"It just struck me as the thing to do," he said finally. "Small town, small job—good place to get my bearings again."

"Again?"

She might look like soft, but the lady was a piranha—big eyes, tousled hair and all. "Look, if it's all the same to you, let's leave my bearings out of this and get on with the business at hand. Do you need a job done, or don't you?"

She took a deep breath, hinting at what lay hidden by a baggy turtleneck sweater that showed signs of age. And he wasn't even a breast man. If anything, he was an eye man, eyes being the window on the soul.

The window on the soul?

Clear case of too much fried food and too much time on his hands.

"It's a remodeling job," she explained. "I doubt if it'll take very long. At least I hope not. I want my downstairs moved upstairs so I can reopen my bookstore downstairs."

Cole thought for a minute, then nodded slowly as a couple of things clicked into place. "The bookshelves you were painting in your garage." The smell still lingered, a combination of burnt cinnamon, fresh urethane and paint thinner—but either his olfactory sense was numbed or the stench was starting to fade.

She nodded. "I thought I'd better refinish them now so that they'll be thoroughly dry by the time my upstairs gets finished so I can move my downstairs upstairs and move the shelves into these two rooms and start restocking."

Okay. He had the general picture now. "You want to

show me what you have in mind?" He hadn't committed himself to anything.

Marty rubbed her right thumb and forefinger together as she considered whether to show him her drawings first or take him upstairs. She'd burned off her fingerprints, which might come in handy in case she couldn't get her bookstore reopened in time and was forced to turn to a life of crime.

"Come on, I'll show you upstairs first so you'll understand my drawings better. You might as well know, you're not the first builder to apply for the job. The others turned it down."

"Any particular reason?" he asked.

Conscious of him just behind her, she made a serious effort not to move her hips any more than she had to. Too much stress was obviously affecting her brain. Just because she'd noticed practically everything about him, from his tarnished brass eyes to the worn areas of his jeans to the way they hugged his quads and glutes and…well, whatever—that didn't mean he was aware of her in any physical sense.

Sasha would have had a field day if she could've tuned in on Marty's thoughts. Her friend was always after her to add a little more vitamin S to her diet. Vitamin sex. "Maybe then," she was fond of saying, "you'd get a decent night's sleep and not be a zombie until noon."

She wasn't that bad. Just because she wasn't a morning person—

He'd asked her a question. He was waiting for an answer. Kick in, brain—it's four-thirty in the afternoon! "Reason why they didn't work out? Well, one never showed up, and the next two, once they found out what I wanted done, told me I was wasting their time. Oh, and one of them said he could only work on weekends because the rest of the time he worked with a building crew at Nags Head." She hadn't yet mentioned the time constraints, but that shouldn't be a problem. It wasn't a major job, after all. Not like starting from scratch and building a house.

"So—here it is." She waved a hand in the general direction of the upstairs hall and the spare bedroom, which she planned to move into so that the larger bedroom could become her living room.

She had painted up here less than two years ago. She'd chosen yellow with white trim on the theory that sunshine colors would help kick-start her brain when she stumbled out of bed and staggered to the bathroom early in the morning.

While he looked around, tapping on walls, studying the ceiling, Marty told herself that it *would* get done. It *was* going to work. Her life was *not* in free fall—it only felt that way because time was wasting. She kept racing her engines but not getting anywhere.

Following him around, she tried not to get her hopes up—tried not to be distracted by the fact that he smelled like leather and something spicy and resinous, and that he looked like—

Well, never mind what he looked like. That had nothing to do with anything except that her social life had been seriously neglected for too long.

They were standing beside the closet she wanted taken out and turned into part of a new kitchen when he said, "You want to show me your drawings now?"

There was plenty of room. It was only her imagination that made it feel as if the walls were shrinking, pushing them closer together. Breathlessly, she said, "Come on, then, but remember, I'm not an architect. You can get the general idea, though." Turning away from her yellow walls, she was aware again of how early it grew dark in late January—especially on cloudy days. "I'll make us some coffee," she said. Heck, she'd cook him a five-course dinner if that was what it took to get him to agree.

Marty saw him glance into the spare bedroom where she'd stored dozens of boxes of paperback books, plus the bulletin boards where she used to tack up cover flats, bookmarks and autographed photos. She hated clutter, always had, and now she was wallowing in the stuff. As Faylene, the housekeeper she could no longer afford, would have said, "You buttered your bread, now lie in it."

Hmm…alone, or with company?

Two

"They're there on the coffee table," Marty said, leaving Cole to look over her plans while she started a pot of coffee. Too late to wish she'd taken time while they were upstairs to pull her hair back with a scrunchy and put on some shoes—and maybe add a dab of her new tinted, coconut-flavored lip balm. Not that she was vain, but darn it, her feet were cold.

Okay, so he was attractive. He wasn't all *that* attractive. Not that she had a type, but if she did, he wasn't it. She'd been married at eighteen to Alan, whose mother had left him this house. Whatever she'd seen in him hadn't lasted much beyond the honeymoon, but as she'd desperately wanted a family, she'd stayed with him. After he'd been diagnosed with MS, leaving was out of the question.

A few years after Alan died she had gotten married again, this time to Beau Conrad, a smooth talker from a wealthy Virginia family—F.F.V., U.D.C. and D.A.R.—all the proper initials. Only, as it turned out, Beau was the black sheep of the family.

Looking back, she could truthfully say that both her husbands had been far handsomer than Cole Stevens. So what was so intriguing about shabby clothes, shaggy hair, and features that could best be described as rugged? Was she all that starved for masculine attention?

Evidently she was. When she'd first mentioned her building plans, Sasha had offered to buy her a stud-finder. Four-times-divorced Sasha, ever the optimist. It had taken Marty several minutes to realize that her friend wasn't talking about one of those gadgets you used to find a safe place to hammer a nail into a wall.

"You see what I mean, don't you?" she called now from the kitchen. There'd been no sounds from the living room for the past several minutes. "Where I want the closet taken out and added to the back wall to make room for a couple of counters and whatever else I need for a small kitchen." She could mention the plumbing and wiring later. She didn't want to scare him off until she had him on the hook. She was rapidly running out of time. If it didn't happen with this one, she might not make the deadline, in which case she might as well have a humongous yard sale, sell off her remaining stock and then look for a job in an area where there weren't any. Either that or pull up stakes and move, which wasn't an option. The closest thing to roots she had was this house. Beau had tried to force her to sell it, but she'd held out. God knows, it was about the only thing of hers he hadn't forced her to sell. The paintings and antiques he'd inherited from his own family had been sold off soon after they'd married, along with the few nice things she'd been able to accumulate.

Damn his lying, thieving hide. She hoped wherever he was now, he was married to some bimbo who would take him for every cent he had.

Marty laid a Tole tray with two mugs, sugar, half-and-half and a plate of biscotti. As a bribe, it wasn't much, but at the moment it was the best she could do.

"Of course, I guess I could always get a camp stove and a dorm refrigerator," she said as she joined him in the living room. "It's not like I did a lot of entertaining."

No comment. Was that a good sign or a bad sign? At least he hadn't walked out after seeing her drawings. The stick figures might have been overkill. Occasionally in moments of desperation she got carried away.

"I guess we need to discuss money," she said, searching his face for a clue. If knocking out a wall or two and putting in a kitchen on the second floor was going to cost too much, she might have to—

Might have to do what? Open her bookstore in the garage? It wasn't even insulated, much less heated.

So then what, rob a bank? Get a loan? She hated debt with a vengeance, having been in it for one reason or another most of her adult life.

He'd taken off his leather bomber jacket. Good sign or not?

Who knows. The Sphinx was a chatterbox compared to Cole Stevens. He wore a faded blue oxford-cloth dress shirt with frayed collar, and turned back his cuffs to reveal a pair of bronzed, muscular forearms lightly furred with dark, wiry hair. She couldn't help but notice his hands, but then, she always noticed a man's hands. They said almost as much about him as his shoes. Shoes were something she had noticed ever since hearing her friend Daisy, who was a geriatric nurse, talk about this doctor who wore neat three-piece suits and silk ties, but whose nails were dirty and whose shoes were always in need of a polish. It turned out that for years he'd been killing off his elderly patients.

Okay, so his carpenter's deck shoes weren't the kind you polished. They were old, but obviously top-of-the-line. He had nice hands with clean nails, and she liked the way he handled her drawing pad, treating it as though the drawings had real value.

How would those hands feel on a woman's body? It had been so long....

Breathe through your mouth, idiot, your brain's obviously starved for oxygen!

She waited for him to speak—to say either "This looks doable," or "No thanks, I'll pass." The faded blue of his shirt made his skin look tan, which made his hair look even lighter on top and darker underneath. She was almost positive the tan was real and not the product of a bottle. Sasha, who was a hair person, could tell in a minute, but Marty didn't want Sasha to get even a glimpse of this guy. Her redheaded friend was a Pied Piper where men were concerned, and Marty intended to keep this one around for as long as it took.

For as long as it took for what?

To finish the job on schedule, fool!

"I didn't know if you took anything in your coffee," she said when he finally glanced up.

Despite a lap full of drawings, he'd made an effort to rise when she'd come in. She'd shaken her head, indicating that he should sit. Obediently, he'd sat, knees spread apart so that what Sasha called his "package" was evident.

You are not *having a hot flash! You're nowhere near ready for menopause!*

"Black's fine," he said, and took a sip of coffee.

"I could open another window. The rain's let up," she said. The odor inside was still pretty awful.

"No need," he said, and went on studying her drawings.

Hopefully he hadn't noticed her burning cheeks. "The stick figures are silly, I know," she said in a rush. "I was just doodling. Sort of—you know, illustrating me washing dishes, leaning over to use the under-the-counter fridge. Anything you don't understand, I can explain." That is, she could if she could manage to get her brain back online.

"They're clear enough. Thing is," he said, "this right here is a weight-bearing wall. I'll need to leave at least three feet of it, but then I can open your entryway right here and shift this wall down to here."

She forced her eyes to focus on the area he was indicating instead of his pointer finger. Then, because they needed to share the same vantage point if they were to discuss her drawings, Marty left her platform rocker and settled onto the sofa beside him.

Even without the bomber jacket he smelled sort of leathery with intriguing overtones. Salt water, sunshine and one of those subtle aftershave lotions that were babe magnets.

"Mmm, what was that?"

"I said the space can be better utilized if you don't mind using part of the closet for your range and oven. Stacking units would fit."

Marty realized their shoulders were touching—in fact, she was leaning against him. She sat up straight, but as he outweighed her by at least fifty pounds, she had to struggle to overcome the slope of the cushion.

Damn sofa. She'd never liked the thing, anyway. Sasha

had bought it at a huge discount for a customer who also hadn't liked it, so she'd let Marty have it at cost.

"Well," she said brightly, wriggling her butt away from his until she could hang on to the padded arm. "Uh, there are a couple more things we need to talk about. That is, if you're still interested in taking the job."

Cole flexed his shoulders and tried not to breathe too deeply. Yeah, he was still interested in taking on the job. Construction jobs were plentiful all up and down the nearby Outer Banks, but then, Muddy Landing was undergoing a small building boom as more and more Virginians moved south of the border. And while wages might be higher on the Banks, working conditions, especially in January, could be a lot worse. Climbing all over a three-story building some fifty or more feet above ground level, with a howling wind threatening to blow him out into the Atlantic? No, thanks. If he had to relearn the building trade after more than a decade in management, he'd sooner start out in a slightly more protected environment, even if his employer did happen to be a bit of a flake.

"The first man who answered my ad told me the job was a boondoggle. I'm not exactly sure what he meant. Actually, I'm not even sure what a boondoggle is, and words are my business—in a manner of speaking. Something to do with the government, I guess."

Cole had to smile—something he hadn't done too much of in the recent past. "I think it's a general description of most bureaucracies. You mentioned time constraints?" He reached for another biscotti—his third. The things were meant for dunking, but he figured he didn't know her well enough for dunking, so he bit off a chunk and tried to catch the crumbs in the palm of his hand.

"Right. There's this deadline," she said earnestly. "New zoning laws go into effect the middle of March, and unless I'm in business before then, I won't be grandfathered. That means—"

"I know what it means."

"Yes, well—of course you do. See, there are already several businesses in the neighborhood, but they won't allow any new ones to open after the fifteenth."

She hooked her bare toes on the edge of the coffee table, then dropped them to the floor again. She kept rubbing her thumb and forefinger together like a crapshooter calling up his mojo. Her eyes darted to the clock, and she bit her lip.

"Ms. Owens, are you sure this is what you want to do? Tear up your house so you can open—what, a bookstore?"

"I have to," she said simply. Then, with another glance at the clock, she quickly explained about Marty's New and Used. "Up until last fall I rented a two-room cinder-block building that used to be a garage and a bait-and-tackle shop and some other things. Anyway, the rent was cheap enough and the location was okay, I guess, but the income still couldn't keep up with the overhead. Some days I didn't even sell a single book." She gave up rubbing her fingers and folded her hands together, resting them on her knees. Her toes were back on the coffee table. "So I thought if I reopened here, I'd at least save the rent because I own my house. It's all paid off. My first husband inherited it from his mama."

Whoa. Her first husband? He was nowhere near ready to share personal histories.

The third time he caught her looking at the clock he asked her if she had a problem.

"Not really, but there's this dog I walk twice a day. I'm running late today because I was waiting for—"

She hesitated, and he filled in the blanks. She'd been waiting for him to show up.

"For the rain to stop," she finished.

The rain had stopped. A few chinks of salmon-pink sunset broke through the dark clouds.

Cole said, "Then why don't I leave you to it? I need to run a few errands if I'm going to stick around the area."

She looked so hopeful, he could have kicked himself. They hadn't even reached a concrete agreement yet.

"Are you? Going to stick around, I mean? Like I said, if things don't work out just right, I'm stuck with a garage full of bookshelves and a spare room filled with thousands of used paperbacks."

"Two things we still need to talk about—your deadline and my wages."

Looking entirely too hopeful, she said, "When can you give me an estimate?"

If he didn't watch it, Cole told himself, those big gray eyes of hers were going to influence his decision. That was no way to start rebuilding a career. "How about we both think it over tonight and I come back first thing in the morning with an estimate. If we reach an agreement, I can start right away. I should be able to bring it in on schedule, depending on how much time you need after the job's completed."

They both stood. Her eyes and her ivory complexion and delicate features called to mind the word fragile, yet he had a feeling she was nowhere near as fragile as she looked.

She said, "Come for breakfast. You're not organic or vegan or anything like that, are you?"

"Methodist, but sort of lapsed," he replied gravely, and heard a gurgle of laughter that invited a like response. He managed to hold it to a brief smile.

They agreed on a time and she saw him to the door and said she'd see him in the morning. It sounded more like a question than a statement, but he didn't reply. He had some serious thinking to do before he made a commitment. One thing for certain—he was nowhere near ready for retirement. As to what he was going to do with the rest of his life and where he was going to do it, that was still up for grabs.

Standing in the doorway, Marty watched as the most intriguing man she'd met in years adjusted his steps to her flagstones. She sighed. What a strikingly attractive man— and yet he wasn't really handsome. It was something else. Something in the way he carried himself, the way he…

Maybe Sasha was right and she was seriously deficient when it came to vitamin S.

Mutt was all over her the minute she opened his gate at the kennel. His owners, the Hallets, who lived three streets over in the development that had grown up around Alan's mother's old house back in the seventies, were on a two-week cruise out of Norfolk. Marty was being paid to pick Mutt up twice a day for a run, as the space provided by the boarding kennel hardly sufficed for a big, shaggy clown that looked as if he might be part St. Bernard, part Clydesdale.

"Whoa, get off my foot, you big ox." She managed to snap on his choke collar while he did his best to trip her up. He'd started barking the minute he saw her, and didn't let up until she opened the front door. Then he nearly pulled her off her feet trying to get outside.

She gave him a full half hour because that was what she'd agreed to do. Not a minute less, but not a minute more this time because she had to have him back by six when the kennel closed for the day. If she missed the deadline she'd have no choice but to take the crazy dog home with her, and that would be disastrous.

There had to be an easier way to earn money. If she were a diver she could drive to Manteo to the aquarium every day and scrub the alligators or maybe floss the sharks' teeth. Unfortunately, her marketable skills weren't all that impressive in a town where, other than flipping hamburgers, jobs were practically handed down from father to son. None of Muddy Landing's farming, fishing and hunting applied to her.

Maybe she and Sasha could start charging for their matchmaking services. Practically everyone in town knew what they were up to, anyway. It was no big secret; they'd been at it too long. They'd been good at it, too—Daisy, Sasha and Marty, with occasional input from Faylene, the housekeeper they'd all shared for years until Marty had gone out of business and Daisy had unexpectedly fallen in love with a good-looking guy who'd come east in search of his roots. A nurse and easily the most sensible of the trio, Daisy had fallen head over heels and ended up marrying Kell and moving to Oklahoma.

Marty and her friends had been good at it, though—all the planning and finagling it took to bring two people together. Three of their most recent matches had actually ended in marriage and two more couples were still involved.

Of course, there'd been a few spectacular failures, too, but it had been great fun. Mostly they'd been forgiven their blunders.

But Sasha was up to her ears in her latest decorating project, so matchmaking was taking a time-out. "And that just leaves me," Marty panted as she struggled to hang on to the end of the leash. She was wearing out her last pair of cross-trainers trying to keep up with Super Mutt. "Slow down, will you? Let me catch my breath!"

If she hurried, she might get home before he left for the day.

Right. Looking like she'd just finished a five-mile run. That would really impress the heck out of Cole, wouldn't it?

By the time Cole got back to the small marina with a take-out supper consisting of barbecue, fries, hush puppies and slaw, the last vestige of daylight had faded. And second thoughts were stacking up fast. Not about the work itself, although it had been a while since he'd done any actual construction work. That wasn't what had him worried.

As he stepped aboard his aged thirty-one-foot cabin cruiser, he waved to Bob Ed, who was outside sorting through a stack of decoys under the mercury-vapor security light.

The friendly guide called across the intervening space, "You see her?"

"I saw her."

"Ya gonna do it?"

"We're still negotiating," Cole called back.

Nodding, Bob Ed went back to checking out his canvasbacks. He was a man of few words. Which was just as well, Cole thought, amused, as Bob Ed's better half appeared to be a woman of many. Cole had met her only briefly, but she'd made an indelible impression.

What bothered him, Cole admitted to himself once he was inside, the lights on and his small space heater thawing out the damp cold, was the Owens woman. Or rather, his reaction to her. Before meeting her he would have sworn he was permanently immunized. Trouble was, Marty Owens and Paula Weyrich Stevens, his high-maintenance ex-wife, were two different species. If Paula had ever lifted a hand to do anything more strenuous than polish her nails, he'd missed it. Even for that she usually depended on a manicurist. Paula's idea of a perfect day started at noon with a three-daiquiri lunch at the club, followed by a shopping marathon, followed by dinner out with whatever poor sucker she could reel in to escort her while her poor slob of a husband worked late. Actually, Cole had been consumed those late nights with digging into the mess at Weyrich, Inc.

Marty Owens, on the other hand, varnished bookshelves in her spare time and tried to cover the smell by setting a pan of cinnamon on fire. She walked a friend's dog—at least, Cole assumed she did it for a friend. If she was hard up enough to do it for money, she probably couldn't afford the remodeling job she wanted done.

On the other hand, if she didn't get it done, what would happen to her business? Reading between the lines, he could only conclude that she was pretty close to the edge. And, like a certain ex-builder he could name, looking for the best way to revive a career that had collapsed through no fault of her own.

Not that he could swear to that last, but from what he'd seen so far, Ms. Owens was industrious, intelligent and not afraid to get her hands dirty. The fact that she was also sexy without making a big deal out of it wasn't a factor in any decision he might make. No way.

Definitely not.

As for the demise of his own career, Cole freely accepted the blame. All he'd had to do was turn a blind eye to what he'd uncovered—the good-old-boy bidding system, the under-the-table payoffs, the shoddy workmanship that had eventually resulted in three deaths and a number of injuries when the second floor of a parking garage collapsed due to insufficient reinforcement.

Oh, yeah, he'd blown the whistle on Joshua Weyrich, but by that time his marriage to Paula was washed up anyway. Looking back, about the only thing he and Paula had ever had in common was a serious case of raging hormones. Once that had died a natural death, there'd been nothing left to sustain a relationship. The only reason they'd stayed together as long as they had was that breaking up required more time and energy than either of them was willing to spend.

But once he'd blown the whistle on her father, détente had ended. He had gladly ceded to Paula the showy house they'd been given as a wedding present, plus all furnishings, including the baby grand piano she didn't play, the art collection she never bothered to look at and a bunch of custom-made furniture designed not for comfort but to impress.

With the help of a good lawyer, Cole had managed to keep his boat, his old Guild guitar, his fishing gear and roughly half his investments—which was all he really needed. He considered himself damn lucky to walk away with that much.

Now he looked around for a place to set his supper. The fold-down table was covered with fishing tackle. He made room for the take-out plate and a cold beer, shucked off his shoes and slid onto the bench. To say his living quarters were compact was putting it generously, but then, he didn't need much space. The wet slip, utilities included, cost a lot less than he'd been paying at his old place on the Chesapeake Bay.

He turned on the twelve-inch TV and caught up on the news while he ate. When the talking heads turned to the latest celebrity trial, Cole's thoughts drifted back to the woman he'd just met. After hearing about the job prospect from Bob Ed and his lady, Ms. Beasley—mostly from the lady—he hadn't known what to expect. Julia Roberts with big gray eyes and a brown squirrel's nest dripping down her back didn't fit the image he'd conjured up when he'd spoken with her briefly on the phone.

When she'd asked to see his references, he'd mentioned Bob Ed.

"Any reason why I should trust your word?" she'd asked.

The answer, of course, was that she shouldn't—but if she didn't know it, he wasn't about to tell her. If he'd learned one thing from the mess he'd been involved in over the past eighteen months, it was to listen to his instincts.

And right now his internal weather vane was telling him there was more at stake here than just a chance to see if he could still do the work. Without bothering to think further, he grabbed a paper napkin and started listing the tools he'd need to buy.

Halfway through the list his mind began to wander, distracted by thoughts of a pair of gray eyes, and the way they could go so quickly from suspicion to amusement to…interest?

Three

Sasha showed up for breakfast with a box of Krispy Kremes and a copy of *Architectural Digest.* "Check out page sixty-eight and think about the color scheme for your front room. I'm headed to Norfolk—just thought I'd stop by on my way." Her cheeks were pink from exposure to the damp, cold air, her eyes avid for anything that even hinted at romance.

While Marty was still trying to nudge her brain awake, her early morning visitor planted beringed fists on her rounded hips and said, "Let's hear it. Start from the first and don't leave out anything. If he's as prime as Faylene says he is, we might want to add him to our list. Is he taller than five-ten? Because Lily Sullivan over on Chelsea Circle is at least that. She towers over me, even in my new green Jimmys. I'm thinking of finding someone shorter to do my taxes. It's bad enough to be intimidated by the IRA without—" She blinked a battery of fake lashes and said plaintively, "Wha-a-at? Oh, Lord, you're still sleepwalking, aren't you."

Still wading through her usual morning fog, Marty refused to be intimidated by the five-foot-three-inch steamroller. "Look, I've got a date with a dog, so make this fast. Exactly what do you mean by 'prime,' and what difference does it make what he looks like?"

"Actually, none, I guess. We just thought—that is, Faye said—and I was thinking that if he was going to be hanging around long enough to destroy your second floor and put it back together again, he might like to join in a few social activities. You know what they say, 'all work and no play'?"

Marty sighed. "It bugs you, doesn't it? The fact that somewhere in three counties there's a competent, independent woman who gets along perfectly without the benefit of a man. Did it ever occur to you that some of us like our lives just fine the way they are?"

The redheaded interior designer tried looking innocent and gave it up as a lost cause. "You're talking like you never did any matchmaking. How about Clarice and Eddie? How about Sadie Glover down at the ice-cream parlor and—"

"How about stuffing a doughnut in it?" Marty poured coffee, adding half-and-half—which her guest called diet cream—to both mugs. "Mutt's waiting, so eat fast."

"Gross. Do you have one of those scoopy things in case he does his business in somebody's yard?"

Marty rolled her eyes. "Sash, I really need to get this job done in record time, and once y'all start messing around with my carpenter, you're going to scare him off—so quit it, okay? Just knock it off. At least wait until I'm finished with him."

Sasha began licking the sugar coating off another doughnut. "Just thinking about poor lonesome Lily, that's all. I ran into her at the post office the other day and she happened to mention that she hadn't had a date since last summer."

"Just happened to mention it, huh? Like you didn't pry it out of her with a crowbar?"

"Would I do that? Anyway, we're running short of bachelors and I thought I'd get your take on whatshisname, your new carpenter. So? What's he like? Faylene says he's a hunk."

"Dreadlocks, whiskers, ragged Brooks Brothers shirt, worn-out L.L. Bean shoes and no calluses. Which probably means he buys his clothes at a thrift shop using money he stole instead of working for it."

"You jest." Sasha licked her fingers, showing off inch-long nails and a glittering array of jewelry.

"I jest not. I might exaggerate now and then—I might even occasionally speculate—but please, Sash, don't go trying to distract my carpenter. He's my last chance."

"No problem, hon, he's all yours during business hours. Did you say he was tall?"

"Let's just say he's taller than you are."

"Everybody over the age of twelve is taller than I am. Is he good looking?" She wriggled her generous curves. "Faye says—"

Marty hesitated just a second too long, and Sasha pounced. "He is! Admit it, you're hot for him and you don't want him exposed to Lily until you've had time to make an impression on him yourself."

"Will you *stop it?* It's nothing like that! He's supposed to come by to give me an estimate early this morning, and I've got to walk Mutt first and get back here—so if you don't mind, you need to leave now and so do I. Five minutes ago, in fact."

Sasha grinned, her eyes sparkling like faceted gemstones. Today they were aquamarine. Tomorrow, they might be topaz or sapphire. The woman had never met an artifice she didn't adore, regardless of the time of day.

Marty, on the other hand, was barely able to find her mouth with a toothbrush, even after she'd stood under the shower for five minutes. A morning person she was not. The time had long since come and gone when she could stay up half the night reading and wake up bright-eyed and bushy-tailed at the crack of dawn.

"Look, just let me get him on the hook and then you and Faye can have your way with him. All I want is his skills."

"What else is there?" the redhead murmured.

"His carpentry skills!" Marty all but shouted.

"Shh, calm down, honey—no need to get all excited. You can have him during working hours, but Faylene and I want whatever's left over for Lily. She needs a little R 'n' R before the tax rush starts. We tried Egbert on her, but it didn't work out."

In the middle of a jaw-cracking yawn, Marty had to laugh. She edged her best friend toward the front door. "No kidding. I wonder why?"

"Hey, when you're wired for one-ten, you don't go fooling around with two-twenty. I learned that from husband number two, the electrical engineer."

"I thought number two was the con man."

"Aren't they all?" Sasha called cheerfully over her shoulder.

Marty watched her friend sashay down the flagstone walk hitting about every third flagstone, not even bothering to look where she was going. That was Sasha—stiletto heels, red leggings and faux fur at a quarter of eight on a cold, gray Monday morning, leaving in her wake a trail of Nettie Rosenstein's Odalisque. She might look purely ornamental, but when she was on a job, she worked harder than any woman Marty knew—including Faylene, Muddy Landing's unchallenged queen of housecleaning.

As soon as the red Lexus convertible disappeared around the corner, Marty grabbed a coat and a pair of gloves. Cole had said he'd be here between eight-thirty and nine, which barely gave her enough time for Mutt's half-hour gallop.

"You'll make it, easy," she assured herself as she waited for her cold engine to turn over. "Think positive," that was her motto. It had to be, because any negative thinking might send her into a serious decline.

There were several doughnuts left in the box. Still breathless from the dog walk—or in Mutt's case, dog gallop—Marty left them on the table as she hurriedly washed the mugs and turned them down in the dish drainer. A moment later she heard the truck pull into the driveway behind her minivan, which meant she'd run out of time. Her hair was a wild, windblown tangle, her nose and cheeks red from the cold, and there was no time to dash upstairs for a quick fix.

Probably just as well. No point in giving him the wrong impression. Inhaling deeply of the air that now smelled only faintly of varnish and burnt spice, she braced herself for bad news. It was called hedging her bets. Deliberately not getting her hopes up. If so-and-so happens, she always reasoned, I can always do such-and-such, and if that doesn't work out, I'll just fall back on my contingency plan.

What contingency plan? This *was* her contingency plan.

She opened the front door before he could knock. "Good morning, have you had breakfast?"

He raised his eyebrows. They were almost, but not quite black. Thick, but not unkempt. "Did I misunderstand? I thought—"

Oh, shoot. She'd told him to come by for breakfast. "The bacon's ready to pop in the frying pan, the eggs ready to scramble and there's doughnuts to start with. Toss your coat on the bench or hang it on the rack and come on into the kitchen."

Oh, my mercy, he looked even better than she remembered! She was no expert, but after two husbands and several near misses, she'd learned a few things about men. For instance, she knew the really handsome ones were about as deep as your average oil slick, having spent a lifetime getting by on their looks. Cole Stevens wasn't that handsome. Whatever it was that made him stand out from all the men she'd ever met, it was far more potent than a pleasant arrangement of features.

"Do you have a phone where I can reach you if I need to?" she asked.

He gave her his cell phone number and she hastily scratched it down on the bottom of a grocery list. Then he followed her into the kitchen.

"Warming up out there," he said. It wasn't.

"Spring's on the way," she replied. It wasn't. "Where are you staying, in case something comes up and I need to reach you?"

"At this place down by the river. Bob Ed's. I thought I mentioned it yesterday—I'm living aboard my boat at the moment."

Right. Bob Ed and Faylene had sent him, after all. There'd been a few distractions yesterday, including the man himself.

"Isn't it cold?"

"Yep."

And that was the end of that…unless she wanted to invite him to move into her warm, insulated house, which wasn't even a distant possibility.

Back to business. "How long do you think it will take to tear out what needs tearing out and turn my upstairs hall into a kitchen?" She placed three strips of bacon in a frying pan and turned on the burner. At the first whiff of smoke she remembered to turn on the fan. The cover and batteries for her smoke detector were still on the counter where she'd left them.

Spotting them, Cole replaced the batteries and clicked the cover in place.

Marty smiled her thanks. "I was just getting ready to do that," she lied.

"As to the tear-down, it shouldn't take more than a day or two."

Was that a yes, he'd do it, or an answer to a rhetorical question? Forcing herself not to sound too eager, she said, "That sounds great."

He stood beside the table staring out the window, his hands tucked halfway into the hip pockets of his jeans as the tantalizing aroma of frying bacon filled the room.

"Forecast is calling for more rain," he said.

Marty glanced over her shoulder. *Oh my, honey, I hate to tell you this, but those jeans are a little overcrowded.* "It'll be February in a few more days, and after that, March—that's when spring starts for real. Of course, we get those Hatteras Lows that can hang around for days, beating the devil out of any blossom that dares show its face."

"Mmm-hmm," he murmured.

Mr. Enigma. The fact that Marty tried not to look at him again didn't mean she wasn't aware of him with every cell in her undernourished body.

She took up the bacon and placed the strips on a folded paper towel. Whipping a dab of *salsa con queso* into the eggs, she tried to focus her mind on the estimate and not on the man. The fact that he'd showed up meant he was ready to talk business. Whether or not she could afford him without taking out a loan remained to be seen.

"Have a seat. D'you need to wash up first? The bathroom's upstairs—but you know that, of course. Or you can use the sink down here if you'd rather. The hand towel's clean—or there's paper."

Excuse me and my big, blathering mouth, I always talk like this when I'm on the verge of losing my mind.

A few minutes later, Marty popped two slices of bread in the toaster and filled two plates. Cole had excused himself and gone upstairs, either to wash up or to take another look at the job before committing himself. Thank goodness she'd made her bed as soon as she'd crawled out of it. Was her gown hanging behind the bathroom door? Had she put the cap back on the toothpaste?

Well, shoot, did it matter? At least she was wearing

shoes and socks today. He had no way of knowing she just happened to be wearing the only pair of jeans she'd ever owned that cost more than a hundred bucks. She'd bought them on sale two years ago, just to prove something or other to Sasha—she'd forgotten now what it was.

"I've got strawberry jam, marmalade and homemade fig preserves," she told her guest when he came back downstairs. "Help yourself."

Hope for the best, prepare for the worst, that was her motto. He would hardly eat her food if he intended to turn down the job, now would he? Or price himself out of the market. Unless he was broke and hungry or totally lacking in ethics.

He might be broke, and he was certainly hungry, judging by the way he was packing away his breakfast—but she'd be willing to bet on his ethics. Something about the way he looked her square in the eye told her that much.

Right. And Beau hadn't looked her in the eye and lied like a rug?

A few minutes later he laid his knife and fork across the top of his plate, poured himself another half cup of coffee and then held the pot over her cup. "It looks feasible."

Not wanting to have to excuse herself and race to the bathroom, Marty declined the coffee. They were finally getting down to brass tacks. "Feasible?" she prompted.

He nodded. "That wall you want removed—I think I mentioned yesterday it's a weight-bearing wall. Structurally, you need it, but I can work around it and still get your basic needs taken care of if you're willing to compromise."

"Compromise is my middle name."

Her basic needs? If he had the slightest idea of what

her basic needs were at this moment, he'd hit the road running. She hadn't even realized she had any basic needs until he'd shown up on her doorstep yesterday— or rather, when he'd burst into her house, yelling for a fire extinguisher.

Forget the fire extinguisher; bring on the cold shower.

"Does this mean you're going to do it?" she ventured.

"You want an hourly rate or an estimate for the complete job?"

"Um…whichever you'd rather."

"Then how about this?" He fingered a folded piece of paper from his shirt pocket—Brooks Brothers again, frayed collar, white oxford cloth, button missing three down from the top. Why did she have to notice every tiny detail about the man? Because she was a Virgo?

Ha. A Virgo with her Venus in Scorpio. According to that article she'd read recently she was supposed to be repressed, but secretly obsessed by sex, which just showed how much stock you could put in all that astrology bunk.

Cautiously, she unfolded the note. The first thing that caught her eye was his handwriting. Or rather, his printing. Actually, it was a combination. Sort of masculine with unexpected grace notes. Like the man himself, she thought before she could stop herself.

His silence weighed on her, making her aware that he was waiting for some reaction. "I don't see any real problem," she said finally.

No real problem if you didn't count her entire nest egg disappearing down a sinkhole. But then, what were nest eggs for? Once hers hatched she could start accumulating eggs all over again. Or if not, she could always sell her house, buy a tent and a bicycle and move to the beach, where summer jobs were plentiful.

"Then," he said, "shall we both sign it, date it and call it a deal?"

Hearing the crunch of tires on her driveway the next morning, Marty fought off a fresh set of misgivings. It was going to cost a bundle and there was no guarantee things would work out in the end. If she could fail in a stand-alone bookstore on the edge of Muddy Landing's tiny shopping district, she could fail even faster in a residential location.

She'd spent the morning moving out of her bedroom and into the smaller spare room. Compared to wrestling all those heavy bookshelves, dismantling a double bed, dragging it into the next room and setting it up again was child's play. She'd learned a long time ago how to lift without endangering any vital organs.

A few backaches didn't count. Life was full of little backaches.

She slid the mattress across the hardwood floor and flopped it onto the box springs just as she heard Cole call up the stairs.

"The door was unlocked, so I came on in. Okay?"

She'd mentioned yesterday that if she wasn't here when he came to work, the front door would be unlocked. He hadn't said anything, but from his expression, she gathered he didn't think it was a good idea.

"This is Muddy Landing," she'd told him. "Crime rate zilch, if you don't count the occasional kids' pranks. But if it makes you feel any safer, I'll start locking the door whenever I leave."

He'd nodded and said that would be safer.

"If you get here before I get back from walking the dog, the key will be under the doormat."

He'd rolled his eyes. Greeny gold eyes, thick black eyelashes, not-quite-bushy black brows. *Be still my heart.*

"Come on up," she called downstairs. "I just finished clearing out the big bedroom." Without thinking, she massaged her lower back with both hands. Occasionally when she was in a hurry she still forgot to lift with her legs.

It took two trips to bring up his tools. He handed her a roll of heavy-duty trash bags. "This first part's going to be messy. I thought about renting a Shop-Vac, but—"

"Oh, I already have one," she said proudly as if she'd just produced the winning lottery number.

"Great. I figure I can reuse most of the studs and rafters, but the rest—"

She nodded vigorously. "I know, plasterboard walls can't be reused. Will we have to take down the ceiling where the wall comes out?"

"First, let's settle this 'we' business. I work alone."

"Oh, but I—"

"My way or no way. I do the cleanup as I go along. If it's not clean enough for you, you can do it over again while I'm on a break."

"But I—"

"Marty—Ms. Owens, I agreed to do the job. I did not agree to have to explain everything I do and then have to argue over whether or not I could have done it another way. I doubt if you have enough insurance—the right kind, at least—to compensate either of us when I trip over you and we both break a few bones."

She took a deep breath, trying her best to ignore the hint of aftershave, laundry soap and something essentially masculine. Dammit, you'd think an aching back would be enough of a distraction. "I only wanted to help."

"Don't. I know what needs doing, I know how to do it. What I'm not good at is having my concentration broken every few minutes by questions."

She felt like telling him he was fired, but she didn't dare. They had signed a contract…sort of. Besides, if she were honest with herself—and she always tried to be—she didn't want him to leave. He was her last hope. He was also…

Well. That was irrelevant. He was her employee, period. They'd settle later which one of them was in charge.

She was backing toward the stairs when the phone rang. It was still sitting on the floor in the bedroom she'd just vacated. Bending at the knees rather than risking further injury to her back, she scooped it up, keeping one eye on Cole Stevens, who was tapping walls just a few feet away.

"Oh, hi, Faylene." With a sigh, she leaned against the wall, resigned to listening as the long-winded friend who had also, until recently, been her once-a-week housekeeper, described the yacht that had recently berthed at the marina just south of Bob Ed's place.

"Two men's all I seen, but we could have us a boatload of 'em. If they're still here for Bob Ed's party Sunday night, I'm thinking 'bout askin' 'em over."

Marty made some appropriate response, which wasn't really necessary. Once Faylene got the bit between her teeth, she was off and running.

"She's one o' these fancy yachts with the kind of old-fashioned woodwork you don't see much anymore. You think I should invite 'em to the goose-stew?"

The goose-stew. Once the holidays were over, stews, fries and candy-boils constituted the main social events until box-supper season. "Why not? No point in wasting a yacht-load of men," she said jokingly.

"That's what I thought. How's your man working out?"

"My—? Faylene, he's not my man!"

"That's what I'm talking about. If the one I sent you don't work out, maybe we can gaff you one of these."

Marty sighed heavily. "Invite them all, married or single. It's up to you." *Just so you leave my carpenter alone,* she added silently.

She listened for a few more minutes while Faylene speculated about all the things an unmarried yachtsman might have in common with either a bookseller or an accountant, most of her ideas being gleaned from various soap operas. Faye was as bad as Sasha when it came to dishing and conniving.

Leaning against the bedroom wall, Marty held the phone away from her ear while she absently rubbed her burnt fingertips together. All the boxes of books she'd shifted from one bedroom to the other still had to be hauled downstairs again. She'd have left them in the garage, but dampness was a book's worst enemy.

When Faylene paused for breath, Marty said, "Okay, hon, invite the entire crew and let the games begin." She hung up quickly before her friend could launch another barrage.

After Daisy had moved, the housekeeper had slipped into the matchmaking trio as if she'd always been a part of it. Actually, she had—even after their misguided effort to match her up with the mechanic, Gus Mathias, had failed so spectacularly.

Rather than risk her back by bending over again, Marty

pulled the phone cord from the wall. Was there a jack in the spare room? If not, she needed to have one installed.

Glancing up, she caught Cole watching her, his expression guarded. "I've got some errands to run," she said. "I'll just put the Shop-Vac at the bottom of the stairs and you can get it whenever you need it, okay?"

He might never win any Mr. Congeniality awards, she told herself on the way to the supermarket, but he was hers, bought and paid for.

Or if not bought and paid for, at least signed and delivered.

Four

Cole waited until he heard her go downstairs before taking down the rest of the crown molding and setting it inside the bedroom she'd recently vacated. The room still carried that subtle fragrance he'd quickly come to associate with the woman. Not polyurethane and fried cinnamon. Nothing overt, like Paula's, but something that reminded him of the kind of flowers you might catch a whiff of while cruising in the tropics on a hot summer evening.

This is Muddy Landing, you jerk. It's January, so cut it out and get back to work.

Replaying her phone conversation in his mind, Cole thought, that was fast work. Some poor guy ties up at a marina and already the local ladies were swarming like sirens. Maybe he should stop by and pass on a word of warning, one sailor to another.

Or maybe he should mind his own business.

What was it she'd said? *Let the games begin?*

He hated to think Marty was involved in that kind of game, but it was none of his business. His job was to do what he'd contracted to do, collect his wages and move on to the next marina, the next job—maybe the next country.

He heard a door shut downstairs as he unscrewed another switch plate and set it aside. He had already taken down one section of plasterboard.

He figured her bungalow for late fifties or early sixties, several decades older than the other houses in the development. Back when this one was built, two bedrooms and a single bath were enough for most young couples. If the family outgrew the original floorplan, they usually built on an addition. That was before the days of starter homes.

But it was her house. She could do what she wanted with it, including turn it into a bookstore. Just because he'd moved out of a five-bedroom, four-bath plastic palace into a boat so small you had to go up on deck to change your mind—

Time to quit thinking so damn much about the house and its owner. Time to do the job he'd been hired to do, then move on.

Before he'd married the boss's daughter and graduated to a corner office where he'd been anchored to a damn desk, Cole had done just about every kind of construction work there was, starting with the boatyard where he'd landed his first summer job. But it had been years since he'd done any hands-on carpentry other than helping Bob Ed with those windows, and the hours he put in on the *Time Out.*

Maybe this had been a mistake. Maybe he should have moved on, waited for more time to pass. He was permanently immunized against sophisticated high-maintenance women who used their sexuality as bargaining chips.

But when it came to the kind of beauty that didn't rely on paint and polish, he might be just a tad susceptible.

What do you bet, he asked himself, amused, that underneath those baggy clothes she's wearing plain white cotton underwear?

The next few hours passed quickly while he measured, marked and cut, his thoughts occasionally straying from the job at hand. Funny how quickly he'd gotten comfortable with her after that near calamity he'd walked in on yesterday. He usually took his time getting to know people. Even before his career, not to mention his personal life, had imploded, he had never been known for his sociability.

Don't get too attached to the place, he warned himself. He happened to like solid, unpretentious houses, and he appreciated those same qualities in a woman—but this was just another job. That was *all* it was.

Still, she was solid and unpretentious, and more. Intelligent but without making an issue of it. If those crazy little stick figures were any indication, she had a sense of humor. He'd never realized what a turn-on that could be. Sharing a few laughs with a woman made you want to get closer, to see what else you could share. It was almost as if they'd been friends for years, but had just never gotten around to meeting until now.

Or maybe his judgment wasn't as sound as he'd thought.

Yeah, well…he'd pretty well proved that, hadn't he?

By the time Marty heard Cole head downstairs in the middle of the day she had set out sandwich makings, a pitcher of iced tea and a pot of freshly made coffee. So far as she knew, he hadn't brought anything with him for lunch. If he took time out to drive to the Hamburger Shanty, it would just put her that much more behind schedule. During the hours when she had him, she wanted *all* of him.

The thought had wings. Before she could turn off her imagination, a mental image began to take shape. She groaned. There was *definitely* something missing in her life.

Passing him in the hall, she avoided looking directly at him, still miffed at being invited to stay out of his way. "Lunch is on the table. If it won't upset you too much, I'll just run upstairs and do some cleaning while you eat." Okay, call her a neat freak. At least it gave her the excuse she needed not to sit across the table and stare at that sexy mouth, those enigmatic eyes.

He said, "Look, I'm sorry if I was a little abrupt, okay? I didn't mean to offend you."

"Abrupt? Not at all," she dismissed. "You made your position perfectly clear, and believe me, I understand. If I let every part-timer I ever hired start telling me how to run things, I'd be out of business by now." Well, she was, wasn't she? "You know what I mean," she muttered.

Upstairs, her irritation evaporated as she took in the wreckage. The exposed skeleton of a wall and the dust and debris that coated every surface. *Clean it up, clean it up quick before someone sees it!*

And just like that, she was a kid again, trying her best to be perfect, hoping against hope that someone would like her enough to adopt her so that she could quit trying to be on her best behavior every minute of every single day, year after year after year. Surely somewhere there was a kind, loving couple who would notice how neatly she kept her few belongings and how perfectly she made her bed every morning. Someone who would recognize that underneath her gawky, homely disguise there was a little girl who was smart, pretty and obedient, who would make them a perfect daughter.

She blinked twice and she was back to the reality of the mess that had, until a few hours ago, been her neat upstairs hall. She'd been so busy looking beyond this particular stage to the result that she'd failed to consider what happened between the Before and the After.

Okay, so now she would deal with Between.

Peeling a trash bag from the roll, she began picking up the big pieces and wondering whether to sweep or vacuum the rest. Was it safe to plug her vacuum cleaner into the wall socket? There were wires showing between the studs or rafters or whatever those two-by-fours were called.

So much for her pretty yellow walls. Once there'd been an elegant little parquet table and an arrangement of pictures on the wall. The table had long since disappeared. Beau had given it to her the first year they were married, bragging that it was just a small part of his heritage. The only time he'd taken her to his home outside Culpepper, her reception had been cool to the point of intimidation. On the way back to Muddy Landing he'd explained everything she'd seen—the house, every stick of furniture, plus all the paintings—were family heirlooms. It went without saying that anything that came from the Owens family couldn't be considered joint property, even if he'd given it to her as a birthday or Christmas gift.

At least her first husband had given her a home. Alan had signed the deed over to her shortly after they were married, almost as if he'd known he had only a few more years to live. She would like to think she'd risen to the challenge of juggling a full-time job with a full-time marriage, because even before he'd been diagnosed with MS, Alan had required considerably more energy than her first book-store. Not because he'd been particularly demanding, but because she'd been so anxious to be the perfect wife.

But then he'd fallen ill and she'd spent the next few years on automatic pilot. With the bills piling up, she hadn't been able to afford to close down. Instead, she'd hired someone to mind the store while she'd stayed home with Alan.

After he died, she had forced herself to set her grief aside and resurrect what was left of her business. Gradu-ally over the next few years, she had started breaking even, slowly moving into the black—but then the recession had hit. Her landlord had raised her rent, claiming increased property taxes, and by that time the online booksellers had started selling used as well as new. The rest, as they say, was history.

Now, unless this plan of hers worked out, she might as well go back to square one. As tired as she was, both men-tally and physically, she might not make it to square two.

With renewed resolve, she plugged in the vacuum cleaner and, when nothing blew up, picked up the wand and promptly knocked over three short two-by-fours. "Well, crud!"

From downstairs, Cole heard the Shop-Vac start up and stop. He heard something clatter to the floor, heard her ex-clamation and shook his head. Who *was* this woman he'd signed a contract with? He'd thought he had her pretty well sized up until he'd heard her talking about some guy's yacht, inviting the crew to some party and letting the games begin.

What games?

A few minutes later when they met on the stairs again, Cole stepped aside to allow her and her bulging sack of trash to pass. "I put the leftovers away," he said, amused at the belligerent set of her delicate jaw. Skin like thick cream…color and texture. He wondered idly what it would taste like. "Thanks for lunch. I didn't figure in meals when I made that estimate."

"No problem," she said airily. Dropping the sack at the foot of the stairs, she clutched her back.

"Got a problem?"

"Nope," she said brightly. "Not a one." Aside from the fact that she was freezing, having turned off the furnace earlier when she'd seen him prop the door open to bring in supplies.

She watched him lope up the stairs, his feet barely making a sound on the oak treads. Those shoulders were made for carrying stacks of lumber. As for his long, muscular legs…

Oh, shut up and get to work, Owens!

The phone rang again just as she opened the door to take the lumpy sack of trash outside. She paused, then decided whoever it was, she wasn't in the mood to talk.

"Want me to get that?" Cole called after the fifth ring.

Probably a telemarketer. "Suit yourself," she called back. Or it could be Sasha, wanting to talk about Faylene's new hot prospects down at the marina. As if she didn't have enough on her mind without getting involved in another matchmaking project. Personally, she'd rather indulge in a small panic attack, brought on by hiring a sexy itinerant carpenter to tear her house apart on a gamble that stood less than a fifty-fifty chance of paying off. A few quiet little screams, a minute or two of beating her head on the garage wall—that should get it out of her system.

In her more rational moments, which admittedly were few and far between these days, Marty was forced to conclude that reading was no longer a favorite pastime. Even for those who still read, there were too many competing sources for books. Flea markets and chain stores, thrift shops and libraries, not to mention the Internet. If only half of her old regulars bought two paperbacks a week from Marty's New and Used, that would mean...

"Oh, shoot," she muttered. Maybe she should have opened up a tattoo parlor.

The next time she saw her carpenter he was gray-haired. She couldn't think of anything she'd said or done to cause it. If he'd torn everything up only to change his mind about the job, she was miles up the creek without so much as a pair of water wings, much less a paddle.

She should have insisted on references. Just because Bob Ed had recommended him—just because he had Faylene's approval...

Oh, boy. To challenge or not to challenge. Only time would tell, but time was exactly what she didn't have.

She decided on the oblique approach. "Who was on the phone?" she asked, closing the front door behind her.

"It didn't say."

"*It?*"

He shrugged. "Must have been one of those 'If-a-guy-answers, hang-up' calls."

Oh, great. Now she was getting hang-up calls.

At four-thirty, when Marty bundled up to give Mutt his afternoon run, Cole was hauling out the last stack of broken plasterboard. "Dog walk?" he asked.

"Yep. Will you be here when I get back?"

When he glanced at his watch, she caught herself staring at the way the muscles in his forearm moved under a film of dust. "I'm at a good stopping place, but I'd like to get some material upstairs, ready to start putting up your new walls tomorrow."

Well, that sounded promising. She held the door open for him, then watched as he stacked the trash and covered it with a plastic tarp. There was something endearing about a man who took such pains with trash. Alan had left newspapers and clothing scattered throughout the house. Beau, after the first few months, hadn't stayed home long enough to litter.

Cole watched her tug on earmuffs and a pair of thick knit gloves. Her nose and cheeks were already reacting to the cold wind. A complexion like that—Scottish or Irish ancestry, most likely—was the next best thing to a lie detector. Not that he thought she'd lied to him, but after Paula he was conditioned to expect any woman to lie if the truth happened to be inconvenient. With Paula, lying had been a catch-me-if-you-can game.

After a while he hadn't bothered to try.

"Want me to lock up when I leave?" he called as she was about to climb into her minivan.

"Not unless you're worried about your tools." Without waiting for a reply, she backed out onto the street just as a gray Mercedes pulled out of a driveway three houses down the street. It waited for her to pass before heading in the same direction. He noticed the car only because it was a few decades old—a nicely restored classic, in fact. The truck he drove now was one of Bob Ed's rent-a-junkers, but he could definitely appreciate a fine piece of machinery.

Mutt was excited to see her. "I guess he's bored," she said to the part-time attendant, a kid with a blue Mohawk and a gold earring, while she struggled to attach the leash to the dog's choke collar. She felt a little embarrassed to be using the thing, but Annie had told her it didn't hurt him at all—it helped to slow him down when he saw something he wanted to chase.

"What he needs is a few trucks to run after," Blue Mohawk said cheerfully.

"Pity the poor truck if he ever caught one."

"Naw, he'd just water the tires. You seen all these big, tall trucks. Now you know how they got that way."

Marty rolled her eyes and led the dog out, nearly tripping over him when he tried to wrap himself around her knees.

"What you need, my dear Super-Mutt, is a crash course in manners," she panted once the big shaggy creature pulled her out to the path that served as a sidewalk. "Take a left! Left! That way, dammit!"

They went right, toward the Hamburger Shanty, where Mutt knocked over a trash container and then tried to tackle her when she bent to collect the blowing garbage.

A gray Mercedes cruised past as if looking for a parking place. There were several available, but evidently the driver didn't care for the specials posted in the window. Triple cheeseburger, double fries, thirty-six-ounce drink? What's not to like, as long as you've got the metabolism of a hummingbird.

Mutt was sniffing at Egbert Blalock's tan Buick. The bank had just closed, and evidently the new vice-president was picking up a take-out supper. Egbert was known to be as stingy with the bank's money as if it were his own—which probably wasn't a bad thing in a banker.

"You want to pee on his tires? Be my guest."

This time the dog obeyed, but she knew better than to take credit for it.

It was barely five-thirty when she got home again, but already it was practically dark. Her lower back was zapping her after trying to hang on to Mutt's leash with one hand while she picked up the garbage he'd spilled with the other. Those platter-size feet of his could probably topple a Dumpster. Fortunately, he hadn't tried.

She was dimly aware of the gray sedan turning the corner of Parliament and Sugar Lane behind her.

"Need a hand?" Cole's face, showing only concern, appeared at the driver's window.

He was still here. Was that a laugh line or a wrinkle in his left cheek? Disgusting how attractive lines in a man's face could be, when women were forced to spend a fortune on wrinkle removers.

She opened the door, but her feet were no longer responding to orders from headquarters. "No, thanks." And then, because he still looked dubious, she said, "Did you ever try wrestling five hundred pounds of untrained mongrel that's determined to sniff every weed along the path? On both sides of the street?" Not to mention pee on every blade of grass along the way. She sighed and managed to extract first one leg and then the other without actually grimacing.

"This is a daily thing? The dog-walking?"

"Twice daily. I'm doing a favor for friends who've been looking forward to this trip for ages. The boarding kennel wouldn't accept Mutt unless someone agreed to walk him at least twice a day, because he's too big for the short runs they provide."

Actually, Mutt's owners weren't really friends of hers. They lived a few blocks over, but Annie had once been a regular customer and they'd been desperate. And Marty had needed the money.

She limped toward the house while Cole deposited another bag of trash on the area he'd set aside. Food first, she promised herself—then a hot soak and bed. Those strong hands of his on her lower back wouldn't be unwelcome, either, she thought wistfully

Quit it! The last thing you need is another man in your life.

As he was right behind her all the way to the front door, she tried not to limp. Tried not to collapse, coat, earmuffs, gloves and all, on the living room sofa. Instead, she turned and asked, "Was there something you needed?"

"You had three more phone calls."

She lifted an eyebrow. At least she still had a few muscles that worked without causing pain. "Well?"

"A Ms. Beasley who said she could come any day next week if you want to start setting up the books. I think she's the one I met at the marina, who told me you needed a builder. You're to call her when you're ready."

Marty murmured, "Bless her heart." Faylene knew very well Marty was nowhere near ready for that.

Standing close enough so that she could smell a combination of freshly sawed lumber and a subtle aftershave, Cole continued. "There was a call from someone named Sasha. At least, that's what it sounded like. Anyway, she has some carpet samples she's bringing by in the morning."

"I'm not nearly ready for carpet and she knows it." More curiosity. "Anything else?"

"Another of those 'If-a-man-answers, hang-up' calls."

Marty closed her eyes. "Oh, shoot, shoot, shoot. I hate that kind of thing, don't you? It ought to be against the law."

"Probably just a wrong number."

When she opened her eyes again, he was still there. Still looking big and solid and protective and all the good things the romance stories described—things that she had never personally experienced. If she'd needed another clue that she was almost ready for an over-the-counter de-stress medication, that was it.

"Look, I closed up the house and turned on the heat again. Why don't you take off a few layers while I make you a pot of coffee? Once you warm up, maybe you'll feel more like—"

Better yet, turn the dog loose, call a cruise line and make reservations for two and you're on. What was it that caused two strangers to bond based on a few casual exchanges?

Or at least, caused one person to bond?

Five

Cole ended up staying for supper, partly because he had nothing better to do and partly because her house, even with a faint lingering odor of polyurethane and burnt cinnamon, was a hell of a lot more comfortable than the *Time Out* with its faint odor of mildew and inefficient space heater.

It has nothing to do with the woman, he assured himself. Nothing to do with the fact that he enjoyed her company—enjoyed even more speculating about what she'd be like in bed. So far as he could tell, she hadn't done a single thing to attract his attention.

Maybe that was it. She used natural bait, not an artificial lure.

He had no business fishing in these particular waters, no matter how tempted he was. On the other hand, she looked as if she needed someone to dump on. Her two friends probably had their own baggage. At least, she didn't seem too eager to speak to either of them.

He happened to be both handy and baggage free. A disinterested party, so to speak.

And you're going to damn well stay that way, right?

Right!

"The thing is," Marty said as she opened a diet drink and a bottle of Blackhook porter, "I really don't have time for fun and games right now." She handed him the ale. "Do you want a glass for that?"

"Bottle's fine." Fun and games? She'd explained briefly about their favorite pastime of matchmaking—which explained part of the conversation he'd overheard. "Don't your victims have anything to say about it?"

"I'd hardly call them victims. I mean, look how many people try to meet other people in chat rooms. And lots of people go on blind dates."

"Of their own free will. Nothing's forced on them."

"We've never forced anything on anyone," she protested. "All we do is arrange for X to meet Y, and they can take it from there."

"X and Y as in chromosomes?"

"Hadn't thought of it that way," she said, gray eyes twinkling. "Anyway, I'm too busy trying to figure out how to fit a bunch of ten-foot bookshelves into my two front rooms to worry about the social life of our neighborhood CPA. Any advice would be greatly appreciated."

"Your CPA's probably about to have all the social life she needs, with tax season looming dead ahead."

"I meant advice with the bookshelves."

"Oh. Right." What the hell, he wasn't one of her busy-buddies. What did he know about matchmaking? "That's not a problem."

"Maybe not in theory. Just whack the shelves in two and close up the open ends. I'm good at theory, just not so great when it comes to the actual whacking and closing."

"I can do one or two for you after supper."

Her doubtful look gradually gave way to a smile that was all the more effective for a tiny chip on the corner of a front tooth. Oh, man, this natural bait was wicked stuff.

"You don't have to do that," she protested.

He was tempted to agree. It wasn't a part of their agreement. On the other hand, he wasn't particularly eager to go back to the marina. This small yellow bungalow, even with a portion of the second floor gutted, was a hell of a lot more comfortable than the cold, damp cabin of a forty-year-old cruiser.

Yeah, sure. The house is the only attraction.

She was saying something about the dog, about how she was already dreading tomorrow's walk. "Rain or shine, he has to get out twice a day for a run, and the Hallets won't be back for… Oh, lawsy, five more days? I'm not sure my arms will survive."

Cole helped clear away the remains of supper as if he'd been doing it all his life. It had been Paula who'd insisted on hiring a combination cook-housekeeper. When he'd protested that with only the two of them they didn't really need it, and besides, they couldn't afford it, she had meekly agreed. A few weeks later he'd received a surprise promotion and a hefty raise.

He'd been excited at first about getting in on the architectural side of the business. That had always been his goal. He'd even managed to get half a degree in architecture before he'd damaged his left knee, putting an end to his football scholarship.

But not even when he'd been relegated to the job of selecting from a set number of styles and floor plans and making superficial changes among them had he tumbled to the fact that he was a kept man.

Once he'd been given the job of working on more challenging projects like the Murdock Office Complex and the Josephine Civic Center, he'd settled in and actually begun to enjoy the work.

That is, until too many accidents had aroused his suspicions and he'd started coming in early and staying late, poking into areas that were out of his jurisdiction.

Now he followed Marty into the living room, where she pointed out the potential placement of her bookshelves. "That wall's the longest. There are eleven of them, and if possible, I'd like to fit them into these two rooms." She waved a hand, indicating the small dining room that currently doubled as a home office. "I thought I'd use the kitchen for an office and box room. The table won't fit upstairs, but it'll be great for unpacking."

Stroking his stubbled jaw—he was a twice-a-day shaver when neatness counted—Cole studied the layout. One thing about living aboard a small boat—you learned to make the most of every square inch of space.

"Sasha has some wild ideas about colors—she's this friend I was telling you about. You spoke to her on the phone? Anyway, she's an interior designer—she's supposed to be tops in this area—but she thinks I need to paint my walls three different shades of red—can you believe it? She says with the north light I need to make it not just inviting, but exciting."

The room was already inviting, to Cole's way of thinking. Walls painted a warm, creamy shade with furnishings a comfortable mixture of old and not-quite-so-old. It looked just right to him. Nothing really outstanding—at least, nothing that screamed, "Keep off the furniture!"

Paula had insisted on an all-white color scheme to show off her art collection. He'd hated the damn stuff, her so-called art included.

Marty had a couple of pictures on the wall. One a reproduction of a marsh scene, the other a factory-produced oil of a cloudy sunset on the water. Both were pleasant enough. Hell of a lot better than Paula's primary color abstracts, anyway.

Walking around the two rooms that, along with the kitchen and a laundry-utility room, made up the first floor, Cole mentally transposed the bookshelves with the furniture that currently occupied the space. Damn shame to crowd all this into one room upstairs, but it was her house.

Marty was following him around like a hungry pup waiting for a handout. He was no miracle worker. He could remodel her second floor, but he couldn't guarantee anything beyond that. Sensing her anxiety, he said, "You've got choices, you know."

"Choices. You mean colors?"

He heard her sigh and turned to find her only a couple of steps behind. Too close. His hand brushed her hip and electricity sizzled. The way she jumped back, she must have felt it, too.

Sounding slightly breathless, she said, "I'll have to fight for them. Did you ever hear of a velvet-covered steamroller? That's Sasha."

"I'm talking about your arrangements, not your color

scheme." Her mouth looked soft, tired and discouraged. Staring at it, he thought, What the hell—a little encouragement wouldn't cost him anything.

Fortunately, before he could act on his impulse, his survival instinct kicked in. Taking a deep breath, he said, "You want to know what I think? I'm betting you can hold your own against any steamroller, velvet-covered or not."

It drew the ghost of a response. Not quite a smile, but at least those full, naked lips didn't look quite so discouraged. "Yes, well…you don't know Sasha."

Nor was he sure he wanted to meet her.

Marty shook her head. "I've tried arranging those darn shelves ever which-a-way on paper, but the proportions are all wrong for here. I had them custom built for my old place, but—" She shook her head again. "Am I crazy to even think of doing what I'm doing? Don't answer that—it's way, way too late." This time she actually chuckled.

It affected him in more ways than he cared to admit.

"People remodel all the time. In a house this age, it's probably overdue."

"Sure, to add a downstairs bath and maybe a room or two over the garage, but turning it into a retail outlet?"

He was tempted to pull her head down on his shoulder and tell her not to worry, that it was always darkest before the dawn, or some other meaningless fairy tale.

"Customers have to be able to move freely, you know? They're not going to browse in a room where they feel claustrophobic."

Moving to stand behind her, Cole placed one hand on her shoulder and used his other to gesture. "Eighteen feet, right? Fifteen of usable space between the door and the corner. How about we cut a few of your bookshelves down to about six feet, butt them up against the wall here, here and here." He indicated the area, his arm brushing against her shoulder. "That should give you plenty of clearance on the open end, and you can use the corner space beside the door for wall shelves."

"Cut them down?" Regardless of what she'd said earlier about whacking, she sounded as if he'd suggested cutting her legs off just above the ankles. Spinning around, she had to step back to keep from stumbling. He was that close. When he put out a hand to steady her, her eyes widened, sucking him into the cloud-gray depths.

Flowers. Even with the faint echoes of paint and burnt spice, he smelled flowers. There wasn't a damn thing blooming in her yard. It had to be the woman herself. No makeup, wild hair, clothes that could have come from any thrift shop—and she smelled like a tropical garden.

He leaned closer. She froze, a deer-in-the-headlights look in her eyes. *Don't do it, man—you're starting something you're in no position to finish.*

"Like we talked about before—shorten them," he said gruffly, stepping back to a safe distance.

Her cheeks flushed with color, she nodded slowly. "And I could use the short ends over here—and here." She gestured toward the space between windows and on either side. "And there's still the dining room."

She gradually lost the bemused look, if that's what it was. He was no expert when it came to reading a woman's expression, but she no longer looked wary. Actually, she looked almost excited, and an excited Marty Owens was a little too infectious for his peace of mind. He moved back and leaned against the door frame while she walked around, motioning with her hands, muttering to herself—soft little sounds she probably wasn't even aware of making.

And who'd have thought gray eyes could darken and sparkle that way? He wondered if that was how she'd look in bed, after—

"I'd better be getting back to the marina." It was one thing to hang around and help her plan her building project. It was another thing entirely to—

Yeah, well…forget about that. "I'd like to get here about seven tomorrow, if that's not too early." That way she'd be out walking her dog and he could start work without any enticing distractions.

Marty watched until Cole's truck disappeared, allowing her imagination free range. What was it about men and the way they dressed? Ninety-nine out of a hundred might as well be wearing baggy bib overalls for all the difference it made. She might even know and like them personally, but there was no chemistry. No *click*.

And then, along came that one out of a hundred—a thousand—wearing faded jeans and a plain black tee, and she immediately started wondering….

Be still, my heart.

A few minutes later she gathered her wandering wits and focused on her immediate problem. At least, one of her problems. She wandered around, studying the available space and jotting notes on the back of an envelope. If she used the utility room instead of the kitchen for—

That wouldn't work. No way was she going to squeeze a washer and drier into her upstairs hall, even after re-modeling. The living room and dining room would provide enough display space, using the kitchen for—

The refrigerator. Oh, shoot. All she'd have room for in her new kitchenette would be one of those dorm-size models.

She could worry about that later. Meanwhile, just when it seemed as if her plan was not going to work, suddenly everything was falling into place, thanks to a sexy carpenter with shaggy hair, greeny gold eyes and a smile that could melt porcelain.

All of which was totally beside the point, she reminded herself forcefully.

Still, ever since she'd conceived the idea, she had thought she'd considered every possible way to fit eleven ten-foot-long bookshelves into the available space. And said sexy carpenter had given her the answer.

On Wednesday morning Marty was up long before daylight, wide awake for once, even though she'd stayed awake far into the night mentally arranging and rearranging her new showroom. The kennel didn't open until seven, which was when Cole was due.

She gulped down a glass of orange juice, winced as it hit her empty stomach, then bundled up and hurried outside, leaving the front door unlocked. The damp, cold northeast wind was still howling like a chorus of banshees. Occasionally they got a day when the temperature hit the seventies in January, but not this year.

Mutt loved the weather. There was probably some polar bear in him somewhere. With his shaggy coat streaming out behind him, he galloped off down Water Street toward his favorite destination, the Hamburger Shanty. Yelling at him was like yelling at a long-haired locomotive. She did it anyway. According to an article in one of the women's magazines Sasha was always bringing her with the pertinent pages turned down, yelling was a great stress-reliever.

Mutt ignored the shouts. If any of the few passersby heard her and wondered if she was stark raving bonkers, one look should clear up the mystery. The damn dog marched to a different drummer.

Or galloped to a different scent. Nary a signpost along the way went un-watered nor a weed un-sniffed between the kennel and his favorite buffet, the trash bins outside the Hamburger Shanty that weren't emptied until later that morning.

There were a few cars in the parking lot. Staff, mostly, as the place wouldn't open for another twenty minutes or so. A semi-familiar gray Mercedes cruised by slowly, probably looking for a place that served breakfast. It was the same one she'd seen yesterday—and come to think of it, hadn't the same car been parked in the Caseys' driveway?

A house sitter, maybe. The Caseys were in Florida, but they hadn't mentioned a sitter the last time Marty had spoken to Ruth Casey before they'd left.

"All right, I'm coming!" she yelled, as Mutt lunged at the stray cat that was nosing around in what he considered his private pantry.

Some twenty minutes later she finally closed the door to his unit at the kennel.

The blue-haired kid grinned at her. "Reg'lar handful, ain't he."

She shot him a dirty look. "You could've at least helped me get him out of his choke collar."

"Not in my job description. Hey, they don't pay me enough to wrestle critters like him."

"What *do* they pay you for?" First she had ruined her lower back on all those heavy bookshelves, and now her arms were in danger of being pulled from the sockets.

"Answer the phone. Take money. Make reservations."

"Don't strain yourself," she jeered.

When had she turned into such a shrew? Was that one of the symptoms of a shortage of vitamin S?

Cole was there by the time she got home, his truck pulled over to one side to make room for her minivan. He was a thoughtful man—she'd already discovered that about him. Whether or not he was a competent carpenter remained to be seen. He was good at tearing up. What else was he good at? she wondered before she could stop herself.

Don't ask. There are more important things in life than sex.
Oh, yeah? Name one.

"Hello, I'm home," she called, wincing as she wriggled out of her coat and dropped it on the hall bench. Later she might hang it in the closet, but first she had to collapse and catch her breath. Once she found the energy she might pop a couple of ibuprofen and rustle up something for breakfast. A spoonful of peanut butter would be quick and easy.

Hearing footsteps, she glanced up to see her carpenter loping down the stairs. In those faded jeans and a black shirt, he was almost too macho to be a male model except maybe in one of those sporting goods catalogs.

"G'morning," she greeted, offering him a tired smile.

"Looks like you just lost a marathon," he observed.

"Came in on the ragtag end, as usual. Believe me, it's not worth the money."

"You, uh…get paid?"

She nodded. "If I'd been introduced to that damn dog before the Hallets left town, never in this world would I have agreed to go near him."

"That bad, huh?" Cole said a moment later when he rejoined her in the hall.

Bless his heart, he'd gone directly to the kitchen and switched on the coffeepot she'd left all ready for when she got back. It occurred to her that no man had ever made coffee for her before—not even one of her husbands.

For some reason, that made her want to cry.

Allergies. It had to be allergies. "He not only outweighs me by a ton, he out-stubborns me by a mile," she said. "Don't laugh, it's not as easy as you might think." She grinned, but her heart wasn't in it.

He was standing. She was still seated. Lacking the energy to turn away, she was faced with a portion of male anatomy that was somewhat dusty but nonetheless impressive.

He said, "I thought this was a personal favor you were doing for friends. Didn't you know what he was like when you offered to walk him?"

"I told you, I'd never even seen him before I agreed. The way Annie talked about him having his own furniture and all, I knew he was a house pet. I guess I expected a poodle, or maybe a cocker spaniel. How many people keep a Clydesdale in their house?" She began flexing her shoulders and heard a disturbing crackling sound near the back of her neck.

"Annie?" Cole prompted as he hung her coat in the closet.

"She's one of my best customers. Actually, I only know her from the bookstore. They live several blocks over, but I've never even met her husband. Faylene says he's a lawyer. She said he'd just won his first case after practicing for nearly six years, which is why they decided to celebrate with this cruise."

"First case, huh?"

She sighed and closed her eyes. "According to Faylene, but that doesn't make it gospel. Anyhow, when Annie called and asked me if I could pick him up at the kennel and walk him twice a day, I said sure." Marty didn't bother to add that the money Annie had insisted on paying her was a large part of the inducement. Opening her eyes, she lifted her gaze to his tanned, weathered face. "You know what? I'll bet they asked everyone else they knew, but all their friends turned them down. Dumb me."

He was smiling at her again. Lordy, the man was too much! He said, "Chalk it up to a learning experience. Next time the guy wins a case and wants to take another vacation, don't be so quick to volunteer."

He moved closer. She felt him touch her shoulder, felt the firm pressure of his thumbs on the rock-hard muscles at the back of her neck. Tipping her head forward, she groaned.

"Don't worry, you couldn't pay me enough to—ahh!"

"This where it hurts, the trapezius?"

"Oh, yesss," she purred.

Cole eased her around so that he could use both hands. She was as tense as a ten-pound test line with a sixty-pound channel bass on the other end. Under three layers of clothing the skin was like warm satin. He sniffed. Flowers again. He wondered if her whole body smelled like that, or...

A final gurgle from the kitchen announced that the coffee was ready. "You want to stay here in the hall or hit the sofa?"

"I'd rather hit a bed or a hot bath," she admitted with a weak chuckle, "but I don't think I can make it up the stairs."

If that was a hint, he wasn't taking it. No way.

Unfortunately, his body had lost contact with his brain. "You had breakfast yet?"

"Just juice." She put a hand on the small of her back and stood.

Come to think if it, he'd seen her grab her back a time or two yesterday. "Hey, are you sure you're all right?"

"I'm fine. Nothing a few ibuprofen won't take care of."

"How many?" Cole had been that route, only in his case it had been a prescription painkiller after he'd been worked over by a couple of thugs hired by his ex-father-in-law. That was all ancient history, but he'd learned a few valuable lessons in the process. Never trust a guy whose neck is thicker than the width between his ears, especially if he calls your father-in-law Boss. And don't risk ruining your brain and your belly with anything more potent than beer, ale, or the occasional glass of Jack's finest.

"How are we doing upstairs?" she asked with a smile that didn't quite reach her eyes.

In other words, he interpreted, *Butt out of my personal business.*

"I'll start closing the end section today. By tomorrow I should be ready to start on your cabinets."

"I don't want anything fancy."

"Just sketch out precisely what you have in mind. We've got a little leeway but not a whole lot."

Did that mean she was allowed to join him upstairs while he worked? How about after hours?

How about concentrating on what's important, Marty reminded herself. While Cole headed for the kitchen, she wandered into the living room and eased herself down onto the sofa. Her stomach didn't exactly welcome the thought of coffee, but she needed something to start her engine.

"Lots of cream," she called out.

"Yes, ma'am."

A polite carpenter. With good hands. Slow, firm hands that knew exactly where to touch and how much pressure to apply, stopping just short of actual pain. Sasha would have a field day if she could tune in on her musings right now, Marty thought, amused.

The coffee was welcome, even if her stomach was pumping acid by the gallon. Weeks ago she'd gone online and checked out everything she could find about stress and the physical manifestations thereof. How to avoid it, or at least how to deal with it. The trouble was, she didn't have time for tai chi. As for yoga, which she used to enjoy, she would never even make it past the Sun Salutes.

Music was another recommendation. Daisy had given her a dreamy New Age CD, but the stuff only made her race her engines, waiting for the music to get to the point instead of rambling all over the scale.

Yelling seemed to be her only option. It was free and the side effects were probably minimal—but she needed something to yell at. She was far too inhibited to step outside and do the primal scream thing.

"I made you some toast."

She opened her eyes. Pavarotti with the frog in his throat was back. He was too good to be real.

"Do you really need that ibuprofen?" he asked.

She sighed. "I guess not." Pills couldn't cure a broken back. She needed the pain to tell her how bad off she was.

"When do you have to do the next dog run?"

"This afternoon. Anytime between two and six when the kennel closes."

"I'll go with you. I need to go by the hardware store anyway for cabinet materials. What breed did you say this dog was?"

"St. Bernard and Clydesdale mix. Maybe some polar bear. Annie said they got him from the pound when he was nothing but a little ol' fuzz ball. Ha!"

"So now he's a big ol' fuzz ball."

Cole switched on a lamp to offset the gray morning. Instead of heading back upstairs, he settled into her one man-size chair. Marty struggled to a semi-reclining position. She'd rather stay flat, but siphoning coffee through a rubber hose wasn't an option, so semi seemed advisable.

"What about—you know?" She nodded toward the ceiling.

"Like I said, I'm ahead of schedule. I allow for a couple of short breaks during the day. Now, tell me what kind of wood you want. It makes a difference in how you want them finished. Raw, painted, pickled or varnished."

"What would you suggest?"

They discussed styles, wood finishes and hardware. "I'll take you to pick that out after I get the things built."

"Oh, so I finally get to voice an opinion. Does that mean I can go upstairs while you're there, or do I have to wait until you leave and write down a work order."

"My, my—snide, aren't we?"

"Yes, we are," she snapped, and took another sip of coffee. Which he had made and served, she reminded herself. After he'd laid hands on her and taken away more of her pain than he probably knew. Taken her mind off it, anyway.

She yawned. Bad back, dream-filled sleep…

The last thing she remembered was feeling the cup eased from her fingers. Then something light and warm drifted down over her body. He didn't turn off the lamp, but tilted the shade so it wouldn't shine in her eyes.

"Don't leave without me this afternoon," he said quietly.

"Mmm," she murmured.

The classic gray Mercedes was gone from the Caseys' driveway by the time they left home just before four that afternoon, Marty noticed. She tried to remember exactly when the Caseys had left. According to Faylene, who knew practically everyone in town and most of their business, they'd gone to Tampa to see their first grandchild. A boy. Named Todd.

"Weather's moderating," Cole observed.

They were in his rattletrap of a truck so he could pick up the lumber needed to do her cabinets and the bookshelves on the way home from walking Mutt.

Or rather, from chasing after the creature, trying to hang on to his lead. For once, Marty thought, relieved, she could trot along behind and let someone else do the hard work. Cole had even offered to go in and fetch the dog from his wire-walled cubicle.

"Be my guest," Marty said, leaning back against the headrest. Through sleepy eyes, she watched his hand on the gearshift. Nice hands...strong, but sensitive. She knew how they felt.

She yawned for the third time since they'd left home.

"Need another nap? What's the matter, does all the mess upstairs keep you from sleeping?" he asked.

Well...maybe his hands weren't what impressed her most, but they impressed her a whole lot.

"I sleep perfectly well," she lied. "It's this weather. Maybe I'm part bear. Cold, rainy days I tend to want to hibernate."

Did bears hibernate two to a cave? Maybe they were onto something, she mused.

A few minutes later when Cole and Mutt emerged from the door at the top of five wooden steps, Marty climbed out and joined them. Mutt was in high fettle. They reached the corner of Water and Third streets and Cole tugged lightly on the lead and flipped his right hand.

Mutt obediently veered right.

Marty stopped dead in her tracks. "How did you do that?"

"How did I do what?"

He was hatless. With the wind ruffling his hair and plastering his leather bomber jacket to his chest, he looked wildly attractive and more than a little dangerous.

"How'd you get him to turn there? I always have to pull my arms out of the sockets getting him to go where I want him to go."

"Don't you use hand signals?"

"Both my hands are occupied. In case you hadn't noticed, he pulls like a six-mule team."

"Marty, you do know he's deaf, don't you? Didn't they even tell you that much?" Cole snapped his fingers. The dog didn't even look around.

She shook her head slowly. She was beginning to believe there was a lot the Hallets hadn't told her—probably knowing that if they had, she might have refused the job.

"He's also got a ripe cataract in one eye."

"Well…shoot."

Mutt sat on his broad haunches, a big, sappy grin on his tricolored face, while Cole explained about his handicaps. "He's still got good vision in one eye. As for his hearing, all you have to do is see how he responds to hand signals."

"But—but I never gave him any hand signals," she protested.

"Not intentionally. He's obviously used to watching for them, though, so when you wave your hands first one way and then another, he's confused. Being a dog, he simply does whatever he wants to do, which is usually to mark his territory and explore any interesting scents."

Chagrined, Marty was still thinking about how many clues she had missed by the time they headed back to the kennel. She'd never owned a dog. Had always wanted one, but first there was school and then there was Alan to look after, and later she'd been too busy all day with Marty's New and Used. It wouldn't have been fair to leave a dog at home alone all day.

Excuses, excuses. The truth was, it took just about all her energy to manage her business without having to worry about looking after a pet.

Some women did it all, some didn't. She'd even managed to kill off a potted philodendron, which, according to Sasha, was all but impossible.

Mutt acted as though he was glad to be back, standing still—or as still as a big dog could when his stub of a tail was flapping a hundred miles an hour.

Cole went through a few basic signals and the big, shaggy dog performed beautifully, after which Mutt was rewarded with a bit of roughhouse tussling before he was shut into his compartment.

Leaving the building, Marty said, "You must have owned dogs, you know so much about them."

But before he could tell her how he'd come by his knowledge, a now-familiar gray sedan cruised past slowly.

Marty stopped, one hand on Cole's sleeve. "You see that car that just passed? If I didn't know better I'd think it was following me. Lately I seem to see it everywhere I go."

Cole watched as the 220SL disappeared around a corner, then he opened her door of his pickup. "They're not all that uncommon, even the older ones," he observed.

"I know that."

"If you didn't recognize it, it's probably an out-of-town visitor."

"This time of year? Any visitors we get in the wintertime are usually hunters, and they rarely drive Mercedes, not even the SUVs. Besides, I've seen this same gray car parked down the street in a neighbor's driveway, and I happen to know they're in Florida."

Six

Marty insisted on going to the lumberyard with him, and Cole indulged her. It was her money, after all. She was still chafing over the dog—over missing such obvious clues. If he hadn't known it before, he did now—she liked to be the one in control.

Most women did. Paula had disguised that side of her nature with a helpless, clinging-vine act that had held up for almost a year after they were married. Helpless like one of those pretty flowering vines that could conquer anything in its path, given enough time.

"Here y' go, sir. That be cash or credit?"

"Credit card," Marty said, pushing her gold card across the desk. "Might as well earn the three cents interest on my money between now and the end of the month."

"Pick up around back," the clerk said, and Marty marched ahead to lead the way through the vast metal building.

Strolling along behind her, Cole deliberately shortened his stride to let her go first. Funny woman. Militantly independent, smart enough to know when to shut up and listen, yet unafraid to admit when she was out of her depth. The way she had watched, listened and learned when he'd demonstrated how to control that big goofy dog was a good example. You had to admire a woman like that.

Somewhat to his surprise, Cole realized that he not only admired her, he liked her.

He loaded the lumber into the back of the truck, secured it with ropes from the toolbox on back, and turned back to where Marty waited. "If you don't mind my working late to make up the time, I'll go with you again in the morning to make sure you can handle him. Trouble with a deaf dog is that once he gets away from you, calling and whistling won't get him back."

"Believe me, I thought of that," Marty said grimly.

Before he could help her up, she grabbed the door frame and swung herself up into the cab.

He closed the door. "You'll do fine, but it won't hurt to be doubly careful."

Once they got back to the house she insisted on helping him unload the truck. "I can carry one end of the boards while you carry the other."

"Be easier if I balance 'em on my shoulder."

She looked at the two-by-fours and the yellow pine boards, then looked at his shoulder. They did it his way, which was far more efficient than having to juggle each plank between them. She went ahead to open the doors, and he watched her simply because she was worth watching, even in a down-filled coat, with her windblown hair tangling around her earmuffs.

By the time the last plank was stacked in the hallway upstairs it was almost dark. Marty insisted he stay for supper.

"It's the least I can do after you taught me dog language. It'll be something quick and easy. I'll just pop a couple of frozen dinners into the microwave."

Bad move, Cole told himself. Really bad move. After three days he was already having trouble thinking of her as just another employer. "You don't have to do this. I can stop off on the way to the marina and get take-out." In fact, he'd sort of counted on it. Meat, bread and two vegetables. Barbecue, hush puppies, slaw and fries. He knew how to take care of himself—had been doing it for nearly forty years now.

He followed her into the kitchen. It was a nice room. It reminded him of his mother's kitchen, only there was no sheet music scattered over every surface. Paula's kitchen had looked more like a laboratory—not that she'd ever spent much time in it. It occurred to him that he'd never thought of it as their kitchen, not even when they'd first moved in a few months after they were married. Her father had insisted on giving them the house, which had prompted Paula's one and only attempt at humor. She'd told him not to look a gift house in the mouth.

Marty left the utility door open while she checked out the contents of a small, chest-type freezer. With her jeans stretched tightly over her rounded behind, she leaned over to scramble through the contents. Cole made himself look away. Against the taut denim he could see the faint outline of her underpants. Definitely not a thong.

Cut it out, Stevens!

So he forced himself to check out his employer's kitchen instead of her personal assets, pretending a great interest in the double-hung windows over the sink, the leafy vine trailing down from a jar on the narrow sill and the sun-catcher hanging from the curtain rod. The yellow-and-white checked curtains matched the tablecloth. She went in for a lot of yellow. On a day like this, with barely enough daylight to wedge in an eight-hour day, it made the room feel warm and cheerful.

"Here we go," Marty announced, holding out two boxes, one a well-known diet brand, the other Salisbury steak with a side of macaroni and cheese. "Your choice."

He appeared to study the two flat boxes before choosing the two-hundred-and-eighty calorie delight.

She looked surprised. "Are you sure?"

Sure he was sure. It would serve as an appetizer until he could stop for his usual barbecue plate on the way to the marina. Odds were she was in for the night, and he didn't want her going to bed hungry.

They didn't talk much over supper. He studied the three tablespoonfuls of whatever it was he was eating and hoped his belly wouldn't embarrass him by protesting too loudly.

A few minutes later Marty shoved her plastic tray aside. "As Faylene would say, it's pretty good, what there is of it, and there's plenty of it, such as it is. You said you'd met her—Faylene Beasley? Bob Ed's friend? That's the way she talks most of the time."

"In circles, you mean," Cole said as he tried to remember what the woman had said about her friend who needed a small remodeling job done. "Look, about tonight—I said I'd work overtime to make up for taking off early, so—"

"You didn't take off early. You were still—that is—"

"Still on the clock?" he suggested, amused because she looked so embarrassed. He knew better than most that knocking down the barriers between employee and employer was asking for trouble.

"In a manner of speaking," she said primly, and he had to laugh.

To hell with the barriers.

And then she laughed, too. He lapped it up like a cat with a saucer of cream—the way her eyes kindled, the way her lips twitched at the corners just before she gave in and laughed aloud. He had a strong feeling that she hadn't done too much of that lately—laughing, that is. He didn't know why it bothered him, but it did.

When she stood and reached across the table for his tray and coffee mug, her hair swung over her shoulders, and he caught a whiff of that mysterious fragrance again. Flowers. Something soft, subtle and sweet—maybe shampoo, maybe hand lotion. Odds were she hadn't bothered to douse herself with perfume just for his benefit.

Jeez, he'd known her all of what—three days? A smart man would get the hell out before he did anything crazy, like touching her. Like seeing if all that rich mahogany hair of hers was as soft as it looked. Granted, he'd been through a long, dry spell—he was probably suffering from a buildup of testosterone. But there was nothing wrong with his brain. He *knew* what he ought to do.

The hard part was doing it.

"Tell you what," he announced, sliding his chair away from the table and glancing down to make sure he could pass muster without pulling his shirttail out of his jeans. "I'll measure up one of your bookshelves and cut the end boards and braces before I leave. First thing tomorrow we can finish it up. Then, while I work upstairs, you can decide if you want the rest of them cut down the same way. What do you say?"

She said yes.

They worked in the garage, with barely enough room to move around. The only way he could keep from brushing against her was to work on the opposite side of the project, but even that didn't prevent contact. As the garage wasn't insulated, Marty had bundled up in an old coat and pulled a stocking cap down over her ears. She should have looked like a ragamuffin kid. Instead, she looked—

Yeah, well…let's not go there, Cole warned himself.

"That ought to do it," he said after the final cut had been made and the short section laid aside. He stood, flexed his back and looked around for a broom.

"Don't bother, I'll clean up in the morning," she told him. "Would you like—that is, the coffee's still warm."

And so was he. Warm didn't begin to describe the way he was feeling after spending the past half hour working in a small crowded space, brushing hands and shoulders, even backing into her a few times. Purely accidental touches, but that didn't make it any easier to ignore the electricity that sparked between them.

He wondered if she'd even noticed, and decided she hadn't. Otherwise, she'd never have invited him to stay for coffee.

"I'd better get on back to the marina and run the bilge pump before I turn in." Yeah, that'd do it, all right. Cram his six feet two inches and one-hundred-eighty-seven pounds into a shower a quarter of the size of a phone booth while he rinsed off the sawdust, and then try to get to sleep on a bunk designed for a guy half his age and half his size.

It occurred to him that the lifestyle that had seemed so great back when he'd first decided not to look for an apartment in the Norfolk area wasn't turning out quite the way he'd planned.

Hell, now he even wanted to get himself a dog.

The first day of February produced a few adventurous crocuses and the promise of an early spring. Marty had slept like a log—dreamed a lot of crazy stuff that left her tingling and vaguely unsatisfied when she first opened her eyes, but the dreams quickly faded as she stood zombie-like under the shower.

Walk the dog. Had Cole said to wait for him? She couldn't remember, but even if he had, she didn't recall agreeing. Better if he started putting her amputated bookshelf back together while she put Mutt through his paces.

Hand signals. Surely she could remember the ones he'd showed her yesterday. Right, left, stop, sit, stay. What else? Quit peeing on the dandelions? Leave that poor cat alone?

She saw headlights flash across the front window before she'd even gotten the coffeepot ready for when she got back. Darn it, she needed to do this by herself, if only to prove that she could.

But it was Sasha's red convertible, not Cole's pickup truck that pulled up behind her minivan. Curbing her impatience, she opened the front door. "Isn't this a bit early, even for you?" Contrary to appearances, her glamorous friend started her working days early and sometimes worked into the wee hours.

"Give me a doughnut and tell me how he's working out," Sasha demanded.

"They're in the freezer. You'll break a tooth. How who's working out?" As if she didn't know. Where bachelors were concerned, Sasha's radar system was the envy of governmental agencies all over the world.

The interior designer stamped the damp earth off her three-hundred-dollar stiletto-heel shoes, then brushed past Marty and headed for the kitchen in a cloud of her favorite Odalisque. "Open your eyes, take a deep breath and wake up, hon."

"Don't you have anything to eat at your house?" Marty grumbled. Sasha knew she was never at her best this time of morning. Today was even worse than usual, thanks to spending half the night dreaming dreams that refused to disperse.

"Why bother? I'm always out for lunch and dinner, and you're right on my way for breakfast." Sasha plopped her well-rounded behind in one of the mule-eared kitchen chairs. "So tell me this—have y'all been to bed yet?"

Marty was tempted to say yes. Technically, it was no lie. She'd been to bed and she assumed Cole had, too—only not together. "Sash, he's my carpenter. That's *all* he is, okay?"

"Just asking. I still want him for Lily. Faye says he's perfect, but if you're interested, I guess we can find somebody else for her."

"I am not interested!" Marty all but shouted. "At least not that way. But if you distract him so he can't finish up my work on time, I'll never forgive you."

"Pish-tush. Course you will, honey. Besides, all we want for Lily is whatever's left after you get through with him."

"Argh," Marty growled.

"Did I tell you I'm doing this place on the bay for the CEO of PGP? Hey, if you don't have Krispy Kremes, how about some cinnamon toast? Lots of butter, lots of sugar, just a dash of cinnamon?"

"Sorry, I burned up all my cinnamon. Plain buttered whole wheat is the best I can do."

"Oh, God, you're just so disgustingly wholesome. Is that him? I heard a truck out front."

Well, shoot. "You hung around deliberately just so I'd have to introduce you, didn't you."

The redhead's smug look was all the answer Marty needed. By that time Cole was at the door and there was nothing she could do to postpone the inevitable.

"You ready to roll?" he called as he stepped into the hall.

"Come on in the kitchen a minute. There's someone I want you to meet." Sure, she did. Like she wanted a face full of zits.

"Sasha, this is Cole Stevens. Cole, Sasha." Through narrowed eyes, she watched for any reaction.

Cole grinned and looked over the short, shapely, over-dressed redhead without even bothering to disguise his interest. Amazement or amusement, she couldn't be sure.

"Nice to meet you, Ms. uh—Sasha. I believe we spoke on the phone."

Sasha all but drooled. "Well, my goodness gracious, aren't you a sight for sore eyes." It was a statement, not a question.

"Sasha," Marty warned softly.

"I just meant, poor Marty's been so desperate for a man—that is, for someone to tear her house up and put it back together again."

"Oops, look at the time. I guess you'll have to stop off at IHOP on the way north," Marty said with a grim smile. Sasha didn't have a mean bone in her body, but mischief was her middle name. "Cole's got work to do, I've got to walk Mutt, and then we've got loads of stuff to accomplish today— Isn't that right, Cole?"

He nodded obediently, those tarnished brass eyes gleaming with amusement. She would have swatted him if it wouldn't have given Sasha so much satisfaction. Nothing the redhead liked better than stirring up a hornet's nest.

"Nice meeting you, ma'am."

"Oh, would you just listen to that. Isn't he sweet?"

"Sasha…"

"Have you thought any more about those colors I showed you?" she asked as Marty urged her toward the front door. "With that big north-facing window—"

"I'm giving it a lot of thought," Marty lied as she all but pushed her friend out the door. And then listened to the throaty chuckles that drifted in her wake like a cloud of her favorite perfume. "With friends like that," she muttered, "who needs enemies?"

"Is she, uh, in show business?" Cole asked when she rejoined him in the kitchen.

"You mean just because she's wearing a red leather skirt, a yellow fur jacket and chandelier earrings, not to mention white lace stockings and those five-inch heels? I think it's the Napoleon complex. She doesn't want to risk being overlooked."

Cole shook his head slowly as he led her out to the truck. "Not much chance of that," he said. "I didn't catch her last name. Does she have one?"

"She has at least five—one of her own and four ex-husbands to pick from. I never know which one she's using, so I usually don't bother to use one."

"Madonna. Cher. Sometimes one name's enough."

"I hadn't thought of it that way, but that's probably it."

Evidently done with the subject of her friend's various

names, he said, "I figure we can put Mutt through his paces and be back by eight, unless you have stops to make."

She didn't. And this wasn't the way she'd planned for the morning to go, but she surrendered to the inevitable. Less trouble that way.

She really should have insisted on taking her car, though, because his truck was a little too cozy. The scent of leather, soap and coffee from the mug in the cup-holder teased her senses. That was before he switched on the engine and the strains of classical piano poured from the speaker.

Classical piano? Had he made a mistake and turned on WUNC, the closest PBS station?

Halfway to the kennel, the music was still playing. She recognized it vaguely as Chopin, but couldn't have named it if her life depended on it. While they waited for one of Muddy Landing's three streetlights—the last two were new, and they hadn't quite got the timing down yet—he whistled softly under his breath, following the melody perfectly.

"You want me to take him?" he asked.

"No, thanks. I can do it now that I know what the problem is."

"Fine," he said cheerfully. "I'll just stick around in case he gets distracted by that cat again. Like I said, if he gets away—"

"I know," she cut in. "Call nine-one-one and get someone to sound the tornado warning."

She knew what to do about the dog. What she didn't know was what to think of a man who drove a truck that had to be at least ten years old and was showing signs of rust. A man who lived on a boat and whistled Chopin.

A man who barged into her private dreams as if he had

every right to be there, leaving her all hot and bothered. If she couldn't manage that damn dog, it would be his fault, not hers, Marty thought rancorously.

In fact, Mutt was on his best behavior. Thanks to the hand signals, he actually allowed her to fasten on his choke collar without stepping on her feet more than a couple of times. Of course he whacked her with his stub of a tail and slobbered on her hand, but, as Cole said, that was only because he liked her.

She hated to think of the damage the creature could do if he didn't.

They'd gone only a few hundred feet down Water Street when the gray Mercedes pulled away from the curb and crept forward.

Cole touched her shoulder and said quietly, "Keep going. I'll catch up with you."

Before she could ask what he was going to do, he wheeled around and jogged back along the weedy path. Turning to stare after him, Marty was nearly pulled off her feet until she remembered the hand signal that meant Be still, you big lug.

Just as Cole got to within twenty-five feet of the car, the driver hooked a left and took off down Third Street. Cole stared after it for several moments before returning to where Marty and Mutt waited.

He said, "Damnedest thing," and shook his head.

"Then you don't think I'm crazy? He really is following me?"

"If so, it's about the worst job of covert action I've ever seen. Not that I've seen all that many, but still…"

"What do you think he wants?"

"What do you have?"

While she was trying to come up with some reason why a stranger would be keeping tabs on her, Cole took over Mutt's lead. He allowed the dog to explore the river's edge instead of continuing to the end of the run, which was usually the Hamburger Shanty.

"I'm just guessing, but if he was looking for something in your possession, he'd wait for you to leave and then search your house." They were facing east. The sun was low enough so that he had to squint, lending him a dangerous look. "You'll have to admit, you make it easy for him."

Marty nodded slowly. "I'm beginning to feel like I'm trapped in the middle of a suspense plot."

"A what?"

"Plot. Books. You know—whodunnit, to whom did they do it, and why? Don't you read fiction?"

"Sure—Cussler, Patterson, guys like that. I see what you mean, though."

Marty made up her mind on the spot to introduce him to a few female authors. Men were good—some a lot better than good—but there was a certain subtlety in woman's suspense that was addictive.

"Well, anyway, I don't have anything worth stealing, and like you say, even if I did, why would he keep following me instead of searching my house? It's not like I ever lock the door."

"But you will from now on, right?"

"Definitely." For the time being, anyway. Until she figured out what this stalking business was all about. Probably a mistake.

"So if it's nothing you have in your possession, what do you know that someone might be interested in?"

"You mean like that famous Senate hearing? What did

he know and when did he know it? Beats me. Maybe he's a headhunter. Waldenbooks wants to hire me to open up a Muddy Landing branch."

Cole took her arm as they headed back to the kennel, a grinning, tail-waving Mutt leading the way. "Until we know better, though, the next time—"

Marty finished it for him. "Right. Next time he comes after me I'll march right up to him and demand to know what the dickens is going on. How much are they offering? Is it going to be a stand-alone store or just a cubbyhole in the mall? Not that we even have a mall, unless you count Dinky's Ice Cream Parlor with the drivers' license place on one side and Paul's Hair Salon on the other."

Cole chuckled, and the sound shivered down Marty's spine, reminding her of those torrid dreams. Reminding her that certain areas in her life had been too long neglected. She said, "Maybe I'll do it while I still have Mutt. That ought to scare the truth out of him."

"I was thinking more like taking Mutt home with you, just in case your stalker decides to drop by. I can run any errands you need so you won't have to go out. If he gets desperate enough, we might be able to force his hand."

Marty halted. Mutt didn't. When she regained her balance, she said, "Hold on. Wait just a cotton-pickin' minute here. If you think I'm letting this hairy elephant inside my house, you're crazy. Things are in a big enough mess without that."

"Yeah, and he'd still need walking." Cole went on as if she hadn't even spoken. "I can take care of that, but that would leave you home alone." He led the way up the kennel steps and took over the unhitching before turning Mutt into his compartment.

Marty waited to respond until he'd hung up the leash and collar. "Actually, I've been thinking about getting a dog now that I won't have to go off and leave him alone all day. Nothing over fifty pounds, though. Smaller would be even better. A Jack Russell, maybe. Or a beagle—even something from the pound, as long as it's small."

She called a greeting to the blue-haired kid who was reading a comic book behind the counter. Once they reached the three-car parking lot she automatically scanned the street in both directions. Two trucks, a delivery van and a rusty Camaro passed by. Marty waved to the woman driving the Camaro.

"Sadie Glover. She works at the ice-cream place. She was one of our, um…projects last fall."

"Projects?"

"Don't ask." Usually it didn't bother her—talking about their matchmaking. Everybody knew what was going on, and nobody really minded. At least, nobody ever said so—except for Faylene, after their botched attempt to pair her up with Gus Mathias before they'd found out she'd already been seeing Bob Ed.

"Look, I still don't like leaving you home alone at night," Cole said as he assisted her into his high cab. "Fasten your seat belt."

She did. "I thought we agreed that whoever it is, he's not after me personally. If that was the case, he could've caught me long before now. It's not like I've been hiding."

Cole walked around the front and got in. "That's what's so puzzling," he said thoughtfully as he pulled out of the parking lot onto the street. "He parks near your house, right?"

She nodded. "In the Caseys' driveway."

"He follows you when you leave, but he hasn't tried to break in and he hasn't approached you. Something doesn't add up."

"Maybe he thinks he knows me, but he's not sure. You know, like maybe we were classmates or something?"

"Possible, I guess."

"Or you know what I think? He's waiting for me to lead him to something. Or someone. The question is, who or what?" She had to laugh. "I guess as detectives, neither of us is ready for prime time, huh?"

He chuckled along with her, and Marty thought how comfortable it was, being able to trust a man enough to laugh with him—to have him worry with her and about her.

Although *comfortable* wasn't quite the word she would have used to describe the sensation that shot through her when they pulled into the driveway and he came around to help her down. She wasn't used to being helped, even from a seat that was four feet off the ground.

She had the door open and was feeling around with her heel to find the narrow chrome bar that served as a step down when he caught her in his arms. He didn't set her down right away.

Laughing breathlessly, she said, "Didn't they used to call those things running boards back in the Dark Ages? And weren't they a lot bigger?"

And then her laughter faded, and so did his. Her breath snagged somewhere in the middle of her chest as his face went out of focus. At the last instant, she closed her eyes.

A voice that echoed none of the panic she was feeling whispered that she didn't even know this man. Yet she knew him in the most elemental sense, as if she'd known him all her life only not in this guise.

Then it was too late to think, as senses too long deprived burst into life. She felt the soft, moist brush of his lips on hers. No pressure, no demands, just…touching.

As the kiss slowly deepened, it was as if she'd been asleep for a hundred years and had woken up in a brand-new world to the tantalizing taste of mint laced with coffee. To the scent of bath soap and leather and sun-warmed male skin. To the iron-hard arms that held her breathlessly close—all elements combined to stoke a powerful hunger that demanded fulfillment.

He did a thorough job of it, she thought fleetingly as his tongue explored her mouth. His lips lifted to brush kisses on her eyelids, her temples, and then returned to the starting place.

Her carpenter. Her kissing carpenter, her upstairs man. Her bodyguard and dog walker and problem solver.

"Well," she breathed. Once he finally lifted his face and she found enough air to speak, she couldn't think of another thing to say. "Well…"

"Got that out of the way."

She noticed that he sounded just a tad shaken, too.

"You want to fire me? Go ahead, I'll understand."

She shook her head. Fire him? No way. Things might be infinitely more complicated after this, but if he walked away now she'd probably chase after him, begging him to come back.

"Got what out of the way?" she asked breathlessly.

"You telling me you haven't thought about what it would be like? Kissing?"

She'd never been any good at lying, so she said nothing.

Seven

With her synapses firing off like Fourth of July fireworks as they entered the house, Marty couldn't organize a single coherent thought. No other man had affected her the way this one did.

At least not since she was fifteen and was exposed to a sullen sixteen-year-old dropout who knew dirty words that hadn't even been invented, who could swear in two languages, had a world-class sneer and carried a pack of Camels in the rolled-up sleeve of his T-shirt. James Dean redux.

"You do the—the—you know—the bookcases," she said, tugging off her stocking cap and massaging her scalp as if it might encourage circulation to her brain. "I need to—to—um…"

Cole nodded as if she'd made herself perfectly clear. If he was suffering any of the same aftereffects, he hid it well. "I'm headed to the hardware store. I shouldn't be gone more than half an hour or so, but I want you to lock up behind me, all right? Don't open the door to anyone until I get back unless you've known them for at least five years."

"Does that include you?" Okay, so she had a few of her wits together now. "Aren't we being a wee bit paranoid?"

A watery streak of sunlight slanted in through a west-facing window, turning his eyes to pure jade. It occurred to her that his hair didn't look quite so shaggy today. Either he'd had a trim or she was getting used to his brand of casual.

"Paranoid? Let's hope so. If we're making too big a deal of it, there's no harm done, but just in case…"

"In case the Muddy Landing Mafia is after a fortune in used first-edition paperbacks, you mean? I promise, at the first sign of imminent attack, I'll call the FBI."

With a quick twitch of his lips, he said solemnly, "Repeat after me, 'I will lock the door. I will not let any strangers inside until Cole gets back.'"

Marty, who had never been given to theatrics, threw out her hands and rolled her eyes. "All right, all right! What is *happening* to my nice, dull, orderly life?" She held up one finger. "I wake up one morning and some creep is stalking me." Held up another one. "My house is falling down around my ears." Third finger. "I'm ordered to lock my door in case the bogeyman tries to get in." All five fingers on both hands.

"Hey," he said softly, capturing her hands and folding them into his own. "It's not as bad as it looks. We big-city guys just tend to be a little more cautious, so humor me, will you?"

She nodded. Didn't even try to speak because she'd probably throw herself in his arms and beg him not to leave her. He was still holding her hands as if he'd forgotten to release them, so she did it for him. Pulled away while she still could. If she'd needed a reminder that too much stress could be hazardous to a woman's health there was no need to look any further for the cause. One kiss from a man who reminded her of all the good things a man could be, but rarely was, and she was trying to twist her uneventful life into a plot for a romantic suspense.

His quick kiss missed whatever he'd been aiming for and slid off the side of her nose.

A moment later Marty watched him lope across the front yard, open the truck door and swing himself up into the high cab.

"You Tarzan, me Jane," she whispered. "Ya-hoo!" It was more rebel yell than jungle cry. She couldn't even get that much right.

In the kitchen, she opened the refrigerator and took inventory. Half a carton of one-percent, four eggs, one of them slightly cracked, bagged salad that was several days past sell-by, Sasha's diet cream, three limp carrots and a few strips of bacon.

Instead of working on various ways of positioning her bookshelves, she started another grocery list, this time with a man in mind. She might be able to live on salad, peanut butter and ice cream, but if Cole was going to be moving in…

Good gravy, Cole was moving in? Into her *house?*

Out of the question. She'd sooner take her chances with a stalker, who probably wasn't one, anyway. Probably a telemarketer who forgot to pay his phone bill and was forced to make his calls in person. Or a spammer whose computer crashed.

One thing she could almost guarantee—if she let Cole Stevens move in with her, she was going to want him in her bed, and that was about as dumb as facing down a deadline by ripping her house apart.

She wrote down *pork chops, potatoes,* and then began doodling while her mind drifted off down fantasy lane. She wasn't the only one who had enjoyed that kiss. Some things a man couldn't hide, enthusiastic arousal being one of them.

Maybe she'd better plow through her boxes and dig out all the erotica titles. After reading the first few she hadn't bothered to read any more. Her tastes ran to more plot and less sex.

G-spots? That mythical so-called "little death" that was supposed to potentially render a woman unconscious for a few seconds?

Forget it. She liked fiction as well as the next person, but she preferred hers to be reality-based. If any man ever got close to her G-spot—that is, if she even had one—to heck with losing consciousness, she wanted to be awake to enjoy it while it lasted.

Meanwhile, she'd better quit fantasizing and get busy.

Some forty-five minutes later she opened the door to Cole and a rush of cold, damp air.

"No callers?" he asked, dropping a six-pack and two plastic sacks on the hall bench.

"Nope. And you know what? The more I think about it, the more certain I am that it's just someone who's new to the area, who's just trying to learn his way around town."

"Using you for a guide? Why not just pick up a map?"

"A map of what? Metropolitan Muddy Landing?"

"Yeah, I guess you're right. It's not exactly the Greater Norfolk area."

"Or even the Greater Elizabeth City area." To keep from staring at his mouth, his shoulders, his chest or anything south of the border—*Lord help me, I'm out of control!*—Marty frowned at his hair and said, "You got a haircut." It sounded more like an accusation than an observation.

"Homemade. Why, did I miss a spot?" When she didn't reply, he went on to say, "Look, I've got what it takes to install chains on both your doors and stops on all the first-floor windows so they can't be raised from the outside. It's far from perfect, but this guy doesn't strike me as an expert."

"Slow up—wait a minute! You're talking like we've got a real crime wave here. I'm sorry now I ever mentioned that damn gray Mercedes."

There must be some law of physics that dictated that the more she overreacted, the more he underreacted. Here she was, flapping her arms like a scarecrow in a windstorm, while he stood there, calm as a marble statue.

"Like I said," he put in quietly once she shut up and stopped flapping, "it's probably nothing, but as long as I bought all this stuff, you might as well put it to use. Once you open for business again, a few precautions make sense."

Calm down. Deep breath. "You mean in case some dumb creep tries to break in and loot my cash drawer? He'd be lucky to find lunch money."

"Insurance won't pay off unless you can prove you've taken certain precautions."

She crossed her arms while she tried to find some flaw in his line of reasoning. The truth was that she should have thought of it herself. She might be casual about her home because she knew her neighbors—her neighborhood—but a business was something else.

"How much did all that stuff cost?" she growled.

He reminded her that it was a legitimate business deduction and handed her the sales slips. "You don't like to lose an argument, do you." Again that twitchy little smile.

That was the trouble with enigmatic men—you could never be certain what went on behind their manly composure.

"Who does?" she countered, waiting for him to fire his next shot. It occurred to her that arguing with Cole Stevens was nowhere near as depressing as arguing with a husband. She and Alan had rarely argued, they'd simply drifted apart…that is, until his illness had brought them together again.

With Beau, it had been different. Beau always started out by wheedling, turning nasty only when he couldn't get his way. Besides his charming self, Beau had brought to the marriage a vintage Jag, a few really nice antiques and several beautiful and no doubt valuable gilt-framed paintings. All but the Jag were gone within the first year, sold to pay off his gambling debts. He'd claimed it wasn't his fault he was always in debt—he was an addict, and addicts couldn't be held responsible, and if she loved him, she wouldn't keep refusing to change the deed on the house. He'd held to that argument right up until she'd had the good sense to kick him out of her house and her life.

But when Cole argued he simply stated the facts and then waited for her to see reason. The crazy thing was that arguing with Cole was stimulating—almost like a sport.

She put the beer in the fridge, then followed him from door to door, window to window while he installed the new hardware, handing him tools and trying to ignore the quiet, efficient way he moved. The way the muscles in his forearms flexed as he twisted the screwdriver.

"Remember, none of this is any good if you don't use it," he warned.

"You don't have to state the obvious. I promise to latch the chains and flip the little brass whatchamacallit on all the windows before I go to bed every night."

Something else to add to her growing list of things to do. So far the list included making sure she turned off everything that needed turning off; making sure the commode wasn't running—it had a tendency to hang up; and slathering on the miracle cream she'd wasted money on because it promised her a dewy, well-moisturized, line-free complexion. How exciting could life get for a woman whose sole interest at the moment was rehabilitating a moribund career?

Marty got out the broom and dustpan while Cole put his tools on the step to go upstairs.

Hands on his hips, he said, "They're not foolproof, but at least you'll have enough of a heads-up to call nine-one-one and get the hell out of the house."

They headed back to the kitchen, which no longer reeked of polyurethane and blackened cinnamon. "Outdoors? But that's where our mythical stalker will be waiting," Marty protested. She would much rather wrap herself in those strong, tanned arms and ignore the whole crazy mess. "You know what? The trouble is, I read too much. Instead of suspense, from now on maybe I'll stick to—" She'd been about to say romances, but then, those weren't the safest reading, either. Not when there was a genuine cover-worthy hero standing only a few feet away. "Biographies," she finished weakly. "I'm pretty sure I just overreacted."

He didn't say a word. Didn't have to—his eyes said it for him.

The first time she'd seen him she'd thought he looked wild, windblown and untamed, like the swashbuckling hero on the cover of a historical romance. Now that she'd come to know him better, he looked…

That was the trouble. He *still* looked like a swashbuckler, only now she saw more than just broad shoulders, narrow hips, greenish eyes that saw far too much, and all that shaggy, sun-streaked hair. Now his appeal was all tied up in a hundred small details, like the soapy, salty scent of his tanned skin and his deep raspy drawl. Like the way he held doors for her and helped her in and out of his monster truck. The way his lips twitched and his eyes crinkled when he was amused, but reluctant to admit it. The way he kissed…

Oh, my mercy, the way he kissed. What on earth was going on inside her small-town, dull-as-mud, semi-educated brain? He should have known better than to start anything he wasn't willing to finish.

Because she *was* willing. Far too willing. The trouble was, the job came with a built-in deadline, and her carpenter came with the job, and any distractions could royally screw up her schedule.

Right. And don't you forget it.

She reminded herself that elevated stress levels were only to be expected under the circumstances. Genuine clinical depression was another thing altogether. She didn't have time to be depressed. She certainly couldn't afford a shrink, and talking it over with her best friends wasn't even a faint possibility. She knew in advance what that pair would recommend.

Bracing her shoulders, she said, "Okay—for insurance purposes, but I still think all this might be overkill."

"Maybe. But like I said, if you hear someone messing around outside, it'll give you time to call nine-one-one."

"Betty Mary Crotts—she's the night dispatcher—she's another of my regulars. If she happens to be awake, she'll probably have her nose in a Regency romance."

"All the more reason to keep you safe. Your regulars need you."

"There's just no winning an argument with you, is there." It sounded almost like a compliment. From the twinkle in his eyes, he knew it, too. Damn him for reading her like a third-grade primer. "Then shall we both get to work? We've already wasted half the day."

"Wasted?"

She couldn't meet his eyes. Instead, she snatched up her floor-plan-in-progress and stalked off toward the living room.

They ate lunch separately. Shortly after Cole went back to work, Marty called up the stairway to say she was going to run to the post office and would be back in an hour or so. She didn't wait to hear his arguments. If a certain Mercedes wanted to follow her while she picked up her mail, plus a few things she needed from the drugstore, all the better. She would damn well force a confrontation and end this silly charade once and for all.

She slowed down as she passed the Caseys' brick ranch. They'd driven his car to Florida. Hers was locked in the garage.

No sign of a Mercedes as she drove to the post office to collect her daily allotment of catalogs and bills. She traded greetings with Miss Canfield, whose tremors were getting worse. "Are you having a garden this year?" she asked.

"Just beans, tomatoes and okra."

"Let me know if you have any trouble with deer. I've found something that works pretty well."

At the drugstore she smiled and nodded to Mr. Horton who lived in the same trailer park as Faylene. Judging from the books he read, the old man was considerably more adventurous than he looked.

Marty headed for the middle aisle where she picked up a bottle of ibuprofen and a microwaveable heat pack in case her lower back started acting up again. Passing the cosmetics display, she impulsively picked out a frosted pink blusher.

And then she saw the condoms.

Oh, for heaven's sake.

All the same, what if…?

A few minutes later she walked out with the blusher, the back-wrap, a bottle of ibuprofen and a box of condoms. With her cheeks burning like fire, she hardly needed the blusher.

It was late afternoon by the time she got back home, having stopped by the bank to order checks for Marty's New and Used at the new address. If everything went according to schedule she would soon be needing them.

Bursting through the front door, she met Cole coming down the stairs with a stack of broken plasterboard. "I told you to toss that stuff out the bedroom window. You don't have to be so careful. I can clean up."

"No problem," he said coolly.

His brusque response did little to quench her optimism. "You know what? I'm going to meet my deadline."

He nodded and waited for her to open the door for him.

She did, and then stood there like a lamppost, clutching her catalogs and her drugstore purchases.

"In case you were worried," she said when he came back inside, "I'm keeping track of all the time you've spent on extras." When he greeted the news with only the lift of one dark eyebrow, she hurried to explain. "I mean stuff that wasn't in our contract."

"Trade it for a few meals. Just remember what I said."

What the devil was bugging him? Remember *what?* She was having trouble remembering her own name at the moment.

"Oh, you mean if I hear someone trying to break in, I'm to call Betty Mary. Got it."

"And then call me."

"Why? You'll be miles away, sound asleep in your boat, and anyway, the local law can handle it. In case they're late and someone does manage to break in, I'll lean over the banisters and drop books on his head." She tried out a perky smile just because he looked so grim.

"Dammit, Marty, I'm serious!"

"Well, you don't have to yell at me. I just meant I could stall him until help arrives. Of course, paperbacks might not do the job. Heavy literature might work better." She was deliberately being facetious and she didn't really know why. Because she was embarrassed? Because she was still clutching her packages, including the box of condoms? Because what she really wanted was for her swashbuckling carpenter to ride in on a white stallion, sweep her off her feet and save her from the bad guys?

That didn't even make sense. What evildoer worth the title drove around town at twelve miles an hour in an elderly Mercedes? The thing didn't even have tinted windows.

As if he had all the time in the world, Cole hooked his thumbs in the low waist of his jeans and waited for a reaction. All eight remaining fingers pointed toward ground zero. When Marty realized she was staring she quickly lifted her gaze in time to see his lips twitch, but when no smile was forthcoming, she thought maybe she'd just imagined it.

Why the heck wasn't the man easier to read? He was a carpenter, for Pete's sake, not one of those superheroes who managed to save the world with one hand tied behind him. The type who could last all weekend in bed without the benefit of any little blue pills.

"Well. That pretty well settles it, then, wouldn't you say?" she huffed. It was the best she could come up with. He could take it any darn way he wanted to.

Oh, yes, that was definitely amusement she saw sparkling in those eyes. If he laughed at her she'd kill him.

He didn't laugh. Soberly, he said, "There's only one more thing I need to do."

She was afraid to ask.

"You might as well come with me to the marina while I throw a few things in a bag. We can pick up some barbecue on the way back."

She took a step back and bumped into the hall bench. Once a klutz, always a klutz. "Oh, now wait a minute, maybe we'd better rethink this—what you said earlier. About spending the night here. Most of my second floor, in case you haven't noticed, is pretty well uninhabitable." Since she'd moved into the spare room, her old bedroom—the one that would soon be her new living room—was the repository for roughly a ton of paperback books, not to mention stacks of assorted building material.

"I'll sleep on the sofa."

She said, "Ha! I can just see you leaping up to go into action with a hammer and screwdriver against an armed intruder."

That drew both a twitch *and* a twinkle. "Just don't go dropping any books on my head if I need to use the john in the middle of the night."

All she could do was shake her head. Wasn't being broke and racing to beat a deadline so she could do something about it enough excitement, without throwing in car chases and sexy carpenters? Who the devil was plotting this life of hers, anyway?

"Another benefit," he said calmly, "is that I won't waste so much traveling time. I can get started as soon as we walk Mutt, and work as late as necessary, or at least until you go up to bed."

It made sense...sort of. "You really do think I need a bodyguard, then?"

"Let's just say it's better to be safe than sorry."

"To coin a cliché," she murmured. "All right, then, but if the perp tries to climb in a window and tramples on my iris bulbs, he's going to wish he'd tackled some other mark. Believe me, I'm not helpless."

This time his amusement was unmistakable. "Right. All those boxes of ammo upstairs. Three guesses which ones you've been reading."

Even if he was laughing at her, it felt good. A kind of warm-and-mushy-inside good. If she had an ounce of survival instinct, she'd be out of here retroactively, stalker or no stalker. Because the real enemy was inside her gates. A Trojan horse of another color.

Marty was used to arguing with her female friends. It

was the way they bounced ideas off each other when they were trying to come up with the best way to get a couple of needy people together. Nobody's feelings ever got hurt. With Alan, they'd been too much alike to argue, even before he got sick. More like best friends—or later, like mother and child.

Arguments with Beau had occasionally been about backgrounds; her lack of one and his illustrious one. More often they had been about money. Win or lose, she'd always ended up depressed. If anyone had told her it was possible to argue with a man and actually enjoy it, she'd have said they were nuts.

It was after dark when they set off. Cole had hammered and sawed and done his thing upstairs, while Marty had worked on her prospective layout downstairs. Sasha would insist on feng shui along with her three shades of red. Paint was one thing, but Marty didn't have room for any feng shui. Her biggest concern was having as many books as possible exposed to as many browsers as possible, all without threatening claustrophobia.

The night was cold and luminous, the three-quarter moon set in a bed of iridescent clouds. They came to a section of soybean fields where the sky was visible practically from horizon to horizon, and Cole slowed almost to a stop. There was no traffic.

"North Star. Check it out."

"Where?" Leaning forward against the seat belt to peer through the windshield, Marty tried to summon up her meager knowledge of astronomy. Thanks to a passing interest in astrology, she knew the names of the planets, but not how to find them.

"See the Big Dipper over by that dead tree?" He waited until she said she did. "Now draw an imaginary line through the two stars at the end of the bowl and there's your North Star."

"I see it, I see it! I'm impressed."

"Yeah," he said smugly. "That's what I'm shooting for. I figured once you found out how smart I was, you'd jump to do my bidding without any more backtalk."

In the faint light of the dashboard, she stared at his just-this-side-of-handsome profile. "Balderdash."

He picked up speed and cut her a quick glance. "Balderdash?"

"It's a literary term. It means bull-pucky."

"Pucky?" He was openly laughing at her now, teeth flashing white in his tanned face.

Crossing her arms over her chest, Marty said, "You know very well what I mean." But then she was laughing, too.

"Looks like Bob Ed's entertaining tonight," he observed a few minutes later as they turned off onto a dirt road that led past the guide's home-office.

"He's surprisingly gregarious for a grizzled old bachelor. I think Faylene might have something to do with it."

They drove slowly along the waterfront, past several short piers to the one on the end where a low-profile boat was secured to the wooden pilings.

"Welcome to the *Time Out*," Cole said, quiet pride evident in his tone.

The deck dipped precariously when she stepped aboard, clutching his hand for balance.

"Easy there, I've got you."

"It's hardly the first time I've ever been on a boat," she

said, trying not to grab him and hang on with both hands. "I rode the ferry to Ocracoke several summers ago, and I've even been deep-sea fishing."

That was the time when one of Sasha's clients invited the decorator and any of her friends who cared to join her to spend a day fishing in the Gulf Stream. She'd been too busy throwing up to appreciate the thousand-dollar treat.

"My, it's…airy, isn't it?" she murmured, holding tightly to a stanchion while Cole unlocked a door and led her belowdeck.

When he turned on lights, she looked around, marveling at the way everything seemed to fit together.

"For an older model, she's in great shape. I've been working on her in my spare time for years," Cole said as he opened and closed various lockers.

Marty continued to look around, curious about what it was that led a man like Cole Stevens to live aboard a boat. It could hardly be called a yacht, but his pride was obvious—even touching.

His hands came down on her shoulder and he shifted her aside in order to open the door to the tiny head. Marty was struck by the same clean, masculine scent she'd come to associate with him. She was no expert on male toiletries, but whatever brand he used, it was nothing at all like the products used by either of her husbands. Alan had favored Old Spice, claiming it reminded him of his father. Beau had doused himself in a potent cologne that she'd quickly come to despise.

"I haven't been down this way in months," Marty said once they left the *Time Out* and headed back to Muddy Landing. "Not since Bob Ed's last birthday bash, in fact."

Cole slowed outside the guide's living quarters, where

a flickering blue light shone through the windows. Watching basketball, probably. Faylene was an avid sports fan.

"That's Faylene's car. You met her, didn't you? She's promised to come once I'm ready to open and help with a final cleaning."

"Blond lady in a pink sequined sweatshirt and white tennis shoes? I met her."

The description was a lot kinder than some she'd heard. Summer or winter, Faylene's unique fashion sense tended to raise eyebrows in those who didn't know her.

Cole slowed as they neared the turnoff. Where the wooden wharf followed the shoreline, a few commercial fishing boats glowed dimly in the moonlight. At the very end, a sleek, dark-hulled yacht rode quietly on the still water. A couple of cars and trucks, rentals most likely, were parked between a stack of crab pots and a chain hoist. Some marina operators kept a few rentable wrecks on hand for layovers.

Cole said, "In case you wondered how I managed to bring both my boat and a truck south, this is one of Bob Ed's rentals. Things are slow, so I got the pick of the litter."

"That explains the rod holders on the front bumper, then," she murmured drowsily.

"Yep. I troll—I rarely surf fish."

This time she didn't bother to comment, lulled by the sound of the tires and the steady presence beside her.

"Barbecue?" he asked a few minutes later as he pulled onto Highway 168 again.

She opened her eyes and yawned. "Sounds good. Tomorrow I need to make a trip to the grocers."

"How about we run by after we do the dog in the morning."

She was too relaxed to bother arguing. At this rate, she thought sleepily, her remodeling job was going to take a back seat to all the other activities, and as much as she enjoyed them, she couldn't afford any more delays. "How about you carp while I walk Mutt and do the shopping?"

"We'll see," he said agreeably.

"Damn right we will," she muttered, but there was no fire in it. Only slumbering coals. If she didn't watch out, her priorities were going to be turned end for end, and the worst thing about it was that she found the threat more exciting than frightening.

Eight

How's a woman supposed to concentrate, Marty asked herself, when her sleeping dragon wakes up after a long winter's nap, only to trip over a sexy dragon-slayer?

Okay, bad analogy. She didn't think too clearly this early in the morning. Never had, actually, but now it was even worse. Now she was hungover after wrestling with a night full of X-rated dreams. Inviting Cole to move in with her had been a major mistake.

Although, come to think of it, she'd never actually issued an invitation.

Wet-haired and bleary-eyed, she made her way downstairs at a quarter of seven on Friday morning and shoved open the kitchen door. And there he was, seated at her table—the star of all those steamy high-definition dreams.

Slowly, he unfolded his taut, muscular body as she entered his room, his narrowed eyes taking in every detail, from her towel-dried hair to her grubby cross-trainers. Four of his square-tipped fingers rested on the tabletop. "You look pale. Sure you're feeling all right? Was it the barbecue?"

Heck no, she wasn't feeling all right. Barbecue had nothing to do with it. She hadn't felt this "not all right" since she'd flunked algebra on account of the boy who sat in front of her, whose voice had already changed and who had had to shave at least twice a week.

She tried to think of something marginally intelligent to say and came up empty. "Sorry 'f I woke you. Tried to be quiet," she mumbled. Her early morning voice was raspy to the point of surliness, but then he already knew that. Any friend who knew her well enough to drop in before noon understood. "Not a morning person. It's January—February—whatever. I'm still hibernating."

Cole nodded. Didn't say a word but looked as if he understood. Sympathy, she didn't need. Sympathy always made her combative. When he continued to stand, she waved him back to his seat. "Just don't expect me to carry on a conversation," she warned.

Silent as an oyster, he nodded again.

She was the only one who was doing any conversing, and for some reason she couldn't seem to shut up. "Circadian rhythms," she grumbled as if that explained everything. Opening a cabinet, she stared at a box of dry cereal, made a face and shut the door. One thing about walking Super-Mutt—it not only woke up her appetite, it helped oxygenate her brain.

Cole sat down again and tipped his chair back. Not saying a word. Just sitting there, watching while she muttered about circadian rhythms.

"It's just that as soon as I get things sorted out," she felt compelled to explain, "we go on daylight saving time and the whole stupid process starts all over again. If I had half a brain I'd find myself a night job. Maybe a convenience store…"

Chatter, chatter, chatter. So much for not being a morning person. She was okay with Sasha and Faylene, who knew her limitations and made allowances, but with anyone else she was hopeless.

She fumbled in the dish cabinet for her favorite mug, wishing she had her house to herself again.

Liar, liar, pants on fire!

Nobody should look that good this early. The brass lamp over the table shone down on his head, making his hair glisten with moisture. He must have already showered. Which meant he'd been standing there stark naked only a few feet away from where she was sleeping. No wonder she'd woken up panting and throbbing.

"What ever happened to the sun?" she muttered.

"It's on the way. Give it a few more minutes." He reached for the drawing pad that was spread open alongside his coffee mug, while Marty filled her mug from the fresh pot of coffee, the fumes of which were just now reaching her caffeine receptors. She added two heaping sugars and a dollop of milk.

"Toast, or something more substantial?" he asked genially as if she hadn't practically snarled at him.

She focused on the two slices of whole-wheat waiting at half-mast in the toaster. "No solids, not this early."

Clearing her throat, she asked him what he was working on, and Cole slid the pad over so she could see it. She stared at the lines on the paper until the elegant drawing began to make sense. "Nice," she murmured. "Compact. Not exactly what you'd call a family room, but I guess it's all there."

Which was actually a fairly coherent response, all things considered.

Okay, so he could draw as well as take things apart and put them back together again. He could talk about things like coffee and toast and still manage to look like the kind of guy who devoured fair maidens for breakfast.

She took another rejuvenating sip of coffee, sat her mug on the table and cleared her throat. "Cole…am I making a monumental mistake here?"

His eyes widened. The dark centers seemed to expand.

"What we're doing upstairs, I mean."

She closed her eyes, Not *that,* she nearly said, stopping herself just in time. They hadn't done a darn thing upstairs—not together, at least. If you didn't count a few territorial skirmishes.

Leaning back, he thumbed his freshly shaved chin and studied the drawing. He'd even gone so far as to indicate a small ceiling fixture over the table. "What's the matter—you're having second thoughts?"

"Only a million or so," she confessed.

"A little late, isn't it?"

"Actually, it's too early. I usually sleep until seven-thirty or so, but since I've been walking the dog, I have to get up in the wee hours."

"Any reason why he can't wait until later in the day?"

Deep breath. Oxygenate that old brain. "Annie said he liked to go out for his first run before breakfast, but that might be so they could both get to work on time." Two slices of medium-crisp whole-wheat toast popped up, and without thinking she reached for the butter and the fig preserves. A little sugar rush wouldn't hurt, since she was being forced to sound rational before she was even awake.

With Sasha, who often dropped by on her way to work, depending on where her current client was located, Marty could be as grumpy as she liked. Her friend understood and never took it personally.

With Cole it was different. She hated for him to see her as she really was—a puffy-eyed, raspy-voiced going-on-thirty-seven-year-old woman.

Oh, yeah? How do you want him to see you? Naked and in his bed, all ready for a few rounds of whoopee?

Shut up, dammit, who asked you?

Who just bought a whole box of condoms?

Still tipped back, with his long legs stretched out before him, he said, "I haven't started on the cabinets yet. If you're not comfortable with the plans we agreed on, now's the time to say so. I can put things back the way they were, but it'll take a few days."

"I'm not," she protested quickly. "That is, I am. Comfortable, that is."

What she was not comfortable with was sharing breakfast with him, smelling his aftershave, his soap—actually her soap. He'd evidently forgotten to bring his own.

That was the trouble with dreaming the kind of dreams she didn't even know how to dream—it left her imagination susceptible to the slightest provocation. One whiff of the same brand of bath soap she'd used for years and she instantly pictured a naked carpenter standing in her shower with water streaming down on his broad shoulders, his narrow hips, his taut butt, his—

Okay, got the picture.

"No, it looks great," she croaked earnestly. "Really. I like what you've done here—this little space over the sink."

"In most kitchens you'd have a window there. You don't want a cabinet in your face."

She didn't particularly want a mirror in her face, either. "There's no room for a dishwasher, I guess." She had one, but never used it. Living alone, she ran out of clean dishes before she could ever get a full load. "That's okay. I'd probably never use it anyway."

"It might come in handy for holiday entertaining."

"Just make room for a double sink, that's all I need."

For no reason at all, he smiled at her across the table then, and she got tangled up in his eyes. His laugh lines, even his squint lines were sexy. Pity the same couldn't be said for her own. Double standards were the pits.

"Finish your toast and let's pick up Mutt. You think he's truck trained?"

"You mean, like housebroken?"

"I mean, if we anchor him in the back of my truck, will he try to jump out?" Rising, Cole reached for the coffeepot, shot her a questioning look and, when she shook her head, switched it off. He glanced at the back door, and seeing the chain still in place, set his mug in the sink and put away the butter, cream and preserves.

How the devil, Marty asked herself, could a man look sexy doing kitchen chores?

"In case your stalker shows up again, we might want to turn the tables and follow him. It'd be easier with wheels."

"Don't even think about it. All these chains and whatchamadoodles on the windows are one thing, but I didn't hire you as an extra in my tiny little melodrama."

"Not even as a walk-on? Not even if I agree to let Mutt have all the best lines?"

She couldn't help but laugh. What else could a woman do? Any way you looked at it, the man was irresistible.

"There, that's better," he said, pausing behind her chair to lay hands on the area where stress had her tight as a bowstring.

One of the areas, at least.

When his thumb began to work on her taut trapeziums she tipped her head back and closed her eyes.

In a soft voice that bordered on a growl he said, "We'd better get a move on. I like to be on the job by eight."

"I told you, there's no need for you to go with me. I've been walking him for a week. Now that I know how to control him, I don't need you."

As if she hadn't spoken, he said, "You want to run upstairs before we leave?"

"We. It's always first person singular when it comes to what you're doing upstairs, but the royal 'We' when it comes to everything else."

He nodded judiciously. "Sounds about right," he said just solemnly enough so that she knew he was joking.

"You're a chauvinist, you know that, don't you?" Brushing his hands away, she got up, rinsed her mug and plopped it in the drainer.

Hips braced against a counter, he grinned. "What tipped you off?"

She felt like frapping him with the hand towel. Instead, she dried her hands and reached for the bottle of jasmine-scented lotion on the shelf behind the sink. Then he got out both their coats and held hers while she slid her arms through the sleeves. She could feel him grinning at her as if she had eyes in the back of her head.

By the time they got out to the truck, the eastern sky was streaked with gold. *February,* she thought. *That's almost spring. Pretty soon it will be summer, and by then I'll be back in business.*

And where would Cole be, cruising down the intrastate waterway? Tied up at another marina, tearing up and rebuilding some other woman's house? For some reason spring didn't feel quite so promising.

The walk went surprisingly well, even after Marty insisted on taking charge of Mutt. The only time things threatened to get out of control was when a pack of strays showed up and the dog went crazy, yapping and jumping, ignoring her shouts, which of course he couldn't hear.

"I forgot how to make him look for my signals," she exclaimed when Cole stood back, making no move to take control.

"Give the leash a sharp jerk," he said.

She did. When Mutt looked around as if to say, "Wha-at?" Marty sliced off a hand signal, the rough translation of which was *Straighten up and fly right or I'll pull your eyelashes out!*

"That dog must be in heat," Cole said when they resumed the brisk pace.

Not that she'd give him the satisfaction of saying it, but Marty hated to think what would have happened if she'd been alone. "Yeah, I figured that's all it was."

"Probably going to be some free pups in a few months. You did say you're thinking of getting a dog?"

"No time soon," she said grimly, shortening the leash when Mutt got a little too interested in inspecting the tires on a rusty Fairlane that was parked illegally. "Speaking of time, we can head back now. It'll be a full half hour by the time we get to the kennel."

"Honor system?"

"Darn right," she said. "Besides, he's a big guy. He needs the exercise."

Outside the canine boarding house, Cole reached for the leash. "You want to wait in the truck while I take him inside?"

"No, thanks." She was cool. In control. Mutt was seated on his overgrown haunches, grinning up at her as if to say *You go, girl!*

So what did Cole Stevens do?

The one thing designed to shatter her composure. Laying a hand on her, he leaned over and kissed her.

Right there in broad daylight, in front of a stream of traffic. Or if not exactly a stream, at least a bread delivery van, a bicycle and Susie-at-the-bank's new hatchback.

Oh, my, if she'd been turned on by his looks, by his voice and his touch, his taste sent her sailing over the edge. Whose heart was it that was thundering between them? Beating hard enough to be felt even through two layers of coat? His or hers?

Or both?

They were standing toe to toe. One of his hands moved up to her back, holding her close. The familiar taste of him—coffee, mint and something essentially personal, was as intoxicating as any whiskey.

Not until he stepped away did Marty realize that she had a death grip on his arms. She stepped back, forced herself to breathe normally and tried pinning on a smile. Her lips were tingling. She only hoped they weren't trembling.

Cole licked his lips and said casually, "Mmm, nice. Coconut?"

But his eyes had gone dark on her again. She took a modicum of satisfaction in that, at least.

A red convertible was parked behind her minivan when they got back to Sugar Lane, so Cole parked on the street. "Pretty early for company," he observed.

"Not for Sasha," Marty replied, not sounding particularly happy at the prospect of company. "She stops by on her way to work sometimes."

There were two women seated in the car. As the top was up, Cole couldn't tell much about them. Leaving Marty to invite them inside—or not—he headed toward the front door. As the door was locked and the key was in her coat pocket instead of under the doormat—he'd insisted on that—he had no choice but to wait.

A minute later both car doors opened and two women emerged. He'd met the redhead before, but not the tall blonde in black pants, black boots, a long, black coat and a purple chenille scarf.

The three women trooped up the front walk, the blonde carefully stepping on each flagstone, the redhead striding out in front, ignoring stepping stones and whatever it was that was shooting up beside the walk. Looked like onions. Probably wasn't.

"Hi, Cole. Lily, this is Marty's carpenter." Short yellow fur coat, black tights and all, the height-challenged redhead charged up the steps, right hand extended. There was at least one ring per finger, including her thumb. "I'm Sasha, remember? We met the other day?"

As if anyone was likely to forget.

By that time Marty and the blonde had made it to the front door. Sasha said, "Lily and I were on our way to

IHOP, and it occurred to me that since Marty's going to be opening again right here in the neighborhood, she might need some professional advice. Home office and all—the IRS is picky about that sort of thing. Believe me, I work out of my home, so I know all about it. They make you jump through flaming hoops, right, Lily?"

"I'm sure Ms. Owens is familiar with the regulations." Her voice, Cole decided, matched her looks. Cool, competent, with an air of superiority that might or might not be merited.

The talk of business records and home offices continued briefly before turning to more general topics. Then the redhead hit him with a few personal questions, to which he gave only minimal answers.

Did he actually live aboard a boat?

Yeah, he did. No, it definitely wasn't a yacht, and yes, he'd met Faylene Beasley. No, he didn't have children, and yes, if he had, he would definitely teach them to swim before they could walk.

Yada-yada-yada. Funny thing, though—even as he was answering her nosy questions, he couldn't help but notice that she seemed more interested in Marty's reaction than to anything he was saying.

The blonde looked cool, even in a long black topcoat that Cole recognized as being a pricey model. Among other things, Paula had taught him something about women's clothing. Without making an issue of it, Ms. Sullivan glanced at a tank watch that Cole recognized as a Tiffany model, either that or a damned good knock-off.

Sasha tapped him on the shoulder. "I suppose you know a lot of people around here, hm? Is that why you decided to lay over here? That is what you call it, isn't it? Laying over?"

"Yes, ma'am, I believe that's what it's called."

"Oh, would you just listen to that! Honey, you're so un-PC you're adorable!"

Cole had taken about all he could take without triggering his gag reflex. Before he could think of a reply that would deflect her attention without being openly rude, she turned away.

"Marty, in case you have any questions, you know who to call. Now remember what I told you about colors. You're not going to have that much wall exposed, so you've got to make every inch work for you." Before Marty could respond, Sasha turned back to Cole. "It's great seeing you again. Faylene's told me so much about you and those lovely windows you put in for Bob Ed."

Lovely windows? Unpainted secondhand double-hung windows in an unpainted building? What the devil had the Beasley woman said about him, anyway? He'd spoken to her for three minutes, tops.

Marty opened the door and more or less hurried them out, promising they'd get together for lunch one day soon. Cole was still trying to figure out what had just happened—hell, it was barely eight in the morning—when he heard the plump little redhead who was striding off down the front lawn saying, "That went well, doncha think? Did you see the way she—"

He didn't catch the rest because Marty slammed the door shut. Oh, boy, the lady was steamed about something. Probably wouldn't do much good to ask, but he asked anyway. "Did I miss something important?"

"What? Oh—no. Yes. I mean, I don't know if you realize it or not, but you're now an official target."

"Whoa, I'm not sure I like the sound of that." He backed a few steps toward the stairway.

"Depends on whether or not you like gorgeous, intelligent, independent women," she snapped. "That's who they're setting you up with."

"Now wait a minute—who's setting me up? How?"

"With Lily. Why else would Sasha bring her by here this early when she knows I'm not even coherent this time of day?" Her cheeks were burning, her soft gray eyes flashing fire. "It's not me and my tax situation they're interested in. No way—it's you."

"Hey, I hardly spoke three words to the woman," Cole protested. "By now she's probably already forgotten my name."

"Don't kid yourself," Marty said dryly.

What the devil was she so steamed about? If she already had an accountant, all she had to do was say so. If anyone had a reason to be steamed, it was he. For a few minutes there he'd felt like he had a target painted on his chest.

"Let's get to work, all right? We've wasted enough time."

Nine

In a cheerfully cluttered room a few hours later, Sasha eased off her five-inch heels and massaged her size-five feet. "Now I know how a ballerina must feel. Oh, quit fussing around! Sit down and talk to me," she exclaimed. "No point in washing the inside when the outside's spattered with winter grunge."

Dutifully, Faylene set aside her spray bottle of window cleaner and the wad of crumpled newspapers. "Next warm spell we have I'll get 'em all done, inside and out. I got me one of them things you screw on to a hose. You ready for iced tea?"

"In the fridge. Pour us both a glass, will you?" Sasha eased her feet up onto the sofa. For the few minutes the housekeeper was out of the room, she let herself sag against the cushions. "Bring those macaroons, too," she called. Faylene had stopped by the bakery on her way to work. She was a whiz at cleaning, but her culinary skills were notorious, as everyone who'd ever employed her quickly discovered.

With refreshments on hand, the two women got down to brass tacks. Faylene touched her Dolly Parton do to make sure the lacquered surface was still intact. "What'd she think?"

"Lily? Who knows? Maybe you can find out, I couldn't get a thing out of her."

"Comes from filling out all them gov'ment forms all day long. She don't talk to me, neither, and I been cleanin' for her goin' on a year now."

"So far all I've been able to find out is that she graduated from Wharton, her father's in the military—probably pretty high rank, although I'm just guessing about that. Oh, and she hates country music."

"Bob Ed says Mr. Stevens's got a guitar on board that boat o' his." She pronounced it git-tawr.

"So we'll broaden her education." Sasha sipped her syrupy tea. "Today's country music was yesterday's folk music. If we tell her something like that, she might be more inclined to expand her horizons. But first he needs some incentive to hang around. That's where we come in."

"It still don't sound much like a match to me, her being college educated and all. Maybe we ought to look around some more. How 'bout one o' them highfalutin business men you work for."

"Married, gay or dull as mud. Don't underestimate our studly carpenter. A friend of mine knows the decorator who did his house, and she says—"

"What house? If he's got a house, why's he sleepin' aboard that old boat? It's not like it was a yacht or anything."

"According to my source, he used to be pretty high up

the ladder with this big development firm up in Virginia. In fact, he was married to his boss's daughter, but then there was some kind of scandal—business, not personal. Anyway, by the time the dust settled, he was out of a job, the company was down the drain and his wife and her lawyers cleaned him out. That's why he's living on board his boat and taking small jobs to make ends meet."

"I don't know 'bout meetin' no ends, but he didn't charge Bob Ed nothin' to fix his windows. Shelled out two weeks in advance for the wet slip, too."

"Even better. I doubt if Mar—that is, if Lily would be interested if he were truly down on his luck."

The light dawned. "Law heppus, it's Marty you're fixin' to match him up with, not Miss Lily." Faylene smirked, rearranging a face that had more wrinkles than a box of prunes.

"Well, what do you think? She hasn't had a man in years, not even a loaner."

"She's sure been awful crotchety lately."

"Mmm-hmm. And Lord knows, he's temptation on the hoof. By the way, are y'all planning your usual birthday bash this year?"

"Stewed goose with rutabagas, collards, barbecue and all the rest, same as always."

"All the rest meaning a supply of aged-in-the-jar moonshine," Sasha teased. It was the hunting guide's standard birthday bash, a tradition in an area where entertainment was usually of the homemade variety. It was also a golden opportunity for matchmaking. Sasha wouldn't miss it for anything. Last year's guest list had included a bank president, the chief of surgery at Chesapeake General and three

Tides players who were slated for big things in the majors, all clients of Bob Ed's—plus Faylene's special friends.

"Just don't wear them spike-heel shoes this time," the bouffant blonde warned. "You get one o' them things caught 'tween the planks on the dock and sic a lawyer on 'im, and Bob Ed's not gonna invite you to no more parties."

"I'll be sure to dress suitably for the occasion. Maybe I'll borrow a pair of your sneakers. But back to Cole Stevens—my source in Virginia said the wife was a real witch, so our hunky carpenter might be just a tad gun-shy."

"Name me a man that's not, 'specially if they think they're being herded into a corral."

"What about you and Bob Ed?"

"You don't see us rushin' to tie any knots, do you? And what about you? You had four husbands and not a one of 'em stuck around no longer'n it took for the ink to dry on the papers." The two women knew each other well enough to get down and dirty without giving or taking offense.

"How do you think I got to be such an expert? And anyway, we're hardly herding them to the altar—all we're doing is encouraging two nice people to take a second look at each other by putting them together in a different context," Sasha reasoned.

Faylene pursed her lips. Actually, they were more or less permanently pursed, as she drew the line at Botox injections. "There's some other fellers invited to the party. Maybe I'll invite Miss Lily and we can see what happens."

"Kill two birds with one stone, so to speak."

"Kill more'n that, if we get lucky. Bob Ed's invited them fellers from that fifty-five footer that tied up the other day." A born-and-bred local, Faylene referred to anything larger than a commercial fishing boat by its length rather than its name. "'You make sure Miss Lily comes, and I'll take care o' Marty."

"It's a deal," Sasha agreed, her expression that of a cream-fed Persian cat.

Marty considered asking Cole for help, but then she heard the whine of the power saw, reminding her that she needed him upstairs more than she did downstairs. She'd moved the damn things into the garage using only her back, her brain and a two-wheel hand truck. If she could just get this one past the single step and into the kitchen, the rest of the way would be easy.

After spending the winter outside, her poor minivan was going to appreciate having the garage to itself again, she thought as she levered the cut-down section of bookshelf onto the cart, balanced it and cautiously began moving backward toward the single step.

Ver-r-ry carefully, she backed up the step and tried to pull the cart up with her. When the damn thing started sliding, she let out a yelp.

Sudden silence from upstairs as the power saw cut off. Marty yelled again. Bracing her back on the door frame, she jammed one knee against the side of the shelf, hoping to keep it from toppling onto the cement garage floor. "Cole! Help me!"

"What in God's name—?" Like a genie out of a bottle, he appeared behind her. "Hang on, I'm coming!"

"You can't get past," she wailed, struggling in the doorway between kitchen and garage to steady the teetering bookcase.

He disappeared briefly. A few seconds later he reappeared in the garage, where he braced the leaning book-shelf with both hands. "What the devil were you trying to do? No, don't say anything. Steady now, I've got the shelf. When I tip it back, pull the cart up onto the kitchen floor, then wait until I come back around to take control."

The look she gave him was the rough equivalent of *Over my dead body.*

The cart was capable of moving a refrigerator as long as it was balanced. But a six-by-six-foot by eighteen-inch bookshelf was, by its very nature, unbalanced.

"Where the hell are you going with it, anyway?"

"Living room."

"Now? Why?"

She just shook her head. If she couldn't explain it to her-self, she knew better than to try explaining it to anyone else. "Through here. Hold it while I take up the rug."

A few minutes later the first of the bookshelves was sharing space in the living room with a sofa, three chairs and two tables. It was monstrous.

It's a first step, she told herself. Every journey begins with a single step—she'd read that somewhere.

The trouble was, she'd read everything somewhere, at one time or another. Including Othello. One look at Cole, standing in the doorway, arms crossed over his chest, brought to mind another quotation. "Yon Cassio has a hun-gry look. Such men are dangerous."

And don't you forget it, she warned herself.

Struggling between discouragement and elation, she stared at the elephant in the drawing room. The rest of the herd was still in the garage. "I forgot how big it was," she whispered. "What am I going to do with all the others?"

"You're actually asking for suggestions? Wait until I have time to cut them down, and we'll make room in here."

Cole moved in behind her and put a hand on her shoulder. His thumb began smoothing away the tension that always seemed to gather at the back of her neck.

"Only trouble here is, you got the cart before the horse. Next time, ask for help."

"What I've got is a twenty-mule team before a buckboard. What you've got is work to do upstairs. I can manage down here."

She could manage a whole lot better if she weren't melting under his magic fingers. A puffy little sigh escaped her as he found the magic spot and began to work on it. Pain…but a good kind of pain…

"Don't be so damn stubborn," he chided.

"I'm not stubborn, but I know what has to be done and I don't see any reason to wait till the last minute to do it."

His hands left her shoulder and his arms slipped around her from behind.

"You're not stubborn. Rain's not wet. The temperature outside's not hovering around the freezing mark, either. Hey, it's almost spring out there, right? Flowers bursting out all over the place."

"All right, so I made a mistake. I should have moved all this stuff upstairs first, but I just wanted to get an idea of how it was going to look."

When he started to chuckle, she stiffened. "Don't say it. So now I've got a huge mess. I've probably made the biggest mistake of my life. Well, maybe the second biggest mistake."

His fingers were moving up the back of her neck to her

hair, stroking, massaging, sapping the strength from her aching bones.

He said, "What was the biggest? Just curious—you don't have to answer that."

"I don't intend to." He didn't need to know that she'd been on a romance-reading binge about the time she'd met Beau Owens. She'd mistaken suave manners, tailor-made suits and a Hollywood-handsome face for the real thing.

The only thing real about Beau had been his total lack of integrity. Wasn't there another quotation about a lesson too late for the learning?

Or no—that was a song, wasn't it?

She sniffed, wishing she had a tissue. Things were piling up too fast, flattening her hopes like a wet tortilla. Just yesterday she'd been happily working on floor plans. Sales counter here by the front window; old romances, billed as classics, in the dining room; new titles, once she could afford to stock them again, facing the entrance. A few posters, her autographed author pictures and maybe even those three-shades-of-red walls Sasha insisted would send customers into a buying frenzy.

Frenzy, my foot, she thought. So far all she'd accomplished was to destroy her single asset—her house. Her eyes blurred and then began to sting.

Without saying a word, Cole turned her so that she was leaning against him, damp-eyed and discouraged. And that was another thing—her emotions were all over the place. Either she wasn't eating right or sleeping enough, or she was sliding into early menopause. Now there was a cheerful thought!

"Hey," he murmured, his warm breath stirring her hair, "we got it this far, didn't we? What if I help you move your furniture upstairs right now? We'll leave your rocking chair here so you can sit and plan how you're going to use your space."

"We can't move upstairs yet—you're not finished up there." She almost wished he would quit being so helpful— so understanding. She was falling into the habit of depending on him, and that, she knew from experience, was a fatal mistake.

"We can throw sheets over the stuff to keep the dust off while I'm working. Until I finish your new kitchen you can still use the one down here, right?"

His tone was sympathetic, and unfortunately, sympathy had always been her undoing. She couldn't remember the last time she'd been undone, because her friends knew better than to push any of her emotional buttons. Once she started crying, which she absolutely refused to do, it was "man the lifeboats!"

He let her bawl her eyes out for several minutes, not even attempting to talk her out of it. Not once did he try to reason with her—not that it would have done a speck of good. His hands moved slowly over her back from shoulders to waist—no higher, no lower.

She sniffed. *Why on earth am I crying? I never cry!*

Her fingers crept across his chest, feeling to see if he had a tissue in his shirt pocket. He stiffened, and she suddenly became aware of the heat engendered by two warm bodies in close proximity. Of masculine hardness pressing against feminine softness. The scent of his skin only made matters worse. Instinctively, she moved against the hard ridge. Pelvis to pelvis. The hard ridge moved.

Omigracious!

She wasn't responsible for *that!* Couldn't be. She had it on the best of authority that she wasn't the type to turn men

on. It was probably just a standard male reaction to the circumstances. Like—like—drinking beer and belching.

"There's a handkerchief in my hip pocket," he said, his
voice sounding strained.

He was probably embarrassed and didn't know how to
let go without hurting her feelings. So she did it for him.
Stepped back and accepted the handkerchief he handed her.

And immediately missed his warmth, his strength, and
everything else she'd been starved for, but hadn't realized
it. She wiped, blotted and blew.

"I'll wash it," she said stiffly, avoiding his gaze.

He didn't say a word, just continued to look at her.

This is a dead-end road, woman. Stop right where you are.

And then he did just what she wanted most and needed
least. He reached out and pulled her against him and...
kissed her again.

This time there was no mistaking the nature of the kiss.
It was carnal from the start. Without lifting his mouth from
hers, he eased her past the bookshelf, backed her toward
the sofa and lowered her onto the cushions.

It was hard and narrow with scarcely enough room for
two to lie down unless they were plastered together. At first
neither of them moved. The sensation that swept through
her was one she hadn't felt in years. The mindless kind of
hunger that demands immediate satisfaction.

Why couldn't she have bought a damn futon instead of
a three-cushion couch? His backside had to be hanging off
the edge. To keep him from landing on the floor, she anchored him by hooking a leg over his hip.

Smart move, Marty. Real subtle.

His hand grazed her breast as he eased the neck of her
pullover away to nuzzle her collarbone. A rash of goose

bumps broke out along her sides. How could he have known about that tiny hollow at the base of her throat? All he had to do was breathe on it and she fell apart.

His hands slipped under her sweater, under her bra. When his fingertips raked over her nipples, she whimpered, "We need to—to talk."

Will the last gray cell to leave the brain please turn out the lights?

Cole's hands went still. Talk? Was she crazy? More to the point, was he? If he was smart he'd get the hell out of here, contract or no contract, while he was still more or less in his right mind. He might drop anchor down around Southport, or maybe Charleston. Or maybe he'd just keep on the move until he couldn't remember her name or what she looked like, much less the way she smelled...or tasted.

He hadn't even begun to suspect how dangerous she was until the second day. Couldn't even remember what tipped him off. It wasn't as if she made any effort to attract him. No makeup, no heavy perfumes, just that flowery smelling soap and lotion.

"Marty," he said through clenched jaws, "I don't want to take advantage of you."

The hell he didn't! Crammed together on the hard-as-rocks cushions, with one thigh over his hips and her sweet little mound rubbing against his erection, he was about to explode.

What with work, worry, plus a hard narrow bunk in a cold cabin that smelled of mildew, Cole couldn't remember the last time he'd been in this condition. His libido had taken a sabbatical about the time he'd realized that Paula was cheating on him. Since then he'd been too busy to worry about getting laid.

The trouble was, this wasn't just a matter of getting laid. This was Marty.

So? She was a woman, wasn't she?

Unless he'd mistaken the signs, she was as eager as he was. And he just happened to have a condom in his wallet.

Right. One that had been there since around the time of his divorce, when he'd had some crazy notion of going out and snagging himself some revenge sex. The use-by date had probably long since expired.

She shifted and somehow managed to bring them into even closer contact where it counted. The crazy thing was that it counted everywhere. If he'd needed a reminder of just why sex with Marty Owens wasn't going to work, that was it. Not only because he worked for her, but because he liked her too much. Respected her. Hell, he even admired her. She was a little too independent for her own good, but then, there was probably a reason behind it.

"Marty—" He tried to ease away, but there was nowhere to go but the floor. He managed to slide off the sofa onto one knee, and felt stupid as hell. *Smooth, man. Really suave.*

"If you're looking for an apology," he said, the words grinding like a rusty hinge, "you've got it. I should never have—"

Sitting up, she laid a finger over his mouth. "Don't say it. Just don't, all right?" Her voiced sounded raw and her eyes refused to meet his.

He looked for other signs of vulnerability, but found none. Unless you counted the neck of her yellow sweater that was stretched out of shape, and the fact that her hair looked like she'd been through a wind tunnel.

With her chilly gray eyes focused somewhere over his left shoulder, she said primly, "Thank you very much for helping me get it in here."

A few wildly inappropriate notions zinged through his head before his brain reconnected. "Yeah, well…next time give me some warning. The short one shouldn't be a problem, though."

As he stood up he watched her face, trying to get a read on what was going on in that squirrelly mind of hers. It was like watching cloud shadows racing over the water, disguising what lay just under the surface.

"Yell when you want help moving this stuff upstairs," he said.

"Let me think about it first. Maybe this afternoon."

You'd think they were two strangers who just happened to be passing the time of day.

Shrugging, Cole climbed the stairs to finish what he'd been doing when he'd first heard her yell for help.

What *had* he been doing? His concentration was now shot, that was for damn sure. It didn't help that the bed she'd slept in last night was only a few feet away. His senses honed to a fine edge, he caught a whiff of the scented soap she used in the morning while she stood naked under the shower.

His power sander was waiting where he'd left it, a clue that he'd been working on her cabinet doors. He picked it up, reminding himself that power tools could be dangerous when a guy's blood deserted his brain and headed south.

Ten

Downstairs, Marty stared at the monstrous intrusion between her coffee table and the ugly platform rocker that was the first piece of furniture she'd ever bought.

My God, she'd almost—

And she'd wanted to. For the first time in more years than she cared to remember, she'd been ready to tear off her clothes and make love. Burning for it. Throbbing for it. She *never* burned, much less throbbed. And besides, her box of condoms was upstairs.

Deep breath. Another one. Now, back to the real world. It took some doing, but she did it, a measure of just how disciplined she could be when she put her mind to it.

After first removing the drawers, she maneuvered her desk through the living room, around the bookshelf, across the hall and into the kitchen, where it blocked the refrigerator. Shaking her aching hands, she told herself she'd find a place for it later. It was only furniture, after all. She'd learned early in life to keep her possessions to a minimum and her goals realistic. Rearranging furniture was realistic. People did it all the time. If you didn't like the results, you could always put things back the way they were.

The way they were? With a garage full of big empty bookshelves, another one blocking her living room, not to mention a ton of paperback books that were growing more out-of-date by the minute?

And do not, she warned herself—I repeat, do *not* even think about the man upstairs!

The maple drop-leaf dining table wasn't all that heavy once she'd unloaded the to-be-read pile of books and the to-be-dealt-with stack of mail, which was mostly catalogs, anyway. By stacking the chairs, she managed to get all four, plus the table, in the utility room. She'd have to clear them all out to get to the washer, but it was the best she could do for now. With more rain—possibly even sleet—in the forecast, she could hardly set them out on the porch.

Hands on her hips, she surveyed the chaos. Was she there yet? At the point of no return? Once she got past that point, there'd be no going back. Until then she could still fire her carpenter, put a hot plate in the bathroom, wash dishes in the lavatory and use the refrigerator downstairs.

That was the trouble with having a galloping case of the hots. It blew any possibility of logical thought.

Dammit, he wasn't even interested enough to take what she'd offered. What did he want—time and a half for overtime?

"Story of my life," she muttered, glaring at the dishes in the sink that she had yet to wash and now couldn't get to without climbing over a mountain of misplaced furniture.

Upstairs, the sound of a power sander continued, blocking out—she hoped—the sound of dragging and thumping, plus several four-letter words awkwardly strung together. Cursing was another area where she lacked expertise.

As she wandered back through her empty front rooms, Marty was surprised he hadn't come downstairs to see what was going on. "Aren't you even curious?" she muttered, eyeing her dusty staircase. "What are you afraid of? That I'll grab you and tear off your clothes and have my way with you before you can scream for help?" She sighed, said, "Fat chance," and shook off the mental image.

Hearing the commotion downstairs, Cole planed away a sixteenth of an inch too much wood, swore and laid aside his plane. Whatever the hell she was doing down there, she obviously didn't need help, else she would've asked for it. Yeah, right.

He was tempted to go see what the devil she was up to, but even more determined to mind his own business. He didn't understand women. Never had, never would. And Marty Owens was in a class by herself.

He waited until he'd swept up shavings and sawdust before he headed downstairs. There was barely enough room to stand.

She confronted him at the foot of the stairs, hands on her hips. "I didn't move it all by myself—a neighbor helped."

Cole was forced to step over a stack of desk drawers. "Are you out of your mind?" he demanded.

"Well, I don't know. What's your diagnosis?"

Her tone was suspiciously reasonable, her eyes suspiciously glittery. Her small, rounded chin jutted out as if daring him to take a swing at her.

As if he would. As if he would ever hit a woman, no matter what the provocation. "You want my diagnosis? Clinically speaking, I think you're scared out of your gourd. I think you're trying to put yourself in a position where backing out's not an option. How'm I doing so far?"

"I hired you as a builder, not a shrink. Is that trash? Give it to me, I'll take it out." After snapping out orders like a small female general, she reached for the bag.

He stepped back and attempted to stare her down. "Your jaw's about to snap out of alignment."

"Just give me the damn trash bag!"

So he handed it over. "Tie your shoelace before you trip."

She took a deep breath, drawing his attention to her upper assets, which were—in his estimation, at least—just about perfect.

She poked the bag back at him. "Then you do it!" Normally her complexion was parchment pale, but now twin splotches of color bloomed on her cheeks. The tip of her nose was pink, and her eyes—

Oh, hell, they were starting to leak again.

He dropped the sack of sawdust and shavings, stepped over two desk drawers, endangering the contents, and before the first tear splashed down he had her safely in his arms. "Hey, it's no big deal, honey. Whoa, now, don't cry. Rainy days are made for doing stuff you don't ordinarily have time for, like rearranging furniture. I knew this woman once who—"

"I don't want to know about your d-damn women," she sobbed, her voice muffled against his shirt.

He was filthy—covered in sawdust, but that didn't keep him from holding her while he made those noises men make when they feel about as useful as tits on a male dog.

"This is twice," she sobbed. "Th—that's a record."

He hadn't the least idea what she was talking about, not that it mattered.

Her hair tickled his chin even as her soft, warm body wriggled closer. If ever a woman needed holding, this one did. He wouldn't even claim any merit badges for taking on the job, because some jobs were their own reward.

"Shh, it's all right, honey. Good idea, in fact."

"What's good about it?"

Feeling her fingers at his waistband, he instinctively sucked in his breath. She was pulling out his shirttail? To do what? *To get to what?*

To use it as a handkerchief.

"I'll wash it," she promised, her elbows poking him in the chest as she tugged his flannel shirttail up to her face to dry her tears.

Without releasing her, he shifted his hips to one side in an effort to hide his body's enthusiastic reaction. Talk about a trial by fire!

He made a few more of the only kind of noises a man can make when his brain skips out leaving no forwarding address.

When she dropped his shirttail and wrapped both arms around his waist, pulling him into alignment again, he closed his eyes and prayed for patience. Forbearance. Maybe sainthood.

"Whoa—that is, uh—why don't I take that trash out while you, uh—find a place to sit down. Then, when I come back I'll make us some coffee and we can talk about what you're planning to do in here. How's that sound?"

He didn't wait for an answer, but gently pried her arms from around his waist. It was either put some distance between them—a couple of continents should do it—or lower her onto the nearest flat surface and let nature take its course.

She sucked in a shaky breath and stepped back. And then, damn if she didn't smile at him. Red eyes, pink nose, wet cheeks and all, it was that smile that cut through all the scars that had built up over the years, making him think thoughts he had absolutely no business thinking.

And not just of sex, either.

So he grabbed the sack of trash and fled.

Talk about cutting off your nose to spite your face— she'd had some crazy idea that by moving out what had to go out and moving in what had to come in she could get ahead of schedule and put an end to all the second thoughts that were driving her batty. The deeper she got into this mess she'd created, the harder it was to extricate herself.

Marty shoved aside the sofa cushions and snatched her coat from the closet. She scrambled around and found a rain hat that was as old as dirt and probably no longer waterproof, but then, it hadn't actually started raining yet. She jammed it on her head, snatched her purse and left. She'd better get in the last dog-walk because later was looking less and less likely.

The car started on the second try, just as Cole came around the corner of the house. He called out and waved his arms. Marty pretended not to see or hear. She didn't want to talk to him now, she really didn't. So she backed over her bulb bed to get around his truck, and just as she pulled out onto the street, the first few spatters of rain struck the windshield.

* * *

Cole watched the white minivan disappear around the corner. He was tempted to follow her. If she needed provisions before the weather closed in, she should have said so. If she wanted to get in a second dog-walk before things got too messy, then she should have told him, dammit, and he'd have gone with her.

Had she forgotten about that Mercedes?

Oh, hell, she didn't need him. If nothing else, she'd proved that much with this morning's exercise. For all he knew, she tore up her house and shifted all her furniture whenever the notion struck her. What did he know about women, anyway? Paula, the spoiled daughter of a construction worker who'd been canny enough—or maybe just crooked enough—to make millions, might have been born with a stainless steel spoon in her mouth, but she'd quickly adapted to sterling.

As for his mother, Aurelia Stevens had been a piano teacher who had never gotten over her dream of being a concert pianist. Cole had watched her grow old, staring out the window day after day, year after year, as one or another tin-eared kid who would rather be outdoors playing ball, abused her precious baby grand.

Both Cole and his father, a security guard with a serious drinking problem who'd had trouble holding a job, had saved for years to buy her that piano. That was one of the reasons it had got to him when Paula had decided she needed a Steinway to fill the corner of what she called her drawing room. She didn't even like music, much less play. She'd majored in cheerleading. Rah, rah, rah...

Back to Marty, he told himself as a soft freezing mist dampened his face. Follow her or get back to work?

He settled for hauling all the furniture he could handle single-handedly upstairs and stashing it in the larger of the two bedrooms, the one she planned to use as a living room. The sofa would have to wait. Maybe once the weather let up he could get Bob Ed to lend him a hand in exchange for the windows he'd installed.

That done, he worked on fitting the cabinet doors, marking and chiseling out for the hinges. Some time later he glanced at the clock. It wasn't as late as it looked, but she'd already been gone nearly two hours. Something between sleet and frozen rain fell steadily, although judging from the few cars that passed by, nothing was sticking to the streets. The temperature still hovered a few degrees above freezing.

At three, he called Bob Ed and asked him to check on the boat. "I left a leeward port open a crack for fresh air. Would you mind closing it? And while you're there, how about listening to be sure the bilge pump's not running. The timer's been giving me some trouble lately. Oh, and I probably won't make it back tonight."

By the time he heard Marty pull into the driveway, Cole had the lower doors ready to hang. He'd tried working on the drawers, but had given it up. Everything was a mess, himself included. His concentration was shot. Damn, it was none of his business where she went, or who she spent her time with.

So how come it felt like his business?

He went downstairs, just as she came in through the front door, bringing with her a waft of cold, wet air. Shaking moisture from her coat and stripping off the ugliest hat he'd ever seen, she stopped dead in her tracks.

"How come you're still here? I thought you'd leave early today on account of the weather." She looked around slowly. "And where's all my furniture?"

"Most of it's upstairs. Your shoes are wet, better take

'em off before you catch cold." The legs of her pants were wet, too, but he wasn't about to go there.

"I'm numb. It's freezing outside!"

She shivered and rubbed her hands together, and Cole forgot all the things he'd intended to say about having a plan and sticking to it, about not going off half-cocked, and especially about not going off without telling him where she was headed and when she expected to return.

"You wouldn't believe the day I've had," she said, shaking her head.

The hat had left her hair plastered to her forehead and frizzed out on the ends. On her, it looked…cute.

"Tell me there's coffee in the pot."

He cleared his throat. "Which part of your day wouldn't I believe? The part where the first elephant invaded your living room, or the part where—"

"Oh, hush up." She tossed her wet coat toward the bench, where he'd stacked the contents of her coffee table before toting the table upstairs. "I haven't eaten a bite in ages, so don't talk to me, okay? I'm mean as a junkyard dog when I'm hungry."

A slow grin spread across his face. "Yeah, I believe you," he said as he followed her into the kitchen and waited for her reaction to the two bookcases he'd cut down while she was gone. All four sections.

Compared with bringing her flowers or candy, it hardly rated. As he waited for some sign of approval, he realized with a degree of alarm just how much her approval meant to him.

Trouble was, there was no easy way he could back off at this stage.

Eleven

So then Cole had to explain how he'd called the marina and left orders to secure the *Time Out*, and how he'd stuck around because he'd been worried about her, and how as long as he was here, he'd figured he might as well accomplish something.

"Accomplish something! You've done all this—?" She waved her hands around the room, where the only alien pieces were the bookshelves. "My God, in—what, two hours?"

"More like four. I'd have had the rest of them done and moved into the living room, ready for you to start stocking with books, if you'd been any later." The truth was, he'd been about ready to go out and beat the bushes looking for her. Muddy Landing wasn't all that big. He figured he could cover it in less than an hour as long as he didn't mind breaking a few speed laws.

And as long as she'd stayed in town.

She could have been anywhere. She could've taken a notion to drive up to Chesapeake with her nutty redheaded friend. To say Marty was maddening didn't begin to describe how she frustrated him, but it was a start.

She refused to look at him. Marty was in no mood to be fussed at. Leaning back, elbows braced on the table, she toe-heeled off her wet shoes. Then, groaning, she bent over and pulled off her socks. Her feet were bluish white, her toes red.

"You walked the dog, didn't you."

Whether or not he meant it as an accusation, that's the way she took it.

"So? I agreed to two walks a day. The times weren't specified." She ran her fingers through her hair and frowned down at the wet ends. "That dumb dog thinks rules don't count on rainy days. Either that or he's already forgotten everything you taught him." Propping one foot on her knee, she tried to thaw it out with massage.

"I didn't teach Mutt, I taught you!"

Dropping her foot to the floor, she glared at him. "Okay, so *I'm* the one who forgot. Or maybe I didn't sleep in the right motel!" When he continued to stare at her as if she'd lost her mind—there were no guarantees on that score— she said glumly, "That TV ad—you know. You don't need any fancy degrees as long as you stay in the right motel? Hotel? Whatever."

And then she sneezed twice in quick succession.

He scooped her up in his arms before she could do more than squawk in protest. Balancing her on an upraised knee, he managed to switch on the coffeemaker with one hand, and then he headed upstairs. "You're the one who started this mess," he growled. "Three guesses who'll get blamed if you don't meet your deadline. You want to catch pneumonia?"

"You don't catch pneumonia from wet feet, you catch it from—"

"From bugs! I know that, dammit! Maybe I didn't sleep in the right hotel, but at least I know that a hot bath, dry warm clothes, and something hot to drink won't hurt you, and it might even help. You got any whiskey?"

If it hadn't sounded so good—if he hadn't felt so good—Marty might have put up more of a fight, but she was so tired and so cold. She'd picked up a neighbor whose car wouldn't start and taken her to the library and then made two more stops. What are neighbors for?

"Under the toaster. I mean, under the counter where the toaster sits. It's in a jar, not a bottle."

Upstairs in the bathroom, he set her on her feet with orders to strip. Then he closed the valve and turned on the water, adjusting it until he was evidently satisfied it was hot enough to kill any cold germs.

"You need any help?" he demanded when she just stood there like a lamppost with the bulb burned out.

Steam rose from the tub, quickly clouding the mirror in the chilly room. When she pulled the sweater off and dropped it on the floor, he picked it up and draped it over his arm.

A tidy man? Would wonders never cease?

"What about stuff women always put in the water? You use anything like that?"

She glanced at the jar of bath salts. She used it not for the scent—well, partially for that, but mostly because it cut down on rings in the tub. Following her glance, he reached for the jar and before she could stop him, dumped half the contents into the steaming water.

"Too much," she protested. "That's way, way too much!"

"Too late," he mimicked. "Way, way too late. You should've told me."

"You should have given me time! By the way, did I tell you you're fired?" Her teeth were chattering, and not just from cold. Heat pumps were no match for this kind of weather, but whoever heard of a bathroom fireplace?

He shook his head. "Get in the tub, Marty. I'll bring you something to put on."

"Didn't you hear me? You're fired."

"Right. I'll pack up my tools and leave just as soon as I finish your new kitchen."

"Just stop being so damn reasonable, will you?"

"Just finish getting undressed and hit the tub, will you?"

She took a deep, shuddering breath, willing herself not to bawl. Again. Caution: streaky-haired men with sexy bodies can be hazardous to your health. The FDA or somebody ought to stamp his side with a purple warning to that effect.

"You need help?"

"Thank you, you've done quite enough," she said stiffly.

"Then hop to it."

"As soon as you leave," she said. Her jeans were wet from the thighs down. She had goose bumps on her goose bumps, but she refused to strip naked with him standing there leering at her.

Okay, so maybe he wasn't leering, but he was still here, and she had no intention of—

With a sigh that reeked of strained patience, he shut off the water just as it reached the overflow drain. "Marty, I'm trying to help you here, but you're not making it easy."

"Then leave. Go somewhere else, I don't care where, just leave before I'm forced to throw you out."

He opened his mouth to speak and obviously thought better of it. Shaking his head, he left, taking her sweater with him, leaving behind the faint scent of fresh-cut lumber and a cedar-citrus aftershave that cut through her vanilla-scented, grocery-store-brand bath salts.

Once the door closed behind him, she wasted no time in stepping out of her clothes and testing the water with one foot. It was perfect.

Well, damn. Along with everything else, he knew how to draw a lady's bath.

She eased herself under the deliciously hot water up to her neck and released a sigh of perfect contentment. All right, maybe not perfect, but close enough. She'd just have to remember to be extra careful getting out, because the tub would be slick as black ice.

Dunking her hair, she felt along the ledge for her shampoo. Normally she shampooed under the shower, but today she just didn't care. She was torn between wanting to get out and confront him in a slam-bang show-down and wanting to hide out here where it was deliciously warm.

By the time she had rinsed away the suds and opened her eyes again, Cole was seated on the stool where she sat to clip her toenails. He held out a hand towel.

"You ready to dry your face?"

She snatched it, blotted her stinging eyes and glared at him. "I told you, you're fired. Go home. Go anywhere, I don't care where, just get out of my house."

"Did I tell you I worked as a lifeguard a couple of summers back when I was in school?"

"Fine. Throw me a life ring and then get out." She crossed her arms over her chest, leaving the rest of her body vulnerable. The water was slightly cloudy, but it was hardly opaque. "Cole, what are you trying to do? I take back your firing, if that's what you want."

He shook his head. Seated on an ivory enameled stool with his knees spread apart and his big feet planted on her pink and white crocheted rug, he should have looked ludicrous. Instead, he looked…

The bath water that had started to cool off seemed suddenly too hot to bear.

He said, "Are you finished? I'll help you out so you don't slip. I should've read the instructions on that bath stuff before I dumped it in."

"You're not going to leave, are you." If she sounded resigned, it was because she knew what was going to happen next. Knew it as well as she knew she was in trouble way over her head. Life rings weren't going to help.

She wet the hand towel and draped it over her breasts. With one hand she shielded her groin from view, with the other hand she reached for his. If she slipped and fell, maybe she'd simply lie there and drown. At least the wake would be interesting, with people setting casseroles and cupcakes on bookshelves and looking for a chair where they could sit and talk about how poor Marty Owens had finally flipped her ever-loving lid.

He'd turned his head when she stood, but the moment both her feet were safely out of the tub he enveloped her in a bath towel. As the water gurgled down the drain, he dropped another towel over her hair and gave it a rub or two.

"You use a drier?" he asked.

She clutched the bath towel around her, shivering, but not from cold. She was warm to the bone. Warm and needy and standing too close to temptation.

And if that wasn't a song title, it should be.

He gave her hair another rub and then started blotting her arms, his face so close she could see the black pupils in those tarnished brass eyes. Pupils that seemed to expand even as she watched. She stopped breathing. So did he. Slowly, she lifted her arms around his neck. When the towel slipped from her shoulders, neither of them noticed.

Under his dark flannel shirt he wore a tee that looked startlingly white against the tanned skin of his throat. She kissed the hollow where a pulse was beating in time with her own racing heart.

"Well, are you going to kiss me, or not?" she asked. Ever the realist, she recognized the inevitable and lifted her face to his.

He was. He did.

Oh, my mercy, how he did.

While his tongue invaded her mouth, his hands slowly slid down her sides, fingertips teasing the sides of her breasts. Then his hands closed over her hipbones and he moved her back and forth, tantalizing her with the hard ridge that thrust against her belly.

When she nibbled the tip of his tongue and then sucked on it, his fingers bit almost painfully into her waist. By the time she broke away from the kiss—only because she had to breathe—his face was flushed, his eyes black with excitement.

She knew the signs, oh, yes. She'd read all about it. She'd just never before seen it, at least not to this extent. After two husbands, that was probably something of a record. Sasha had tried to tell her there was a whole world out there, just waiting to be explored.

"Bed?" he panted.

"Please. I have a box of—"

"Good," he said. "A big box?"

They made it to the bedroom, and she was thankful for all those early years when she'd made her bed to perfection each morning. He carried her past the jumble of furniture, peeled back the neat covers and lowered her to the mattress. And then, while she watched, he stripped off his clothes in what had to be record time.

"I'll go slow," he said, his voice thick, almost grim.

"Don't."

She held up her arms, but instead of taking her invitation, he knelt beside her, his breathing audible even over the slithery sound of sleet pelting the windows.

His gaze was as hot as molten steel as it led the way, followed by his hands, and then his lips. He kissed her eyelid, her ears and her nose. His lips moved down her throat, lingering on that spot that drove her wild.

How could he know?

When he reached her breasts, he cupped them, squeezing them gently, then used his thumbs, his teeth and his tongue on the nipples to drive her totally wild.

Only at that point, she didn't yet know what wild was. Not until he came up on his knees again and she caught a glimpse of...

Oh, my. The word *magnificent* came to mind. So did all those pop-ups on her computer, and the magazine articles she'd scoffed at, believing them to be fiction, if not outright fantasy.

When he buried his face in her quivering belly and then moved south, all hope of rational thought disappeared. In blind supplication she lifted her hips and whimpered,

"Please…" She wanted him inside her while she was still conscious. Already she was feeling rainbows—

Not seeing them, but *feeling* them!

She tugged at his ears, and then his hair, and then her fingers raked over his slick shoulders, dragging him up to where she wanted him. "Please," she begged.

"Give me a minute," he said hoarsely.

Never had a minute seemed so endless, while he ripped open a packet and covered himself. She would have loved to do it for him—only she was no expert and this was no time to further her education.

He kissed her again, tasting of mint, coffee and musk. On his knees and one elbow, he guided himself in place, thrust once and was still.

Hurry, hurry, she wanted to scream when a year passed and he didn't move again. And then he did move, tracing the hills and valleys of her body, burying his face between her breasts, stroking her with his tongue. Utterly boneless, she melted as he suckled her nipples.

Somehow, their positions reversed, and he guided her eager hands down his taut body, lingering where he wanted her attention.

And then it was her turn…again. All too soon she caught her breath—caught it again—forgetting each time to exhale. He thrust faster, harder—she cried out.

He whispered her name, his voice sounding as if he were in pain.

Long moments later she felt a drift of cool air on her back when he rolled over onto his side, taking her with him. His eyes were closed. His skin was slick with sweat, and he was breathing as if he'd just run a three-minute mile.

As echoes of her first truly magnificent orgasm slowly faded, Marty took the opportunity to stare wonderingly at his face—at the laugh lines and the squint lines, and those deliciously long, dark lashes.

This is the face of the man I love, she thought, stunned by the realization.

They must have slept, because the next thing he knew the phone was ringing. It was still in Marty's old bedroom, waiting for a phone jack to be installed in the room where they now slept.

Cole rolled over onto his back when he felt her leave. He squinted at the wristwatch that was all he was wearing at the moment.

A little after half-past four—a.m. or p.m.? Must be p.m., judging from the light outside. Still gray, but not completely dark.

He considered getting up, but lacked the energy. Without intentionally eavesdropping he heard her say, "Oh, he's great. Mmm-hmm, twice already today."

Twice, hell. That near miss downstairs didn't count.

"Well, you don't have to do that—really, I enjoyed it."

Yeah, me, too, he thought, satisfaction oozing from his pores.

He must have dozed. Hearing her opening a dresser drawer, he forced himself to sit up. "Problem?" he asked.

"What? Oh, no—nothing like that." She took out a set of underwear and then shook out a sweater, frowned at it and exchanged it for another one.

He continued to watch her in the mirror. "You want to come back to bed?"

Without looking at him, she shook her head. How come,

he wondered, women considered bed-head a bad thing? On her it looked great. Soft and sexy and a little wild.

"You want to go downstairs and roll those bookshelves into the living room?"

"Mmm-hmm," she said.

She was wrapped in a quilt that had been on the foot of the bed. Sooner or later she was going to have to look at him. The sex had been too good to ignore.

But Marty was…well, she was Marty. He had a feeling she'd been through almost as long a dry spell as he had. She would come to terms with it in her own sweet time. Meanwhile, he could afford to wait. She still hadn't told him who'd called…not that it was any of his business.

It snowed for about twenty minutes just after dark. They stood at the window and watched it swirl around the streetlight. Cole's arm was around her shoulders as if it had every right to be there.

Marty wanted to believe it did, but she was too much a realist. Regardless of what the constitution said, not all men were created equal. At least, not where sex was concerned. Sex with Alan had been…well, not exactly boring, but limited, to say the least. With Beau, it had been exciting at first, but afterward she'd always felt as if the bus had come and gone, and she'd missed it. She'd never complained, knowing there'd be another bus a few days later, but she'd missed most of those, too.

With Cole…

She sighed. "I forgot about supper."

"Anything in the freezer? I doubt that anything's open tonight. There's no traffic."

Half an hour later they had shared freezer pizza with

dabs of this and that from the refrigerator. She had drawn the line at horseradish on her half. After a call from Faylene, reminding her of Bob Ed's birthday party tomorrow night, they had moved a few more of the bookcases into the living room.

Now Marty was torn between standing in the doorway looking at them and telling herself it really was going to happen, and grabbing Cole and dragging him upstairs to bed. Upstairs wasn't even a priority. Anywhere would do. The table...the living room rug...

Cole offered to bring down her boxes of books, but she explained that before she could even think about stocking her shelves she needed to paint the walls and do a final cleaning. "Sasha has this crazy idea—"

"Red walls, right?"

"Three shades of red. I'm probably going to compromise and do all four walls in the palest shade of peach. That's warm enough for a northern exposure, don't you think?"

He stood there looking both sexy and thoughtful in his jeans and navy flannel shirt with only a hint of sawdust around the collar. He had showered and now he smelled of her soap, but he hadn't taken time to shave. She was tempted to stroke his bristly jaw, but she knew better than to touch him again. This was one case where the hair of the dog didn't count.

"The Hallets are back," she said. "That's who called, so no more dog-walking."

"I thought you had another week."

"Everybody got sick, so they cut the cruise short. Big disappointment." She was grinning. "So...how about if I help you hang the cabinet doors?"

"How about if you help me cut down the last two book-shelves?" he countered.

"Deal," she said, and held up a hand, palm outward.

He slapped it with his, and his fingers threatened to interweave with hers, but he dropped his hand. "Deal," he said softly.

Evidently, she wasn't the only one who knew better than to tempt fate.

Twelve

Feeling absurdly self-conscious for a woman of thirty-seven—a woman who had been married twice—Marty pulled on her third outfit, a pink wool turtleneck and maroon slacks. She checked her image in the dresser mirror and decided it would have to do. Her bed was piled with outfits she had tried on and discarded, which was just as well, because now she could look at her bed and think of what she needed to do instead of what she'd already done.

Yesterday. And again last night. Twice!

Cole had woken early and driven back to the marina to check on his boat and collect a few clean clothes. She'd woken up when she'd heard his truck drive off and had sat there for several minutes reliving every kiss, every embrace, every tingling, bone-melting climax.

That was it? she'd thought, stunned. He was leaving? At six-oh-whatever in the morning? Her eyes wouldn't focus well enough to tell the exact time, but thinking she might never see him again, she'd been devastated. She had forced herself to get up, shower and dress. Life went on. If she hadn't learned that lesson after Alan and Beau, she'd darn well better learn it now…after Cole.

She'd just been touching her lashes with mascara when she'd heard him drive up again. Mascara! At seven-twenty in the morning!

You have flat out lost it, lady, she'd told herself.

As it turned out, he had stopped by the grocery store on the way back, bringing enough provisions to last an entire platoon a week.

"Are you *that* hungry?" she'd demanded. Relief came out sounding like irritation…which was probably just as well.

Without answering, he waggled his eyebrows and grinned.

Not a word about last night. Not a word about stealing her heart, her body, and anything else she had of value.

Together, they had worked all day, taking time out only to make sandwiches. At five she had come upstairs to shower and start getting ready for the birthday party, while he'd continued to rearrange shelves, leaving space to work around them to repaint her walls.

Once he'd heard the shower cut off, he had joined her upstairs. "Casual?" he'd asked, poking his head into the bedroom.

"Definitely."

"Good. Otherwise, I'd have had to rush up to Virginia Beach and get my tux out of storage."

He had whistled while he showered, shaved and dressed, taking half the time it had taken her just to decide on what to wear to Bob Ed's party. While she'd stood in front of the mirror trying to do something with her hair, he had leaned in the doorway, again offering advice. She'd finally run him downstairs, but her heart had done cartwheels. If he'd so much as touched her, they'd have ended up back in bed.

All day long, while they'd whacked off and nailed on end boards in the garage and moved shelves into the house, she'd felt as self-conscious as a fourteen-year-old on her first date. That unsure of herself—which was absurd in a woman of her age. An experienced adult who'd had two husbands. You'd think they'd done something bizarre and a little kinky instead of just making love—

Not making love. Having sex. Big, big difference, she reminded herself sternly as she fastened a pair of gold hoops on her ears.

"Do we need to take anything? Beer? Wine? Food?" Cole called upstairs just as she started down.

"Lord, no. He'd be highly insulted. One of his clients has a brewery and another one has a barbecue catering service. That'll give you an idea of what the menu will be tonight." She joined him in the hall, glancing at her watch. Being a Virgo, she was always punctual, but that was before time had stopped three times during the night.

"I thought it was stewed Canada goose with all the trimmings," he murmured, leaning over to inhale the scent of shampoo, soap and jasmine-scented body lotion.

He even claimed to be addicted to her coconut-flavored lip balm.

"That's only the beginning," she said breathlessly as she slid her arms into the sleeves of her warmest coat. She was about to tell him he looked good—and oh, my mercy, he did!—when he beat her to the punch.

"You look beautiful, Marty. I like what you've done to your hair."

She had twisted it into a knot, anchored it with a fancy craft-show comb, and pulled out a few tendrils to curl at the sides. Ordinarily, she settled for a scrunchy. She could feel her face reddening.

Making a big deal out of checking her purse for necessary items, she thanked him.

Yesterday's sleety rain was now only a damp memory. Streaks of gold and lavender brightened the western sky. To the east, the Hamburger Shanty's neon sign cast a cheerful glow against the fast-disappearing storm clouds. Faylene swore that in all the years she'd known Bob Ed, it had never rained on one of his parties.

Marty had a feeling it could be raining buffaloes and she wouldn't notice. "Your car, mine, or both?" she asked. Code for *Will you be coming back here tonight, or are you moving back aboard your boat now that the weather's let up?*

"Mine—if that's all right with you?"

A semi-self-conscious silence prevailed the rest of the way to the marina. Halfway there, Cole put on a CD. This time instead of Chopin, it was classical guitar. It could have been Spike Jones and his City Slickers and it wouldn't have made a speck of difference. Any music shared was romantic music.

The parking area was jam-packed with vehicles of all descriptions. Sasha's red convertible was parked close to the wharf. She had evidently come early to help with the preparations, although she knew better than to offer Bob Ed any decorating advice. Faylene still laughed about the time Sasha had made him a centerpiece using port and starboard running lights, a small anchor and three fat candles.

Cole found a place down near the end of the wharf, near his own boat. "Man, I had no idea it was this big a deal," he murmured as he helped her from the truck, taking her arm and leading her toward the big, unpainted building that served the guide as both home and office.

Marty hugged his arm to her side. "It might not look like it, but Bob Ed's place is famous all up and down the coast. His clients like to believe it's their own private discovery—this little hole-in-the-wall marina just off the beaten track." They dodged a puddle, necessitating a bumping of hips and shoulders. He smiled down at her, causing her heart to skip a beat, and she quickly looked away. Tonight was going to be tricky. One look and Sasha would know exactly what had happened. The woman had the internal radar of a bat.

Every window was lighted, guests spilled out along the wharf on both sides, and from the sound—and the smells—the party was well underway. They had just sidled between two pickup trucks, both bristling with rod holders, when she happened to catch sight of a familiar car. She stopped dead in her tracks and stared.

"Is that what I think it is?"

It was a gray Mercedes, far from new, but in excellent condition. Among all the SUVs and pickups, it stuck out like a sore thumb.

"Yep. Coincidence?" Cole murmured. "I don't think so." He moved around to check the license plate. "This should be interesting."

It was all the excuse she needed to hang on to his arm, tucking her hand against his side to feel his comforting warmth. "Look, I probably made too big a deal of the whole thing," she said. "Otherwise, whoever it is wouldn't be right out here where anyone could spot him."

"He was right out in plain sight when he was following you. He didn't mind being seen when he parked in your neighbor's driveway."

"So he's a gutsy stalker." She attempted a carefree laugh, but it wasn't very convincing. "Or maybe he's new at it. Maybe he's just got a learner's permit."

And then someone said, "Excuse me," and they stepped back to allow one of the locals to pass. He was carrying a washtub filled with ice.

"Well, hey there, Miss Marty. My wife says when you going to get your bookstore open again?"

Her wariness faded. "Oh, hi, James. Tell her soon, I hope." Looking back at Cole, she murmured, "It occurred to me that I'll need to advertise. Mail out cards or buy radio time. Maybe even a trailer on the local weather station."

By then they'd reached the door, which was propped open. They were immediately enveloped in a noisy, good-natured crowd, and Marty forgot about both advertising and her wacky stalker. Snatches of string music could be heard over the sound of laughter and dozens of voices all trying to be heard. The mingled scent of hickory barbecue and something gamier mingled with Brut, Old Spice and Eau de Whatever.

Someone yelled, "Marty, you're the expert. Tell this here dumbhead that Clive Cussler's been diving around these parts for years."

"Expert on popular fiction, maybe, but not on diving. But yes, actually, I think he has."

A strident voice yelled, "The potatoes is done!"

Someone else said, "We got enough Texas Pete?"

"Oh, lawsy, I lost an earring in the stew pot!"

As a dozen conversations swirled around her, Sasha sidled

over and whispered in her ear, "Oh, honey, do I have a hot prospect for Lily! He's right over there, talking to the sheriff." On social occasions, local law enforcement overlooked minor infractions of certain laws. Tonight was obviously one of those occasions, as the man in question was holding a glass of clear liquid. Chances were, it wasn't vodka.

Faylene joined them. "Gus and Cassie, whaddya think? Her boobs and his beer belly ought to be a fit. Picture it."

Marty did. She giggled.

Sasha said, "The mind boggles."

From several feet away, Cole winked at her. He'd been buttonholed by old Miss Katie, a retired schoolteacher who considered anyone under the age of fifty to still have a few things to learn. She was probably right, Marty thought ruefully. About some of us, at least.

The party was in full swing by the time Marty broke away more than an hour later. Several people had stepped outside for a breath of cool air, among them an attractive middle-aged man wearing flannel and tweed and smoking a pipe. Probably a college professor, she thought. He didn't look like a hunter or fisherman—but who ever knew?

She watched idly as he stepped down from the wharf and made his way past two trucks and an SUV. A moment later she saw a light come on as he opened the door of the Mercedes. Without taking time to think, she hopped down and followed. Just as she reached him, he closed the car door and turned away, holding what looked like a tobacco pouch.

"Stop right there," she commanded.

He stopped. He stared. In the cold green glow of the mercury-vapor security light, she could almost believe his face reddened, but she could have been mistaken.

"Ms. Owens?" he said.

"Have you been following me?" While she waited for a denial, she tried to think of a way to make him confess. How did they do it in books? Threats? Torture? Both out of the question—but he was the one, all right. She knew it.

Proving it was another matter. "Just tell me this—why is it that you turn up everywhere I go? Even here." All right, so he'd been here when she'd arrived; that was a minor technicality.

He tucked the pouch in the pocket of his tweed jacket and she caught a hint of vanilla-scented pipe tobacco.

"Ms. Owens, do you have any sisters?"

Puzzled, she tilted her head. "Sisters? Look, whoever you are, I'm not answering any questions until you tell me what's going on."

Only a few feet separated them in the crowded parking area. The man didn't look all that dangerous—she might even be able to take him in a fair fight. But she'd rather not put it to the test. Her knowledge of martial arts had come from reading suspense and watching Jackie Chan.

"I do," he said, sounding almost resigned.

"You do what?" That's right, she thought—throw me off balance.

"Have a sister. Her name is Marissa Owens and she lives outside Culpepper. Kenyon Farms—at least it used to be a farm. All that's left is the house and one empty stable. You might know the place."

Oh, my God. She did. Beau had taken her there just once, right after they'd been married. His mother, who had not attended the wedding, had been frigidly polite throughout the brief visit.

"Then you're…"

"Beau's uncle, James Merchison. I'm truly sorry if I've frightened you. That was never my intention, but when my sister heard I was headed down to Hobe Sound, she asked me to lay over here long enough to find out if you still had any of the things Beau took from home. They're family pieces, you know. We'd be more than willing to buy them back."

"Then why didn't you come right out and ask me?"

"I should have, but I didn't know what to ask. It's embarrassing to be put in the position of accusing someone who was once family of—well, I suppose it could be called receiving stolen goods."

Marty took a deep breath and expelled it in a sharp huff. He looked so apologetic that she was inclined to forgive him, but not before she told him exactly what a piece of work his nephew was.

"Do you know he even stole my wedding ring? Not that it was all that valuable—it definitely wasn't a family heirloom, because I was with him when we picked it out. He told me he was going to have it checked to be sure none of the stones were loose, and then he claimed the jeweler lost it." She glanced down at her bare finger. "As for the paintings he claimed his mother gave him because she didn't have room to hang them, they hung on our walls for—oh, maybe five months. He claimed he was going to have them appraised for insurance purposes. I never saw them again."

They were still comparing notes on the lying, gambling-addicted wretch she'd had the misfortune to marry when Cole found her. His eyes narrowed as he took possession of her arm.

"Is there a problem here?"

Marty introduced the two men. The older man said, "Merchison, Saunders, Vessels and Wilson, Attorneys at Law."

"Then I guess I don't have to tell you what you've been doing is probably actionable," Cole said evenly.

"It was personal. I've apologized and explained to the lady."

"He has, Cole, and I understand. Really, I do." She patted James Merchison on the hand. "If I were you and I were looking for Beau, I'd cruise on up to Atlantic City. Or anywhere there's gambling."

The three of them rejoined the party in time to fill paper plates with everything from stewed goose and dumplings to barbecue, to grilled tuna and crab cakes. Beverages ranged from soft drinks to beer to gallon jugs of white liquor of the no-questions-asked variety.

While Cole worked his way closer to the musicians, Marty cornered Faylene to compliment her on her new hairstyle, which was more Farrah Faucett than Dolly Parton.

"Law heppus, if this wind don't let up, I'm gonna get me one o' them WeedEater cuts. Whatcha think of that feller over there with the Mercedes for Miss Lily? She's some taller, but some men like that in a woman."

It was long past midnight when they got home. Neither of them questioned the fact that Cole would be spending the night there; otherwise he'd have suggested that they drive separately. For the past few hours they had mingled, sometimes separately, sometimes together. Cole had wandered over to talk to the musicians, but even across the room she'd felt his gaze return to her again and again, his eyes glowing with a message she was almost afraid to interpret for fear she'd get it wrong.

Looking around her house now as she shed her coat, she shook her head. "It still comes as a shock when I see the chaos. Can you believe I used to be compulsively neat?"

"Yeah, I can believe it."

His smile held sympathy and more understanding than she was ready to accept.

"You want a nightcap?"

"After that feast? I don't think so."

"I don't, either."

And then neither of them could think of anything to say. Marty reminded herself that she'd lived with the man—well, practically lived with him—for a week. They had shared meals and dog-walks and shopping; she had introduced him to her friends, argued with him and even fired him.

She had made love to him, for heaven's sake.

So why was she acting like an idiot? Why was she quaking inside? Was she afraid he was going to tell her goodnight and drive all the way back to the marina?

"Look, do you want to go to bed, or not?" she blurted. "With me, I mean. You can always sleep on the sofa. It's a mess in there, but I can give you a pillow and a blanket and—"

He hushed her with a finger over her lips. His eyes were laughing. At her, or with her?

Oh, Lord, you'd think she'd eventually learn, wouldn't you?

Upstairs, Cole helped her hang up the clothing she'd left scattered across the bed. Then he undressed her, carefully easing her turtleneck sweater over her head.

"Sorry I messed up your hair. It looked pretty, but I like it the way you usually wear it, too." He was so close she could feel the heat of his body through the navy flannel and whatever he wore under it.

When he stood her up again and unbuttoned the waistband of her slacks she noticed how unsteady his hands were. "You don't have to do this," she whispered. Whispered because she couldn't seem to breathe properly.

"Yeah, I do. Measure twice, cut once. It's an old carpenter's saying."

She clutched his shoulder and stepped out of her slacks. "You're not all that old," she teased, but she knew what he meant. The evidence was…well, evident. Aroused all the way up to his belt buckle, he was taking his time with the preliminaries, doing his best not to rush.

His own clothes came off quickly, though. Khaki, flannel and cotton knit, tossed at a chair, half of it falling to the floor. Marty pulled out her box of condoms and took one—and then another one. And then a third. Just in case. Sooner or later they were going to have to talk.

Or not.

Color stained his angular cheeks. His hands trembled, but there was nothing at all hurried or unsure about his kisses. Slowly, he explored her mouth, his tongue dueling with hers, then thrusting in a seductive promise of things to come. He kissed her eyelids, her ears, suckling the lobes. The moment his lips found that sensitive place at the side of her throat, she sucked in her breath, goose bumps racing in waves down her flanks.

"I…can't…wait," she managed to whisper when his tongue traced a pattern around her nipple. While her fists flailed the sheets and her head moved from side to side on the pillow, he proceeded to drive her wild, first with his hands, then with his lips and his tongue.

"I need you...now!" she whispered fiercely. If he would just come inside her and ease this intolerable ache he'd created, then she might survive. Otherwise, there were no guarantees.

"You don't know how much I've wanted this," he said in a raspy voice, nipping her belly with soft ferocity. "I've waited all night—all day—all week."

He aligned her underneath him. As if they'd done it a thousand times, her toes pushed against his, then her knees lifted to clasp his hips and she breathed in the clean musky scent of his body. She felt the tip of him move intimately against her.

He hesitated. "Tell me what you want," he said, lifting his head so that he could watch her reaction.

She didn't know whether to laugh or cry. After years of thinking of herself as lukewarm in matters pertaining to sex, in a single night this man had turned her into a woman she didn't even recognize. A woman who was daring and desirable, a creature of her own fantasy with a fantasy lover all her own.

"I don't know," she wailed helplessly. Unfortunately, her fantasy was circumscribed by her own lack of experience.

Kneeling over her, Cole took her hand in his and carried it to his chest. She felt the diamond pattern of crisp dark hair that arrowed down to his waist and below. Slowly, he moved her palm over his small hard male nipples, then guided it lower, to where he wanted her attention.

She gave it freely, lovingly, testing his powers of resistance and her own powers to arouse—first with feathery fingertip caresses, then with the judicious use of fingernails. Finally—irresistibly—with a lingering series of kisses that brought him to a state near catatonia.

"God in heaven, woman, what are you trying to do, cripple me for life?"

"How'm I doing so far?" She teased him with a smile.

"You need to ask?"

He moved away abruptly, and she remembered the small, important packets on the bedside table. A moment later, he turned to her again. This time, instead of positioning himself over her, he settled back against the headboard and lifted her astride his thighs. "All right?" he murmured. His hands cupped her breasts while his tongue made love to her nipples.

Moments later they were both breathing harshly, quivering on the edge of the precipice. He cupped her hips and lifted her again, this time positioning her perfectly. It was like setting a torch to dry grass. Together they set a pace that could only be described as fast, frantic and furious. All too quickly, she felt herself flying over the top, heard the series of soft, wild cries that issued from her throat.

And then she collapsed against his chest, her head on his shoulder. Eventually they toppled together onto the bed. Cool air gradually chilled the perspiration on both their bodies, not that either of them noticed.

At some point before morning, one of them—later, neither could remember doing it—managed to pull up the covers.

The first thing Marty saw when a shaft of spring-scented sunshine found its way into the room was the two unused condoms on the bedside table. Cole was watching her, his expression a little cocky, a little wary. "Waste not, want not?" he suggested.

"Um…measure twice, cut once?" she returned.

"Ouch. I'm not sure I like the sound of that."

She grinned. "It's your saying."

"Yeah, well, I can't think of one that fits the circumstances, so how about if I make one up for the occasion?"

"Does it have anything to do with food? Because I missed out on dessert last night, and I'm hungry."

He nodded thoughtfully, his streaky-blond hair standing on end, dark bristles covering the lower half of his face. "Yeah, me, too. But first, tell me this—have you got any objection to being proposed to over bacon and eggs?"

Her heart stuttered, skipped a beat and began to pound. "That depends on what you're proposing," she said cautiously.

"Because I can do it just as well over waffles, even the frozen kind, if you'd rather."

She recognized the glint in his eyes now. "Does this have anything to do with your contract?"

He nodded. "Manner of speaking, I guess it does. See, what I'm after is an extension. Maybe fifty years or so, with an exclusivity clause."

She pretended to think about it while she fought against the absurd urge to cry. She'd had moonlight and roses. She'd had candlelight and French cuisine. None of those had lasted. She had a feeling this was the real deal—finally.

"Bacon and eggs sounds, um, reasonable," she ventured.

"Is that a yes or a no?"

They were still bare from the waist up, covered only by a yellow print sheet and a quilted spread from the waist down. "What are you waiting for? You want me to go first?"

Well, she did and she didn't. Talk of fifty-year contracts

was scary enough; she would prefer a bit of plain-speaking before she jumped to any conclusions. "I want to know if you've got the courage to say it in plain English."

"You mean the L word? As in lust?"

She had to laugh, because they both knew which L word she'd meant. And then he said it—the right L word—and her throat thickened up again with tears. Oh, God, she hated it when her emotions took over this way. What had happened to the pragmatic Virgo who always followed the rules and tried to stay out of trouble?

"Cole, you might as well know that I never rush into things. I'm far too practical for that."

He lifted one dark eyebrow. She rolled her eyes.

"Okay, maybe 'practical' isn't the right word, but I do know better than to act on impulse."

This time his other eyebrow lifted.

She gave up. "All right! But there's a lot about me you don't know. Such as I never—that is, I usually don't…rush into things. Honestly."

"Gotcha. We take it easy, get to know each other—you tell me all your bad habits, I gloss over mine." His smile was purely wicked.

She swatted him, and he laughed. "You want to hear it again?"

"Hear what again?"

"The L word?" he teased.

She shook her head, her heart too full for words. She knew the difference between loving and falling in love. One was permanent. The other was all too often an illusion.

She suffered from both.

But when she saw him reach across to the bedside table, she had to laugh, too.

"How hungry did you say you were?" he asked.

"Not all *that* hungry. Not for food, at least."

His eyes said it all. "That's my woman. My Marty. My love."

* * * * *

Look for Her Fifth Husband? *next month
also by Dixie Browning to see how Sasha finally
picks the right man.*

SILHOUETTE®
Desire™ 2 in 1

HER FIFTH HUSBAND? by Dixie Browning

Four failed marriages were a testament to her lousy judgement.
So when interior designer Sasha Lasiter met stunningly sexy Jake
Smith she fought their mutual attraction. But Jake was convinced
Sasha's fifth time would be the charm—if he was the groom!

THE LAST REILLY STANDING by Maureen Child

Three Way Wager

For Aiden Reilly three months without sex meant one thing: spend
a *lot* of time with his best gal pal, Terry Evans. But eventually
temptation proved to be too much. The last Reilly standing lost the
no-sex bet, but could he win the girl?

BABY AT HIS CONVENIENCE by Kathie DeNosky

She wanted a strong, sexy man to father her child—and waitress
Katie Andrews had decided that Jeremiah Gunn fitted the bill
exactly. Trouble was, Jeremiah had some terms of his own

OUT OF UNIFORM by Amy J Fetzer

Marine captain Rick Wyatt and his wife, Kate, were great together
—skin to skin. But beyond the bedroom door, Rick closed Kate out
emotionally, and she wanted in. So she passionately set out to win
the battle for her marriage.

BUSINESS AFFAIRS by Shirley Rogers

An impulsive bid at a bachelor auction had won Jennifer Cardon
a romantic weekend with her sexy boss, Alex Dunnigan. Alex was
more of a fantasies-fulfilled rather than a forever sort of guy but
now Jennifer was pregnant with his child…

RIDING THE STORM by Brenda Jackson

Firefighter Storm Westmoreland used love-making to blow off
steam. Until a torrid weekend with a too-hot-to-handle virgin left
him craving something other than mere physical gratification…

On sale from 17th March 2006

Visit our website at www.silhouette.co.uk

0106/SH/LC130

❖ SILHOUETTE®

Desire™

DYNASTIES: THE ASHTONS

*A family built on lies...Brought together
by dark, passionate secrets.*

**Visit the Napa Valley in California and
watch the struggle, scandal and seduction.**

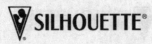

SILHOUETTE®

SPECIAL EDITION™

LORI'S LITTLE SECRET
by Christine Rimmer

Bravo Family Ties

Rumour had it that Lori Billingworth's son was the result of a one-night stand. She and her twin sister had traded places on prom night, and *nobody*— but Lori—knew that she had her dream date with Tucker Bravo.

TRADING SECRETS by Christine Flynn

Going Home

Jenny Baker is back home, hired by handsome local doctor Greg Reid, who ignites feelings she'd thought she'd put to rest and when Greg uncovers Jenny's deepest secret, he makes her an offer she can't refuse...

QUADRUPLETS ON THE DOORSTEP
by Tina Leonard

Maitland Maternity

Everyone is wondering about the abandoned quadruplets left at Maitland Maternity Hospital. Is it mere coincidence that Caleb McCallum's new bride, April Sullivan, wants to raise the babies as her own?

Don't miss out!
On sale from 17th March 2006

HIS WEDDING
by Muriel Jensen

The Abbotts

When Janet Abbott found out that she was adopted she vowed to find out the truth about her origins. Aided by the handsome 'illegitimate Abbott' Brian, Janet begin to unravel the mystery of her past...

HIS BROTHER'S BABY
by Laurie Campbell

When lawyer Connor Tarkington escaped to his family's holiday home, he found Lucy Velardi and her baby daughter abandoned by his brother. Living under the same roof, Connor and Lucy soon wonder if they've found just what they needed – each other.

ALMOST PERFECT
by Judy Duarte

A commitment-phobic best friend like Jake Meredith could not be the perfect match for elegant Boston paediatrician Maggie Templeton – not even when he inherited his tiny niece and nephew...?

Don't miss out!
On sale from 17th March 2006

Available at WHSmith, Tesco, ASDA, Borders, Eason,
Sainsbury's and most bookshops

www.silhouette.co.uk

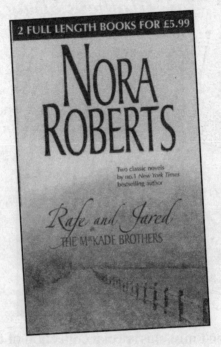

FREE!
2 Books
and a surprise gift!

We would like to take this opportunity to thank you for reading this Silhouette® book by offering you the chance to take TWO more specially selected titles from the Desire™ series absolutely FREE! We're also making this offer to introduce you to the benefits of the Reader Service™—

- ★ FREE home delivery
- ★ FREE gifts and competitions
- ★ FREE monthly Newsletter
- ★ Exclusive Reader Service offers
- ★ Books available before they're in the shops

Accepting these FREE books and gift places you under no obligation to buy, you may cancel at any time, even after receiving your free shipment. Simply complete your details below and return the entire page to the address below. You don't even need a stamp!

YES! Please send me 2 free Desire books and a surprise gift. I understand that unless you hear from me, I will receive 3 superb new titles every month for just £4.99 each, postage and packing free. I am under no obligation to purchase any books and may cancel my subscription at any time. The free books and gift will be mine to keep in any case.

D6ZEF

Ms/Mrs/Miss/Mr ....Initials ....

BLOCK CAPITALS PLEASE

Surname ....

Address...

....

....Postcode ....

Send this whole page to:
UK: FREEPOST CN8I, Croydon, CR9 3WZ